FALL WITH ME

"Thank you," I said, smiling a little.

He sat the glass down and before I knew what he was doing, he placed both hands on the bar top and rose. Stretching over, right in front of everyone in the bar and God, he leaned in, and I thought for a second he'd kiss me, and then I'd melt into a pool of gooey nothingness. He was going right for it. Anticipation swelled sweetly. I was seconds from grabbing his cheeks as my gaze centered on his mouth. I was so ready to melt into that pool.

Reece didn't kiss me. He tilted his head at the last moment, placing his lips near my ear. When he spoke, he sent a tight, hot shiver right down my spine. "Two more hours, babe, and you'll be all mine."

Also by Jennifer L. Armentrout

The Covenant Series

Daimon
Half-Blood
Pure
Deity
Elixer
Apollyon

The Lux Series

Shadows
Obsidian
Onyx
Opal
Origin
Opposition

By J. Lynn

Stay With Me
Be With Me
Wait for You

Gable Brothers Series

Tempting the Best Man
Tempting the Player

JENNIFER L. ARMENTROUT

FALL WITH ME

An Imprint of HarperCollins*Publishers*

This is a work of fiction. Names, characters, places, and incidents are products of the author's imagination or are used fictitiously and are not to be construed as real. Any resemblance to actual events, locales, organizations, or persons, living or dead, is entirely coincidental.

AVON BOOKS
An Imprint of HarperCollins*Publishers*
195 Broadway
New York, New York 10007

ISBN 978-0-06-236274-2
www.avonromance.com

First Avon Books mass market printing: April 2015

Printed in the U.S.A.

10 9 8 7 6 5 4 3 2 1

For the readers.
Hope you enjoy!

Acknowledgements

Writing acknowledgements can be the hardest part of completing a novel. You never want to forget to thank someone, but ultimately you know you will. So I'd like to keep this short and sweet. Thank you to my agent, Kevan Lyon, and the team at HarperCollins—awesome editors, Tessa Woodward and Amanda Bergeron; the amazing marketing and sales support team; and Inkslinger, who worked tirelessly to bring this book to you.

A big thank you to you, the reader. Without you, this book would not be possible. None of this would be possible.

Chapter 1

Only ten minutes had passed from when I'd plopped myself down in a plush cushioned chair inside the sunny waiting room until I saw scuffed white sneakers creep into the line of my vision. I'd been busy staring at the wood floors and thinking that private care facilities must bring in a lot of money to have such expensive-looking dark wood.

Then again, Charlie Clark's parents had spared no expense when it came to their only son's long-term care. Got him in the best facility in Philadelphia. The amount of money they spent yearly had to be astronomical—and definitely more than I made bartending at Mona's and doing web design on the side.

I imagined they thought it made up for the fact they visited Charlie only once a year, for like twenty minutes. There were better, more forgiving people in the world than me, because the familiar burn of irritation I felt whenever I thought about his parents was hard to ignore as I dragged my gaze up to the welcoming smile plastered across the nurse's face. I blinked once and then twice, not recognizing the copper hair or the fresher, younger hazel eyes.

This lady was new.

She glanced up at the top of my head and her stare lingered on my hair for a moment longer than normal, but her smile didn't falter. It wasn't like my hair was that crazy. I'd switched out the deep red streaks for chunky purple ones a few days ago, but it did look like a hot mess in the quick bun I'd twisted the long lengths into. I'd closed down the bar last night, which meant I hadn't gotten home until after three in the morning, and getting up, brushing my teeth, and washing my face before I made the drive into the city was a hell of a feat.

"Roxanne Ark?" she said as she stopped in front of me, clasping her hands together.

My brain screeched to a halt at the sound of my full name. My parents were bizarre. Like there was a good chance they were cokeheads in the eighties or something. I was named after the song "Roxanne," and my brothers were Gordon and Thomas, which mostly made up Sting's real name.

"Yes," I said, reaching for the tote bag I'd brought with me.

Her smile remained firmly in place as she motioned to the closed double doors. "Nurse Venter is out today, but she explained that you come every Friday afternoon at noon, so we have Charlie ready."

"Oh no, is she okay?" Concern pinged around me. Nurse Venter had become a friend over the last six years I visited. So much so that I knew her youngest son was finally getting married in October, and her middle child had just had her first grandchild last month, in July.

"She's come down with an end-of-summer cold," she explained. "She actually wanted to come in today, but we all figured it would be better if she took the weekend to recover." The new nurse stepped aside as I stood. "She did tell me that you like to read to Charlie?"

I nodded as I tightened my grip on my tote.

Stopping at the doors, she tugged off her clipped name badge and swiped it over a sensor on the wall. There was a popping sound and then she pushed the door open. "He's had an okay couple of days. Not as great as we'd like," she continued as we stepped in the wide, brightly lit hall. The walls were white and bare. No personality. Nothing. "But he was up early this morning."

My neon-green flip-flops smacked off the tile floors but the nurse's sneakers made no noise. We passed the hall I knew led to the community room. Charlie was never a fan of hanging out in there, which was so strange, because before . . . before he'd been hurt, he'd been such a social butterfly.

He'd been a lot of things.

Charlie's room was down another hall, a wing specially designed to have views of the sprawling green landscape and the therapeutic pool that Charlie had never enjoyed. He hadn't been much of a swimmer before, but every time I saw that damn pool outside, I wanted to punch something. I don't know what it was about it, maybe because it was something the rest of us took for granted—the ability to swim on our own—or maybe it was the fact that water always seemed so limitless to me, but Charlie's future was severely limited.

The nurse stopped outside of his closed door. "When you're ready to leave, you know the drill."

I did. When I left, I had to stop by the nurses' station and check out. I guessed they wanted to make sure I wasn't trying to steal Charlie away or something. With a happy little nod in my direction, the nurse spun in her sneakers and power walked back down the hall.

Staring at the door for a moment, I drew in a deep breath and let it out slowly. I had to every time I saw Charlie. It was the only way to get the messy ball of emotion—all that disappointment, anger, and sadness—out of me before I walked into the room. I never wanted Charlie to see that. Sometimes I failed, but I always tried.

Only when I thought I could smile without looking slightly crazed, I opened the door, and like every Friday for the last six years, seeing Charlie was like taking a throat punch.

He was sitting in a chair in front of the large floor-to-ceiling window—in *his* chair. It was one of those papasan chairs with a vibrant blue cushion. He'd had it since he was sixteen, got it for his birthday just a few months before everything changed for him.

Charlie didn't look up when I stepped into the room and closed the door behind me. He never did.

The room wasn't bad at all, rather spacious with a full-sized bed neatly made by one of the nurses, a desk I knew he never used, and a TV that I'd never, in the six years, seen turned on.

Sitting in that chair, looking out the window, he was so thin, beyond willowy. Nurse Venter told me that they had trouble getting him to eat three square meals a day, and when they tried to change it to five smaller meals, that hadn't worked either. A year ago, it had gotten so bad they had to do a feeding tube, and I could still taste that fear, because I thought I'd lose him then.

His blond hair had been washed this morning, but it wasn't styled and was much shorter than how he used to wear it. Charlie had favored that artfully messy look and he had rocked it. Today, he was wearing a white shirt and gray sweat pants, not even the cool kind. No, these had those elastic bands at the ankle, and God, he would've thrown a fit if he knew he'd be wearing them now—rightfully so, because Charlie . . . well, he had style and taste and so much.

Walking toward the second papasan chair with a matching blue cushion I'd bought three years ago, I cleared my throat. "Hey, Charlie."

He didn't look.

There was no disappointment. I mean, it was there, that "this isn't fair" feeling, but there wasn't a new wave of the breath-stealing dismay, because this was how it always was.

Sitting down, I placed the tote beside my legs. Up close, he looked older than twenty-two—years older. Face gaunt, skin washed out, and deep, unforgiving shadows under once lively green eyes.

I drew in another deep breath. "It's ridiculously hot out there today, so don't make fun of my cut-off shorts." Back in the day, he would've made me change out of them before even daring to step out into public. "The weather people are saying the temps are going to be record breaking by the weekend."

Charlie blinked slowly.

"Supposed to be really bad storms, too." I clasped my hands together, praying that he'd look at me. Some visits he wouldn't. He hadn't for three visits, and that terrified me, because the last time he'd gone that long without acknowledging me, he'd had a horrific seizure. Those two things probably had nothing in common, but still, it caused knots of unease to form in my stomach. Especially since Nurse Venter had explained that seizures were fairly common in patients who'd suffered that kind of blunt-force trauma to the brain. "You remember how much I like storms, right?"

No response.

"Well, unless it spawns tornados," I amended. "But we're in Philly, basically, so I doubt there'll be many of them roaming around."

Another slow blink I caught from his profile.

"Oh! Tomorrow night at Mona's, we're closing the bar to the public," I rambled on, unsure if I'd already told him about the plans, not that it mattered. "It's a private party thing." I paused long enough to take a breath.

Charlie still stared out the window.

"You'd like Mona's, I think. It's kind of trashy, but in a weird, good way. But I've already told you that before. I don't know, but I wish . . ." I added, pursing my lips. as his shoulders rose in a deep and heavy sigh. "I wish a lot of things," I finished in a whisper.

He'd started rocking in what appeared to be an unconscious movement. It was a gentle rhythm, one that reminded me of being in the ocean, slowly pushed back and forth.

For a moment, I struggled with the impulse to scream out all the frustration rapidly building inside me. Charlie used to talk a mile a minute. Teachers in our elementary school had nicknamed him Mighty Mouth, and he laughed—oh goodness, he had the best laugh, so infectious and real.

But he hadn't laughed in years.

Squeezing my eyes shut against the rush of hot tears, I wanted to throw myself on the floor and flail.

None of this was fair. Charlie should be up walking around. He should've graduated college by now and met a hot guy who would love him, and go on double dates with me and whatever man I dragged along. He should have done what he'd sworn he'd do and published his first novel by now. We would be like we were before. Best friends—inseparable. He'd visit me at the bar, and when it was needed, he'd tell me to get my shit together.

Charlie should be alive, because this—whatever *this* was—was not living.

Instead, *one* fucking night, a strand of a few stupid words and a goddamn *rock* had destroyed everything.

I opened my eyes, hoping he'd be looking at me, but he wasn't, and all I could do was pull it together. Reaching down, I slipped a folded sheet of watercolor out of my tote. "I made this for you." My voice was hoarse, but I kept going. "Remember when we were fifteen, and my parents took us to Gettysburg? You loved Devil's Den, so that's what this is."

Unfolding the painting, I held it up for him even though he didn't look. It had taken me a few hours over the course of the week to paint the sandy rocks overlooking the grassy meadows, to get the right color of the boulders and the pebbles in between them. The shading had been the hardest part since it was in watercolor, but I like to think it came out pretty damn cool.

I stood and walked the painting to the wall across from his bed. Fishing a tack out of the desk, I hung it next to the other paintings. There was one for every week I visited him. Three hundred and twelve paintings.

My gaze traveled over the walls. My favorites were

the portraits I'd done of him—paintings of Charlie and me together when we were younger. I was running out of room. Would have to start with the ceiling soon. All of the paintings were of the . . . past. Nothing of the present or the future. Just a wall of memories.

I made my way back to the chair and pulled out the book I'd been reading to him. It was *New Moon*, and we'd gotten to see the first movie together. Almost got to see the second. As I cracked it open to the last page I'd left off at, I was convinced that Charlie would've been Team Jacob. He would never go for emo vampires. Even though this was the fourth time I'd read the book to him, he'd seemed to like it.

At least, that's what I told myself.

Not once during the hour I spent with him did he look at me, and as I packed up, my heart was as heavy as that rock that had changed everything. I leaned down close to him. "Look at me, Charlie." I waited a heartbeat as my throat clogged. "*Please.*"

Charlie . . . all he did was blink as he rocked slowly. Back and forth. That was all, as I waited a full five minutes for a response, any response, but none came. My eyes dampened as I pressed a kiss against his cool cheek and then straightened. "I'll see you next Friday, okay?"

I pretended he said okay in return. It was the only way I could walk out of that room and close the door behind me. I checked out and as I made my way outside into the blistering heat, I found my sunglasses in my tote and slipped them on. The heat did wonders for my chilled skin, but didn't warm my insides. It was always like this after I visited Charlie, and it would take until my shift at Mona's started before I was able to shake off the coldness.

As I walked toward the back of the parking lot where my car was, I swore.

I could see the heat wafting off the pavement, and I immediately wondered what colors I'd need to mix to capture the effect on canvas. Then I saw my trusty Volkswagen Jetta, and all thoughts of watercolors vanished. My stomach flopped heavily and I almost tripped right over my feet. There was a nice, practically new truck sitting next to mine.

I knew that black truck.

I'd driven it once.

Oh Man.

My feet refused to move so I came to a complete standstill.

The very bane of my existence was here, who oddly was the same person who had a reoccurring starring role in all my fantasies, even the really dirty ones—especially them.

Reece Anders was here, and I didn't know if I was going to punch him in the nuts or kiss him.

Chapter 2

The driver's door opened smoothly, and my heart—my damn, traitorous bitch of a heart—skipped a beat as a long denim-clad leg appeared, along with flip-flops with a tan leather thong. Why did I have to have a thing for guys who were ballsy enough to wear flip-flops, because, oh dear, I really did think that was entirely sexy paired with faded jeans. Another leg appeared, and the door blocked the torso for a moment—only a second. The door closed, and I got an eyeful of a worn Metallica shirt that did very little to hide a well-defined, totally yummy-in-my-tummy six-pack. The shirt was practically mating with his stomach, clinging to each ripple. It was doing the same to his biceps, essentially taunting me.

That was it. The shirt was being a spiteful man-bitch.

I dragged my gaze up over broad shoulders—the kind of shoulders that could bear the brunt of the weight of the world, and *had*—to his face. He was rocking some sexy black sunglasses, looking damn good doing so.

God, Reece looked great in casual clothes, panties-on-*fire* hot when he was wearing his police uniform, and when he was naked, he could seriously induce a visual orgasm.

And I'd seen him naked. Well, sort of. Okay, totally saw his goods, and they were goodie-gumdrops kind of good.

Reece was classically handsome, the kind of guy with the bone structure that had my fingers itching to sketch—angular cheekbones, full lips, and an honest-to-God jawline that could cut cheesecakes all day long. And he was a cop, serving and protecting, and there was just something entirely badass hot about that.

Unfortunately, I also hated him, absolutely loathed him. Ah, well, most of the time. Sometimes. Pretty much whenever I gazed upon his perfection and started lusting after him. Yeah, that's when I hated him.

My girlie parts were feeling that vibe right now, meaning in this moment, I disliked him. So as I tightened my hand on the tote bag I carried, I popped out a hip like I'd seen Katie, a . . . well, odd friend of mine, do when she was about to deliver a verbal smackdown.

"What are you doing here?" I demanded, and then promptly shivered—shivered in the hundred-degree temperature, because I hadn't spoken to Reece in over eleven months. Well, not counting the words *Fuck off,* because I'd probably said that to him, oh, about four hundred times in the last eleven months, but whatever.

Dark brows shot up over the frame of the sunglasses. A moment passed and then he chuckled, as if what I said was the most amusing thing ever. "How about you actually say hi to me first?"

Curse words would've flown from my tongue like birds migrating south for winter if he hadn't caught me off guard. I'd asked a totally valid question. From what I knew, Reece never, in the six years I'd been seeing Charlie, had visited the facility, but a smidgen of guilt bloomed and my momma raised me better than this. I forced out a "Hi."

He pursed well-formed lips and said nothing.

My eyes narrowed from behind my sunglasses. "Hello . . . Officer Anders?"

A moment passed as he cocked his head to the side. "I'm not on duty, Roxy."

Oh man, the way he said my name. Roxy. How he curled his tongue around the R. I had no idea how, but it made me all squishy in areas that so did not need the squishiness.

When he didn't say anything else though, I was close to punching myself in the girlie areas, because he was seriously going to make me do this. "Hello . . ." I drew the word out. *"Reece."*

Those lips curved up at the corners, a smile that said he was proud and he should be. Me saying his name at this point was a major accomplishment on his part, and if I had a reward cookie for him, I'd shove it right in his face. "Was that so hard?" he asked.

"Yes. It was hard," I told him. "It blackened a part of my soul."

A laugh erupted from him, which surprised the hell out of me. "Your soul is all rainbows and puppy dog tails, babe."

I snorted. "My soul is deep and dark and full of other infinite meaningless things."

"Meaningless things?" he repeated with another deep laugh as he reached up and scrubbed his fingers through his dark brown hair. It was cropped close on the sides, but a little longer on top than most cops had. "Well, if that's the truth, it hasn't always been that way." The easy, somewhat—okay, totally— charming grin eased off his mouth and his lips formed a flat line. "Yeah, it wasn't always like that."

The next breath hitched in my throat. Reece and I . . . we'd known each other for a long time. When I'd been a freshman in high school, he'd been a junior, and even back then he'd been everything a girl could obsess over, and I'd crushed on him *hard*. Like, I had drawn hearts with his name in the center, my earliest and lamest doodles, across my notebook and treasured every time he'd smiled at me or looked in my direction. I'd been way too young and didn't run in his circles, but he'd always been kind to me.

Probably had to do with the fact that he and his older brother, along with his parents, had moved into the house next door to my childhood home.

Anyway, he'd always been good to me and to Charlie, and when he'd left to join the Marines at eighteen, I'd been heartbroken, utterly devastated, because I'd convinced myself we'd get married and populate the world with lots of babies. Those years he was gone had been hard, and I'd never forget the day Mom had called me to tell me he was injured while at war. My heart had stopped and it took a long time for that suffocating ball of dread to lift, even after we were assured that he'd be okay. When he finally came home, I was old enough not to be considered jailbait and we'd actually become friends. Close, good friends. I'd been there for him during the worse moments of his life.

Those terrible nights he'd drunk himself into a stupor or become so moody he was like a caged lion ready to bite the hand off anyone who approached him—anyone except me. But then one night with too much whiskey had ruined everything.

I'd spent years infatuated with him, always believing he was unobtainable, and no matter what had transpired between us that night, he would still never be mine.

Frustrated with where my thoughts had gone, I resisted the urge to chuck my tote at him. "Why in the world are we talking about my soul?"

One broad shoulder rose. "You brought it up."

I opened my mouth to argue, but he was right, I had and that was kind of weird. A fine sheen of sweat had broken out across my forehead. "Why are you here?"

Two steps and his long legs ate up the distance between us. My toes curled against my sandals as I forced myself not to whirl around and scurry away. Reece was tall, coming in around six feet and three inches, and I was an unofficial member of the Lollipop Guild. His size was a wee bit intimidating, also a tiny bit sexy. "It's about Henry Williams."

In a split second, I forgot about the messy history Reece and I shared and the current shininess of my soul as I stared up at him. "What?"

"He's out of jail, Roxy."

The sweat turned to sleet on my skin. "I . . . I know he is. He's been out for a couple of months. I kept up with the parole hearings. I—"

"I know," he said quietly, intensely, and my stomach dropped to the ground. "You didn't go to his last parole hearing, when he was released."

That was a statement, more than a question, but I

still shook my head. I'd gone to the one before that, but had been barely able to stomach the sight of Henry Williams. And from how the talk was cycling around, there had been a good chance he'd be released at the next hearing and low and behold, he had been. Rumor had it that Henry found God or something like that while in prison. Good for him.

But it didn't change what he'd done.

Reece took off his sunglasses and startling blue eyes met mine. "I went to the hearing."

Surprised, I took a step back. My mouth opened, but there were no words. I hadn't known that—hadn't even crossed my mind that he would do that or even why he would.

His gaze remained latched to mine. "During the hearing, he asked to—"

"No," I said, almost shouted. "I know what he wanted. I heard what he wanted to do if he got out, and no. No times a billion. *No.* And the court can't give that kind of permission anyway."

Reece's expression softened and something—something close to pity filled those eyes. "I know, but sweetheart, you also know you don't have any say over it either." There was a pause. "He wants to make amends, Roxy."

My free hand tightened into a fist as helplessness rose like a swarm of bees inside me. "He can't make amends for what he did."

"I agree."

It took me a moment as I stared up at him to realize what he was getting at, and it was like the ground shifted under my feet. "No," I whispered, stomach twisting into knots. "Please tell me that Charlie's parents did *not* give him permission. Please."

A muscle tightened along the strong curve of his jaw. "I wish I could tell you that, but I can't. They did, just this morning. I heard about it through his probation officer."

Raw emotion poured into my chest, and I turned to the side, not wanting him to see it. I couldn't believe it. My brain refused to process that Charlie's parents had given that . . . that bastard permission to visit him. How incredibly callous and crude and just so wrong. Charlie was the way he was now because of that homophobic asshole. Those knots spun tighter in my stomach, and there was a good chance I was going to puke.

Reece's hand folded over my shoulder, causing me to jump, but he didn't remove his hand and the weight of it . . . there was something grounding about it. A tiny part of me was grateful for the pressure and it reminded me of how it used to be between us. "I thought it would be better for you to hear it first and not be sidelined by it."

I squeezed my eyes shut and my words were hoarse. "Thank you."

He kept his hand there as another moment stretched out between us. "That's not all. He wants to talk to you."

My body jerked out of his reach on its own accord. I faced him again. "No. I do not want to see him." In a second, that night came roaring back, and I backpedaled, bouncing into the side of my car. Things had started out lightly. Joking. Teasing. Then everything escalated so quickly, so badly. "No way."

"You don't have to." He moved toward me, but drew up short, lowering his hand to his side. "But you needed to know. I'll tell his officer that he needs to steer clear of you. Or else."

The "or else" barely registered, as was the low threat

to his deep voice. My heart pounded in my chest, and I suddenly needed to be far away from where I was, alone, to process this. Edging along the passenger side of my car, I brought the tote bag up to my chest like some kind of shield. "I . . . I have to go."

"Roxy," he called out.

I made it around the front of my car, but somehow, like a ninja or something, Reece was in front of me. His sunglasses were still off and he was focused on me, his eyes the color of clear, precise blue.

Both of his hands landed on my shoulders, and it was like sticking my finger in an electrical socket. In spite of the news he'd just delivered, I felt the weight of his hands in every cell, and I don't know if he felt it too, but his fingers curved, anchoring me in. "What happened to Charlie," he said, voice low. "It wasn't your fault, Roxy."

My stomach flopped as I broke free, and he didn't stop me this time as I darted around him and all but yanked open the car door and threw myself in behind the wheel. My chest rose and fell heavily as I stared at him through the windshield.

Reece stood in front of my car for a few seconds, and for a moment, I thought he was going to climb in the car with me, but then he shook his head as he slipped his sunglasses on. I watched him turn and stalk his way to his truck, and only then did I speak.

"Mother pucker," I spat at the steering wheel as I gripped it with shaky hands. I didn't know what the worst thing that had happened was. That Charlie hadn't acknowledged me again. That Henry Williams had gotten permission to visit Charlie. Or the fact I was reminded that I wasn't sure if Reece was right.

If what happened to Charlie really was my fault.

Chapter 3

There was a part of me that wished I drank while I bartended, because after the kind of day I had, I'd get good and plastered tonight. But alas, I was pretty sure the owner of Mona's would so not appreciate me passing out behind the bar, tucked in next to the service well.

Jackson James, more commonly known as Jax and who truly did have a name that sounded like he belonged on the cover of *Tiger Beat,* had cleaned up Mona's with nothing more than elbow grease and pure grit and determination. The bar had been a crap hole before he came along, rumored to be nothing more than a druggie hangout, but not anymore.

He circled his arms around his girlfriend Calla's waist. Her response was immediate and so endearingly natural. She leaned into him as they stood not too far from the worn pool tables, grinning at another couple.

Hell, there were couples everywhere. It was like it

was couples night at Mona's and someone forgot to tell me.

Cameron Hamilton and his fiancée, Avery Morgansten, sat at one of the tables, a beer in front of him and a glass of soda in front of her, being their normal super cute. Avery had this amazingly gorgeous red hair and freckles, looking like she could be a walking ad for Neutrogena, and Cam was handsome in that all-American way.

It was Jase Winstead and Cam's younger sister Teresa who Jax and Calla were talking to. Those two were simply striking together, like the Brad Pitt and Angelina Jolie of Mona's. Then there were Brit and Ollie, blond bombshells, the latter who was explaining to one of the guys holding a pool stick that there are fifty-two Fridays in 2015 . . . or something equally bizarre as that. The last time I'd talked to Ollie, he told me about how he was starting up a business where he was selling leashes . . . for tortoises. Wow.

Adjusting the glasses I probably should be wearing all the time, I let my gaze drift back to Calla and Jax, and I felt my lips spread into a smile as I reached for the bottle of Jack. Witnessing two people who truly deserved to be loved fall *in* love was probably the most amazing thing to see. It made my teeny-tiny heart all mushy when she tipped her chin up and Jax dropped a kiss on her lips.

Tonight was about them—well, about her. She was leaving on Monday, heading back to Shepherd and Jax had closed the bar down tonight for a little going-away party—the private party that I'd told Charlie about.

Pouring a Jack and Coke for Melvin, who was older than Father Time and practically had his own stool at the bar, I grinned as he winked and grabbed the short glass. "That's love right there." He spoke over the old rock-and-roll song that was playing, nodding in the direction of Calla and Jax. "The kind that lasts."

Actually, it was like love threw up in the bar. Even Dennis, who worked with Reece and his brother, was here with his wife. They were all cuddled up together. But Melvin was right, and it made me a little sad, because I'd be pouring myself into bed all by my lonesome tonight.

Oh well.

"Yeah, it is." Sliding the bottle back on the shelf, I leaned against the bar top. "You want wings or anything?"

"Nah, sticking to the real deal tonight." He lifted the glass as I raised a brow. "It's good about those two," he added after taking a drink. "That girl, you know, she ain't had the easiest life. Jax will . . . yeah, he'll take good care of her."

I was of the mindset that Calla didn't need Jax to take care of her, that she could do it all by herself, but I got what he was saying in that old-fashioned way of his. One just had to look at her to know that some bad—real bad—things had happened. She had a scar on her left cheek, one she didn't try to hide so much anymore, and she'd told me what the fire had done to the rest of her body. It had happened when she was a young girl, and she'd ended up losing her whole family. Her brothers had died, and her mom dived off the deep end, while her dad had bounced, unable to deal.

So like I said, it was amazing seeing someone who really deserved love find it.

Melvin tilted his grizzly cheek toward me as I straightened the glasses perched on my nose. "So what about you, Roxy-girl?"

Looking around the half-empty bar, I frowned. "What do you mean what about me?"

He gave me a toothy grin. "When you gonna be out there with your arms around some man?"

I snorted. Couldn't help myself. "Not anytime soon."

"Famous last words," he replied, tipping his glass to his lips.

Shaking my head, I laughed. "Ah, no. Not famous. Just true."

He frowned as he slid off the stool. "I saw you going into that Italian place with that one boy last week. What's his name?"

"I like to think I don't date *boys*," I teased. "So I have no clue who you're talking about."

Melvin finished off his drink in a way that must've made his liver proud. "You date a lot, little lady."

Shrugging a shoulder, I couldn't argue with that statement. I did date a lot and actually some of the guys did act like boys, thinking that a cheap dinner at the Olive Garden meant they were getting some action afterward. I mean, geez, it should be a rule somewhere that said filet and lobster had to be on the menu before second base could be achieved.

"Yeah, well, what about the one who looked wet behind the ears? The redhead kid," he said. "Yeah, he had red hair and some peach fuzz on his face."

Peach fuzz? Oh geez, I bit down on my lip to stop from laughing, because I knew who he was thinking of and the poor guy seriously couldn't grow facial hair. "You're talking about Dean?"

"Whatever," he said dismissively. "I don't like him."

"You don't know him!" I pushed off the bar, grinning as he rolled his eyes. "Dean's actually a pretty nice guy, and he's older than me."

Melvin grunted. "You need to get with a real man."

"You volunteering?" I threw back.

That got a deep, throaty laugh out of him. "If I was younger, girl, I'd show you a good time."

"Whatever," I laughed, folding my arms across the lettering on my T-shirt, which said HUFFLEPUFF DOES IT BETTER. "You want another drink? Beer, though, because it's obvious you don't need any more liquor."

He snickered in my direction, but quickly got all serious face with me. "You got someone walking you to your car when you get off?"

I thought that was a weird question. "One of the guys always walks me to my car."

"Good. You need to be careful," he went on. "I'm sure you heard about the girl over in the Prussia area? She's around your age, lives alone, and works late. Some guy followed her home, messed her up pretty badly."

"I think I remember hearing something about that on the news, but I thought it was some guy she knew. An ex-boyfriend or something."

He shook his head as he took the bottle of beer I offered. "Last I heard, he was cleared. They think it was a stranger. Prussia ain't far from here, and you remember that girl who disappeared about a month ago. Shelly Winters, I think was her name. She lived over in Abington Township? They still ain't found her." He tipped the bottle at me, and I vaguely remembered seeing Missing Persons photos shared on Facebook. If my memory served me right, she was a pretty girl with blue eyes and brown hair. "Just be careful, Roxy."

Leaning against the bar, I frowned as Melvin ambled off. Now that was kind of a creepy turn in our conversation.

"Wanna make a bet?"

I turned and looked waaay up at Nick Dormas. He took tall, dark, and brooding to a whole new level, and the girls who came in here ate it right up. He had an "I'm gonna break your heart" allure, and yet the girls kept on flocking to him. I was a little surprised he was talking, because he rarely spoke to anyone besides Jax, and I had no idea how he hooked up with so many chicks when he was as quiet as a mime. Nick was a hit-it-and-never-see-your-face-again kind of guy. I once overheard Jax telling him he couldn't ban chicks he'd banged from the bar just because Nick didn't want to see them again. "For what?"

Grabbing the bottle of tequila, he nodded in Jax's direction. "He'll be down to Shepherd before the week is out."

A grin tugged at my lips as I stepped back, giving him access to the rack of glasses. "Yeah, I'm not making that kind of bet unless I get to say yes, he'll be down there."

Nick laughed softly, which was another strange sound, because it was also something he rarely did. I didn't know what his deal was, he could be moody and he was really bad boyfriend material, but I liked him. "Hey," I said. "Guess what?"

He raised a brow.

"Banana."

One side of his lips kicked up. "Is that like a code word for something?"

"Nope. Just felt like I needed to say it." I grabbed a towel and swiped up a bit of spilled liquor. "But wouldn't that be a weird safe word during BDSM play? Like the chick yelling banana in the middle of sex? That would be so awkward."

Nick stared at me.

"I read this book once where the girl yelled *cat* right before they were about to get some bow-chicka-bow-wow," I told him. "It was high-larious."

"Okay," he murmured before wandering away.

Jax was standing by the bar, both brows raised. "What in the hell are you two talking about?"

I grinned at him and Calla. "Safe words used during BDSM."

Calla's eyes widened. "Um, all right, wasn't expecting that."

A giggle escaped me, and in the moment, I felt a lot lighter than I had the whole day. "You two want something to drink?" I looked at Calla and smiled like the Joker on meth. "How about tequila?"

She drew back, and I almost expected her to hiss at me. "Hell no. I don't want any of that devil's juice."

Jax chuckled as he dropped his arm over her shoulders and tucked her against his side, almost protectively. And that brought forth an *aww* moment from me. "I don't know. It's kind of cute when you cuddle a bottle," he said.

Her cheeks flushed as she placed a hand on his lower stomach. "I think I'll just stay away from that."

I ended up forking over a Bud Light for him and a hard lemonade for her. "Like the shirt," Calla commented as she cradled the bottle close to her pouted rosy lips. "I'm gonna miss you and your shirts."

"I'm going to miss you, too!" I shrieked, and if I could actually climb over the bar, I would've thrown myself on her. "But you're coming back, right? We have like joint custody of you."

She laughed. "I'll be back before you know it. You won't even miss me."

But I would totally miss her.

"I'm tagging along with her when she comes back." Tess appeared beside her, smoothing a hand down the glossy length of her dark hair. "I like it here."

Calla glanced over to where Jase was talking to Cam. "I hope you aren't planning to leave him behind, because I don't think that will work out well for you."

"I'd never do such a thing." Tess looked over at me. "He's great arm candy to have around."

My gaze traveled back to the silver-eyed hottie known as Jase. "True dat."

"Okay, I think it's time for me to go." Jax dropped his arm as he pressed a kiss to Calla's cheek. "Jase is dreamy, though! I'd do him."

He'd said that loud enough that Jase sent us a confused look that he somehow managed to make look sexy, and I cracked up into a fit of hyena-type giggles.

Tess shook her head as she leaned into Calla. "All seriousness, both of us really like it up here. So do Cam and Avery. Good place to get away to."

"And you can always come visit us," Calla said to me.

I nodded absently as the door swung open. Only people who were close to Calla and Jax would be coming in tonight, and I expected it to be Katie since she hadn't made an appearance yet, but that wasn't who it was.

Reece walked in, wearing a variation of what he had on earlier today, and my stupid heart did a little jump. It was Friday night, and being a deputy, shouldn't he be working?

Dammit.

He didn't even look to where the guys were crowded around one of the tables. His attention immediately went to the bar. Our eyes locked. Girlie parts instantly engaged.

Double dammit.

Like every time I saw him, he took a bit of my breath away. Maybe it was the way he walked—oh hell, he was heading right for the bar! I veered around, my gaze landing on Nick. "I'm going to go check stock."

"One of these days you're going to tell me why you do this," Calla muttered, and I didn't hear what else she said, because I was hightailing my bony butt out of the bar.

Maybe it was a bitchy thing to do, because he'd been really thoughtful coming to find me this morning. It was something I'd thought about all afternoon. Well, about that and Henry Williams wanting to make amends.

Amends—as if that were truly possible.

God, I wanted to laugh as I dashed down the hall and dipped into the stockroom. Closing the door behind me, I leaned against it and blew out a breath, stirring a chunk of purple and brown hair that had fallen in my face. I didn't want to think about Henry right now and as terrible as it sounded, I didn't want to think about Charlie either. My mood was up, and I still had several hours left before my shift ended and I could crash.

So my mind danced its way over to Reece, and I still had no idea why he'd made a special trip to tell me about Henry. Granted, we'd been really good friends at one point, but for eleven months, there'd been a no-fly zone between us. He'd breached that, and I really didn't know what to think about what it meant. It probably meant nothing—it couldn't mean anything, because Reece . . . well, he'd really taken a hunk out of my heart eleven months ago.

And he didn't even know it.

I waited a good five minutes, deciding that Reece would've gotten a drink from Nick by then. Pushing off the door, I tucked the strand of hair behind my ear and opened it.

"Criminy!" I shrieked, stumbling back into the stockroom.

Reece stood there, hands braced against the door frame, his chin dipped low and jaw hard. He did not look happy. "Are you done hiding?"

"I . . . I wasn't hiding. N-not at all." Heat flooded my cheeks. "I was doing stock."

"Uh-huh."

"I was!"

He arched a brow.

"Whatever. I need to get back out there, so can you kindly remove—"

"No."

My mouth dropped open. "No?"

He straightened, but instead of backing off, he stalked forward, catching the door on the way in. The bicep in his right arm flexed as he slammed it shut. "You and I need to talk."

Oh dear. "Buddy, there's nothing we need to talk about."

Reece kept coming toward me, and I was moving backward before I even knew what I was doing. I bumped into a shelf. Bottles rattled behind me, and then he was right in front of me, so close that when I inhaled, I could practically taste the crisp, fresh scent of his cologne.

Two hands landed on the shelf on each side of my shoulders and then he managed to lean in even further. His warm breath danced across my cheek. A fine shiver curled its way down my spine. Whoa. Girlie parts engaged, locked, and ready for takeoff.

I was so going to hit myself later.

"I've let this go on between us for far too long," he said, and his stare snared my wide-eyed gaze. The blue . . . dang, it was cobalt—a blue that was hard to mix and capture with watercolors.

My tongue felt heavy. He hadn't been this close since that night with all that whiskey. "Nothing is going on between us."

"Bullshit, Roxy. You've been avoiding me for months."

"Nuh-uh," I said, and yeah, that was lame-sounding, but his mouth was right there, and I remembered clearly what his mouth felt like against mine. A wonderful combination of firm and soft, and I also recalled how strong he was. How he'd lifted me right off the floor and . . .

And I really needed to stop thinking about that right now.

"Eleven months," he said, voice deeper. "Eleven months, two weeks and three days. That's exactly how long you've been avoiding me."

Holy crap, did he just count that out to me? Because he was totally right. That was exactly how long I'd been steering clear of him, in between the moments I'd told him to screw off.

"We're going to talk about the last time you and I had a decent conversation."

Oh no, we were so not going to talk about that.

He dipped his head, and his voice was right in my ear. When he spoke, my fingers tightened on the edge of the shelf I was hanging onto. "Yeah, babe, we're going to talk about the night you drove me back to my place."

I swallowed hard, unnerved. "You . . . you mean the night you were drunk off your ass, and I had to drive you home?"

Reece lifted his head and those eyes bored into mine. Neither of us spoke for a long moment, and I was thrust back eleven months, two weeks and three days ago. He'd been at the bar, and we'd been flirting with each other like we'd been doing every time we saw each other since he returned from overseas. But when he came back, it was like those years he'd been gone had washed away. Visions of marriage and making babies had danced in my head despite the fact I'd ordered myself not to read into the harmless flirting. But I'd been infatuated and I'd also been an idiot. That night, he'd asked me to drive him home, and I'd thought he was finally making a move—a really weird way to make a move, but I hadn't really thought the whole thing through. I'd been crushing on this guy forever and I had been greedy with his attention, so I did it. When we'd gotten to his place, I'd followed him inside and I . . . I had been the one to *really* make the move.

Gathering up all the courage I had in me, I had kissed him, right inside his apartment, the moment he'd closed the door. Things had escalated quickly. Clothes had come off, body parts were most definitely touching, and I . . .

"I'd give anything to remember that night," Reece continued, looking me straight on, and that voice got richer. "Anything to remember what it felt like being inside of you."

Several things happened to me all at once. Muscles low in my belly tightened at the same moment disappointment swelled like a tide, washing away the anger flushing my system. I closed my eyes as I bit down on my lip.

Reece believed that eleven months, two weeks, and three days ago, we'd had sex—wild, animalistic against-the-wall sex, but he'd been too drunk to remember it. Too shitfaced to remember anything past the moment we'd gotten naked in the hallway.

I just hadn't realized he'd been that far into his cups, which was stupid, because I bartended and knew when people were plastered and needed to be cut off. Hell, he'd asked me to drive him home, for crying out loud, but I had been so . . . so caught up in him. So damn hopeful and so beyond crushing, because it was more than that. I had fallen in love with him when I was fifteen and that hadn't changed in all those years.

I'd stayed the night with him, and when he'd woken up the next morning, hungover and so damn apologetic, regretful and seconds from chewing his arm off to get away from me, my heart had cracked. And in the immediate weeks following that night, when he'd avoided me like I was infested with the plague, my heart had shattered.

The sad thing was Reece had it all wrong.

We hadn't even gotten to the point where slot A fit into slot B. We hadn't had sex that night. He'd barely made it to the bedroom before passing out, and I had stayed with him because I'd been worried and I thought . . . it didn't matter what I thought, because we hadn't had sex.

Chapter 4

What was worse than Reece thinking we had sex and regretting what never happened? And seriously, what could be more messed up than that? Reece Anders despised lies of any kind. White lies. Little lies. Necessary lies. Forgiving lies. Any lies.

Mine was kind of a white lie since I never said we had sex, I just never said we didn't. Even though he'd known me since I was fifteen, he'd been there during the aftermath of what happened to Charlie, and the first night back from being in the Marines for four years, he'd shown up at my parents' house. To this day, Mom swore he'd been looking for me, but our families had grown close, so I doubted that was the case. I'd moved out at eighteen and I wasn't there, but when my parents called and demanded that I come home, I'd been expecting something terrible, because Mom sounded like she'd been seconds from stroking out. I had no idea Reece was home, and he gave me . . . oh wow, the best hug ever. And in spite of the friendship we'd built since he became a deputy in the county, he would be so pissed.

His absolute hatred of lying had started way before I'd met him and had to do with his father. I didn't know the details, but I figured it involved cheating since he'd moved in with his mom and stepdad while his father was a serial dater.

So, yeah, lying to Reece equaled shitstorm of the century.

Reece stared down at me, waiting for a response, and I didn't have any. So many times during the last eleven months I wanted to shout the truth in his face. That we hadn't had sex, but the hurt he created based on the way he'd acted that following morning, then ignoring me for weeks was compounded by the fact he had to get so drunk for him to think he had sex with me. The pain had cut deep.

I was embarrassed—horrified, really—and if Charlie were aware of the situation, he probably would've smacked me upside the head. Because I should've known better, but I hadn't and I had paid for that in spades. Days passed while I was under the influence of an ice-cream coma. Weeks when I thought I'd burst into tears whenever I heard his name mentioned. For months, I couldn't look at Reece without my face turning blood red.

And that hurt had lingered.

Gathering up that pain and humiliation, I held it close as I drew in a deep breath that sharpened my tongue. "Like I said, Reece, there's really nothing to talk about. I barely even remember that night myself." Lies! All lies! I forced a shrug. "Nothing to write home about."

He arched a brow. "I don't believe you."

"Do you really think your prowess in bed is so stellar that I'd remember one night with your drunk ass?" I fired back.

"No." His lips curved in a tight half smile, and I couldn't believe he was still standing there. "What I'm saying is that you obviously remember a whole lot if you've been avoiding me all this time."

Hell, he had a good point. "Actually, it's more of an I'd-rather-not-remember kind of thing." The moment those words came out of my mouth, I wanted to take them back, because they were *mean*. Even though I avoided him at all costs and could be pretty spiteful toward him, it wasn't something I enjoyed.

His lips thinned as he tilted his head to the side. The bright fluorescent light glided over the sharp curve of his cheek. A heartbeat passed, and I expected him to fling an insult back in my direction. I would've deserved it after that slam, but that wasn't what I got. "I wish I could say I know it was good for you, and babe, I know I could've made it real good for you," he said, his voice dropping again, and those coils low in my belly spun even tighter.

Memories swamped me, stealing my breath. Even plastered, he'd been well on his way to making it *outstanding*. Like never gonna forget this night in a good way. My lips parted on a soft inhale as a slow burn invaded my veins. His gaze moved to my mouth, and my chest rose sharply. His stare stayed there long enough that a wild idea exploded in my brain, like the king of all wild ideas, because obviously when I got a wild idea in my head, it ended epically bad. But that knowledge did nothing to stop it from taking hold.

I thought Reece looked like he wanted to kiss me as his hooded gaze zeroed in on my mouth. And when I took my next breath, I wasn't sure if I'd stop him. What the hell did that say about me exactly? I was a glutton for punishment.

He cleared his throat as he dragged his gaze up to mine. "But knowing how trashed I was, I'm not sure about any of it. I don't—"

"I need to get back out there." There was no way I could continue in this conversation. I needed to get out of there before a mixture of desire and a need to make him feel better hijacked my common sense. I started to dip under his arm, but he shifted his body. As tall and built as he was, there was no way I was getting past him.

"For Christ sakes, stop running from me."

My hands closed at my sides. "I'm not running."

His eyes met mine, and once again, I was trapped as he carefully placed the tip of his finger against the center of my glasses and pushed them back up my nose. My heart flip-flopped in response to a gesture he used to do all the time.

"I need to get them adjusted," I would say, and he'd always respond with, "Nah. I like being your official keeper of your glasses." Goodness, remembering that made my heart ache.

"Did I . . . did I do wrong by you, Roxy?"

I stiffened as if steel had been dropped down my spine. "What?"

Everything about Reece's posture had changed. He was still close, his hands still on the shelves on either side of me, but the lazy arrogance that seemed to bleed from his every pore was gone. Every part of him was alert and tense. "Did I hurt you somehow?"

My mouth dropped open. Had he hurt me? Yes. He'd bruised my heart, smashed it into pieces, but I didn't think that's what he meant. "No. God, no. How could you even think that?"

His eyes closed briefly as he exhaled harshly. "I don't know what to think."

Oh God, my entire chest clenched. I needed to tell him the truth, because it didn't matter how badly my feelings and pride were bruised, I couldn't let him think something like that about himself. The words formed on the tip of my tongue.

"It should've never happened," he continued. "You and I . . . not in that way."

The words fizzled up on my tongue, going out like a spark in a downpour. I knew how crazy it was to be upset, because he said it shouldn't have happened when it had in fact never happened, but it was the *point* behind it all. A different set of words flooded out of my mouth. "You really do regret it, don't you?" My voice sounded too hoarse. "I know I can't be the first chick you got so drunk—"

"That I don't remember being with?" he cut in. "Yeah, you're the only girl I've done that with."

I didn't know if I should be relieved to know that or be really insulted. Shaking my head, I grappled with the mixed bag of emotions. "You . . . you wish that night never happened, right?"

"Yeah, I do." The blunt honesty was like taking a bullet straight to the chest. "Because I wa—"

The stockroom door suddenly opened. "Man, I have really bad timing when it comes to this shit," announced Nick. "Sorry to . . . yeah, intrude. I just need to grab some . . . stuff."

My escape was in the form of dark and broody, and I wasn't going to look a gift horse in the mouth. I used the distraction to my benefit. Reece had dropped his arms as he faced Nick, who was grabbing the new napkins with Mona's logo splashed across them. I darted away from Reece and hauled butt through the open door. I didn't look at Nick and the blood roaring in my ears drowned out anything either of them could've said.

The odd burn in the back of my throat had to do with allergies. Probably mold somewhere in the building, I told myself as I headed behind the bar and forced a wide smile when I saw the girls sitting there.

"You guys need drinks?" I asked cheerily, reaching almost blindly for a bottle.

"We're good." Calla's gaze drifted over my shoulder, and I didn't need to look to know that Reece had exited the stockroom. I saw him within seconds, crossing the barroom floor. He dropped into the empty seat next to Cam, his profile stoic.

"You okay?" she asked, voice low and sincere.

My smile was going to split my cheeks. "Of course."

Doubt crossed her face, and as I turned around and pushed my glasses up to my forehead, I told myself to pull it together. This was her night—her and Jax's. I didn't need her worrying about me. Scrubbing my hands over my face, I probably wiped off what was left of my makeup. Oh well, didn't matter at this point. I fixed my glasses and whirled around.

Calla, Tess and Avery stared at me.

I drew in a shallow breath that scratched at my throat and then grabbed the hem of my shirt, pulling it straight. "So, do you guys want to know why Hufflepuffs do it better?"

Avery grinned as she leaned forward. "Do we *want* to know?"

I nodded eagerly. "Oh, yes—yes you do."

Tess bounced once, way enthusiastic to hear my reasons for why being sorted into Hufflepuff was a good thing, and I think I fell in love with her in that moment, but Calla wasn't fooled. She nibbled on her lower lip as she watched me refill Avery's glass with soda. And I couldn't stop myself from glancing over to where all the guys sat. Cam and Jax, who appeared to be on the verge of an epic bromance were deep in conversation with Jase, but the moment my gaze drifted across the table, I forgot what I was doing with the ice scoop. Holy hell, I didn't even remember picking it up. Why was I holding it?

Reece's eyes met mine, and the air slowly leaked out of my lungs. The intensity in his stare traveled across the distance between us. It struck me then—why had he picked tonight to finally breach the standoff between us. Not that it really mattered, but I was curious.

I didn't need to have any of Katie's ability—she was convinced that when she fell off the pole while, um, dancing and hit her head, she developed psychic power—to know what he was thinking and what the concentrated power in his stare meant. I might have dodged him in the stockroom, but he was far from done with me.

Vibrant blue eyes, the shade of the sky seconds before dusk washed away the startling color, peered out from a thick fringe of dark brown lashes surrounded by golden hued skin. Those eyes were set in a face that still held a hint of boyish charm, but the hard line of the jaw, stubborn and dominant, and those expressive, well-shaped lips spoke of masculinity. A beauty that could be as harsh as it was majestic.

My gaze moved over the canvas and then to the paintbrush in my hand, the ends of its bristles stained blue.

Dammit all to hell in a handbasket. And not a cheap handbasket, one of those Longaberger baskets like my mom collected.

I did it again.

Resisting the urge to throw the brush at the painting, I wondered if the handle was sharp enough to give myself a lobotomy, because seriously, that was the only valid response to painting Reece's face.

Again.

As in way more than once.

Not only was it really kind of pathetic, it was also sort of creepy if I thought about it. I mean, I doubted he'd appreciate knowing I was painting or sketching his face. I'd freak out if some dude was secretly painting my face and had several versions hidden away in his closet. Unless it was Theo James or Zac Efron. They could totally paint my face all they wanted and then some. Reece also probably wouldn't want to know that I woke up this morning with his eyes burned into my thoughts because I'd dreamed of him again.

Also as in way more than once.

Maybe he wouldn't mind, an evil little voice whispered. After all, last night in the stockroom he'd gotten all up in my personal space. He totally fixed my glasses for me. There was a moment when I thought he might kiss me.

He also told me the night he thought we had sex should've never happened.

So, that evil little voice was a misleading bitch who liked to stir up shit.

Pushing my glasses up my nose, I sighed as I

dropped the brush next to the little jars of watercolors sitting on top of the old nightstand that looked like the primary color wheel threw up all over it.

I really needed to stop painting his face.

Why couldn't I be a normal wannabe artist, painting rolling hills and vases of flowers or some other stupid, abstract stuff? Oh no, I had to be the artist people would think had stalking tendencies.

Sliding off my stool, I wiped my hands along my denim shorts and then carefully peeled the sheet of watercolor canvas free. Some people liked to paint on recycled paper, but I'd always preferred the texture and look of canvas, and all you had to do was gesso the canvas so the watercolor would work.

What I needed to do was roll it up, trash it so no one in the world could see it, but like every time I committed any image to canvas, no matter how embarrassing it might be, I couldn't part with it.

Painting, the same as sketching, well . . . it became a part of me.

"I'm such an idiot," I muttered as I walked the almost dry painting to the makeshift clothesline I'd strung the length of the bedroom I'd converted into a studio.

I hung the portrait from clothespins and then backed out of the room, closing the door behind me and swearing that if anyone ever stumbled inside the room and saw that painting—or any of the others—I'd curl up in a little ball in the middle of the interstate.

The soft hum of the TV in the living room tickled my ears as I started down the narrow hallway. Ever since I was a kid, I didn't like silence, and it got worse after what happened with Charlie. A TV or a radio always had to be turned on. At night, I always had one of those standing fans running, not so much for the cool factor, but mostly the noise.

Two steps took me past my bedroom and the one and only bathroom. My apartment was a bit on the small side, but it was nice. Ground level, hardwood floors throughout, an open floor plan combining the kitchen and living room, and a door that led out from the kitchen onto a neat deck and green area, as well as front access.

It really wasn't an apartment complex either. Just a huge, old Victorian smack-dab in the middle of the Plymouth Meeting, a town a few miles outside of Philly. The Victorian had been remodeled back in the early 2000s and converted into four two-bedroom apartments. Charlie would've called it quaint and he would've loved it.

An elderly couple, Mr. and Mrs. Silver, lived in the other ground floor apartment, some dude I rarely saw had just moved into the apartment above me a few months back, and James, a guy who worked at the local insurance place lived in the other apartment with his girlfriend, Miriam.

My phone dinged, drawing my attention to where I'd left my cell on the arm of the couch when I got home from the bar. I saw it was a text.

I winced and almost hid behind the couch. It was from Dean and all it said was: *Love to see u again.*

Yikes, I suddenly felt spazzy. I didn't even want to touch my phone.

Last week, when I brought Dean home—the guy from Olive Garden who had peach fuzz according to Melvin—things hadn't gone as I'd hoped.

The night had ended with some kissing. Kissing in a good location, out on the small deck, under the stars, but nothing more. Probably had to do with Mr. Silver hobbling out on the deck shared with the apartment next door. The elderly man looked like he was going to beat the poor guy with his cane.

But even if we hadn't been interrupted, nothing else was going to happen between Dean and me. He was a nice guy, if not a wee bit overcommunicative, but when I thought about him, I didn't feel anything.

Maybe had to do with . . . God, was I going to finish the thought? That the kiss I shared with Dean was lackluster because it was nothing like when Reece had kissed me—*crap!* I'd finished the stupid thought.

Funny thing was, I wasn't in the business of looking to feel anything in the first place, so in a way, Dean was safe. He was fun to hang out with and there was absolutely no chance in holy hell of my heart getting involved, but that wasn't fair to him.

I sighed as I passed the couch, leaving my cell phone where it was. Dean was nice, but there was going to be no second date. I had to find my lady balls and tell him that, but I needed a nap before I did that. Maybe a bowl of chips and—

My stomach flopped as I came to a stop in the dining area, facing the kitchen. Movement outside of the small window above the sink caught my attention. It was quick—a flash of gray or dark brown, but it was gone too quickly for my craptastic eyesight, even with glasses, to register what I saw. When I made it to the window, I clutched the edge of the cool steel of the sink and stretched up on the tips of my toes. Peering out the window, the only thing I saw was the basket of pink flowers I'd bought from the market last week, sitting on the wrought-iron bistro set that had seen better days, petals swaying in the breeze. I thought I heard a door shut, but as I settled on my feet, I shook my head.

Now I was seeing things.

Turning around, I leaned against the sink and drew in a deep breath as I moved my neck from one side to the other. Closing down Mona's last night meant I hadn't gotten home until after three in the morning and I'd woken up way too early.

Woken up with that feeling in the pit of my stomach, that . . . that horrible emptiness that had no real cause behind it. Just there, making me restless and itchy in my own skin. It had lingered until I picked up the paintbrush, and I knew it would come back again.

It always did.

Pushing off the sink, I grabbed a banana from the sad fruit basket that was mostly filled with pieces of chocolate just as a knock came from the front door. One look at the clock near the fridge told me who it was.

Every Saturday, since I'd moved out when I was eighteen, four years ago, my mom and sometimes my entire family stopped by at noon. Just like every Friday I visited Charlie.

Thank God I'd closed the studio door, because the last thing I needed was anyone in my family—Mom, Dad, or my two brothers, to see paintings of Reece. They knew who he was.

Everyone knew who he was.

Unlocking the door, I threw it open to have a wave of heat smack into me and a gallon of brown liquid shoved in the general direction of my face. I stumbled back. "What the . . . ?"

"I made you sweet tea," Mom announced, thrusting the still warm plastic container in my arms. "Figured you'd be out."

I could make any drink at the bar known to man, but I couldn't make sweet tea to save my life. For some reason, I couldn't get the sugar to tea bags to water ratio correct. It was beyond me.

"Thanks." I cuddled the jug close to my chest as Mom blew into the house like a five-foot-and-three-inch tornado with short, spiky brown hair. "It's just you today?"

She closed the door in a whirl and adjusted her red-rimmed glasses. Not only did I get my lack of height from Mom, I also got her crappy eyesight. Yay, genetics! "Your father is golfing with your brother."

I assumed "your brother" meant my older brother, Gordon, because my younger brother, Thomas, was going through some kind of goth stage and wouldn't get within five miles of a golf course.

"He's going to have a heart attack in this heat, you know? It's absolutely ridiculous that he's out there. Same with Gordon," she carried on, making her way to the secondhand couch I bought when I moved into the apartment four years ago. She dropped down. "He needs to be more responsible—your brother, since he has my grandbaby on the way."

I had no idea how playing golf in August had anything to do with his wife being three months pregnant, but I let that slide as I carried the jug to the fridge. "Want anything to drink?"

"I drank so much coffee that I'm surprised I didn't float my way here."

My nose wrinkled as I opened the door. Taking a startled step back, I stared into the fridge, my fingers tightening around the handle on the jug. "What the . . . ?" I muttered.

"What are you doing, honey?"

Unsettled, I stared in the fridge. On the top shelf, next to the case of soda, was the remote control to the

TV. I'd never in my life ever accidentally put the remote or any other non-consumable goods in the fridge. I didn't know anyone in real life who'd even done that, but there it was, sitting on the shelf like a tarantula perched to attack.

I glanced at the sink window, stomach tumbling as I thought of the blur of movement I'd seen outside earlier. It was nothing, and I had to be a lot more tired than I thought I was, but still it was weird—very weird.

I shook my head as I snatched the remote from what I was beginning to think was the fridge in *Ghostbusters II*, and put the tea in to cool.

Twisting on the couch, Mom patted the cushion next to her. "Sit with me, Roxanne. We haven't talked in a while."

"We talked on the phone yesterday," I reminded her as I closed the door and brought the remote back to where it needed to stay, on the coffee table, like a good little remote.

Her brown eyes, just like mine, rolled. "That was forever ago, honey. Now get your ass over here."

I got my butt over there and the moment I sat down, she lifted a slender hand and gently poked at the messy ponytail I was rocking. "What happened to the red streaks?"

Shrugging, I reached up and tugged out the hair tie. My hair was long, reaching my nonexistent breasts. Other than the purple streaks, my hair was a deep brown. I messed with it a lot, so much so I was surprised it hadn't fallen out of my head yet. "I got bored with it. You like the purple?"

She nodded as her eyes narrowed behind the glasses. "Yes, it's very much you. Matches the paint stains on your shirt."

Glancing down at my old Twilight shirt, I saw that there was quite a bit of purple splattered across Edward's face. "Ha."

"So . . ." Mom drew the word out in a way that had warning bells ring-a-dinging in my head. "You know, the offer still stands. Right?"

My spine stiffened as I met her earnest stare. The offer. Ugh. The offer was a living, breathing crutch that I sometimes—okay, almost always—wanted to lean on. The offer was to move back home, at twenty-two, drop the computer graphics classes and the bartending and the web design I did on the side, and devote 100 percent of my time to my real passion.

Painting.

I was seriously lucky that my parents would be willing to support a broke-ass artist, but I couldn't do that. I needed my independence. It was why I moved out and it was why it was taking me ten billion years to finish my classes at the community college.

"Thank you," I said, clasping her warm hand in mine. "I mean it. Thank you, but you know . . ."

She sighed as she pulled her hand free and clasped my cheeks. Leaning in, she pressed a kiss to my forehead. "I know, but I just need to make sure you haven't forgotten." Drawing back, she tilted her head to the side as she smoothed a thumb just below my glasses. "You look so tired, worn out."

"Geez, Mom. Thanks."

She gave me a pointed look. "What time did you get off from Mona's?"

"Three in the morning." I sighed as I leaned back against the cushion, letting it swallow me up. "I got up early."

"Couldn't sleep?" Sympathy tinged her tone.

My momma knew me. I nodded.

There was a pause as she folded one knee over the other. "You saw Charlie yesterday?"

I nodded again.

"Of course you did," she said quietly. "How is my boy?"

Hearing her refer to Charlie like that made the wound of seeing him the way he was now so much harder. My parents . . . God, they were more parental figures to Charlie growing up than his own parents were. Sighing heavily, I told her about my visit with Charlie and how he hadn't acknowledged me again. Concern filled her dark eyes, because she too remembered what happened before.

When I was done, Mom pulled off her glasses and fidgeted with the slender arm. "I heard about Reece."

My eyes widened until I thought they'd pop out of my head. She heard about Reece? About our hookup that was not really a hookup? Mom and I shared a lot, but I drew the line there.

"I thought it was very nice of him to find you yesterday and tell you about Henry," she continued, and relief punched me in the stomach.

Thank God she wasn't referencing the shenanigans. "How did you know about that?"

She smiled. "His mother told me last night." The look about her became shrewd. "I think he went out of his way to do so. Out of his way, Roxy. Hmm, don't you find that interesting?"

"Oh, Mom." I rolled my eyes. Of course, she knew I had a huge crush on him from the moment he'd moved in next door. I was convinced that she and Reece's mother might have plotted to get Reece and me together last year over Thanksgiving, because they'd been dropping hints about both of us being sadly single to the point Reece's brother almost choked on mashed potatoes because he was laughing so hard.

It had been an uncomfortable joining of the two families, which meant it was going to be even more awkward this year, since the almost-hookup happened not too many moons after the Thanksgiving dinner.

"He's a good boy, Roxy." Mom droned on, sounding like an infomercial for Reece. "He fought for his country and then came home, took a job where he puts his life in danger. And what happened last year, with that boy. He had to make a tough—"

"Mom," I moaned.

I was able to steer the conversation away from Reece and toward the upcoming debut of grandbaby number one. When it was time for me to get ready for my evening shift at Mona's, I got a warm and squishy hug from Mom.

As she pulled back, she looked me straight in the eye. "We didn't talk a lot about Henry and what he wants, but I wanted to let you know that your father and I support you, no matter what you decide."

Tears rushed me, and I blinked them back. Aw man, I loved my parents. They were too good to me. "I don't want to talk to him. I don't even want to see his face."

Her smile was sad as she nodded, and I knew what she was really thinking. They wanted to see me let go of the big old baggage of hate that sat on my shoulders. "If that's what you want, then we are right behind you."

"It is," I confirmed.

She patted my cheek and then roared out of the house the same way she'd come in, and as I closed the door behind her, I realized there'd be no time for a nap.

Which was a good thing, because I'd probably end up dreaming about Reece again, and that was the last thing I needed to do. Right that second, I developed a list of priorities.

Number One: I needed to shower. Baby steps.

Number Two: I needed to stop dreaming about him. Easier said than done, but whatever. It was high on the priority list.

Number Three: I also needed to stop painting his stupid—albeit sexy—face.

And finally, Number Four: I needed to be up front with Reece the next time I saw him and tell him the truth about that night. I could do that, at least. Let go of *that* baggage of hurt. I needed to, because I couldn't stop thinking about what he had asked me.

Did I hurt you?

Pressing my lips together, I tried to ignore the nugget of guilt that bloomed in my belly as I started down the hall. Reece had dealt with enough guilt. He didn't need me adding to it. Once inside my bedroom, I stripped down, leaving my clothes remaining where they fell as my thoughts were circling around how I was going to break the news.

I had a sinking suspicion he wasn't going to be happy with me.

But if I had known he thought something like that this entire time, I would've cleared it up long ago. Seriously. Me being butt sore over it was nowhere near as bad as him thinking he did something really bad.

Chewing on my lower lip, I padded across the room, passing the deep closet. The doors were open, and a cold draft wafted on the bare skin of my stomach, creating a wave of goose bumps on my flesh. The bad thing about the Victorian was the draftiness, even in the summer. Mr. Silver once told me that there were hidden passages in the house from back in the day, pathways under the staircases and hidden doors behind plastered-up walls.

Come to think of it, the main staircase leading to the upstairs apartments abutted up to my bedroom.

Wheeling around, like a dork I quickly closed the closet doors. Pretty pointless considering I was buck naked, but I did it anyway.

As I got ready for work, I went right back to obsessing over the caring and sharing session I was going to have to have with Reece. Deep down I knew it wasn't going to end well, and I shouldn't care, but I did.

And I knew he was not only going to regret the night that never really happened, but once he realized I hadn't told him the truth, he was also going to end up hating me.

Chapter 5

Mona's was slammed Saturday night. With Jax already at Shepherd University in West Virginia with Calla, we were a man down when it came to the bar. Clyde was still out of commission due to doctor's orders after suffering a heart attack last month. Sherwood, our part-time cook, was running around like a madman.

We were so busy I barely caught the moment Nick slid his phone number scribbled on one of our new napkins to a girl in cut-off jeans.

"Another one bites the dust," I sang as I shimmied past him to grab two beers.

His eyes narrowed on me.

I giggled as I spun back, placing the bottles on the bar. The two guys waiting looked legit and normal, dressed in dark jeans and plain shirts, but I knew they didn't run in the friendliest of circles. I'd seen them both with Mack, who'd worked for a guy in Philly named Isaiah, who everyone in and near the city knew to stay away from. *Worked* as in the past tense, because over the summer, Mack had ended up with a bullet to the head on a lonely back road. From what I gathered, he'd been the one messing with Calla, threatening her over what her mom had gotten into, and Isaiah hadn't been too keen on the unwanted police attention being thrown his way.

So I smiled brightly up at them. "On the house."

The older one with coal-black hair winked. "Thanks, darling."

I figured it was a good idea to have potential mobsters in your back pocket. Never knew when one needed someone to take a cement swim. Ha.

I was guessing Reece was working, so completing Priority Number Four was on hold. I'd be a liar, liar, pants on fire if I said I wasn't relieved, because I was so dreading that moment of truth. And I had his phone number, so I could've totally texted him and asked to meet up. Or I could've texted him the truth.

But that would've been so lame I'd have to give myself a cement swim.

Good news was I wasn't really dwelling on it, since I was bouncing from one customer to the next, racking up tips. It was after midnight when I looked up from making a wicked sex on the beach and saw Dean standing at the corner of the bar.

Oh crap.

The moment I looked up, he saw me. Duh. I was standing right there and he was looking right at me. Briefly, I considered diving behind the service well.

"Hey," he said, finding what had to be the only unoccupied bar stool in the world. "Busy tonight."

I could feel heat creeping into my face. I so had not responded to his text earlier. After Mom had left, I'd forgotten about it. "Yeah, it's been a really busy . . . day." As I placed the pineapple juice back, I winced. A day so busy I didn't have time to send a text? Lame. When I faced him, I kept my bar smile firmly in place. "What can I get you?"

He blinked slowly. His eyes were blue, not as vibrant as Reece's—dammit! I was not thinking about his eye color. "Um, a Bud would be great."

Nodding, I quickly hurried off to grab him a beer. On the way back, Nick raised his brows at me but said nothing. I slapped a napkin on the bar and placed the beer on it. "Tab or pay as you go?"

Again, he blinked and then leaned back, fishing out his wallet. "Pay now." He slipped a ten over. "Keep the change."

"Thanks," I mumbled, wanting to leave the money on the bar, but there was rent and that new set of watercolors I wanted to get, so . . . Taking a deep breath, I glanced up at him as I folded my hand over the cash. "Look, Dean, I had a really good—"

"Hey! Roxy-moxy, my girl!"

My bones nearly jumped out of my skin at the sound of Katie's voice. I turned, surprised that she'd been able to sneak in. Then again, the bar was that crowded, and she was actually dressed down tonight. Kind of.

Katie worked across the street at the gentlemen's club. In other words, she was an exotic dancer and loved every minute of it. Normally she was wearing something that most wouldn't even consider wearing out in public. Tonight, her long legs were encased in bubble-gum pink leather and her halter top was like a purple disco ball.

Dean eyed her like she was an alien who had just strolled into the bar.

"Yo," I recovered quickly, and out of habit, grabbed the bottle of Jose and a shot glass. "How's work tonight?"

Elbowing her way between an older woman and Dean, she squeezed into the miniscule space. "So boring I almost fell asleep while sliding down the pole."

"That would've ended badly." I poured the shot.

"So, you're off on Sunday, right?" Dean cut in, clamping his arms close to his sides as if he were afraid of touching Katie and catching something from her.

I did not like that.

Katie snickered as she curled fingers with an icy blue manicure around the shot glass. "She is off, but she ain't going to be spending it with you unless your last name is Winchester." She arched a brow as she checked him out, and my mouth dropped open. "And you are so obviously not Dean Winchester."

"Excuse me?" he sputtered, his cheeks flushing red.

"What?" She shrugged tanned shoulders. "Honey, I'm just telling you in a nice way you don't stand a chance with her."

"Katie," I hissed.

Dean turned to me.

"Awkward," murmured Katie.

I shot her a look.

She pursed her lips, kissed the air, and then downed the shot of tequila in one gulp. "Remember what I told you." She slammed the glass on the top, and the woman next to her watched her back her way out of the spot with raised brows. Katie tapped her finger off the side of her head. "You've already met the man you're going to spend the rest of your life with."

Oh dear. I so remembered her telling me that I'd already met the love of my life, basing it on the psychic powers she claimed she developed when she fell off a greased-up pole while dancing.

These kinds of things only happen to people I know.

I was highly doubtful—or at least hopeful—that I hadn't met the love of my life yet, but that wasn't the only thing she told me. One of the things she had told me had come true.

And it had to do with Reece.

Katie made a face at Dean's back. "And it ain't him. Anyway, Roxy-moxy, we still on for waffles for lunch tomorrow?" When I nodded, she wiggled her fingers. "Toodles."

Sort of struck stupid, I watched her prance her way out of the bar. I'd known Katie for a long time, but she still managed to throw me for a loop.

"There is something wrong with that girl," Dean said, voice razor-edged with irritation. "I don't know how you deal with her."

My gaze swung on him. "There's nothing wrong with her at all." His eyes flared with surprise. "I'm sorry, but I'm pretty busy right now."

He did that blinking thing. "It's okay. We'll talk later."

I opened my mouth to tell him that wasn't going to happen, but he pivoted around and disappeared into the crowd. Shaking my head, I moved to the other side of the bar. I didn't have to say a word to Nick, because he switched sides and I threw myself into filling orders. Sometime later, I glanced up and awkwardly made eye contact with Dean. After that, I didn't see him.

The rest of the night zoomed by. We did final call, and then cleared out the bar before we cashed out tips and settled the register. Normally when Nick and I did this together, we did so with nothing but music to keep us company. Usually I'd find the most annoying song known to man and play it, but I wasn't really feeling it tonight.

And apparently Nick was in a chatty mood. "Who was that guy who was in here talking to you?"

I shut the register door and scribbled the totals on the spreadsheet Jax had created. One day, Mona's would grow up to be a real bar and we'd get a POS system. A girl could dream. I sighed as I faced him, leaning against the bar while he cleaned up. "He was just some guy I went out on a date with."

"Only going to be one date?"

I shrugged. "Yeah. Not interested."

Flipping the towel he was using over his shoulder, he walked over to me. "Is he going to be a problem?"

Both of the boys—Jax and Nick—could be a wee bit overprotective, as could Clyde. "No, he won't be a problem. I think he got the message tonight." I cocked my head at him. "Besides, I'm not your little sister and you've got to run all the boys off."

"I don't have a little sister."

"Whatever."

"I have a younger brother, though." He placed his hands on either side of me and dipped his chin. As close as we were, I could see that his eyes were more green than brown. And holy mother of pearls, we were as *close* as My Little Ponies. "And Roxy, I do not see the word *sister* when I think of you."

"Oh?" My glasses started to slip down my nose.

"I'd totally get with you," he announced. Just like that. Bam. Right in my face.

My eyes widened as shock jolted through me. Never

in a gazillion years had Nick shown any interest in me. "Um . . ."

His lips curled up in a half grin. "But then I couldn't work here anymore, so that isn't going to happen. I'd probably make an exception for you, but that's not the main reason why I wouldn't . . ." He moved one hand and tapped the tip of my nose. "Go there with you."

I stared at him a moment, flattered, and . . . yeah, dumbfounded. "Thanks. I think."

He winked and then pushed off the bar. Grabbing the towel off his shoulder, he picked up a spray cleaner and spritzed the bar top. It took a moment for my brain to start working again. I fixed my glasses.

"Well, I'd . . . totally do you, too, but then it would just be awkward."

Nick chuckled.

"So . . . you really, truly just hook up with chicks and then never see them again?" Curiosity might've killed the cat, but it was my best friend.

"I don't do commitments."

"Seeing someone more than once isn't a commitment," I reasoned with what I thought was valid logic. "I mean, I can almost get not hooking up with someone more than once, but seeing them?"

He looked over his shoulder at me. "It's just the way I am."

"Okay," I murmured, shaking my head. "Aren't you just a heartbreaker?"

A snicker was my only response. We finished up shortly after what I was considering to be a really weird night at Mona's. I had the keys, so when Nick opened the door, I wasn't paying attention to what was outside. I was busy struggling with the lock, and first thought the low chuckle that rumbled out of him had to do with me. It was when I dropped the heavy key ring in my purse and turned around, that I saw what he was laughing at.

"Wha . . . ?" I trailed off as my heart began pounding.

There was a county cruiser parked next to my car and there was a really freaking hot cop propped against the passenger side, long legs crossed at the ankles and arms folded across a yummy chest.

Reece was waiting.

I wasn't really thinking about my list of priorities as I stared at him in the dimly lit parking lot. The muggy night air settled over me as he unfolded his legs and pushed off the cruiser. My gaze roamed over him. I was really just thinking about how the polyester material of his work pants moved along his thighs.

God, he walked with the kind of lethal grace that should be illegal.

Nick leaned in and whispered in my ear, "And right there is the main reason why I wouldn't get with you."

I tripped over my feet.

"Hey man." Nick clapped Reece on the shoulder as he strolled past him. "Have a good night. See you Wednesday, Roxy."

"Bye-bye." I didn't take my eyes off Reece. What was he doing here, at two thirty in the morning? It wasn't the first time I'd stepped out of the bar late at night and found Reece waiting. Back before "the night thou shalt not repeat," he used to do it every once in a while, when he was working the night shift and was taking lunch.

But it was something I hadn't expected him to do again.

The sound of Nick's motorcycle rumbling to life

echoed throughout the otherwise silent parking lot. I needed to say something, because we were standing there, a few feet between us, staring at one another. "Hi."

Well, that was spectacular.

One side of his lips kicked up as his gaze dipped. "What . . . ?" He laughed, and there was a flutter deep in my belly, like a nest of butterflies had suddenly taken flight.

"What does your shirt say?"

I glanced down, trying to stop the smile tugging at my lips. "It says 'Ladies' Man.' What's wrong with that?"

Long, thick lashes lifted and then he laughed again, that nice and light laugh that wrapped around me. "You are . . . you're something else, Roxy."

Shifting my weight from one foot to the next, I bit down on my lip. "I'm not sure if that's a good thing or a run-in-the-other-direction kind of thing."

He took one step closer, his arms loose at his sides—his right arm brushing against the handle of his duty gun. The star on his chest seemed shinier than possible, and was eye level with me. "It's . . . yeah, it's a good thing."

I sucked in an unsteady breath as a balmy breeze tossed a strand of hair across my face. What in the world was happening here? I glanced around the empty parking lot and to the line of cars beginning to stream out of the strip club across the street. "Are you . . . on lunch?"

"Yeah. I work until seven in the morning," he replied, and then he moved so quickly, I didn't register what he was doing until the tips of his fingers grazed my cheek. He caught the wayward hair, and as the breath literally got lost inside me, he tucked the strand behind my ear. His touch, it lingered briefly along the sensitive skin behind my ear, drawing out a sweet shiver.

My pulse was somewhere in cardiac territory. "What . . . what are you doing here, Reece?"

A slight smile graced his poetic lips. "You know, I really didn't know at first. I was out driving around, knowing I needed to take my lunch, and I found myself pulling into the parking lot. And I thought about how we used to do this."

My insides got all mushy, because it was dumb, but I was amazed that he actually remembered doing this. Here I was thinking that I was the only person who held on tight to those memories. I looked up at him, feeling dizzy, and it had nothing to do with the heat or his height. "And?"

"You tired?"

That wasn't an answer to my question, but I shook my head. "Nope."

His eyes, such a deep blue they appeared black in the low light, fixed on mine. "Well, I got to thinking. Crazy thoughts."

My brows rose. "Crazy thoughts?"

He nodded as his grin went up a notch. "Crazy insane thoughts, such as why can't we just start over?"

"Start over?" I was turning into a puppet that repeated everything he said.

"Yeah, you and me."

I'd figured that much.

"And I think it's a damn good plan," he continued, and he was somehow one step closer, which put him as close as Nick and I had been standing earlier, but I'd felt nothing earlier. Now, there was a riot of sensations invading my system, shorting out my nerve endings. "I'm hoping you agree."

"What plan?"

He reached out again, this time fixing my glasses. "Let's forget about that night. I know we can't really pretend it never happened, but you said I . . . that I didn't do wrong by you and I know you wouldn't lie about that," he went on, and my heart dropped to my navel. Lie? Me? Never. "But we can move past it, right?"

"Why?" The question blurted out of me, and one of his brows arched. "No. I mean. Why now?"

A heartbeat passed. "We were friends, and I'm going to be real up front with you, babe, I miss that. I miss *you*. And I'm tired of missing you. So that's the why behind the now."

My heart did a round of hopscotch. He missed me? He was tired of missing me? Oh my God. Now my brain was spazzing out. I had no idea how to respond. I'd literally spent eleven months cursing at him and hiding from him, and now I was simply speechless. He regretted that night that kind of didn't happen, wished it never happened, but he was here, wanting to start over.

And hope—oh man, there was a spark of hope in my chest, flickering to life. It was like being fifteen again, when he first smiled at me across the lawn. Or when he used to walk me to class at school. It was like the hug he'd given me upon his return.

It was most definitely like the night I'd given him a ride home.

And it was the same hope that I'd thought I'd extinguished over the course of eleven months, but it was obviously still there, blazing through self-preservation, confusion and the guilt.

"Is that a good enough reason for you?" There was a teasing tone to his question, one that made me want to smile, but I was floored.

I needed to tell him what really happened that night. I knew I did, but he wanted to start over, and how could I start over by delving back into the past—into the night he wanted to move on from the past?

Reece lifted his hand once more, and this time, his fingers found mine. He threaded them together. My heart was done with hopscotch and had moved on to back flips. Maybe a roundoff. He gently tugged on my arm. "What do you say, Roxy? Eat lunch, dinner, breakfast—whatever you want to call it at three in the morning—with me?"

How could I say *anything* other than yes?

Chapter 6

Sitting with Reece in the all-night diner down the road from Mona's was familiar . . . and yet strange. It was like slipping into someone else's life I was intimately acquainted with.

The diner was virtually dead with the exception of a table of college guys who were trying not to appear too drunk while in the presence of an officer and a few truckers. Coffee was delivered for Reece and sweet tea for me with a quickness. We'd decided on getting breakfast.

Things were a wee bit awkward at first. I sat across from him, Indian style, in the harsh overhead lights, my hands fidgeting crazily in my lap. I didn't know what to say or do, and I kept focusing on the low conversation that crackled through his shoulder radio every five seconds.

Reece broke the awkward sauce though. "So I saw that Thomas added another piercing to his arsenal."

Moving one hand to fiddle with the cool glass, I

nodded. "Yeah, he got the eyebrow piercing last week. Every time I see him, I want to take a chain and connect the piercing above his eye to the one in his nose and then to the one in his lip."

He chuckled lightly. "I'm pretty sure he'd be down with it. Your dad was calling him 'Metal Face.' "

I shook my head. "Thomas is turning eighteen in a few months, and he has our parents convinced that he's going to get a facial tattoo. Something to do with a zipper on the back of his head that starts at the nape of his neck and ends between his eyebrows?"

His eyes widened. "He's not serious, is he?"

I laughed. "I don't think so. He'd have to cut off all those pretty curls, and I don't think he'd do that. I think he's just messing with them. Well, for the . . ." I trailed off as a loud *thunk* traveled across the diner.

Leaning against the red cushioned seats, Reece tossed his arm along the back of the booth as he glanced over at the college table. Someone had spilled a drink, and apparently it was insanely funny to the entire table, because they sounded like a pack of hyenas. My gaze darted back to Reece. He gave great profile. It was the jawline, I decided, that really just made his face exquisite. Capturing the hard line would be so easy with a stroke of a paintbrush or with charcoal. Ah, I could totally do his portrait in charcoal! Wait. I was pretty sure I'd added the whole "stop painting his face" to the priority list.

I really sucked at that priority list.

Reece's gaze slid back to mine, and I felt my cheeks heat. Because I was totally staring at him, and he totally caught me. The grin that tipped up his lips was full of boyish charm. There was a flutter in my chest. "You're still taking graphic design, right?"

Huh? It took me a moment to realize he was talking about college. "Oh, yeah. I'm doing online classes. Only two this semester." I shrugged. "Those damn classes are expensive."

"How much longer do you have?"

"A couple of more years." I took a drink of tea. Ah, sugar. "Since I'm only taking two classes a semester, it feels like I'm taking the scenic route, but when I'm finished, I'll . . ."

"Then what?"

I opened my mouth, but then I frowned. "You know, good question. I really have no idea. Guess I need to figure that out."

Reece chuckled again as he dropped his arm and placed his elbows on the table. "You're twenty-two, Roxy. You really don't need to figure anything out at this point."

My expression turned bland. "You make it sound like I'm still in diapers. You're only twenty-five.

Maybe he was right, but there was a niggle of panic in the center of my chest. Once I graduated college, would I keep working at Mona's? Doing web design on the side? Or would I get a "real" job as some people, especially nosey people, lovingly advised? "I like working at Mona's," I announced.

"Why wouldn't you? Jax is a great guy to work for," he said, head tilted slightly to the side. "And you're good with people."

I grinned. "I make some damn good tips."

His gaze dropped to my mouth and then slowly rose. "I bet you do."

A pleasant buzz trilled through my system at the light, almost offhand compliment. Was I that desperate for praise that if I had a tail, I'd be wagging it? Or was it just because it was coming from Reece?

Thick lashes lowered, shielding cobalt-blue eyes momentarily. When he looked up again, his eyes practically burned with the intensity uniquely his.

Oh yeah, it was because it was coming from Reece. Who was I kidding?

I shook those thoughts right out of my head as I grabbed hold of the paper the straw came in and started tearing it up into tiny pieces. "But how bad is it that I graduate with a degree in graphics and still work at Mona's?"

"How bad is it for you to stop doing something you enjoy for something you don't?" he countered.

My lips formed a perfect O. Well, when one summed it up like that, it really didn't make sense.

"Look, do you remember how badly my stepdad freaked when he realized that both my brother and I had no plans of ever going to college?"

I nodded. Colton, his brother, and Reece never had any aspirations of being a college grad, something their stepfather, Richard, was not too keen on, considering he'd been all about higher education and law school.

"And not to this day do I regret never stepping foot in a college. I'm glad I joined the Marines and came back to this," he said, shrugging one shoulder. "I'm satisfied with being a cop, even when there are moments when it's . . ." A shadow crossed his face, and I held my breath, thinking he was going to talk about what happened—the shooting that had spun his life out of control for a little while.

Peeking up at him, I thought about how . . . how cut up Reece was after he was involved in the shooting a year and a half ago. Who knows what he faced at war, and I did know that he'd taken quite the hit while over there, something I didn't like to think about . . . it was why he came home, but the shooting he'd been involved in as a cop had rocked him hard. While Reece hadn't pushed me away at that time, it had been Jax who'd pulled him out of the downward spiral.

"Even when it's fucking difficult, I don't regret my choice."

For some reason, I was disappointed that he hadn't mentioned the "difficult" situation. Even though Reece had allowed me to get close to him while he was dealing with that crap, he'd never talked about it, and I guessed he still didn't.

"Not everyone has to do the same thing to be happy," he continued. "It took Richard a while to get over it, but he did. And he's fine, because he knows Colton and I are happy." He paused. "And I know your parents wouldn't care if you kept working at Mona's or whatever. They just want you to be happy."

"I know." And that was the God's honest truth.

Reece reached across the table and wrapped his long fingers around my wrist. Slowly, he pulled my hand away from the pile of paper I was creating. "You know, you don't have to live Charlie's life for him."

My jaw hit the table.

"Just because he can't go to college, doesn't mean you have to do it for him." Turning my hand over, he smoothed his thumb along the inside of my wrist. "Charlie would never have wanted that for you."

There were many days where I wondered what the hell I was doing or why I was doing it, and Reece nailed it on the head right then, after us not exchanging a single civil word to one another for almost a year. Shocked me right to the core, because there was a part of me that didn't want to acknowledge why I did some of the things I did.

Or why I didn't do other things.

His thumb made another swipe, drawing my attention. The pads of his fingers were calloused, telling me he used his hands a lot. The contrast of the roughness to the smooth movements and his words had me squirming in my booth.

Before I could think of a response suitable to that statement, our food arrived and he let go of my wrist. But when he did, his fingers were slow to leave my skin, trailing over my hand and the length of my fingers. Unable to stop it, I shivered.

The topic of conversation changed to a much lighter one. "So how long do you think Jax is going to be up here before he takes his ass back down to Shepherd?" he asked, digging into his biscuit drowning in gravy.

I laughed as I picked up a slice of turkey bacon. "Nick was wondering the same thing. Jax is supposed to be back home middle of next week, but I doubt he'd make it a whole week without running down to see her."

"I don't either." His grin was just too much. "Man, he's got it bad for her."

"They're good for each other."

"True," he agreed. "Jax deserves it."

When we finished eating it was close to four, and Reece had to go back on duty. He took care of the check, ignoring my protests with a mischievous grin that made me feel sixteen again.

He walked me to my car, parked next to the cruiser. "I'll follow you home," he said, opening my car door for me.

I blinked. "You . . . Reece, you don't need to do that."

"I'm back on call. If I get one, I can take it. And it counts as patrolling, so it's no big deal." He placed his hand on my shoulder and looked me straight in the eye. "It's late. You live alone. I'm going to follow you home and make sure you're safe. Either you can be okay with it or I can follow you like a total creep."

My brows shot up.

That damn grin was back as he dipped his chin. "Don't let me be the creep."

A laugh burst out of me. "Okay. Follow me." I started to slide into the seat and glanced up at him. "Creeper."

His answering chuckle had me grinning and then had me wanting to bang my head off the steering wheel the short drive to the Victorian. What was I doing? Why was I all happy and fuzzy? Just because he wanted to start over didn't mean anything other than being friends. And that was totally cool, and I guess it was also cool to be . . . happy about that and letting go of the anger and all the messy crap that surrounded that night. I could totally do the friend-zone thing with him.

As long as he stopped grinning at me like he was, and touching me. Friend zone meant a no-touch policy.

When I parked at the curb, the cruiser was right behind me, and I wasn't entirely surprised that, when I stepped out of the car, he was already out of his, waiting for me. "Walking me to the door?" I asked, slinging my purse over my shoulder.

"Of course." He closed the car door for me. "After all, I'm all about protecting and serving."

I lifted a brow.

The scent of the late-blooming roses Mrs. Silver took care of filled the air as Reece placed his hand on my lower back, steering me up the old cobblestone walkway to the front porch. The weight of his palm seemed to sear right through my thin shirt. The whole no-touch policy went right out the door.

The lights were off in the Silvers' and James and Miriam's place, but a small yellowish glow radiated from the apartment above mine. I really needed to introduce myself. I added that to the ever-changing priority list.

Stopping in front of my door, I fished out my keys, desperately wishing I didn't notice how his hand still remained on my back or that we were standing so close, his right thigh almost brushing my hip.

I glanced up at him and drew in a sharp breath. Out of all the things streaming through my head, I couldn't pull out a single coherent sentence.

"See, you safely made it to your door," he said, his tone light.

My skin felt too warm in the balmy air. "Thanks to you."

"I'm good for something."

"You're good for a lot of things." For some reason when those words jumped out of my mouth, they sounded a lot more perverted than they did before I spoke them.

In the dark, I could barely make out his expression, but he shifted so that we were face-to-face. Doing so caused him to drag his hand from my back to my hip. "Ah, Roxy, I wish I could say that I believed you knew just exactly what I was good at, but I can't."

Ack! Okay. The words really did come off perverted-sounding, because he was talking about that night, and we were supposed to move on from that. But we were right smack-dab in the middle of that mess. And my tongue got completely out of control. "You were good," I said, remembering the way he'd kissed me. Drunk off his rocker or not, the man knew how to kiss. "I mean, *really* good."

Those damn lips curved up, getting my lady bits all kinds of excited and wishing he'd move his hand a few inches to the left and down. "Now, Roxy, I thought it was nothing to write home about?"

I had said that. And I also realized we were thinking about two very different things. Kissing versus sex. I really needed to tell him what happened. "Reece, I—"

"There's something I want to be up front about," he said, cutting in. He dipped his head so that when he spoke, his breath danced along my cheek. "I told you that I missed you and I was done missing you."

My brain emptied. "Yeah, yeah you did."

"But that's not the only thing," he explained while my heart started to pound. "Obviously there is something between us. Drunk or not, that night would've never happened if there wasn't."

"Wait. You said you regretted that night. That you—"

"Yeah, I wish that night didn't happen, Roxy. Only because I want to remember the first time I got inside you. I want to recall every second of thrusting into you, inch by inch, and commit that to memory, babe. That's why I regret it and fully plan on rectifying that situation."

Oh, holy balls, what he just said was light-me-on-fire hot. So steaming hot I wasn't even focusing on the fact he'd never been *in* me. No guy, not even Reece, ever talked to me like that.

I liked it.

So did my girlie parts.

Katie once told me she knew this guy who could make her wet just by speaking to her, and I seriously didn't believe her. Now I did. Totally did. Definitely no longer an urban legend. It was possible—wait a sec. He planned on rectifying the situation?

"You know what the fucking hardest thing the last eleven months was to watch?"

"No," I whispered.

His voice was rough, a low rumble. "Seeing you with guys who weren't even worth a minute of your time—people that make me wonder what kind of shit choice in guys you have."

I started to defend my taste in men, but I snapped my mouth shut. Yeah, the last couple of guys I'd gone out with were kind of bad. Not Dean. He was just . . . blah. Boring.

"You go out with these tools while you'd turn and run from me."

"You're worth my time?" I asked, unable to stop myself from doing so.

The tilt to his lips was knowing, arrogant and annoyingly sexy. "Babe, you have no idea how worth your time I am." The hand on my hip tightened. "I'm not wanting to be just friends with you, Roxy. Hell no, but if that's all you want, then I'll deal with it. I just need to lay it all out there. So we're both on the same page. You know what I want."

Static transmitted through his shoulder radio, a dispatcher calling in a traffic accident on a back road not too far from here. Keeping his eyes on me, he moved his hand and hit a button I couldn't see on the radio. "This is Unit Three-oh-one," he said. "I'm en route."

When Reece removed his hand, he said to me, "Just think about it." Then he dipped his head, brushing his lips across my cheek, to my temple. He placed a honeyed, all too brief kiss there. "Now get your sweet ass inside."

In a daze, I did just that. The only thing that stopped me was when I turned in the open doorway and he was already halfway to his cruiser. "Reece!"

He looked over his shoulder. "Roxy?"

My cheeks heated. "Be careful."

I couldn't see him smile, but I heard it in his voice. "Always, babe."

Then he was gone.

The pleasant trill was back, stronger than I could remember. It was like having sugar land on my tongue. I floated as I closed my door, seconds from throwing out my arms like the chick in the *Sound of Music* and twirling around when I drew up short, just in front of the hall. There was a low hum coming from the kitchen, the sound of gears—of a machine turning over.

Reece and his I'm-not-just-wanting-a-friendship speech forgotten, I quickly flipped on the light. Everything looked normal, but that sound . . .

Dropping my purse on the couch, I slowly made my way through the small dining room, flipping on lights as I went. My stomach twisted as I reached the kitchen, quickly finding that light switch.

Light flooded the kitchen and I sought out the source of the noise, immediately finding it.

"What in the world?" I muttered.

Directly across from me, the dishwasher was getting down, doing its business. Nothing weird about that . . . except I hadn't turned the dishwasher on before I left for work. And even if I had, it wouldn't have been running this long. Tiny hairs rose along the back of my neck as I stared at it.

With the breath hitched in my throat, I crept toward the dishwasher, expecting it to spring to life and start singing like appliances did in *Beauty and the Beast*.

Swallowing hard, I slid my fingers under the handle and yanked it open, interrupting the cycle.

Steam poured into the air, and I jerked my hand back. The door creaked and then fell all the way open. There were only two things in the dishwasher. The cup I'd used for the tea before I left for work and the plate I'd eaten a bagel on.

Nothing else.

Leaving the door open, I backed away as I shook my head. I didn't get it. Had I accidentally knocked on the timer? Sounded plausible, but hell, I honestly didn't even know how to turn it on.

A cold chill snaked down my neck as I folded my arms across my chest. Turning in a wide circle, my gaze sought out every nook and cranny in the kitchen. Then, more than a little freaked out, I darted out of the kitchen, leaving all the lights on, and I didn't stop running until I was in my bedroom, door shut *and* locked behind me.

Chapter 7

"Do you still believe in ghosts?" I asked Charlie.

He was staring out the window, no response, but I was dauntless—totally like that chick in that movie everyone was talking about. Couldn't remember her name, but Theo James was in it, so score.

"I remember us playing with the Ouija board stuff," I continued, sitting in the chair across from him with my legs tucked under my butt. "But we were, like, thirteen, and a year before that, we swore we saw the *chupacabra* outside, but whatever, I think my apartment might be haunted."

Charlie blinked slowly.

I took a deep breath. "The remote control ended up in the fridge last Saturday, and when I came home from my shift, the dishwasher was running. Then, after my shift on Thursday, I came home and the TV . . . in my bedroom was on. I didn't leave it on when

I left. So, either there's a ghost in my house, someone else is living there that I'm completely unaware of, or I'm losing my mind. And I know, going crazy doesn't seem too unbelievable."

My nervous laugh echoed around the otherwise silent room, taunting me. Truth was, whatever weirdness that was going on in my apartment was freaking me out. I'd told my mom about it when I talked to her this morning on the way to visit Charlie, and she was totally convinced it was a ghost. Although, I'd never seen one, I believed in them. I mean, way too many people—healthy, normal, and completely sane people—in the world had claimed that they'd seen a ghost for some cases not to be real. But nothing had happened in my apartment before. Why would it start messing around with stuff now? Or maybe it had done things before, and I just never noticed? God, it was super creepy to think that my place could really be haunted.

I needed to get some salt the next time I was at the grocery store, like a bucket's worth of salt. That seemed to work for the guys on *Supernatural*.

I sighed as I pulled out the painting I'd brought with me and showed it to Charlie. I'd done another landscape, this time of Rehoboth Beach, where our parents would take us for the summer. The sand glittered on the canvas, like a thousand tiny diamonds had been sprinkled over it. The ocean had been fun to paint, but wasn't entirely accurate.

Because no ocean was as deep as Reece's eyes.

I needed help.

Charlie didn't acknowledge the painting, so I got up and tacked it to the wall, next to the one of Devil's Den. Then I turned, scrubbing my hands down my face.

Without my glasses, I felt weird. Naked even. Mmm. Naked. That made me think of Reece.

I seriously needed help.

Dropping my hands, I resisted the urge to bang my head against the wall. Several moments passed as I stared at Charlie, wishing that he'd turn and look at me, if only for a few seconds. But he didn't.

"Reece wants to move past that night," I announced to the silent room. Of course, Charlie knew everything that had and had not gone down that night. "He cleared up the whole regret thing, which"—I laughed—"would've solved a lot of problems if he'd just, you know, said that back then. Clarified it a little. And he doesn't want to be just friends with me. He pretty much stated that clearly. He said . . . he said he was worth my time."

I imagined Charlie agreeing with that.

Shuffling back over to the chair, I plopped down. "He didn't say he wanted to be my boyfriend or that he wanted to date me. Our conversation really didn't get that far, but he came into Mona's Wednesday night and we talked like we used to. He flirted with me." I pulled my knees up to my chest and propped my chin on them. Closing my eyes, I let out another sigh. "I haven't told him what really happened. You know how he hates lies of any kind, and really, when was I supposed to tell him that? Hey, I know you thought you got some, but you didn't. So long has passed that it's hard to even go there."

Charlie said nothing, but I knew if he could talk, he would've understood where I was coming from. Eleven months of miscommunication wasn't as easy as anyone would think to fix, but even understanding that, he would—if he could—tell me that I needed to fess up.

The one-sided conversation went on for a while and then I picked up *New Moon*, spending the rest of the time reading to him. When it was time for me to leave, I tucked the worn book back inside my tote and stood.

Charlie was the only person outside of my family that I truly loved and going through what I've gone through with him . . . well, the idea of loving someone as much as I loved Charlie and experiencing this kind of pain again terrified me.

Hell.

If I was being honest with myself, it was probably why I had such shit taste in guys I dated. None of them were long-term material. None of them were dangerous to my heart, none except Reece, and he's always been obtainable. Even if he wanted to knock boots with me, once he found out that I lied, that would be the end of that. So, in a way, he was a safe choice. Someone I could lust and dream over, but always knew would slip out of my grasp before I fell hard.

I couldn't pull my eyes from Charlie as I stood silently by his side. Shadows were deeper under his eyes and cheekbones. In a week, he seemed frailer and gaunt. The hair along his temples appeared thinner.

Guilt churned my stomach, and I couldn't help but think he wouldn't be in this position if I had . . . if I had kept my mouth shut that night. Simply just walked away from Henry Williams and his friends. If I hadn't been goaded by his crude remarks. I hadn't picked up that rock and I hadn't been the one who'd thrown it, but in a way, I had played my part.

And Charlie had paid the price.

A terrible, horrific thought bloomed. I didn't want to even finish it, but it had already whipped through me. I smacked a hand over my mouth, muffling a choked sound.

Would it have been better for him to have not survived?

Oh God, I couldn't believe I even thought that. It was so wrong. I was a terrible person. But a voice whispered in the back of my head in spite of me telling it to shut up.

Was this really living at all?

That was the question of the century, and as I stood there, I thought about what Reece had said to me about living my life for Charlie. If I wanted to get really deep and reflective, really honest with myself, I knew that some of the decisions I made were because Charlie couldn't.

And maybe . . . maybe because I . . .

I couldn't finish that thought either.

Helplessness unfurled in the pit of my stomach. Nurse Venter had explained when I had checked in that they were still having difficulty getting Charlie to eat enough during the day. She'd given me a bowl of mashed potatoes, something he'd normally eat, but I had spent the better part of our visit trying to get him to eat it to no avail. If it continued, they'd bring in a feeding tube, probably before the end of the weekend, and he hadn't been a fan of that. Last time, he'd managed to pull it out and ended up having to be restrained. There was nothing I could do to really help him, but I had to try.

I picked up the bowl and plastic spoon, scooping up some of the lumpy white stuff. As soon as the spoon neared his face, he twisted away. I didn't get it. He wouldn't acknowledge me, but he'd turned his face from food. Ten minutes of this went on before I placed the bowl on the small table by his chair.

Slipping between his chair and the window, I knelt

in front of him. "I need you to do something for me, Charlie." Our eyes connected, and it was like a punch to the stomach, because even though he was looking at me, he didn't *see* me. Emotion clogged my throat. "I need you to eat, okay? When they bring you dinner tonight, you need to eat."

Not a single flicker of emotion crossed his blank expression.

"If you don't, they're going to use a feeding tube. Remember how you hated that before?" I tried again, reaching up and cupping his cheeks. He flinched, but nothing more. "So, please eat, Charlie."

I kissed his forehead as I rose. "I'll be back Friday, sweetheart."

Nurse Venter waited for me outside. Her dark hair, liberally streaked with gray, was pulled back in a hasty bun. I figured she was waiting to see if there had been any change in Charlie's behavior.

"He's the same way he's been for the last month," I told her as I started down the wide corridor. "I couldn't get him to eat the mashed potatoes. Totally don't get it. He hasn't been responding to me at all, but he sure as hell responds when a spoon gets near him."

"Roxy—"

"He used to love those yogurt Popsicle things," I suggested as we neared the double doors leading to the waiting room. "Maybe I can bring some by before work tomorrow? I have the time."

"Honey," she said, catching my arm in a gentle grasp. "I'm sure Charlie loved a lot of things, but he's . . . well, he's not that Charlie anymore."

"Charlie's . . ." I stared at her a moment and then pulled my arm free. "I know he's not the same, but he's . . . he's still Charlie."

Sympathy dug its way into the lines around her eyes and mouth. "Honey, I know, but that's not the only thing we need to talk about. There's—"

Whatever she wanted to talk about I really didn't want to hear at that moment. Probably had to do with the feeding tube, and I just couldn't think about it, because I knew how Charlie would react. I also knew that his parents wouldn't be here to see it, and often wondered if they even cared.

Looking away, I pushed open the doors.

My whole world stopped.

Sitting on the same couch that I'd waited on a handful of hours ago was Henry Williams. The strap from my tote bag slipped out of my fingers and the tote hit the floor with a loud smack. I was frozen right where I stood.

"Roxy," whispered Nurse Venter. "I was trying to tell you that he's here."

Henry unfolded his massive length. He'd grown since the last time I'd seen him. Before, he'd been average height, maybe five feet, nine inches. Now he was well over six feet.

Prison hadn't been kind to him, not that I really cared.

His dark brown hair was buzzed close to the skull and his skin was paler than I remembered. Then again, you didn't get to see the sun in prison a lot. There were bags under his eyes, making him appear older than he was, which had to only be twenty-three or twenty-four. And he was bigger. Sounded totally cliché, but he had to have been pumping iron behind the bars because his shoulders stretched the plain white shirt he wore in a way it never did when he was younger.

My muscles were completely locked up as I stared at Henry.

He smoothed his hands along the sides of his khaki shorts. "Roxanne," he said, and my skin crawled like an army of cockroaches had swarmed me.

A huge part of me wanted to flee the waiting room, run straight for the doors and get as far away from Henry as I could, but I couldn't. Henry wasn't here for me. He wanted to see Charlie, and like a mama bear, I was so not going to let that happen.

My muscles unlocked and I moved so that I was standing in the center of the double doors. "You're not welcome here."

Henry didn't look surprised. "I don't imagine that I would be."

"Then why are you here?" I demanded, my hands closing into fists. "This is the last place you should be."

He glanced over to where Nurse Venter stood. Luckily no one else was in the lobby, but that would soon change. "I know. I'm not trying to start anything—"

"You shouldn't even be out of prison. You were in there for how long? Five years tops and you're out now, walking around and enjoying whatever, but Charlie has lost everything?" I shook my head, breathing heavy. So freaking unfair. "You're not going to see him."

"Roxy," Nurse Venter said quietly. "I know you realize you—"

I whirled on her. "So, you're okay with this? Siding with him?" Betrayal was a bitter acid in the back of my throat. I knew it was unreasonable. She was just doing her job, but frustration and helplessness were a second, irrational being inside me. I did not care about her job. All I cared about was how unfair this was to Charlie.

Her brows pinched with sympathy. "It's not an issue of siding with anyone. Charlie's parents—his guardians—gave permission. And unless Charlie says he doesn't want to see him, and I know how that sounds, he's allowed."

My mouth dropped open. "Charlie hasn't spoken more than a sentence in six years! And now he's suddenly going to express his discontent with something?" I whipped around, facing Henry. "Did you know that? That Charlie hasn't spoken in years?"

He looked away, a muscle thrumming in his jaw.

I stepped forward. "Oh, is that too hard to hear? Because you did that to him?"

"Roxanne." Nurse Venter grasped my arm with her cool fingers. "I think it will be best for you to leave."

Yanking my arm free, I was seconds away from erupting in a stream of fiery insults and curse words, but my wild gaze met hers. She wasn't just looking at me, she was pleading with me to let this go—to walk out of the facility, because there was nothing she could do.

There was nothing I could do.

I drew in several deep breaths that went nowhere. All I could do was nod in her direction before I picked up my tote bag. It was like walking through quicksand. Every cell in my body demanded that I not walk out of the building, but I did. Calling on every ounce of restraint I had in my body, I managed to walk my ass out of that building, under the overcast skies, and was halfway across the parking lot.

"Roxanne."

My eyes widened. Oh hell to the motherfucking no. Dumbfounded, I turned around slowly.

Henry was right behind me. "I know you're upset—"

"You're so fucking observant."

He ignored that. "And you have every right to be upset."

Staring up at him, I knew I was going to do something stupid if I didn't remove myself from this situation just as much as I knew those dark, plump clouds were going to break.

"Leave me alone," I said, tightening my hand on my tote as I pivoted around. I picked up my pace, skirting around a van.

Lightning lit up the dark clouds overhead and the thunder cracked, so loud it rattled my chest. As another cloud flashed like a disco ball, I focused on counting the seconds between the streak of light and thunder.

Then I saw my car.

Better yet, I saw what was sitting next to my car. It was an old Mustang—a cherry red muscle car straight out of the 70s. The vanity plate was familiar, too. It read BBRB, and I knew what that stood for, too.

Bad Boys Are Better.

Motherfucker, it was Henry's car—the same car he had in high school that he and his father had restored. The same car he and his friends used to roll around in to pick up girls, like something straight out of a cheesy movie.

Henry got out of prison after destroying my best friend's life and his fucking, stupid car—his pride and joy—had been waiting for him.

"Please, just give me a few seconds. That's all I'm asking." Henry grabbed my arm.

I lost it.

Fury exploded inside me, like a lit match carelessly dropped on a puddle of gasoline. My brain clicked off and common sense did a swan dive off a building. I just wasn't thinking, only feeling rage, so much so that it was like being outside of my body. I reached down into the tote bag, pulled the first substantial thing my fingers touched and I cocked my arm back like a pro pitcher in the MLB.

The heavy, hardcover edition of *New Moon* flew through the air like a rock—much like the rock that had destroyed lives—and connected with the windshield of Henry's Mustang.

Glass shattered.

Much like all our lives had shattered that night at the lake.

Chapter 8

I had a mean case of déjà vu.

Kind of.

Sitting inside my car, I stared through the rain-drenched windshield—totally intact windshield—as Dennis finished up with Henry. Well, it wasn't the just-got-married Dennis who often came into the bar. Right now he was Officer Dennis Hanner.

Out of the hundred deputies that worked this county, it had to be someone who knew me. Of course. Because that was how life worked.

Ugh.

I didn't know if Henry would've called the police on me for breaking his windshield, because he hadn't gotten the chance to do so. Since I had impeccable timing, an elderly couple visiting someone had just gotten out of the car the very second *New Moon* broke the sound barrier and the windshield. Not only had they called the cops, but they'd also parked themselves in front of my car, like I would run off, until Officer Hanner showed up.

Apparently, I'd hit the windshield at the right place. Or maybe it was the wrong spot. Since most glass was reinforced, I must have hit the one and only weak area. Or maybe I was really a mutant and could turn books into weapons of windshield destruction.

Then it rained, all the while Dennis—nope, Officer Hanner—had glared at me like he wanted to pick me up by the ankles and shake some sense into me. I was soaked; so was he, even though he'd donned one of those plastic anti-rain things.

Both Henry and Officer Hanner turned to look at me.

Squeezing my eyes shut, I rested my forehead against the steering wheel. I was such . . . such an idiot—an impulsive, irresponsible idiot. What had I been thinking? I couldn't even believe I'd done that. Granted, I had a hell of a temper. Got that from my mama, too, but I'd never committed an act of vandalism. Shame rode me hard, making my skin clammy and icky.

How was what I'd done any different than what Henry had done? I mean, I didn't hurt someone, but I lost my shit and I reacted in a way that was violent and stupid.

Uncomfortable with that comparison, I felt a shudder shake my shoulders.

The passenger car door opened suddenly, causing me to jerk back against the seat. Wild eyed, I watched Dennis slip into the seat next to me. My gaze bounced to the front of the car. Henry was gone. So was the Mustang. Reluctantly, I looked back at Dennis.

He tugged off the hood of the plastic, yellow poncho. "What were you thinking, Roxy?"

I opened my mouth.

"Don't answer that question," he snapped, scrubbing his hand along his jaw. "I already know. You weren't thinking a goddamn thing."

I snapped my mouth shut.

"I cannot believe you. You of all people should know better than to do what you did."

Casting my gaze to the steering wheel, I pressed my lips together as I nodded. I did know better.

"You're so damn lucky," he said. "Henry's not pressing charges."

My gaze swung toward him. "What?"

He shook his head as he flipped his stare to the window. "He decided not to press charges. Which is great, because I really don't want to explain to Reece why I had to arrest you."

Oh God. Reece.

"Or have to deal with your parents, who I'm sure would be hella proud of what you did," he added, laying it on thick. But hell, I deserved it. "However, your ass is going to pay for that window to get fixed ASAP. You got it?"

"Yes," I replied immediately. "As soon as I know how much it costs, I'll pay it."

A moment passed. "Henry's going to get an estimate, and it'll go through me. I think that's for the best right now."

I agreed 100 percent.

"Dennis, I'm . . . I'm sorry. I wasn't thinking. I was just so angry that he was there, and he grabbed my arm—"

"He said he grabbed your arm right before you threw the book," he cut in. "By the way, I think that's the first time I've seen a book take out a windshield, so thanks for that. But he didn't make it sound like it was an aggressive move. And you didn't bring it up when I first got here. Is there something I don't know?"

"It wasn't an aggressive move. He wanted to talk. I didn't."

"And that's your right, Roxy. You don't have to talk to him," he agreed. "But you can't damage his property."

"I know," I whispered.

Dennis sent me a long, sideways look. "I wasn't around when that shit went down with Charlie. Hell, I didn't even live in this state, but I've heard the details. I know what happened, and if it were my decision, the punk ass would still be sitting in jail. But it's not my decision." In the cramped seat, he twisted toward me. "And I get that it's majorly fucked up that he's out and he gets to come around here, but little girl, you've got to pull it together. You can't do shit like this. It doesn't help anyone, especially yourself."

I stared at him.

"You feel me?" he asked.

"Yeah, I feel you."

Needless to say, I was late for my shift, which sucked ass, because it also meant I wasn't going to get the design done for a blogger before I left for work. It was going to be a long night, because I was going to have to finish it up when I got back home.

Surprisingly, Jax hadn't known about my very powerful throwing arm, but when I told him what I had done and he caught me by the hem of my WALKERS NEED LOVE TOO shirt and dragged me down the somewhat quiet hall, I knew I was in for Lecture Number Two of the night.

"Girl, what in the hell were you thinking?" he demanded.

"I wasn't thinking anything," I told him. "That was the problem. I just got so pissed and stopped thinking."

He stared at me, brows raised. "That isn't a good enough reason."

I almost jumped up and down out of frustration. "I know it's not. Trust me. I totally know that. I'm going to pay for the damages."

"Roxy . . ."

Ducking my chin, I folded my arms across my chest. All day I'd felt like crap for what I had done. It wasn't a pitying type of feeling like crap. Oh no, it was the I'm-such-a-fucker feeling like crap. I hadn't felt this way since the last time I had to dodge my landlord when I was late on rent.

Once again, I found myself wishing I could drink at work.

"Well, there's one thing at least." He cuffed my chin, and I looked up. "You obviously got a hell of an arm."

I rolled my eyes as a dry laugh parted my lips. "That's what happens when you grow up with two brothers."

"True. You tell your parents yet?"

"No. I'm leaving that until tomorrow."

"Good luck with that."

"Thanks," I moaned.

Shaking his head, he gestured at the closed office door. "By the way, there's something in there for you."

"There is?"

His lips quirked. "Yeah, and after the day you've had, it'll be a nice surprise. Check them out and get back behind the bar."

"Yes, sir!" I gave him a jaunty salute, which he promptly ignored.

Since I'd been late getting in, I had gone straight to

the bar, stowing my purse there, so I hadn't stepped foot in the office. I opened the door and drew up short.

"What the . . . ?" I murmured.

There was no way Jax was talking about the flowers sitting on the desk. I looked around the small room. Nothing else stood out to me. The couch was there. The file cabinet. The bowl of possibly stale beer nuts.

My eyes traveled back to the flowers.

The roses were nice—way over a dozen, bright crimson, and had just bloomed. The light scent wafted over me as I walked toward the desk. A square envelope poked out between the baby's breath and green stems. My name was clearly written on it. Somewhere deep in my belly, there was a bunch of wiggling going on—happy wiggling. I carefully plucked it up and opened it.

Next time will be better.

My brows inched up my forehead. Uh, what? I flipped the card over. No name. I turned it back over and read the message again. A slow smile tugged at the corner of my lips. It had to be from Reece. The message was kind of weird, but it had to be from him.

I curled my fingers along the edges of the dainty card as I bit down on my lip. Reece was normally off on Fridays, or at least, that's what I thought. It was hard to keep track of his schedule. He'd been in the bar on Wednesday, and we had talked, but he hadn't mentioned the whole wanting to be more than friends thing, and I hadn't brought it up either, because I didn't know what to do with that.

Well, I had plenty of ideas of what I could do with that. A lot of them involved getting naked and contorting our bodies into yoga-type positions and such, but as cliché as it sounded, I didn't know how to handle wanting something/someone for so long and then finally getting it.

Maybe I could text him about the roses.

Grinning like a complete doofus, I slipped the card into the back of my jeans and headed back out to the bar. There was a crowd waiting to get served, and poor Pearl was running back and forth as fast as her legs would carry her.

Hours flew by before I even realized it or had a chance to pick up my phone and the crowd was finally thinning out a little. I took the precious downtime to gather my hair up into a quick ponytail and to grab a fresh Coke from the tap.

When the door opened one more time, the scent of summer rain tickled my nose, and I glanced up and over.

My heart flailed in my chest.

Reece walked in, his brown hair plastered to his forehead, the ends curling. Tiny drips of rain cascading down his temple and onto his shirt. As he reached up and smoothed his large hand over his head, brushing those wet strands back, he reminded me of Poseidon rising from the ocean.

Holy hotness.

He looked over, and our gazes collided. Held. As he crossed the floor, walked around the bar and came behind it, toward me, he didn't look away for one second.

"Okay." Nick stepped back before he got mowed over.

My lungs constricted as Reece took my hand and then turned, walking out from behind the bar, tugging me along.

"Nice to see you, too, Reece." Jax shared a look with Reece and then nodded in Nick's direction. "Don't mind us. Take a break. We got it."

Normally, I would've protested, especially since sarcasm dripped from half of what Jax said, but the wiggling in my tummy was back in full force. It was like that somewhat scary show I watched as a kid—*The Wiggles*.

Someone—was it Melvin?—catcalled as Reece led me down the hall, and my cheeks flushed. "Okay, he-man, I can walk all by my little self."

He cast a look over his shoulder at me as he opened the office door. "I'm sure you can."

Then he pulled me inside.

My gaze flipped to the roses—the roses!—but before I could say a word, he closed the door and my back was pressed against it, his hands planted on either side of my head and his face right in mine. Like right there, within kissing distance.

Wow.

"So, I was at my father's place in New Jersey most of the day, and you know, he lives out near the Pine Barrens, so service is shit."

I nodded even though I really wasn't processing what he was saying as I was too busy staring at his mouth. Those lips, fuller on the bottom, drove me to distraction.

"I pull out of his driveway and I have all these messages from Dennis," he continued, and I finally caught on to what he was talking about. "I honestly thought he was messing with me at first."

I cringed. "He . . . um, he wasn't."

He shot me a bland look. "That much I figured out." His hands slid on the door, stopping just shy of touching my shoulders. "What did he do to you?"

"What?" I blinked.

"What did that bastard do to make you throw a book through his windshield?"

Oh. *Oh*. My heart was now wiggling along with my stomach. "He really didn't do anything. I just lost my cool. He wanted to talk to me, and I didn't want to talk to him."

"You don't have to talk to him."

"That's what Dennis said, but I shouldn't have damaged his car."

A muscle flexed along his right jaw. "That's true." He shook his head. "Damn, Roxy, can't say I'm surprised."

My brows flew up. "You're not?"

He laughed under his breath. "Babe, you've always had a hell of a temper on you."

Ah, that was kind of true. "Is that a good thing or a bad thing?"

Reece cocked his head to the side. "A sexy thing, but vandalism and destruction of property doesn't look good on you, sweets."

"No. It doesn't match my manicure." I raised my hands, flashing him the blue nails.

He laughed again and then he sobered up, just like that. Cop Face was on, and yeah . . . the low coiling in my stomach told me I found Cop Face arousing. "You're lucky. He could've pressed charges, and this conversation would be going in a whole different direction."

My own half smile slipped off my face. "I know. It's . . . I was just with Charlie, and he's . . ." Unable to continue, I forced a casual shrug I didn't feel. "What are you going to do with me?"

His lips parted as his chest rose with a deep breath, then his gaze dropped to my mouth, and his expression tightened. He looked . . . he looked hungry. "I have lots of ideas."

Warmth invaded me in the form of a slow burn. His

thick lashes lifted, and I was lost in the depths of his blue eyes. My fingers itched to touch him like I had that night so long ago—to sink my fingers into his damp hair, to smooth my hands over his hard chest and stomach. I bit down on my lip as he moved his left hand and caught a piece of hair that had slipped out of my ponytail. He smoothed it back, and a wave of tight, hot shivers coursed down my spine. In an unconscious, oddly instinctual move, my hips lifted off the door, moving closer to his. That did not go unnoticed by Reece, and I wondered, what would he do if I touched him now? Dragged my hand down his chest, under his shirt? Touched his bare flesh?

God, just thinking about it almost made me moan.

A half smile formed on his lips as the blue of his eyes deepened. "What are you thinking, Roxy?"

Naughty, dirty thoughts I'd never share, so I said the first thing that came to mind. "Thank you for the roses."

He arched a brow as some of the heat faded from his stare. "I didn't send you roses."

"Oh. *Oh*." The moment between us was officially broken. "You didn't?"

Pushing off the door, he dropped his arms to his sides. "No." His lips pursed as he turned sideways, eyeing the roses on the desk. "Those flowers?"

"Yeah, those flowers. I thought they were from you." I edged away from the door. "Are you sure you didn't send them?"

The look on his face basically said what a dumb question that was.

"Well, this is awkward." I shifted my weight from one foot to the next. "The card didn't have a name on it, and I honestly don't know who they'd be from."

He approached the flowers, running a finger over a dewy petal. "What did the card say?"

"Um, something like it'll be better next time."

Looking over his shoulder at me, he grinned. "I can see why you'd think it would be from me, but it wasn't."

I wondered if he thought it would be weird if I grabbed the flowers and threw them out of the office. Okay. No more throwing stuff.

"Should I be worried?" He faced me fully.

"Huh?"

The grin was full of boyish charm. "Do I have competition?"

It took me another moment to get what he meant, and a laugh burst out of me as I glanced at the flowers. "Yeah, I guess so."

The flowers had to be from Dean, and that meant even though I hadn't responded to any of the four texts he sent me, he still hadn't gotten the message.

"I'm going to have to do something about that," Reece said, leaning against the desk. He crossed his arms, drawing my attention to the shape of his upper arms. "Which reminds me. Back to what I'm going to do with you." His blue eyes glimmered.

My mind jumped in the gutter.

"I didn't drive here tonight," he announced.

"You didn't?"

"Nope. Went home first. That's why I wasn't here earlier. Needed to get changed since I was helping Dad clean out his garage. Then I got Colton to drop me off," he explained as he tilted his head to the side. His gaze dipped, and I felt it all the way to the tips of my toes. "I'm going home with you tonight."

Chapter 9

My heartbeat had not slowed down a moment since Reece announced he was coming home with me. Nervous energy buzzed throughout my system as I finished up my shift with . . . with Reece sitting at the bar.

Drinking water.

It didn't take long for Jax and Nick to notice that Reece was more waiting by the bar than really hanging out.

"I feel like I've missed something important," Jax commented dryly as he glanced in my direction and then back at Reece. "Like really missed something."

Reece chuckled. "You missed everything."

Walking by, Nick snorted.

Jax raised his brows as he grinned. "Well, it's about damn time."

My mouth dropped open. What the what on a monkey butt?

Reece nodded as he picked up his glass, eyeing me over the rim. There was that glint again, mischievous and boyish. "Truer words have never been spoken."

For once in my life, I was absolutely flabbergasted, which seemed to work for everyone, because between fulfilling drink orders, Jax and Reece chatted it up. I bounced from customer to customer, excited and nervous and hopeful and a thousand other things.

He was going home with me.

I was okay with this.

I was also freaked out about this and what it meant. As I mixed drinks like a bartending ninja, I tried to remember if I shaved my legs that morning. Or if I'd have time to do a quick touch-up in other areas. These were pressing concerns, because that's why he had to be coming home with me, right? It wasn't to knit a blanket at three in the morning.

Handing over a cocktail to a girl I'd seen in the bar a few times, I stole a quick glance at Reece. His head was bowed and in his hand was his cell phone. My heart stuttered in my chest as it suddenly became hard to swallow. I was totally willing to hook up with him. I mean, I'd wanted to before and this was what people our age did, and I'd moved on from what happened that night between us. Just thinking about being with him caused parts of my body to tighten and my breath to shorten. I'd wanted Reece since I first saw him, when I was fifteen.

Except this would be the first time with him for me, and it would be the second time with me for him, and something was just so wrong about that.

Plus, was I going to be satisfied with hooking up with Reece and nothing more? I . . . I wasn't sure. And that was scary. Not because he might not want something more, but because he might, and I didn't know if I could handle that.

I focused on getting drinks out to combat the ball of dread building in the pit of my stomach. There was a lot floating around in my head and if I didn't clear it out, I'd be a mess by the time I got off.

When I neared Reece and Jax again, the latter stopped me. "I want you to hear this, too."

Confused, I propped my elbows on the bar as I stood next to Jax. "Okay?"

Bright blues eyes fixed on mine. When Reece spoke, his voice was low enough for just us to hear. "I was just telling Jax about the call that came in this week over in Huntington Valley. I know you aren't watching the news, so you probably haven't heard about it."

"Hey, I watch the news," I defended myself, but as a bland look crossed his striking face, I sighed. "Okay, well I don't always listen to it."

Jax shook his head. "I hadn't heard it either. Been busy and haven't been paying attention to the news, but Reece told me that another girl was attacked."

I pressed my hand against my chest. "Oh God. Is . . . is she okay?"

Reece pursed his lips. "As okay as I guess she could be. She was roughed up and then tied up. From what I heard, the ordeal went on for hours before the guy simply left the vic. Her boyfriend ended up finding her and calling it in. She didn't get a good look at the guy, but they're thinking it's connected to the case in Prussia."

"So you aren't stepping foot outside this bar alone," Jax stated. "Neither is Calla when she's here."

I shivered as I nodded. God, the idea that someone could be out there stalking girls was more than just creepy. It was horrifying.

"Hell, I think I'm going to take Calla to the shooting range. Get her permitted."

Reece took a drink. "Doesn't sound like a bad idea." His gaze flipped to me. "I think you should consider that."

"Me? With a gun?" I laughed at the absurdity of it. "I'd end up accidentally shooting myself or some poor, innocent sap. Me and guns do not mix."

He reached over, capturing my hand. He tugged me forward, so that my hips were pressed against the bar. His eyes met mine again, and I totally forgot Jax was standing right there. "I want you safe," he said, his thumb sweeping the inside of my palm and doing funny things to my belly. "And I want you to at least seriously consider protecting yourself. Okay?"

Reece held on until I nodded and then I ambled off to the other side of the bar in a daze. A little after midnight, some college-aged guy approached the bar. His smile a little too wide, his step a little too wobbly, he leaned against the bar next to Reece. Immediately, I knew the guy was so not getting another drink. I had no problem cutting off people who were stumbling.

"Hey, baby, you are looking so damn . . . cute," the guy slurred, blinking slowly as he weaved unsteadily. "Yeah, your glasses. Hot. Like a dirty . . ."

I raised my brow as I waited.

"Yeah, dirty girl," he finished with a laugh. "I bet you are, too."

Working in a bar, I've heard some stupid pickups, which were usually met with polite disinterest, but that was gross. My mouth opened to deliver a well-placed verbal put-down when Reece swiveled on his chair and made eye contact with the guy. Cop Face was back. Except the stern, hard jaw and glinting blue eyes were not directed at me.

"Apologize," he ordered.

Drunk Guy swayed left and then right as he straightened. "What?"

"Apologize to her," Reece demanded again.

"Are you serious?" the guy replied, face ruddy.

Reece leaned back, raising his brows. "Do I look like I'm fucking joking? You don't know her at all and you say something like that, you dickhead. Apologize."

Absolutely stunned, I watched the guy turn to me and stutter out an "I'm sorry."

"Now fuck off," Reece added.

The dude fucked right off.

I turned my wide-eyed gaze to Reece. "I had that handled."

"I know you did." He picked up his glass of water again and smiled up at me, the picture of freaking innocence. "But I'm not the kind of guy to sit here while some dickhead is being disrespectful. And that was disrespectful."

"Totally was impolite," Nick commented as he walked behind me.

"It was," I said over the sudden cranking of music. My eyes met Reece's. Part of me wanted to tell him again that I had it handled, because I was woman, hear me roar and all that girl power, but he stood up for me . . . and that was important. It really was important for guys to do that when other guys were getting out of line.

"Thank you," I said, smiling a little.

He sat the glass down and before I knew what he was doing, he placed both hands on the bar top and rose. Stretching over, right in front of everyone in the bar and God, he leaned in, and I thought for a second he'd kiss me, and then I'd melt into a pool of gooey nothingness. He was going right for it. Anticipation swelled sweetly. I was seconds from grabbing his cheeks as my gaze centered on his mouth. I was so ready to melt into that pool.

Reece didn't kiss me. He tilted his head at the last

moment, placing his lips near my ear. When he spoke, he sent a tight, hot shiver right down my spine. "Two more hours, babe, and you'll be all mine."

On the way to my place, Reece kept the conversation light and flowing. Sticking to a topic such as the stormy forecast for the weekend worked to calm me enough not to drive off the road and plow into a mailbox. Reece, on the other hand, was 100 percent relaxed.

Every time I peeked over at him, he was the picture of lazy arrogance. Knees bent and spaced wide, one arm rested on his leg, the other against the window. His profile was open, jaw relaxed as his head was tipped back against the headrest. There was a slight, almost knowing grin that settled on his lips.

My heart was doing jumping jacks by the time I pulled in front of the Victorian. As I turned the key, cutting off the engine, he reached over, folding his long fingers over mine. Surprised, I glanced over at him, my breath stuck in my throat.

His eyes were the color of midnight in the dark interior of my car. "I'm gonna ask you a question and you're gonna be honest with me, okay?"

"Okay," I whispered.

He leaned over the center console, keeping his hand on mine. "If you're not okay with me coming in or staying, I can call a cab. You just tell me when you want me to leave and I'll leave."

Not surprised that he was giving me an out in case I wasn't kosher with him being in there, I nodded. "Okay."

His lips tipped further up on one corner. "But I have a feeling you're gonna ask me to stay."

I drew back, eyes narrowing. "Cocky bastard."

"Confident bastard, actually." With a chuckle at my exasperated look, he slid his hand off mine and climbed out.

Shaking my head, I followed suit. His long-legged stride got him to the porch before me and he opened the storm door. Grinning at him, I unlocked the door. "Such a gentleman," I told him.

"After you," he said.

I stepped into the silent, cool house, letting out a tiny squeal when he swatted my behind as he walked in after me. His answering chuckle sent a riot of shivers over my skin.

"Couldn't help myself," he said as I flipped on the living-room light. "Had to equal out my good-guy side with my bad-guy side."

"Wow." I dropped my purse on the worn recliner. "Do you keep a tally or something?"

His gaze found mine. "Only with you."

Those three words were like taking a shot of tequila. They raced through my body, causing my head to float up to decorative plaster moldings near the ceiling. I wet my lips, entirely too delighted when his gaze zeroed in on my mouth. "Are you flirting with me, Officer Anders?"

Reece's grin grew as he tilted his head to the side. "What do you think?"

"I think you are." I moved away from the lamp, heading toward the kitchen. Thankfully, the dishwasher wasn't possessed or anything. "You want something to drink?"

"Got tea?"

I grinned. "I do."

He trailed me into the kitchen, leaning against the counter as I grabbed a glass. As he peered out the kitchen sink window, I had a moment of panic. Was the kitchen a hot, dirty mess? After a quick scan of the countertops, I only spotted a few crumbs by the toaster and my paintbrushes were drying on a sheet of paper towels—thank God. Normally there'd be cup rings, plates, and maybe a bowl of leftover cereal.

"Here you go." I offered him a glass of iced tea.

"Thank you." His fingers grazed mine as he took the glass, and a blanket of sudden shyness wrapped around me. "Mind if I use the bathroom?"

I stared at the thick, leather strap on his flip-flops. "Help yourself." I took a step back, glancing up as I clutched my glass of tea to my chest. I sucked in a sharp breath when my eyes met his. He wore a look—a hot and hungry one—that said he wanted to take those two words I just uttered and apply them to a whole lot of other things.

In that moment, I sort of wanted to smack myself. I'd seen that look before, many times over the last eleven months whenever he was in the bar. We'd both made a lot of assumptions about that night we shared, but I felt like an even bigger idiot as I stood in front of him. There was no mistaking the way he looked at me.

"I'm . . . I'm going to get changed real quick," I said, sidestepping around him. "You know where the bathroom is."

He said something, but there were way too many things floating around in my head to pay attention. I left my tea on the end table I'd painted a deep blue last fall and then all but flew into the bedroom, stopping long enough to make sure the studio-room door was shut. Even though the portraits I'd done of Reece weren't hanging in there, I really didn't want him roaming into that room because they wouldn't be hard to find.

Closing the door quietly behind me, I whirled around and stared at the queen-sized bed I'd scrimped and saved for, managing to purchase about two years ago. Now, I'd be saving to replace Henry's windshield.

Ugh.

I didn't want to think about how tired and . . . and *done with it* Charlie looked today. I didn't want to think about Henry and how badly I'd lost control. I wasn't going to think about any hard things, unless those hard things were a part of Reece's anatomy.

I smacked a hand over my mouth, but a giggle escaped nonetheless.

Reece was actually out there, waiting for me. He was here.

Squeezing my eyes shut, I did a little butt shimmy as I balled my hands into fists, clenching my teeth together to prevent a high-pitch squeal from escaping. This went on for a good twenty seconds, and then I snapped out of, springing forward. What I wanted to do was shower, but that would seem too excessive and take too much time. Stripping down, I lotioned myself up until I was as soft and shiny as a baby seal, then pulled on a pair of fresh yoga pants and one of those camis with a built-in bra.

I yanked a brush through my hair once I let it down and then opened the closet door to check myself out in the mirror hanging on the inside. Giving myself a quick cursory glance, I thought I looked comfortable. Okay even. My hair fell to my breasts, and due to twisting it while still wet, it had messy waves in it. The outfit was laid-back, but flattering. Not like I was trying too hard or expecting anything. That was good. I think.

What was about to happen could end in so many different ways that I wondered if my parents ever had to worry about the many stages of possibly dating when they met. Tonight, Reece and I could hook up and it could just be a one-night stand. Or it could turn into the casual booty call—the one that only took place at three or four in the morning. But that could also progress into the friends-with-benefits stage or the "I think we're dating, because we're going out and doing things that don't always involve sex but nothing has been established" stage. From there, we could end up dating or going our separate ways. We could end up married with babies or we could just fade apart from one another. I doubted we'd be friends with benefits, because Reece knew my family and I knew his, so that could just get awkward.

There were so many different ways this could end that I was starting to stress myself out.

I wasn't going to overthink any of this.

Sticking my tongue out at my reflection, I stepped back and closed the closet door. Taking off my glasses, I placed them on the bedside table and then headed out of the bedroom, leaving the door ajar just in case we needed to make it back to the bedroom with a quickness.

I flushed, because I'd totally do him on the couch, floor, kitchen counter—wherever. A bed was not necessary.

I was going to be down for whatever happened tonight.

Chapter 10

Reece was sitting on the couch, long legs stretched out in front of him, feet kicked up on the coffee table. The TV was on, volume down. For a moment, all I could do was stare at him as my stomach fluttered madly and dangerously, because I could . . . I could get used to seeing him sitting on my couch, waiting for me to get off work. Me waiting for him. Preferably naked.

"Um." He looked up, brows raised. "Is there something you want to tell me?"

I stiffened. "What?"

A slow grin crossed his face. "Your toilet seat lid was up."

"What?" I repeated.

"When I went into your bathroom, the toilet seat was up. I was wondering if there was something you weren't telling me. Like if you were trying a new method or something," he teased.

What in the world? The only time I'd ever accidentally left the toilet seat up was when I cleaned it. My mind raced to find a plausible explanation to how the seat lifted up by itself. Poltergeist. It was official. The Victorian was built on an old Indian burial ground. We all were screwed.

Could I call Ghost Hunters? Or The Dead Files people?

"Sit with me?" he asked, stretching his arm along the back of the couch.

Reece had easily dismissed the toilet-seat thing, and I almost blurted out my Haunting in Plymouth Meeting suspicion, but decided against sounding like a lunatic for the time being. I'd prefer to talk to my mom or Katie about that. He probably wouldn't believe me, and think I was being kooky Roxy.

Making my way over to him, I sat down with what I considered was appropriate space between us. When I pulled my legs up and crossed them, there was at least an inch. Plus, if I leaned back, it would be against his arm.

Why was I even thinking about this?

"What are you watching?" I asked, picking at the hem of my pants.

One shoulder rose in a shrug. "Looks like an infomercial for music of the eighties. Thinking about buying it."

I snorted. "I don't even own a CD player."

He sent me a sideways glance. "You don't own a DVD player either."

When I'd been in his apartment, he'd had an impressive collection of DVDs. Not that I got a chance to scope them out, but I bet he had every movie from the last two decades. "Why would I, when I have On Demand?"

Shaking his head, he picked up his glass. "You don't

have a DVD collection and you still got your momma making tea for you. What am I doing here?"

"Whatever!" I smacked his thigh—his extremely hard thigh. Wow. My fingers tingled when I drew my hand back. "How do you know I didn't make that tea?"

"It tastes just like your mom's tea," he countered, blue eyes twinkling. "Plus, the last I remember, your sweet tea tastes like watered-down engine fuel."

A laugh burst out of me. "It does not."

He arched a brow.

"Okay. Fine. The ratio of tea to sugar always throws me off."

Reece chuckled. "You know, I was being serious about learning how to shoot a gun earlier. It's just a smart thing to do."

"I don't know. Guns . . . I don't have a problem with them, but they scare me," I admitted. "It's having the power to end a life in your hands. All you have to do is pull a trigger." I shook my head. "That's just . . . that's just too much power."

"Babe, you damn well know a rock in the hands of the wrong person can change lives, end them even. A gun is no different."

Unsettled, I had to admit that he was right. But guns were also a part of his life and they weren't a part of mine. Growing up, Dad had hunting rifles, but I rarely ever saw them. He kept them locked up, and never once did it cross my mind to get one for myself.

"You just have to be responsible," he continued. "Just think about it. For me?"

"I'll think about it." Smiling, I looked at the TV. Some dude with a Mohawk was waving a CD around. "So, what were you doing at your dad's house?"

Reece took a long drink and as he sat the glass

down, the ice clinked around. A moment passed, and I wanted to kick myself. Reece . . . yeah, he was never a fan of talking about his dad. Shock rippled through me as he looked over at me and answered a second before I tried to change the subject.

"Divorce Number Three."

I gaped at him. "What? When did this happen?" That was kind of a stupid question, because I hadn't exactly been friendly with him for the last eleven months.

"You know, I really don't know. Everything was fine at the beginning of summer. He and Elaine were going on vacation in Florida." He tipped his head back against the cushion, flipping his gaze to the ceiling. He barked out a short laugh. "Then again, Dad doesn't know how to be up front about anything. So him telling me or Colton that things were good doesn't mean shit. The man's nothing but a liar."

I pressed my lips together for a moment. "Did he say what happened?"

His gaze returned to me. "What do you think?"

A sigh rose. "Did he cheat on her?"

"Yep." A second passed and then I felt his hand in my hair, causing me to suck in a short breath. The touch was light, as if he was just running his fingers over it, but every cell in my body became hyperaware. "With a younger woman he met on a business trip. Told me that it was only a one-night thing and that Elaine was overreacting."

"Overreacting to being cheated on? How does one overreact to that?"

"You know my dad. The man knows no wrong," he said, shaking his head. "While I was there, he left his cell phone on the hood of his car. The thing rang.

A woman's name was on the screen. Never heard of her before. I'd bet my savings account it was the 'one night stand' chick. I'm not surprised his marriage is ending that way. By the time my mom wised up and left his ass, he'd been with five other women. And not a 'wham, bam, thank ya ma'am' kind of thing either. Five other relationships."

"That's so sad," I murmured, lowering my chin. Franklin—his father—was a habitual cheater. At least, that's what I had heard his mom saying once. "I'm sorry. I know you're older now, so is Colton, and maybe it doesn't hurt as much as it did when you were younger, but it still sucks."

Instead of denying it, he smiled softly. "Yeah, it does." His fingers had left my hair, but his arm was still there, warm and beckoning me to lean back. "I didn't get too close to Elaine, but she seemed like a good woman. She didn't deserve that. No one does."

Taking a deep breath, I leaned back. His arm was right behind my neck. Not a second seemed to pass before his hand found its way to my shoulder. "Do . . . do you think he'll marry again?"

"Probably." He grabbed his glass, taking another drink. I'd completely forgotten about mine. "I think the worst thing, though, isn't the fact that he'd stick his dick in anything that walked, but that he constantly lies about it, even when he's caught. I don't get that. Never will. Anyway," he said, drawing out the word with a grin that didn't reach the beautiful eyes I had such a hard time capturing. "So what have you painted lately?"

Holy shit, was he a mind reader? Blood flooded my cheeks as I searched in my head for something that didn't include his face. "Um, well I've been doing a lot of landscapes. Beaches. Gettysburg. That kind of stuff."

Good answer, Roxy!

His gaze tracked over my face, almost like a physical caress. "You still painting for Charlie?"

Of course, he'd remember that. Nodding, I wasn't surprised when the familiar sadness washed over me as I thought of all those paintings hanging on his wall.

The hand on my shoulder tightened. "So when are you going to paint something for me?"

"When you become my official pool boy," I retorted.

He stared at me. "You don't have a pool."

"I know. So it's when I get a pool and you become my official pool boy." I grinned. "You think I'm kidding."

Tipping his head back, he laughed deeply as he used the hand on my shoulder to tug me over to him. One second I was leaning into him, and the next I was on my back, my head resting in his lap, and all I could think as I stared up at him was that was one hell of a smooth move.

"Did you learn that move while training to be a cop?" I asked, breathless.

"Yeah, they teach that special kind of takedown in the academy." His thick, dark lashes lowered as he settled a large hand on the curve of my hip farthest from him. "Couldn't wait to use it on you."

I smiled up at him as my heart started jumping around in my chest. The hand on my hip seemed like an unconscious thing to him. "I feel honored."

"You should." Using his other hand, he carefully brushed a strand of hair out of my face. Something about what seemed like an absent-minded touch sent my heart careening. As his lashes lifted and all I could see were brilliant blue eyes, I knew in that moment that being satisfied with just a hookup here and there was going to be really hard.

Before I could really dwell on that realization, he spoke. "Can I ask you a question?"

"Sure." I wished he'd ask if he could kiss me. That would've been a resounding yes.

The hand on my hip shifted and his thumb smoothed over the hem of my cami, and I shivered. "What were you thinking when you threw that book, Roxy?"

Whoa. Total change of subject I wasn't prepared for. Here I was thinking about him kissing me. I opened my mouth, but it took me a few seconds to answer. "I really . . . really wasn't thinking."

He picked up a strand of my hair, twisting it around his fingers. "Babe, I don't think there's ever truly a moment when we're not thinking."

I averted my gaze as I chewed on my lower lip. Thinking back to the moment Henry had grabbed my arm, there was a lot in my head. So much that it felt like there was nothing. My chest tightened.

Reece dropped my hair and ran his finger over my lower lip, startling a gasp out of me . . . and a response. "I hate him," I blurted out, feeling the words swell inside me like a blood promise. "I seriously hate him, Reece. I never really hated someone before, but when I see him, I want . . . I want him to hurt like Charlie hurt. That's what I was thinking when I threw the book."

The lines of his face softened. "Roxy . . ."

"I know it's wrong." I closed my eyes, exhaling slowly. "I know what I did wasn't that much different than what Henry did."

"No," he argued, and when I opened my eyes, he

was staring at me intently. "What you did was throw a book at a windshield, not at him. Henry picked up a rock and threw it at the back of Charlie's head when you two walked away."

I flinched.

"You never had any intentions of harming Henry," he went on as he kept swiping his thumb along the hem of my cami. "And if Henry really didn't mean to do the kind of damage he did to Charlie, he still made the conscious decision to throw that rock *at* him. Not at the ground or a nearby car. He threw it at another living being. You'd never do that."

Cold air whirled its way down my chest, into my stomach. The thing was, I wasn't too sure of that. When I had tasted that anger, that red-hot bitter anger, I knew I was capable of doing something heinous. Everyone was capable of it; some moral compass ingrained in me had prevented it, but would it always stop me? If I saw Henry again, there was a good chance I'd lose my cool once more, and really, how did that make me any better than him?

"Deep thoughts," I murmured, edgy from where my thoughts were heading.

His lips quirked up at the corners as his thumb brushed against the thin sliver of skin exposed under the hem now. The touch was like an electric shot. "Yeah, too deep for four in the morning."

Reece's tone was light, but everything in me was heavy. It was like a door being unlocked inside my head. Painful memories of the night with Charlie and Henry were unleashed. They stacked up inside me, like a tower about to topple over. They started with what I had done, the verbal rock I had thrown, that had started it all.

And here I was, lying in the lap of the man I'd . . . well, I'd been lying to for eleven months. A man who hated nothing more than he did a liar. That wasn't right.

Pushing myself up, I started to roll onto my side so I could pretend to go to the bathroom, to give myself time to clear my head, but I didn't make it.

Reece curved his hand behind my neck and the hand on my hip slid up my waist, stopping just below my breast. My eyes popped wide as he held me there, my shoulder pressed against his chest.

"Don't," he said, voice rough.

That one word was like a lightning bolt. Sometimes I forgot how well he did know me. Even though we hadn't spoken for almost a year, he still knew when I was getting cagey, recognized that my mood could flip as quickly as a coin spinning through the air.

Our eyes locked as I placed my hand on his shoulder. I started to push off, but then he lowered his head. I looked up as his lips brushed mine. It was a slow sweep. He made the pass with his lips once and then twice. I couldn't breathe as I felt the heat of his mouth increasing the most gentle pressure as he held me in place. There was an almost questioning feel to how his lips moved over mine, as if it were for the very first time. And it wasn't, but the night at his place, he hadn't kissed me like this—not as tender, not so sweet that a ball of stupid emotion formed in the back of my throat. That kiss . . . it was like he cherished me.

My fingers curled into his shoulder, bunching the thin cotton of his shirt as my heart raced. When I thought about him kissing me, I didn't think it would be like this. No guy had ever kissed me like I was a treasure.

"Reece," I whispered against his mouth.

Something about hearing his name snapped a part of him. The hand along the back of my neck tightened, as did the one at my waist, and the kiss . . . oh wow, the kiss deepened. I remembered this kind of kissing, but it was different, stronger and deeper. There was no hint of liquor on his tongue, just sugar and tea and 100 percent male. He nipped at my lower lip, wringing out a soft moan that echoed straight to my core, then he parted my lips, tasting me. The kiss was like touching fire, igniting a deep-seated desire. I no longer needed the space to clear my thoughts. My head was an empty road with one destination in mind.

Reece.

Sitting up, I wiggled around until I managed to get a knee on either side of his legs. He watched me with heavy hooded eyes. "I like where this is going," he said, grasping my hips. "I really fucking do, but I want—"

Done with talking and deep thoughts and well intentions, I cupped his cheeks and got down to business. I kissed him—kissed him just as deeply and as hotly as he'd kissed me.

A deep growl rumbled up and I felt it in his chest as the grip on my hips tightened, sending a wave of hot shivers through me. His mouth opened immediately, and I tilted my head, tasting him. My fingers made their way to the soft brush of hair clipped closer to the sides and then into the longer strands. He made another sound that sparked a fresh wave of desire through me.

His hands slid up my back, following the line of my spine before tangling in my hair for a few precious moments. There wasn't a second that we stopped devouring one another with long, wet kisses and shorter ones that sent heat flooding my body.

Reece glided those hands back down, over the small of my back, and then he cupped my rear, squeezing until I was gasping for breath. The kiss turned hungry as he guided me down on his lap. Another wave of lust slammed into me at the feel of him, straining against the denim jeans. From the brief moments spent together before, I knew he was long and thick, but I had forgotten just how good he felt.

I rocked my hips, pressing myself down on him, and was immediately rewarded with a blast of sensual pleasure. Resting my forehead against his, I moaned as I tugged on the short strands of hair.

"God, you're going to drive me insane." His voice was thick, raw. He pulled my hips down as he grinded up, hitting the right spot through the thin yoga pants. "I don't think you're going to be happy until you do."

Panting, I let my hands slip down the sides of his neck, to his shoulders. "I want you insane for me," I admitted, biting down on my lip as he brought our hips together again.

"Baby, I'm already insane for you." He captured my lips in another scorching kiss before breaking away, trailing a hot, shivery stream up along my jaw. "I think you know that."

Tipping my head back, I held on tight. "Nuh-uh."

He moved those kisses down my throat, stopping to nip above my pulse. He soothed the erotic burn with a soft kiss. "Every time I saw you this past year, I wanted you here. Right *here*." To punctuate what he said, he rolled his hips, pressing the bulge in his jeans against my core. "And every time you turned and walked away from me, I wanted to give chase."

I shook as he brought his hot mouth to the line of my collarbone. He drew his hands up, letting them roam over my stomach and then farther up, over the swell of my breasts. My back arched as exquisite sensations rippled through me.

"You have no idea how many times I thought about throwing you over my shoulder and taking you back to the stockroom." His thumbs swept over the tips of my breasts, and they were already hard and aching. "I'm thinking I should've just done that. Then we could've left all this bullshit behind us earlier."

My head was swimming, lost in the pleasure he was drawing out of me. "Sounds like . . ." I gasped as his tongue flicked over my pulse. "Sounds like it would've . . . been a good plan."

He lifted his head as he brought his hands to my shoulders, slipping his fingers under the thin, delicate straps. His eyes snared mine. "May I?"

God, he could be asking for anything at this point and I'd hand it over. I nodded, beyond words.

One side of his mouth curved up, and again, there was a pang deep in my chest as he grinned at me, all boyish charm and sensuality, and I knew I'd fallen for him all those years ago. There was no changing that, even though I knew he hadn't fallen with me, maybe never would, it didn't undo that he was already under my skin, a part of me.

With his burning gaze locked with mine, he slid the straps of my cami down to my elbows. I didn't hesitate. Dropping my arms, I slipped them out, allowing the material to settle around my waist.

Reece kissed me softly and then he pulled back. His lashes lowered and I knew he was staring at me, and a bit of the haze lifted from my thoughts. Did he remember what I looked like from the alcohol-filled night? Vulnerability slipped over my skin like an itchy sweater. I was barely a B cup and that was probably stretching it.

But he shuddered as he wrapped his hands around my bare breasts, touching me almost reverently. I looked down, breathless as he held me, his skin a darker tone against the pale and pinkness of mine.

"You're beautiful," he growled, grazing the pads of his thumbs over the hard nubs. I jerked as his lips kicked back into that grin. "You like that?"

"Yeah," I whispered, and then nodded just in case he didn't get the message.

"I don't remember what makes you move," he said, catching my tip between agile fingers. "I don't remember what drives you crazy." He tugged gently, and I cried out. His lashes lifted, eyes full of hunger. "You're sensitive."

I was. Always had been sensitive there. Katie, stripper extraordinaire, once told me I was lucky because most women she knew really weren't too big on foreplay of the busty kind.

Unable to look away, I watched him touch me. There was something highly erotic about this. Never before had I ever done this. Then again, most guys hadn't really taken this much time, and when he lowered his hands to my hips, I thought he was moving on.

I was wrong.

He lifted me up so I was stretching above him and as I steadied myself by placing my hands on the back of the couch, he closed his mouth over the tip of my breast.

"Oh my God," I cried out as he drew the puckered nipple into his mouth. "Reece, oh God . . ."

One hand flattened between my shoulders, pulling on my hair. A series of sharp, sensual tingles radiated across my scalp as he savored me. I was trapped, but there was nowhere else I wanted to be as he moved from one breast to the other.

My fingers dug into the cushions as he suckled deep, causing the muscles inside me to coil tightly, until I couldn't take it anymore. I tried to pull away.

"No," he groaned. "I'm not done with you yet."

I gasped as he caught the tip between his teeth. The tiny nip sent molten lava through my blood. I trembled against him, my body hot. "I can't . . . I need you. Please."

He released me, and I went wild. Clenching his shoulders, I pressed myself back down against him, finding his mouth blindly. His hands were back to my hips as I rocked against him. The soft material of his shirt teased the tips of my breasts, and the friction between my legs against the hardness was too much.

I couldn't remember the last time I had an orgasm like this, with most of my clothes still on—without the guy even getting a hand on me, but I could feel it building inside me as I grinded on him, as he pushed up, the thrusts of his hips matching that of his tongue.

Release spun through me, exploding out from my core and rippling through every part of my body. His mouth muffled my moan, but he knew what had happened, because a purely masculine sound rumbled out of him. When the last of the pleasure ebbed through my veins, I was flushed and trembling.

"Look at you," he said into my ear, his voice harsh. "Nothing hotter, Roxy. You're like holding on to fire."

It took me a couple of moments to come to my senses enough to realize that he'd seriously gotten me off, and when I pulled back a little, I pressed a tiny kiss against the corner of his lips. "What do you want me to do?"

His eyes were full of blue fire. "Baby, watching you come made my night."

I shuddered, thinking he was being kind of perfect, but I glanced down and there was no mistaking the bulge in his pants. Hands still shaking as I rocked back, I reached between us, half expecting him to stop me.

He didn't.

A lazy, sated smile pulled at my lips as I ran my fingers over the covered length of him, feeling my insides clench all over when his hips popped up in response. I glanced up at him, breathing deeply. "You didn't get off."

He shook his head, jaw locked down.

My heart was racing all over again as I undid his button and carefully tugged down the zipper. The material parted, revealing black boxer briefs. Without saying a word, he lifted his ass and me right off the couch, a silent demand. I wasted no time, tugging down his jeans and boxers.

I stared as he sprung free, thick and heavy. Truthfully, this part of a guy's body wasn't always the most attractive thing in the word, but Reece . . . oh yeah, it was just as yummy as the rest of him.

Speaking of the rest of him.

As he settled back down, I tugged up the hem of his shirt and he lifted his arms, letting me pull it off. I tossed it somewhere where I hoped he never found it, and got a huge eyeful of what it looked like when a man was no longer a boy and worked his body hard to stay in shape.

Golden skin stretched smooth and tight over his pecs and then down on a chiseled, rock-hard stomach that was tightly rolled. A trail of dark hair ran under his navel, down to where he waited. I dragged my gaze back up. There was a scar just to the left of his navel, skin puckered in an irregular circle. There was another above that. And I knew if I got his pants off, there'd be a third.

My breath caught as I thought about how close I came—how close all of us came—to losing him. Leaning forward, I kissed him, wishing I could take back eleven months of being stupid, because time . . . it was short and never promised.

"What do you want me to do?" I asked again.

His eyes searched mine. "There's a lot I want you to do, Roxy."

"Pick one." Or two. Or three. I'd do them all.

Reece reached down, wrapping his fingers around his cock. Holy smokes, I felt the need to fan myself as his grip tightened. My lips parted as he slowly brought his hand up to the head and then back down. "This is what I want you to do."

Blood was pounding in my ears and I barely heard myself say, "You . . . you are so freaking hot, Reece."

He groaned as his hand swept up again and his back bowed, and I couldn't help it. I moaned. His gaze flew back to mine, a different kind of fire burning in their depths. "I think I know what you want."

"What?" I breathed.

Reece reached out with his other hand, curling it around the base of my neck as he stroked himself again. A bead appeared at the tip. "You want to watch me."

Every part of my body burned. Not out of shame, but because it was true. "I've never watched a guy—"

"That's all I need to hear," he said, moving his hand.

My breath shortened in my chest as I watched him, his grip getting stronger and stronger. I couldn't believe that I was doing this—couldn't believe how arousing it was—or that I was still in his lap, my cami forgotten around my waist, my skin flushed. I started to look up.

"No. Watch me," he ordered, and I shivered at the demand in his voice.

And I watched him as his hand pumped and his hips moved more furiously. I had to place my hands back on his shoulders to hold, and I didn't look away, not until his hand around my neck yanked me forward.

Reece kissed me as he found his release. No—he didn't just kiss me, he devoured me as he rocked into his hand. "Fuck," he drew the word out as his one arm closed around me, gathering me close to his bare chest and holding tight. I buried my head in the space between his neck and shoulder, breathing in the crisp scent of his aftershave as I felt his heart start to slow.

Neither of us spoke for a long moment and then he laughed softly, the sound bringing a smile to my lips.

"Damn, Roxy." He cleared his throat. "You're going to make me want to keep you."

My heart was tugged in two opposite directions as my befuddled head tried to make sense of what that meant. Already, I was beginning to apply a crazy amount of meaning to what he said. Did it mean that he wasn't planning on it? This was just for fun? But he'd said he wanted to be more than friends. Did it even matter? No, it didn't, because there was no lying to myself.

I wanted him to keep me.

Chapter 11

I hadn't meant to doze off, but somewhere between watching Hilary remodeling an old farmhouse and David showing a peculiarly picky couple houses on HGTV, I'd fallen asleep on my side, with my back curled against Reece's front.

I'd never fallen asleep on a couch with a guy before. Seemed like such a simple thing that I imagined millions of people took for granted, but it was something entirely new for me.

At first, I wasn't sure what woke me up. I blinked open my eyes, confused. There was an infomercial on TV, selling the newest Bowflex machine. I stared at it for a moment, seconds from drifting back to sleep, when I felt Reece jerk behind me.

My heart jumped at the unexpected movement. His arm was lax under me, but when I looked over my shoulder, I could see the tension practically pouring off him. He was on his side but his face was turned up to the ceiling. His jaw was locked in a tight, hard line and his brows were furrowed. Every couple of seconds, those thick lashes would twitch. His lips moved, the words silent, but his chest rose with a sudden, ragged, and broken breath.

"Reece?" I whispered, but he didn't hear me. His chest rose again, the breathing more rapid. I twisted onto my other side, facing him as I pressed my hand on his chest. "Reece."

He jolted away, his gaze fixed on the ceiling, and for a moment, he looked so far away, as if he wasn't even aware of where he was. Seconds ticked by and then he turned his head toward me. His expression relaxed. "Hey," he murmured.

"Everything okay?" I asked.

He swallowed. "Yeah."

I didn't really believe him. "You sure?"

Reece's arm curved around me as he tucked me against his side. "Yeah, sweets, everything is fine." As he threaded his fingers through my hair and guided my cheek to his chest, he sighed deeply. "Everything is good now."

"You got some this weekend."

I nearly choked on my soda as I looked up. Katie slid into the booth across from me, a bright pink-checkered bandana wrapped around her head. Her off the shoulder fuzzy blue sweater looked like it had it out with a bedazzler and lost the battle. She wasn't alone.

Calla sat down next to Katie. She'd come back into town yesterday morning and had worked at the bar last night. Grinning, she tugged her blond hair up into a ponytail. I remembered, when I first met her she'd always kept her hair down to hide the scar. Not so much anymore.

Ignoring Katie's somewhat astute comment, I nodded at Calla. "I'm surprised Jax let you out of his house to have breakfast."

"He knows better than to get between me and food and my friends." Flipping open the menu, she raised delicately arched brows at me. "So, is Katie right? You get some?"

Katie grinned. "I'm always right."

I rolled my eyes as I sat back against the booth. Reece had fallen back asleep after what I guessed was a nightmare, and I'd taken him home yesterday morning. Before he'd climbed out of my car, he'd leaned over and kissed me. Just thinking about that scalding kiss made me want to fan myself, and then it made me think of what I'd watched him do.

Goodness, I needed a cold shower.

He'd worked the night shift, and I figured he was probably sleeping right now. He'd texted me right before I'd gotten off, a quick message telling me to let him know when I got home, and I did. The request was . . . cute, like he was thinking of me, and it made me feel all girlie.

"The tips of your ears are burning," Calla pointed out, eyes narrowing. "Come on, fess up."

The waitress saved me for a few minutes while she took our orders. Katie ordered half the diner, going for every version of bacon and sausage they had. "I need my protein," she said as Calla and I gaped at her. "Dancing and climbing a pole is one hell of a workout. You guys should try it."

I giggled. "No thanks."

Katie rolled cornflower-colored eyes. "You guys are

no fun." She twisted toward Calla. "When is Teresa coming back up? She wanted to learn how to shake it until she breaks it."

"I think she and Jase are coming up in a few weekends with me." Calla smiled as the waitress returned with two coffees and a fresh soda for me. Then she pinned me with a look. "Did you and Reece hook up?"

"What?"

At the same time, Katie answered, "Yes."

I shot her a baleful look. "How do you know if we hooked up? Were you hiding in my house?"

"I know things," she replied. "I know lots of things. And you totally just assumed that I'd be hiding in your house, which means something of the fleshy kind went down in your house."

Calla propped her elbows on the table. "And Jax told me Reece came in on his night off and waited for you to get off. That you drove him home."

"Jax gossips like a thirteen-year-old girl," I retorted, but I wasn't upset with the line of questioning. I was glad both girls could do breakfast this morning, because I really, *really* needed to talk to them.

A moment passed and then I leaned forward, unable to keep quiet about it a second longer. "Okay. We kind of did hook up Friday night. We didn't have sex, but . . ." I trailed off, pulled back to those early-morning hours. I could see him then, his hand wrapped around—

"All right, you guys definitely did something of the fun and naughty kind based on the way you suddenly look like you just took a hit of ecstasy," Katie said.

Calla clapped as she bounced in her seat. "For real? Okay, girl, I'm happy for you, because Katie is right, you look like you just slipped into a sex coma."

"Something you know a lot about," I said under my breath.

She itched her nose with her middle finger. "But you wouldn't even talk to him just a few weeks ago. Every time he walked in or even looked in your direction, you bailed. I've always known something was up between you two, but I'm confused as to what is going on here."

I gave a wobbly smile. "Well, it's a long story."

"Since I ordered half a pig, we have time," Katie replied.

"And you guys are going to think I'm a terrible person."

"Doubtful," Calla reassured me.

I wasn't so sure about that, but I hadn't told a soul except Charlie about what had gone down between Reece and me, including the huge misunderstanding. I took a deep breath and then I told them *everything* about the night with Reece, pausing long enough for our food to be delivered.

"So, yeah, that's . . . that's where I'm at with everything," I finished as I cut the rest of my syrup with a side of waffle into tiny squares.

Calla stared at me, a piece of extra-crispy bacon dangling from her fingertips.

Even Katie gaped at me, which was saying something, if I managed to shock her into any realm of silence. I shrunk back against the booth, feeling sheepish and crappy. "I'm a terrible person, aren't I?"

"No," Calla said immediately. "You're not a terrible person."

"Wait." Katie held up one hand. Somehow a thick piece of sausage had made it to her fingers. "So, let me make sure I have this correct. You've basically been in love with Reece since you were fifteen."

"I wouldn't say *in* love," I muttered, but my heart thumped.

"Whatever. I've known you've been in love with him," she insisted, and I didn't protest it, because I figured it would end up with a discussion about her super-stripper powers. "Anyway, you've been *in love* with him, but he always treated you like the annoying kid next door."

My eyes narrowed on her. "I wouldn't say he treated me like the annoying kid next door either."

She ignored me. "He finally starts treating you like the hot chick that you are, he comes to the bar one night, gets shitfaced, but because you're madly, deeply, and irrevocably in love with him and because you're a girl, you don't realize he's shitfaced."

My eyes narrowed further on her.

"You two go to his house, because he asked for a ride for his drunk ass, things get hot and heavy. You see his sausage." She waved the sausage she held, and Calla made a choking sound as she reached for her coffee. "You guys make out all the way back to his bedroom, where he passes out. Am I following this so far?"

"Yeah." I folded my arms. "Kind of."

Katie nodded sagely, and I had no idea what she was being sage about. "First off, that's lame of him to get that freaking drunk, so he gets a cool point taken from him."

"Cool point?" Calla turned wide eyes on her. "We're still adding and taking away cool points?"

I snickered.

"In my world, we are," she replied, and then she bit into the sausage, chewing thoughtfully for a moment. "So he passes out, you stay with him, and then he wakes up, thinks you guys had sex and is apologetic and regretful?"

Nodding, I popped a piece of waffle into my mouth.

"And you thought he regretted having sex with you," Calla tossed in. "But he regretted getting so drunk and having sex with you?"

"Yep."

Katie shook her head as she picked up the salt and dumped it on her half-eaten sausage. "But you two didn't have sex."

"No. And I started to tell him that when he first made the assumption, but he was so damn sorry about it all that I thought he was talking about the actual sex."

"And that hurt your feelings," Calla said gently. "That's understandable. I probably would've thought the same thing."

"But you could've cleared it up right then," Katie pointed out.

"No shit," I replied. "But I didn't. I was so embarrassed and . . . yeah, my feelings were hurt, so I left his place and just so much time passed, and I was still all butt sore about it that I never cleared it up."

Katie finished off the sausage and then moved onto the smaller links. "And Reece has this thing with lying? That's not good."

I pinned her with a bland look.

She leaned forward, waving the link around like a wand. "Look, I totally get why you haven't said anything. It's like telling one little lie and then telling another little lie to cover that one and so on. Then it all builds up. I get that. A lot of time has passed and how would you explain what really happened? Hey Reece, would you like to play with my tits? Oh, by the way, we never had sex."

Calla almost choked again. "That . . . that sounds like an awkward conversation."

I sighed as I pushed my plate away from me. "I do

feel terrible. I wish I'd pulled my head out of my ass long enough to give him a chance to explain why he reacted that way, and I wish I'd just told him the truth."

"He ain't completely innocent in all of this," Katie argued. "Remember, he was so drunk he thought he had sex. I've drunk a lot in my day. A lot. Like so much, I'm pretty sure I've turned into a brewery, but I've never been so drunk that I didn't know if I had sex."

Calla nodded as she poked at her scrambled eggs. "True."

Neither had I ever drunk that much, but that was beside the point. Taking a sip of my soda, my shoulders sank as the weight of the situation settled on them. I straightened my glasses as I sighed. "I . . . I really like him, guys. I really do."

"Duh." Katie rolled her eyes. "You're in love with him."

I ignored that comment, because love . . . love was a scary four-letter word. "He's a good guy, a really good guy. And you remember the last dude I kind of seriously dated?" I asked Katie.

She wrinkled her nose. "Before Dean the ginger?"

"Oh my God," Calla murmured, stifling her giggle with the back of her hand.

I shook my head and then took a drink. "Yes. Remember Donnie, the—"

"The really nice guy who took you to the Eagles game and you totally got with in the parking garage, but turned out to be married?" Katie supplied happily.

My lips pressed together. "No. That was Ryan the fucker and thanks for reminding me about him. He also had a kid he never told me about. I was talking about Donnie the starving artist who stole my jewelry my grammy left me."

Calla blinked several times. "Wow. A married guy and a thief?"

"I normally don't attract the greatest people." I shrugged, but I thought of Henry, and that made my skin crawl. The thing was, I knew I dated guys like that for a reason. They were safe. "But Reece is not like them, and a part of me . . ." I let out a slow breath. "I have spent years lusting after him." And I'd probably spent years feeling something stronger than that.

Sitting there, I shook my head. What was I even doing? I just needed to tell him the truth. Let this thing between us die before I got burned big time, but I couldn't . . . I couldn't not try with him. Not after all these years of wanting him.

God, I sounded like I had a split personality. Go after him. Don't go after him. Tell him the truth. Don't say anything. I was giving myself whiplash.

"You need to tell him the truth," Calla advised. "As soon as possible. But I wouldn't worry about it too much."

I arched my brows at her.

"Seriously," she insisted. "It's not like you lied about something major."

"I think not telling him we didn't have sex is pretty major."

"Not really." Calla smiled at me. "Trust me, there are worse lies out there. It's not like you lied about being with someone else while with him or anything like that. He'll understand. Right, Katie?"

She watched me, pouty lips turned down at the corners.

Calla elbowed her as she frowned. "*Right*, Katie?"

Frost coated my insides as Katie's eyes clouded over. "I don't know, Roxy. Tell the truth before he gets in those pants of yours for real. If you don't, I think you've gone too far."

Agreeing, I nodded slowly. The same dread I experienced the first time I realized I needed to tell Reece what really happened returned.

Calla cleared her throat. "It'll be okay."

"She's right," Katie agreed, stabbing her last link with her fork. "Besides, you broke Henry Williams's window and he still gave you an orgasm. You'll probably get an even better one out of this."

Smacking my palm off my forehead, I groaned. "Oh God. Who doesn't know about that?"

"No one, honey." Katie bit off half the link. "Absolutely no one."

Calla and I watched Katie speed out of the parking lot in her Mini Cooper, almost clipping a minivan that had a Baby On Board bumper sticker, but when the van parked, an elderly couple climbed out.

"You're really not going to hold a séance, are you?" Calla asked.

I laughed loudly. I'd told them about the strange things happening in my apartment. Luckily neither of them thought I was crazy or that I was weird for thinking that my place may be haunted. Of course, Katie had lots of ideas of how to address the strange happenings, and one of them was by calling someone in town who supposedly communed with spirits and could host a séance.

"Ah, you know, I don't think that will be a great idea," I said, grinning. "If there really is a ghostie roaming around, it hasn't tried to scare me. In a way, it's been strangely helpful."

Calla snorted. "I bet more people would like to have a ghost like that."

"And the whole idea of séance or allowing a psychic in the house just—I don't know, if that's what it really is, I don't want to know what's there. As long as I don't wake up in the middle of the night and find it staring at me, then I'm cool with it."

"Oh my God." She shuddered. "That's so creepy." There was a pause. "But what if it isn't a ghost?"

"What else could it be? Seriously, though? Unless I have people living under my stairs like in that creepy eighties movie, it's either a ghost or I'm losing my mind."

"You're not crazy." She squinted. "But maybe you should have Reece just take a look at your place. Or Jax?"

Yeah, I could picture both of guys never letting me live it down if I told them I thought I had a ghost in my house.

"So how long are you going to be up here?" I asked, changing the subject as I leaned against my car, pulled off my glasses, and used the hem of my shirt to clean them.

"My morning class is cancelled tomorrow so I'm going to head back then." Calla glanced up at the overcast skies. The scent of rain was thick in the air. "Which is probably a good thing, since I think they're calling for pretty bad storms today."

I slipped my glasses on, smiling when I didn't see any smudges or spots. "You and Jax got anything planned for today?"

"I think we're just going to hang out at his place." She twisted a length of blond hair between her hands as she shrugged. "What about you and Reece?"

"I don't think we have anything planned. It's weird. I don't know if we're dating or if we're just . . . hooking up. He texted me last night, asking me to let him know when I got home and I did that." I folded my arms, pursing my lips. "So I really don't know."

"You just text him, invite him over if he doesn't work or something. Keep it casual," she offered, and then laughed softly. "Honestly, I'm the last person who should be giving you advice when it comes to this."

"No." I reached out and squeezed her arm. "You obviously know what you're doing. You hooked a guy like Jax, so . . . ?"

Her cheeks flushed and she laughed again as she propped her hip against the passenger back door. "You know damn well I had no idea what I was doing when it came to him."

I grinned. Calla had been pretty clueless. "True."

"But you know, I think it's always like that when you really like someone. It was the same with Teresa and Jase. Liking someone makes us stupid. That's what I'm going with."

"Sounds accurate."

"Oh!" she exclaimed. "I forgot to ask you last night. Who got you the roses? They are beautiful."

Feeling creeped out by the roses since I assumed they were from Dean, I'd left them in the office. Now that room smelled like a florist shop. Ha. "You know, I have no idea, if they're not from Dean."

She arched a brow. "You really think they're from him?"

I shrugged. "I guess so."

"What did it say?"

"Something like next time will be better," I told her, frowning. "Weird, huh?"

She nodded as she pushed off the car. "Maybe the flowers were meant for someone else if they weren't from Dean."

"I don't know. They had my name on it. Maybe it was just a mistake."

Calla smiled and she reached down and gave me a hug. "I've got to run, but I'll call you later, okay?"

I waved good-bye and then climbed into my car. On the way home, I was surprised when Dennis called. Since it was Sunday, I wasn't expecting to hear from him, but cops didn't work normal Monday-through-Friday schedules. He let me know that Henry had gotten an estimate for the windshield damages and it was going to cost a couple of hundred to fix.

I groaned, thinking of how much I had in my savings account, which wasn't a lot at all. But this was my bed I made, so I had to roll around in it and pick up more web design to make back the cash.

When I got home, I was halfway across the sidewalk when the sky ripped open and rain pelted me, soaking me in seconds. Squeaking, I dashed up to the porch. My wet sandals hit the floorboards, and I slipped. Arms wheeling like a windmill, my purse hit the porch and I lost my balance.

I was so going down.

Before I crashed, the entrance door swung open and a blur shot across the porch. Strong arms caught me around the waist and jerked me up. The sudden impact against something hard and dry knocked my glasses off my face and punched a grunt out of me. For a moment, the only thing that moved was my pounding heart.

"You okay?" asked a low-pitched male voice.

Lifting my head, all I could make out through the

curtain of my dark hair was that it was a guy with blond hair. Definitely not James, who had coal-black hair cut short. "I'm so okay. Thank you for . . . um, catching me." Feeling like an idiot, I pushed my hair out of my face, and got a good look at the guy.

His face was vaguely familiar—cheeks a little round with a nose that was slightly crooked, obviously broken many years ago. His eyes were a dark brown and sharp. Intelligent eyes.

And he was still holding me by the waist.

Geez.

Stepping back, I laughed awkwardly as he dropped his arms. "Sorry about that. Usually I don't almost kill myself when I try to walk on to the porch."

A tight-lipped smile formed. "That's good to know. Wait," he said as I started to step to the side and reach for my purse. I froze while he swooped down, snatching up my glasses. "You almost stepped on these."

Double geez.

"Thank you again." I took them and smiled as he handed me my purse. Tucking my dripping hair back behind my ears, I squinted up at him. "I don't think we've met."

The tight smile expanded, flashing a little of white teeth. "I'm Kip Corbin. I live upstairs. Moved in a couple of months ago."

"Oh!" I exclaimed. "That's why I thought you looked familiar."

"You did?" Surprise colored his tone.

I nodded. "Yeah, I must've caught a glimpse of you coming or going or something. Anyway, I'm glad we finally got to meet."

"Same here." He glanced out toward the street. Rain was coming down so hard, I could barely see my car parked along the curb. "Well, I've got to go." He pulled out a set of keys from his pocket as he sidestepped me. "It was good meeting you."

I turned to my door as I wiggled my fingers at him. "Same here."

He hesitated at the top of the steps. "Be careful, Roxy."

Unlocking the door, I pushed it open as I sent him a smile over my shoulder. "You, too. Don't get washed away."

He was already racing down the sidewalk as I stepped inside, closing the door behind me. Dropping my purse in the recliner, I stopped in the middle of the living room and frowned. Wait. He knew my name. I didn't think I'd told him what my name was.

A knot of unease formed a tiny ball in my belly. How did he—? Okay. I was being stupid. James or Miriam could've told him my name. It also could've been the Silvers.

I needed to stop being an idiot.

Glancing at my purse, I also needed to stop being a baby and text Reece. But first, I needed sweet tea.

After making myself a glass, I flipped on the TV and turned it to the HGTV channel. Property Brothers marathon for the win. Grabbing my cell out of my purse, I took it with me to my studio room.

No sooner had I headed down the hall, when the phone rang while I held it. I glanced down and cursed when I saw that it was Dean. Part of me wanted to hit the reject button, but I forced myself to answer the phone.

"Hello?" My voice sounded as flat as a sheet of paper.

There was a beat. "Roxy?"

I rolled my eyes. Who else could it be? He called me, and I answered. As soon as those thoughts wrapped up, I felt bad. Dean hadn't done anything wrong. "Yeah, it's me. I'm getting ready to . . ." I looked around the room frantically, trying to come out with an excuse. "To . . . take a shower."

I winced. Jesus. God. I sucked.

Dean laughed softly in my ear. "Well, thank you for planting those images in my head," he said, and I cringed. "I don't want to keep you. I just wanted to know if you were free tonight?"

"Dean," I sighed, wanting to bang my head off a wall. Instead, I pushed my glasses up to the top of my head. "I actually do have plans tonight—"

"What about tomorrow?"

I leaned against the wall, closing my eyes. "Dean, I'm sorry, but I'm not really interested in a second—"

"I know we didn't have the greatest first date, but I think we hit it off," he insisted, and in my mind, I could almost see him blinking as he spoke. "And I think if we have another date—"

"I'm seeing someone else," I blurted out, and that wasn't a lie. Not really.

His inhale was heard through the phone. "What? Since when?"

"I'm sorry. You're a great guy. It's nothing personal—"

"What the fuck, Roxy?"

My eyes popped opened as I pushed off the wall, stiffening. I'd never heard him cuss before. Not that I had sensitive sensibilities, but hearing him talk like that was jarring.

"You've been seeing someone else?" he charged on. "Don't you think you could've told me that in the beginning? I wouldn't have wasted my time with a slut."

"Whoa. Yeah, that's not okay. Fuck off," I said,

and then hit the end call button. My skin crawled as if a dozen fire ants were climbing all over me. I was so angry, my head was going to spin. It took several minutes for me to calm down enough to walk into my studio.

The plastic-like scent of the watercolors and the cedar brushes tickled my nose as I nudged the door open. I breathed in deeply, letting the fumes that might irritate someone else relax me, push away all thoughts of Dean. Some of my favorite paintings hung on the walls, above magazine clippings—words and phrases that I'd found over the years that I'd thought matched the paintings.

Placing the tea and cell phone on a small table by the door, I shuffled over to the easel as I pulled out a hair tie. My steps slowed, and I stopped in front of the easel as I tugged my wet hair up into a quick ponytail.

Wait a minute.

Lowering my hands, I wiggled my fingers as I stared at the easel. When I'd pulled off the painting I'd completed on Friday to take to Charlie, I hadn't replaced the canvas, and I hadn't had time Saturday to do anything. Come to think of it, I hadn't even stepped foot in my studio yesterday.

But a blank piece of canvas was stretched onto the frame, sitting on the easel.

Cocking my head to the side, I retraced the last forty-eight hours. Was it possible that I had done that when I finished the last painting? It was possible. I did things a lot that I didn't realize I was doing out of habit, but I was pretty positive I hadn't done this.

I thought about the remote in the fridge, the dishwasher, the toilet seat and so on . . .

I really needed the Ghostbusters.

Then again, this ghost has been super helpful—creepy but helpful.

Turning from the canvas, I shook out my shivers as a chill snaked its way down my spine. My gaze fell to the cell phone. Forcing myself over to it, I picked it up and tapped on the message icon. Just holding the phone and opening Reece's last text got my heart pumping ridiculously fast.

Texting a guy was not a big deal.

Texting a guy who'd seen my boobs and had gotten me off shouldn't be hard.

Texting a guy I really, really liked was scary as hell.

I texted him a quick hey before I wussed out and then dropped the phone on the table like it was a snake and *then* felt like an ass because he was probably still asleep.

Hurrying away from the phone, I'd just grabbed my stool when I heard the phone ding. My stomach dropped.

"Oh God," I whispered, turning around. The screen was lit up from a message. "I'm being such an idiot."

I made my way back to the phone. As expected, the text was from Reece. Seven words—only seven words—and my lips split into a giant, goofy smile.

Hey babe, was just thinking of u.

Clutching the phone, I took several deep breaths. *I was thinking of u too.* My cheeks heated, because my response sounded so corny when his was all swoony.

The reply was almost immediate. *Of course u were.*

I laughed at his cockiness and felt my stomach dip again, because I knew what I had to do. I needed to talk to him before any of this went further.

Before I could respond, another text came through. *& I really was just thinking abt u. Guess what I was doing while I was thinking abt u?*

My eyes widened as I typed back *Oh my.*

There was a pause. *Is that too real to admit that?*

No. And I shook my head and sent back *No.*

Good, came the quick reply. Followed by *Glad to know u don't think I'm a pervert.*

Nah, I still think ur a pervert.

A hot one at least?

I laughed out loud at that. *Definitely a hot one.* I waited a whole second and then sent, *I think my house is haunted.*

What?

The tips of my ears burned, and I wished I could somehow unsend that text. *Never mind. I'm being stupid. Are u free tonight?*

There was a pause before his response, which caused my stomach to twist. *Got to work 2night, but I'm all yours 2morrow if u'll have me.*

Is that a joke? I typed back. Doing that stupid smile thing, I allowed myself a hobble and a shimmy before I added *Tomorrow wld be perfect.*

We exchanged a couple of more texts, deciding on meeting at my place around seven in the evening. He was going to bring food, and maybe I should go get some wine since I was probably going to need some liquid courage and something, in case it went bad, to drown my tears in.

Chapter 12

"You know, I'd expect one of your brothers to do something like that, because damn, sometimes those boys have shit for brains."

Sitting on the edge of my recliner, I winced as my father passed in front of my couch. This was not how I expected my Monday morning to go, but I wasn't surprised. Somehow, my parents hadn't heard about me, the book of doom, and Henry's windshield. Today was obviously reckoning day, and I'd called and told my mom what I'd done.

Thirty minutes later, my father showed up.

Gavin Ark wasn't a tall man, but he was stout and he had the build of a defensive linebacker. Only a little bit of gray spotted the hair above his temples, and it made me wonder if he was experimenting with Just For Men hair color.

"Especially that younger brother of yours." His rant was really gearing up. "Sometimes I think Thomas doesn't have two functioning brain cells he can rub together. Do you know what he did yesterday?" He stopped at the corner of the couch, planting his hands on his hips. "He went down to get some pop out of the fridge in the basement and left the damn door wide open, like he was trying to cool the entire house."

My brows rose.

"And then I hear you threw a book through a windshield?" Lifting a hand, he scrubbed his fingers through his dark brown hair. "I didn't even know you can throw a book through a windshield."

"Apparently you have to hit the right spot," I murmured.

His eyes narrowed, and I zipped it shut. "We raised you to be smarter than that. And your mother told me that you said Henry didn't provoke you."

"That's true," I admitted sheepishly.

He sighed as he stalked over to where I sat. "Honey, I know you are not a fan of Henry. No one in this damn town is, but you cannot go around vandalizing his property, and I know you know that."

I nodded.

Dropping a heavy hand on my shoulder, he squeezed gently. "Do you need the money to take care of the window?"

My mouth opened, but emotion closed off my throat. Tears burned the back of my eyes. My parents were ticked off to discover I'd done something so stupid, but more than anything else, they were disappointed. Dad was right. They had raised me better than what I'd done, and yet, my dad was still willing to jump in and bail me out.

Like they had when I'd been living on my own for a month and my car had broken down. Like they had when I filled out my financial aid too late my sophomore year and covered my first semester of online classes until the aid kicked in. Like they had virtually all my life.

Man-oh-man, I loved my parents. I knew how lucky I was. Not everyone could have such an awesome parental unit, but I did. I really did.

Swallowing the ball in my throat, I smiled up at him. "Thank you, but I have the money."

He pinned me with a knowing look. "How much will it deplete your savings?"

"Not much," I lied. Truthfully, it would be a hit, but . . . but I wasn't their little girl they needed to swoop in and save anymore. Besides, they worked hard for their money and I'd like to see my dad retire at some point in this century. I fixed my glasses since they'd started to slide down my nose. "I'm going to be okay."

Dad stared at me a moment longer and then he stepped back, folding his arms. Something about the sudden hard set of his jaw had me worried. "So, what's this I hear about you and Reece?"

"What?" I shrieked, hopping up from the recliner.

He narrowed his eyes. "I heard that you two have been spending some time together."

I gaped at him. Reece and I had only hung out one night, and I so was not going to even think about that night in the presence of my father. Ew. "Who told you that Reece and I have been hanging out?"

"I ran into Melvin at the hardware store yesterday morning. He told me that Reece was seen waiting for you to get off work a few nights back."

Crossing my arms, I rolled my eyes. "Melvin is delusional."

"So it's not true?"

Was that disappointment I was hearing in my dad's

voice? Of course it was. I'm pretty sure Dad wanted to adopt both Reece and Colton.

"Now, I don't want any details and maybe he was just being a good guy and making sure you were getting home safe since what happened to those girls in the town over . . ." He trailed off, waiting.

"Maybe Melvin needs to stop gossiping." I tucked a loose strand back as I glanced out the front window. It had finally stopped raining this morning, but it was a dreary day. "Reece and I . . ." How did I explain what Reece and I were when I had no idea? "We're hanging out," I finished lamely.

His brows furrowed together.

"We're friends," I rushed on, feeling my cheeks heat. "We're supposed to have dinner tonight."

A slow smile crept over his face. "Is that so?"

"Yeah." I shifted from foot to foot.

He nodded slowly. "You know, he's a good boy. I've always thought that you and him would be good together."

"Don't tell Mom."

The smile spread and his dark eyes danced.

"Dad! Don't you dare say anything to Mom. She'll read into it, start planning our wedding, and she'll call Reece's Mom!"

"They'd both probably start knitting booties for a nonexistent grandchild," he agreed with a chuckle.

"Oh God," I groaned, wrinkling my nose. "Not funny."

"I won't say anything," he replied, but I so knew he was lying. As soon as he left, he'd be on the phone to Mom. "I've got to get back to the office. Come give me a hug."

After squeezing the living daylights out of me, he

headed outside, stopping on the porch. "Lock the door, Roxy."

Nodding, I did just that when I closed the door. Even though those two girls and the one who was missing—Shelly Winters—didn't live here, I wasn't stupid. And as I headed back to my studio, I mulled over Reece's suggestion of getting a gun.

"No," I said out loud with a laugh. "I'd seriously end up shooting someone accidentally."

Plus, the incident with the book showed I didn't have the best self-control when my emotions were running high. Granted, throwing a book and pulling a trigger were two very different things, but it still wigged me out, the idea of having that kind of end-game level of power in my hands.

As I poked around the paintbrushes, my thoughts drifted to tonight. Excitement hummed through me, but the happy buzz was coated with unease. I was going to have to tell the truth about what happened between us, and knowing how much Reece hated lying, it was a huge risk.

I could lose him before . . . before I even really had him.

But there wasn't a part of me that seriously considered continuing with the lie even though I doubted Reece would ever know the difference. To do so was wrong and cowardly, and I had decent-size lady balls.

I just needed to find them.

I spent the rest of the afternoon working on a painting of Jackson Square in New Orleans. I'd never been, but I was obsessed with the place ever since I read an epic paranormal romance that mostly took place there.

I'd made Charlie read the books, too, and when we were younger, NOLA was on our bucket list. One of these days, I promised myself I'd go there, not just for me but also for Charlie.

Then I'd be able to tell him all about it.

I'd printed out many different views of the square, and had decided on the view where the three steeples from the gorgeous church rose above the statue of Andrew Jackson on his horse. This would probably be one of the hardest paintings I'd decided to embark on, based on the amount of detail and layering it required.

Hours flew by as I worked on the ring of white flowers that were planted in front of the bronze statue of Jackson. My wrist ached from the thousand or so tiny flicks that ensured the petals had definition, but the dull pain was worth the results so far. However, I still wasn't sure I was really going to be able to pull it off with watercolors.

It was close to five when my phone rang, startling me. Coming out of the daze I was always in when I was painting, I hopped up from the stool as I wiped my hands on my old jean shorts.

A giddy smile appeared when I saw it was Reece calling. "Hey," I answered as I picked up one of the brushes.

"Hey babe, I got some bad news," he said. There was a rustling of clothing, as if he were pulling a shirt on over his head. "I'm going to be late tonight. Just got called out for a hostage situation."

I froze, stomach dropping. "A hostage situation?"

"Yeah, it's probably nothing but some drunk redneck who needs to be talked down, but they're calling out SWAT."

Blinking rapidly, I placed the paintbrush back down. "You're on the SWAT team?"

"Been on it for about the last three months," he

explained, and I squeezed my eyes shut. I would've known that if we'd been talking to one another. "Babe, I'm really sorry to have—"

"No. You don't need to apologize." And I meant that. "I just hope everything is okay and that . . . that you're safe."

"Babe," he said again, and the way he said it caused my heart to do a standing ovation. "I'm always safe. You don't have to worry about me."

"I know . . ." I whispered, swallowing.

"I've got to run, but if you're up for it, I can swing by afterward, as soon as I can. I want to see you, with or without Chinese food."

I smiled as I crossed the room, pulling the curtain back. All I could see was a huge oak tree. At least, I thought it was an oak tree. "I want to see you, too. Come over whenever."

"It could be really late," he warned. "It might not even be until tomorrow morning."

"It doesn't matter. Just text me in case I'm asleep," I told him. "Just come when you can."

"Will do. I'll see you then."

My breath caught as I clenched the phone. "Please be safe, Reece."

There was a pause and then, "I will. See you soon."

"Bye."

Turning from the window, I placed the phone on the table as I stared at the painting. Sure, I was disappointed that I might not get to see him, but what I was feeling had nothing to do with that. It paled in comparison actually.

Reece had told me not to worry and he honestly sounded like this wasn't a big deal, but it was a *hostage* situation. How can that not be a big deal? I had no idea he was on the SWAT team. Not that being a police officer wasn't dangerous all on its own, but throwing SWAT team in there? God, I hadn't really thought about how dangerous it was for him.

My stomach in knots, I folded my arms across my waist. It was like being thrust back to when Reece was first in active combat and dealing with the constant gnawing dread that something terrible would happen.

This was why I could not really fall for him. Sex was okay. Dating was great. But really falling for him, letting myself get so deep with him? Hell no. I could lose him like I . . . like I was losing Charlie.

Like I'd already lost Charlie.

And that was a different kind of love, and look how painful that was turning out.

I returned to the painting, and whenever my thoughts started to wander, I refocused. It was close to seven when I took a quick shower just in case Reece wasn't that late, and when nine o'clock rolled around, I made myself a tuna sandwich and ate while obsessively staring at the phone.

Against my better judgment, around eleven, I pulled up the local news on the Internet. A breaking news headline flashed under a picture of red and blue lights outside of a heavily wooded area.

My stomach tightened as I scrolled through the short write-up. There wasn't a lot to be known about the standoff Reece was currently at except that it was a man holding his wife and—it was believed to be—two small children in the home against their will.

"Oh God," I whispered, unable to imagine what that woman and her kids must be going through and how anyone could put their family through something like that.

Restless and unable to watch TV, I ended up changing into one of the oversized shirts I'd lovingly borrowed from my older brother. It reached just below my thighs, long enough to pass as a dress. It was covered in dried paint, perfect to work in. I pulled my hair up and back from my face and then got back to work on the painting.

Hours blurred together, a haze of mixing together shades as I tried to capture the right tone for the bronze statue and began the almost painful sketching of the horse and Andrew Jackson. Drawing it in faint pencil on the canvas was the only way I could do it, but once the paint was on, I didn't think people would notice it had been sketched first. Sometimes I felt like a cheat for doing that, because there were artists who could paint anything freehand. Me? I was so not one of them.

I probably should've spent the time working on the web project, but I promised myself I'd do that Tuesday evening. I had several days left before the deadline on this one, and painting . . . well, it was what I needed right now.

Paint was dried on my aching fingers when my phone dinged, alerting me to a text message. I shot off that stool like it bit my behind and grabbed the phone. It was from Reece. Two words.

You up?

I responded quicker than a gunslinger in the Wild West, firing back a *yes*. After a moment, he shot back *be over in a few*.

My heart was racing as I glanced up to where the time showed on the phone. Holy crap, it was almost three in the morning. Hurrying out into the living room, I placed my phone on the coffee table and was about to haul ass back to the bedroom to change when I saw headlights through the front window.

I dashed over and yanked the curtain back. The headlights were right in front of my car. They'd stopped. A second later, they turned off. Deep inside, I knew it had to be Reece, and he must've texted me while he was on his way here.

Like a wild animal that had run out in front of a car, I couldn't move as I watched a tall shadow take form and head across the sidewalk. When a soft knock on my door sounded, I might've squeaked. A little.

Spinning around, I dropped my glasses on the coffee table and then darted over to the door and stretched up. I couldn't see crap out of the peephole, but knowing it had to be Reece, I opened the door.

Holy hot guy . . .

It was Reece and he was dressed like something out of my fantasies. A tight black shirt accentuated the broad shoulders, defined upper arms and chest. There was no mistaking how cut his tapered waist was. The shirt was tucked into black tactical pants and the black boots he wore completed the badass ensemble.

Okay. I was totally down for this part of the SWAT uniform.

I dragged my gaze up as I stepped back, letting him in. He stalked forward, a large duffel bag in his right hand. His knuckles were bleached white. So caught up in eyeball screwing him, I hadn't realized he was checking me out in the same hungry, intense way I'd been doing to him. It was in that moment I realized I was only wearing the shirt.

I so did not even need to look down at myself to know I looked like a hot mess.

Reece closed the door behind him, locking it without peeling his eyes off me, which I thought, took some talent. I drew in a deep breath. "Is . . . is everything okay?"

There was something in the way he stared at me as he placed the duffel bag behind the recliner. It was raw, wholly unfiltered and a bit . . . unstable. As if he were a band stretched too tight.

He shook his head. "No."

I didn't know what to say as I stared up at him. A shiver danced over my shoulders.

His chest rose and fell with a deep breath. "The guy—the hostage situation. There was no talking him down."

I held my breath.

"When he started shooting out the windows, we were ordered to go inside." As he spoke, his blue eyes darkened to a stormy sky. "It was too late. He'd shot his wife and himself. Wasn't a small caliber, either. The kids saw it. One of them was too young to understand, but the boy . . . yeah, he knew what happened. He'll always know."

Tears rushed my eyes as my mouth dropped open. "Oh my God, Reece, I'm so sorry. I don't know what to say." Not a part of me had thought that night would end like this for him. I'd known it was a serious situation. Obviously, I'd known it could end badly, but it was hard to fathom how he'd felt waking up this morning and making plans, then getting that call, having no idea he was about to see someone end another person's life and then their own. The same with that poor woman and those kids.

But then, in a way, I guess I did know.

When I woke that morning when I was sixteen, it had never crossed my mind that I'd lose my best friend that night. One never knew when their life was about to be irrevocably altered. There was no warning. If anything, it always came when everything was calm and good.

"What can I do?" I asked, blinking back tears—tears for a woman and family I had never met, tears for the fact Reece had to be within ten miles of that situation, especially given his history. I wanted to ask if he was okay, make sure that he was, but before I could do anything, he was on the move.

Reece said nothing as he crossed the distance between us. Tension poured into the air, thickening it. He grasped my cheeks, the touch so incredibly gentle. He lowered his mouth to mine, and there was nothing soft about the way he kissed me. No slow seduction of my senses. He hijacked them with a kiss that swept through me, heating me up like I'd spent the entire day under the sweltering summer sun.

"You," he said, lifting his head. "I want you. Badly. And I need this—need *you* right now." His fingers splayed across my cheeks. "But if you want to slow this down, I can do that. I *will* do that. Just tell me now, Roxy, because I'm feeling like a live wire and when I get you naked, there's going to be no fucking around. I'm going to be in you."

His words sent a jolt straight from my heart to my core. I trembled as my eyes met his. "Don't . . . don't slow down."

Chapter 13

As crazy as it sounded, I knew what Reece needed to do. When everything had happened with Charlie, there was so much pent-up frustration born out of helplessness and the only outlet had been painting. Sometimes that wasn't enough, and I'd fill the bathtub up, slip under the water and scream. That frustration had grown to horrific levels, once Charlie started to slip away into what was nothing more than a husk of a living person.

Reece had felt that tonight.

Life was there one second, gone the next. Like a train running off the tracks. He hadn't been able to do anything to stop it. He bore that same frustration, that same helplessness I felt with Charlie, and I understood that need . . . that almost instinctual drive to remind yourself that you're still alive.

Reece kissed me again, and if I thought he'd turned my senses inside out before, I'd been wrong. This kiss left me weak in the knees and wanting on a level that was almost painful.

His hands slid into my hair, deftly undoing the bun. My hair fell as he dragged his fingers over my scalp. He tilted his head, taking the kiss deeper. As he dragged his hands down, over my arms and to my waist, I gasped into his mouth.

A deep sound rumbled out of him as he lifted me up. My legs curled against his waist, like they'd been itching to do since forever. Whispering his name, I looped my arms around his neck.

"I've got to get you to a bed," he said, and he started walking. "Or I'm going to take you right here on the floor."

I shivered, probably more excited by that prospect than I should have been. I pressed a kiss to one corner of his lips and then against his jaw as he walked us back to my bedroom. My fingers slipped over the soft brush of his hair and then to the taut muscles of his upper back. There was so much power in him.

Stopping long enough to flip the bedroom light on, he sat me down so that I was on my knees on the bed. Heat flowed into every cell as he stepped back, tugging his shirt out of the tactical pants. I was almost panting as he lifted his shirt over his head, and dropped it onto the floor.

God, he was beautiful, every square inch of him, from the way his muscles tightened along his stomach to the way his biceps flexed as he undid the belt.

So I told him as I settled on my haunches. "You're beautiful."

A half grin appeared. "Beautiful?"

"Yes. You're beautiful."

Leaving his belt, he clasped my cheeks and tilted my head back. When he kissed me this time, it was soft and sweet, like a benediction of sorts. It worked me up just as quickly and fiercely as his harder kisses did.

Reece straightened once more and proceeded with his personal strip show, which I wished I had hundred-dollar bills for. I'd be waving those suckers like a crazy person.

Grinning, he undid the button and then the zipper. He paused long enough to toe off his boots and his socks, then off went his pants and boxers.

He was . . . wow, I couldn't even think as I drank him in.

"Up." He wiggled his fingers.

I rose up onto my knees. His eyes met mine as he reached for the shirt and then tugged it off. The only thing left on me was a pair of boy-short undies. If I had been smart, I would've definitely grabbed something sexier. Like the lacy black thong I had. But oh no, I was wearing pinstriped boy shorts. Didn't seem to matter I quickly realized.

His hot gaze tracked over me. "Now this . . . this is beautiful, Roxy." He reached between us, smoothing his thumb over the puckered tip of my breast. "Not me. You. All you."

My back arched, and I reached for him, where he was swollen and hard, but he caught my wrists, shaking his head. "I want to touch every part of you with my hands and my mouth." He dropped my wrists and ran his fingers across my breasts, lingering on the aching tips. "Especially these. And I want to taste you."

Pulse pounding, I wet my lips as he gently pushed me backward, guiding me onto my back. "I especially want to taste you here." Reece lowered his hands, dragging them down my stomach. Between my thighs, he cupped me with one hand, and my back came straight off the bed. "Yes. This. I really want to taste this." He knew what he was doing when he rubbed through the thin cotton. "But I can't wait."

"Don't wait." I lifted my hips.

His eyes flared with heat and then he pulled my undies off. And here we were, both of us in the buff. We'd been to this point before, but we didn't make it far. My stomach dipped. I needed to tell him about that night, but how could I do that right now, after what he'd dealt with tonight? After he said he needed me right now?

Wrong or right, there was no way I wasn't going to be here for him.

Reece placed a knee on the bed and came over me in a way that reminded me of a great panther stalking its prey. His arms flexed as he lowered his mouth to mine. I reached up to touch his face but halted.

"Touch me," he ordered softly. "I like it when you touch me."

"My fingers are covered with paint," I said between kisses. "I'm sorry."

He caught my hand, threading his fingers through mine as he captured my mouth in another deep, scorching kiss. "Don't apologize. It's you. It's sexy as hell."

I had no idea how my heart kept beating as he then brought the hand to his mouth and pressed a kiss against the center of my palm. God, he had me in that moment, he truly had me.

Lifting his mouth to mine once again, his tongue delved against mine. Red-hot pleasure whipped through me as he slipped his hands under my arms and lifted me up, placing me so I lay down the center of the bed. Never once breaking contact between our mouths. The strength in him was mind blowing, actually electrifying.

His body settled over mine, and I could feel the hard length of him pressing against my hip. His kisses running deeper, more urgent, and as he lifted his head, he nipped at my lip. His voice was thick with need when he spoke. "Do you have a condom?"

"Yes." I nodded as I ran my hands over his shoulders and upper arms. His skin was fantastic, smooth like satin stretched over steel. I imagined that was how the bronze statue of Andrew Jackson felt. Absolutely flawless. "There should be some in the top drawer of the nightstand." The moment that came out of my mouth, I worried what he'd think since it was obvious that I had a stash of condoms. "I can get—"

"No. I'll get it." He kissed the tip of my nose and then my forehead, the sweetness of the act almost overshadowing the relief easing the tension in my neck. He didn't care at all. Didn't stop to even wonder why. The man was perfect.

Really perfect.

Because as he planted a hand into the bed next to my head and lifted up, his muscles did all kinds of amazing things. He stretched over me and to the side, and I was fascinated with how the muscles along his sides moved. I barely heard the drawer open over the pounding of my heart. Never before had I been so aroused.

"Thank God you're prepared." His rough voice sending a wave of light shivers over me as he reached into the drawer. "Because I'm not—oh *fuck yeah*."

My brows pinched. "Are you that excited over a condom?"

"No. Hell no." He stretched further and shifted, raising his hand. My gaze fell to what he held. "I'm excited about *this*."

"Holy shit," I muttered. In his hand was my trusty

and often handy vibrator. How in the fuck did I forget my vibrator was in the same drawer? Face burning, I stared at what had been my boyfriend for a while. And it was one of those really nice ones. A Rabbit. And it was pink—hot pink. "I need a bridge to jump off of. Now. Right now."

One side of his lips curved up. "No. I love this. I love the idea of you using this." That grin turned into pure wickedness. "And we are so going to use this."

My eyes widened as parts of my body got all kinds of excited about that. "Now?" I squeaked.

"You'd like that, huh?" He dipped his head, kissing me quickly. "Not tonight. I need to be in you, but we're so going to use this. That's a promise."

"I like that promise," I admitted, flushing to the roots of my hair. No guy I'd ever dated had shown any interest in using toys during sex. I didn't even know that a guy would be down for that.

He chuckled deeply. "I bet you do."

Reece returned the vibrator to where he'd found it and then rolled onto his side, condom in hand. He paused after ripping the foil off, his blue eyes finding mine. "Do you ever think of me when you use that?"

The truth burst out of me as I rose onto my elbows. "Yes."

"Fuck," he grunted.

My avid gaze watched him roll the condom on with a quickness that was rather impressive. Then he placed his hand along my jaw, tilting my head back. When he kissed me this time, it was slower, languid and sensual as he guided me back down. Part of me expected him to climb on and get to the point. I wouldn't complain if he did either, but that wasn't what he did in spite of his words.

Reece trailed the tips of his fingers down my throat,

over the tip of my breast, and his lips chased those fingers. He blazed a path of hot kisses and nips that had my nails digging into his shoulders. When he reached my breast, he lingered and he sucked and nipped, licking to soothe the erotic mix of pleasure and a decadent bite of pain. And as he moved to the other breast, his hand drifted over my stomach and between my legs. I spread them, giving him access to what we both wanted. My breasts were heavy and aching as he eased a finger inside me, wringing out a keening whimper.

"Oh yeah, you're already ready." Reece rose up again, dipping his chin so he looked down the length of our bodies. Molten lava swept through my veins as he watched what he was doing to me.

The combination of the physical touch and the sight of him almost sent me over the edge. I couldn't think as he teased me with his touch.

"God, I love the way you feel." He slipped another finger inside, and my hips jerked in response, my toes curled. "I bet you could come just like this."

I gripped his wrist, not stopping him, but to hold on. The feel of his tendons moving against my palm drove me crazy. He was so right. I could feel the tension coiling low in my stomach. I don't know what it was about him that made it so easy for him to work my body. It was like he had a secret map that gave him every step necessary. It had never been like this before. A lot of times I'd never even get this aroused by the time everything was over and done with.

My gaze flicked up to him, and for a second I couldn't breathe. He was still fixed on watching what he was doing, and yeah, that alone was hot, but I knew he didn't see the moment where I think my heart might have imploded. I wanted him on a physical level. Heck,

I'd wanted him for as long as I could remember. I was physically attracted to him, but it was more than that. It ran a hell of a lot stronger than that, and what Katie had said about how I felt about him might not have been too far from the truth. Pressure clamped down on my chest as I stared at him.

I'd be lying if I said this didn't go beyond lust. I'd be lying if I said the history between us didn't matter. It did—to me, at least.

Reece could break my heart.

Then he did something with his thumb that blew all thoughts out of my head. My back arched and my hips rose, pushing against his hand. He chuckled as he eased his hand away from me.

"I've got to get inside of you." He rolled on top of me, the tips of my breasts sensitive as they brushed against his hard chest. Every part of me was heightened. Each brush of his fingers I felt throughout my entire body.

I tucked my legs against his hips and I felt him between my thighs. This was finally happening. Part of me couldn't believe it and half expected him to fall asleep.

Staring down at me with eyes so blue they didn't seem real in that moment, he curved his right hand around my hip. I shivered as our gazes held and I looped one arm around his neck.

Without breaking eye contact, his hips thrust forward, and a small cry escaped me. There was a quick bite, a feeling of pressure that wasn't painful, that told me that no matter how good that vibrator was, it had nothing on Reece.

"Damn." Reece rocked his hips as I hooked my ankles, delighting in the groan that shook his entire body. He was still for a moment, both of our chests rising and falling rapidly. He was seated deep, and I could feel him in every breath I took.

Then, with his gaze locked with mine, he slowly pulled almost all the way out and then he slid back in, dragging the motion out. I clenched his arm as he shifted his weight to it. He cupped my breast, his thumb circling the sensitive bud.

I was lost in his eyes, lost in the way his body was making me feel. His body trembled with restraint. "You have no idea how badly I just want to fuck you," he said, giving a little shake of his head.

Which was what he had warned he wanted to do, but he was holding back. I stretched up, kissing him. His lips parted, and my tongue spiked against his. "It's okay," I whispered, my lips brushing his as I spoke.

His forehead rested against mine as he pumped his hips slowly. "Roxy . . ."

"Fuck me," I told him softly. Those two words burned my body in many different ways.

Reece groaned as his hips reared up and then slammed back down. His mouth found mine as whatever control he had completely snapped. He moved furiously, the rhythm almost impossible to keep up with.

He reached up, capturing my hand. Like before he brought it to his lips and then threaded his fingers through mine. He pressed our joined hands to the mattress as he ground his hips against mine.

Acute pleasure pounded through me. I kicked my head back, squeezing his hand as the tension coiled tighter and tighter. Unbelievably, his pace picked up and the headboard smacked against the wall. That and the sounds of our bodies drove me over the edge.

I came with a sharp cry that echoed throughout the

room, my body shuddering around his. The release kicked the air out of my lungs. The pleasure came in waves, tossing me up until I thought I'd float right through the ceiling or that my bones would turn to mush.

For a wondrous moment, I knew how I could capture this . . . this feeling on canvas. It would be a sky shaded in violets and deep blues—blues that matched his eyes. It would be the sky moments after a tumultuous storm.

Reece dropped his head into the space between my neck and shoulder as he let go of my hand. Sliding his arm under my lower back, he lifted my hips off the bed. He moved over me and in me feverishly. When he pressed in as deep as he could go, his breath was against my ear. He grunted out my name as his body spasmed, his embrace tightening until there wasn't any space between us, and I held on, running my fingers through the soft ends of his hair. I held him as that storm passed, as my pounding heart slowed.

Many moments passed before Reece rolled onto his side. His arm was still around me. He was still *in* me. "Sorry," he murmured thickly. "I was probably crushing you."

My cheek was plastered against his chest. "I didn't mind."

His other hand found the way into the dense mess of my hair and cradled the back of my head. "I didn't hurt you, did I?"

"No. Quite the opposite," I murmured. "It was . . ."

"Fucking perfect?"

My giggle was muffled. "Yes, it was fucking perfect."

He tipped my head back, and I blinked my eyes open. He was grinning down at me in a way that twisted my insides into delicious, little knots. Dipping his head, he kissed me softly. "Let me take care of this, okay?"

I bit down on my lip as he pulled out. He swung his legs off the side of the bed and stood, and I got a great view of a perfect male backside. He disappeared out into the hall, and I all but sprawled across the bed. A cool breeze drifted over my bare legs, and it must've been coming from the closet, but I was too exhausted to reach down and pull the blankets up or shut the door.

Closing my eyes, I let out a sated sigh. My muscles were absolutely useless and there were parts of my body that were slightly sore, but it did nothing to detract from the wonderful happy buzz that was trilling through me.

"Beautiful," Reece murmured, returning to the bed. Placing his hands on either side of me, he nuzzled the stretch of my neck not covered with my hair. "Is there any way I can convince you to sleep like this every night?"

Another silly giggle wiggled its way out of me as I peeled one eye open. "Maybe."

"If I ask nicely?"

"Sounds about right."

He tugged the comforter out from under my lax body and then the bed dipped under his weight. A huge part of me expected him to make a quick exit at this point. I guessed because I wasn't sure what we were doing, what he thought we were doing, so I was surprised when he pulled the cover up over us and then rearranged me so my back was pressed against his chest.

This was . . . it was good, and I thought it had to

mean something more than just hooking up or needing to work out his frustrations.

Sleepy, I looked over my shoulder at him. He'd turned the light off upon his return, but I could make out the sharp slope of his cheekbone. "Are you doing okay?"

He didn't respond for a moment and when he did, he proved that he got what I was asking. "A lot better. Sorry to come into your house like that. It's just that . . . seeing lives end for no real reason and not being able to do anything to change it doesn't get easier."

"You don't need to apologize." I wiggled around so I was facing him. His eyes were open and there was a soft smile on his face. "I'm glad that I could . . . that I could be here for you."

"Me, too."

"I know it has to be hard." Before I could think about what I was doing, I placed a quick kiss against his lips. "I wish it was different."

The arm around my waist tightened. "Me, too." He kissed my forehead. A moment passed as my eyes fell shut once again. "Make you a deal? If you let me borrow some eggs in the morning, I'll make you a kickass omelet you'll be wanting me to make every morning."

I grinned as I snuggled close. "Then it's a deal."

Chapter 14

I woke up before Reece.

It was still early and only a thin sliver of sun was peeking through the blinds from the window across from the bed. We were tangled together, our arms and legs forming a pretzel. Somehow, I was on my side, my back tucked close to his front.

When I dared a peek at him over my shoulder earlier, I probably ended up staring at him for an unsuitable amount of time, but it was rare to catch him so relaxed. The sculpted lines of his face were relaxed. No trace of Cop Face whatsoever, but there was still no mistaking he was a man—a man who'd fought overseas for our country and had come home and put his life on the line every time he clocked in for work.

If I was honest with myself, he was probably the first man I'd been with. Not that all the other guys were boys, but none of them took on the kind of responsibility that he did. The worst any of them faced was a delayed plane or their Internet stalling out on them while they were playing Call of Duty.

But he was more than just the sum of what he did for a living. Yes, he was brave and strong, but he was also kind and honest. He was loyal. He was wicked smart, and he knew how to work my body like it was built just for him.

Rehashing last night in my head, I felt my cheeks heat as I clearly recalled asking him to do me, but replace the do with a fuck, and I'd never said that to a guy before.

All I remembered was falling asleep facing him, talking about omelets and deals, and now all I was thinking about was how . . . how great our first time was.

Our first time.

I ran the tips of my fingers over his still hand, tracing the strong muscles and bones. I'd been fantasizing about having sex with Reece for a fairly decent amount of time. Years, really. Even though we'd gotten close to doing it almost a year ago, and even after what we did the night on the couch, none of it came close to what it was actually like with him, which was *amazing*.

Our first time.

That was what I was thinking when I woke up. With the way everything was last night, I'd made the decision to delay the conversation I needed to have. I had no regrets about that. It was the right choice, but I was going to drive myself crazy if I didn't clear the—

Reece shifted behind me without warning. His fingers curled around mine as his leg drew up between my thighs, spreading them. In under a second, his hips were pressed against my rear and his face was buried in my neck. I could feel him, hot and hard, slipping between my legs, resting where I was suddenly throbbing for him.

"Mornin,' babe," he murmured, nuzzling my neck as he let go of my hand and gripped my hip, pulling me back against his erection.

Biting down on my lip, I moaned. "Morning."

His teeth caught my earlobe, and I gasped. He chuckled as he rotated his hips, pressing right against my core. My body arched all on its own, and he let go of my ear, making his way down my throat. Wow, he was frisky in the morning.

"I'm having a dilemma," he said, voice rough with sleep and arousal.

So was I, because I was so torn between stopping him and having a much needed conversation, and seeing where this was heading.

"I really want an omelet," he continued, nipping at my shoulder as he rolled those magical hips again. "I think I might have dreamed about that omelet."

"Really?" I gasped.

"Yeah, babe." He slipped his hand up my waist and then under me, cupping my breast. He squeezed gently. "But I also want to fuck you senseless."

Oh my God.

I was so wet it was freaking ridiculous, and it didn't help when he caught my nipple between his fingers. Okay. I really needed to focus on what was important. "Reece, I—" A cry cut me off as he rubbed against me, hitting *that* spot. "Oh God . . ."

"I know you want that omelet, and let me tell you, I make a damn good omelet." His knee spread my legs further apart, and I braced myself on my forearm. "You'll have a mouth orgasm once you have the pleasure of that omelet."

There was a good chance I was about to have an orgasm now.

Brushing my hair over my shoulder, he pressed a kiss at the base of my neck. "But how in the hell do I walk away from this?" His fingers did something truly sinful with my breast, and my hips pushed back again, and it happened. I don't know how. Call it an act of God, but the very tip of him slipped in. "Damn," he groaned, holding himself still. "Fuck the omelet."

In a heartbeat, he was inside me, buried all the way.

"Reece," I cried out, my body a riot of sharp, splintering sensations. From this position, the fullness and length of him was so much more.

"I love the way you call out my name." He kneaded my breast as he began to move, his hips pumping slowly and hitting every nerve ending my body was blessed with. "Do it again," he ordered, his voice settling over me like velvet.

I did it again.

Pleasure licked across my skin as I rocked my hips back against his. Dragging his hand down my stomach, he thrust in, sealing my body to his as he shifted, positioning me on my knees. The feeling of him behind me was intense, overwhelming and wonderful.

I rocked my hips back against him, shivering at the sound of his approval. His grip tightened and then he started to move, his pace fast and hard. My hands slipped across the bed, reaching the spindles in my headboard. I grabbed them, holding on as he slammed into me.

My head was swimming. I couldn't make sense of where his body ended and mine began. We were both moving frantically until his strong arm slipped under my breasts and he hauled me up. My hands hit the wall above my bed, and his hips pistoned up.

Reece was totally in charge as his hand cupped my chin, guiding my head back and to the side. His thumb dragged over my lower lip, and I caught it, sucking it in deep.

He shouted something that would've blistered the ears of sailors and then he brought my mouth to his. His kiss—the way his tongue stroked mine—was no way near as fast as he moved inside me, but it was in no way less beautiful or devastating.

"I want to feel you come," he said, his voice rough in my ear. "Do it for me, Roxy."

Never in my life had a guy talked to me like that during sex, and I discovered in that moment, it did something for me. It did a whole lot, because when he pressed his mouth to the spot below my ear, release thundered through me, whipping through me, and his heavy groan in my ear was the first warning as his hips jerked wildly a second before he pulled out. Wet warmth spilled over my lower back. Tiny aftershocks swirled through me as his hand drifted lazily over my stomach. Neither of us moved for a few moments and then he carefully smoothed my hair over my shoulder, catching the strands that were falling into my face. I lowered my head to the pillow, letting him slowly ease me back down onto the bed, flat on my belly.

My head was buzzing when I heard him say, "Don't move."

Only a handful of seconds passed before I felt him wiping something soft across my lower back and rear. It dragged what sounded like a mewl out of me, because I was pretty sure every part of my body was overly sensitive now.

The bed shook as he flopped down next to me, and it took great effort for me to turn my head in his direction.

One arm was tossed over his eyes, and my gaze got hung up on that heavy bicep for a moment. He was smiling.

I smiled.

"Roxy," he said, lowering his arm. He looked at me, his dark lashes so incredibly thick. I realized I never quite captured them that well when I painted them. "Are you on the pill?"

As the haze cleared from my head, my limbs suddenly went stiff as his question filtered through my thoughts. Are you on the pill? Yes. I was on the pill. I took it. When I remembered. There'd been a dry spell this last year, and I always used condoms, *sooo* I sometimes forgot to take it. When was the last time I forgot? Two weeks ago? Was it more than one pill? Oh dear baby Jesus, my heart started to pound.

"I wasn't thinking." He reached over with his other hand, rubbing his palm against my back. "I've never done that before. Swear to God, I've never forgotten to wear a condom."

"Neither have I. I'm on the pill," I said quietly. "But I . . . I think I missed a day or something a couple weeks ago."

Reece didn't spring out of the bed like his ass was on fire. He studied me a moment, then leaned over and rose up so he was hovering over me. He kissed my cheek. "I pulled out. We'll be fine. And if that didn't work . . ." He kissed the corner of my lips. "We'll still be okay."

Oh God.

Oh fuck me! Tears crawled up my throat. I don't

know why. I was so stupid. Maybe it was because he wasn't freaking out about the slight chance that some sort of insemination just went down. Or maybe it was because he was so damn fucking—ugh—fucking everything.

I had sex with him again—unprotected sex—and I let my hormones get the best of me, and I *still* hadn't told him the truth about that night.

He kissed me again and then playfully smacked my bum as he rose. "Come on. An orgasmic omelet awaits us."

I stared at him from my prone position on my belly.

A boyish grin crossed his features as he rolled off the bed. He bent over, grabbing his pants off the floor. Pulling them on, he winked at me. "Mind if I use your toothbrush?"

At this point, did it matter if he did? "No."

"Your ass better be out of this bed by the time I get done." He then winked and turned, walking out of the bedroom.

Barefoot. Shirtless. His pants weren't even buttoned!

I lay there for a moment, unsure of what I should freak out more over. The fact I was a bitch for still not telling him the truth or that I could've just gotten myself knocked up?

Okay. The knocking up part was highly unlikely and I needed to devote my freak-out energy to something more relevant—the whole bitch part.

When I heard the water turn off in the bathroom and the door open, I was the one who sprung from the bed like my ass was on fire. I'd just grabbed a pair of cotton shorts and a tank top when he appeared in the doorway.

I was still buckass naked, and he totally noticed.

Striding back into the bedroom, he wrapped one

arm around my waist and lifted me up off my feet and kissed me. He tasted of mint and male, and I almost dropped my clothes.

"You're moving too slow this morning." Bending at the waist, he hoisted me up over his shoulder. "I have to intervene."

I let out a shriek that was a half-startled laugh. "Oh my God, what are you doing?"

"Taking your sweet ass"—his hand landed on my ass, causing me to jerk—"yeah, this sweet ass to the bathroom."

He pivoted around as I held on to my clothes for dear life and then walked my sweet ass to the bathroom, depositing me on my feet. His hands lingered though, on my bare hips and then my breasts. He made a deep sound in his throat as he lowered his forehead to mine. "Now I'm thinking about getting you in that shower and—"

"Go," I laughed, pushing at his chest. "As much as I like the idea of us getting all wet and whatnot, we're never going to get that omelet."

Or get to talk.

"Hmm." His hand slipped to my rear. Tugging me against him, he squeezed, and as crazy as it was, my body started to rev up all over again. The man was living, breathing sex! He brushed his lips to the skin just above my eyebrow. "I'm thinking about saying fuck the omelet again."

Oh my. The idea was tempting. Everything about him was tempting, but I managed to get him out of the bathroom. While I cleaned up, brushed my teeth, and then washed my face, I made myself promise I was not going to let anything get in the way of talking to him.

Taking a deep breath, I caught my reflection in the mirror as I tugged my hair up in the ponytail. Where in the heck were my glasses? Good question. My cheeks were flushed, my eyes wide, and my lips had that swollen, totally been-kissed-for-hours look.

I straightened the blue and white polka-dotted toothbrush holder and then made a serious expression at myself in the mirror.

I looked half stupid.

Everything was going to be okay. Reece . . . well, he wasn't going to be happy, but he would be okay. I mean, hell, he didn't flip out about the unprotected sex thing, and he basically said if we just created a baby Reece or baby Roxy, then we'd be okay. So he had to be okay with this. I was just making a mountain out of a molehill. Like Charlie would've said, I was being a drama queen.

Time to pull it together.

Sighing, I whirled around and left the bathroom. Spying my glasses on the coffee table, I snatched them up and slipped them on.

Reece was in my kitchen and he'd already found the frying pan, which wasn't hard since it wasn't like I had that many cabinets. The eggs were already on the counter. He looked at me over his shoulder as he grabbed fresh peppers and a bag of shredded cheese out of the fridge.

Seeing him in my kitchen, shirtless and barefoot with all that golden skin on display was something I could really get used to.

I wanted to paint him—like this. With his back to me, the muscles corded and strong.

"I was thinking," he said, tossing those items on the counter. He went for the milk next. "I got to work tonight and you're working Wednesday through Saturday, right?"

Edging into the kitchen, I nodded.

He cracked a couple of eggs into a bowl he'd dug out of the cabinet. "That makes doing dinner and a movie hard." He paused, glancing back over at me. "By the way, I really want to fuck you when your glasses are on."

Warmth swept across my cheeks. "You are so naughty."

One side of his lips kicked up. "Babe, you have no idea all the things I want and plan to do to you. Years' worth of ideas."

I gaped at him. "Years?"

"Years," he insisted. "Anyway, back to the dinner and the movie. I was thinking we could do more like a lunch and then grab a movie another day since it will be hard to work both in with our schedules."

All I could do was stare at him as he found seasonings and made the omelets. He was making plans for us—multiple days' worth of plans. That damn swelling feeling was back in my chest.

"It's either that or wait until we're both off next Monday," he said, raising his arms over his head and stretching as the omelets cooked.

Dear Lord, that sight—all the muscles rippling, the pants hanging indecently low—was pure sin.

"But I really don't want to wait until Monday. Do you?"

"No," I whispered.

Omelets finished, he pulled the pan off the burner, and I finally moved. I grabbed two plates and glasses out of the cabinet. "So how does Thursday sound?" he asked, slipping one perfectly folded omelet onto a plate. "I know Friday will be tough for you with visiting Charlie. So we can grab lunch."

I blinked back sudden tears again. Dammit, he was . . . so thoughtful. Hurrying to the fridge, I grabbed the tea. "Thursday would be great."

"You okay?" he asked.

When I turned, he was placing the plates on my table, but his eyes were on mine. Clearing my throat, I nodded as I walked the jug over to the table and then grabbed the silverware. A look of doubt was on his face.

"I'm okay," I said as I sat. He was slow to sit down across from me. "It's just that . . ."

"What?" he asked, watching me closely.

"It's just that . . . I've liked you for so long, Reece. A really long time."

The grin was back. He picked up a fork and offered it to me. "Babe, I know you have."

I stared at him blandly. "Did you now?" I cut off a piece of omelet and popped it my mouth. "Oh God," I moaned. "This is good."

"Told you. But yeah, I spent a good part of that time ignoring that you liked me, because there was a high chance your father would've gutted me if I made a move on you before you were old enough to buy liquor. And by the time that rolled around, well . . . shit was going on . . ." Reece frowned as his features tensed. "Wait. Damn. I just thought of something. Did we use a condom that night?"

My stomach dropped all the way to my toes. If I hadn't been sitting down, I probably would've fallen over. Oh shit. Shit. Shit. Shit. I had total shit for brains as I stared at him.

Blood drained from my face as I clenched the fork. The tasty omelet turned to dust in my mouth.

"Fuck," he said, scooping up egg. "We didn't use a condom, did we? Guess that's water under the bridge at this point."

Taking a deep breath, I straightened my shoulders. It was truth time. Hopefully not crash and burn and sob time. I placed my fork on the table. "There's something I need to tell you."

Perhaps that wasn't the best way to start this conversation.

A piece of fluffy egg dangled off his fork as he sat back against the chair. His brows rose. "Is there?" The tone was level, but it made me shiver nonetheless. "About what, Roxy?"

"That night." I swallowed, and the small amount of omelet I had eaten soured in my stomach. "When I drove you home."

He stared at me a moment and then finished off his omelet. Pushing his plate back, he rested his bare arms on the kitchen table. "What about that night?"

My heart was pounding like I'd just done sprints up and down my hall. "I honestly don't even know how to say this, other than I wish . . . I wish I'd talked to you sooner and realized that you weren't regretful of sleeping with me. That it was more of you regretting being so drunk. I was just so embarrassed and mad—"

"Yeah, I know you were mad. That's nothing new," he cut in. "And like I said, I wish I had clarified what I was saying when I had the worst hangover known to man."

Me, too, but that wasn't the point. Like Charlie had always said, I was kind of the act-first-and-never-ask-questions kind of gal. This mess was mostly my fault. "That night, once we made it back to your place, things got . . . well, they got really hot and really quick."

"I figured as much," he commented dryly.

Lowering my gaze, I blew out a long breath. "When we got back to your bedroom—which is a really nice bedroom by the way. Totally loved your bed. It's huge. Nice comforter, too."

"Roxy." His lips twitched.

I dropped my hands to my lap, curling them into tight fists. "We didn't have sex, Reece." There. I said it. Like pulling off a band aid.

His brows knitted together as he tilted his head to the side. "What?" he laughed.

"You . . . . you passed out before anything could happen. We didn't have sex." Saying it out loud made it easier to keep going. I met his disbelieving stare. "We started to, but you passed out, and I stayed with you to make sure you were okay. I didn't realize you were that drunk until then."

Reece stared at me.

"And when you woke up in the morning, you . . . you thought we did have sex," I explained quickly. "You had looked at me and said last night shouldn't have happened, and I wasn't thinking about the fact we didn't actually do it."

Leaning back against the chair, he pulled his hands off the table and then put them right back. Silence.

Unease blossomed. "The morning just got away from me. You know why, and I left, and . . . I just . . . the whole situation got away from us—from *me*. You were avoiding me. And I told myself that I needed to tell you as soon as we started talking again, but . . ." A ball formed in the back of my throat, making my voice hoarse. "I'm sorry. I should've told you that morning. I should've pulled my head out of my ass and told you then. I was going to tell you last night, but it didn't seem right to do so. But that . . . that was our first time, Reece. There was no other time before that."

Reece slowly shook his head as he laughed again, but the laugh—it was short and full of incredulity. "I . . . I just need to make sure I understand this correctly."

The unease spread like a noxious weed as he shook his head one more time, closing his eyes briefly. "For the last year, you have been pissed off at me because you thought I regretted having sex with you, when in fact, we never even had sex?"

I opened my mouth, but what the hell could I say to that?

"So, you've ignored me. You've called me names." He laughed that abrupt, abrasive laugh again. "You've cussed me out over what you thought I meant about an act that never even happened?"

I squeezed my eyes shut for a moment. "I was upset because I thought you regretted having sex with me."

"But we didn't have sex."

I shook my head.

A muscle flickered along his jaw. "Are you fucking kidding me?"

Chapter 15

I always suspected that Reece was not going to be thrilled once he learned the truth, but I still flinched.

Reece stood, walking away from the table. I had no idea where he was heading, but he stopped in the middle of the kitchen and faced me. A long, pregnant pause stretched out between us. "Do you even know how crazy I've been driving myself, because I couldn't remember that night? Remember what it felt like to hold you—to be *inside* you, and fall asleep and wake up with you? That after the shitty year I had, I'd topped it off by not remembering sleeping with the only girl I've ever cared about. Do you even understand how that fucked with my head?"

My breath hitched around the messy knot in my throat.

"I can't even count how many times I've tried to remember it and God knows how terrible I felt for not remembering our first time. For fucking thinking I might've hurt you somehow," he said, rubbing his left hand over his chest, above his heart. "And this whole fucking time, nothing even happened between us? Are you seriously fucking joking right now?"

"No," I whispered, blinking back hot tears. "I should've told you—"

"Hell's yes, you should've told me. You had eleven months to tell me, Roxy. That's a long time."

I stood. "Reece—"

"Instead you've been lying to me this whole time?" His brows rose, and for a moment, I saw everything I never wanted to see written across his striking face. Pain. Hurt. Disbelief. All of those mingled with the anger that tightened his jaw. "Wait. Not actively lying. Just letting me *believe* in a lie."

I started around the table. "I'm sorry. I know that sounds lame, but I am so sorry. It's just at first you weren't talking to me and then so much time passed and—"

"And you didn't know how you'd be able to talk yourself around that lie? Sounds fucking familiar," he spat. I knew at once he was talking about his father. "Honest to God, Roxy, I never thought . . ."

He didn't finish his sentence, but he didn't need to. He'd never thought I'd so brazenly lie to him, and I had. Pain sliced through my chest. I wanted to crawl under the table, but I forced myself to stand there and take it like a grown adult.

Reece opened his mouth, but the muted sound of a phone ringing interrupted him. Pivoting on his heel, he stalked over to where he'd dropped his bag last night. He yanked his phone out of the side pocket.

His eyes were on me as he answered the phone. "What's up, Colt?"

It was his brother on the other line, and I wasn't sure if it was personal or cop-related.

"Shit. You serious?" Reece raised his free hand and

scrubbed it through his hair. He dropped his hand. "That's not good."

I had no idea what was going on, so I turned and picked up his empty plate. Opening the dishwasher, I almost dropped the plate.

A pair of my undies was in the utensils holder, stuffed into the square cubby. My hand shook as I stared at them. They were—oh my God—they were the black lacy thongs that I wished I'd worn last night.

How in the world did they end up in the dishwasher?

I hadn't opened the dishwasher since Sunday, if I remembered correctly. Yesterday, I hadn't used any dishes and I'd left the cup I'd used in the sink.

Shaken, I placed the plate inside, but I didn't grab the undies. I didn't even want to touch them. Casper was haunting me, and he was a pervert. If I'd placed them in there having no recollection, I needed to get an X-ray of my head. Maybe I needed to take Katie up on that séance idea.

"Yeah." Reece's voice startled me. "I can do that. Talk to you soon."

Closing the dishwasher, I left the undies inside. The last thing I wanted to do was whip them out. I had enough explaining to do than try to explain *that*. Turning around, I caught the tail end of Reece pulling a shirt out of his duffel bag and slipping it on over his head. He wasn't looking at me when he buttoned up his tactical pants.

"Is everything okay with your brother?" I asked.

Reece lifted his head as he straightened out his shirt. His handsome face was blank, devoid of all emotion as his clear blue eyes met mine. "Yeah. Everything is cool."

The knot in my throat expanded at his apathetic

tone. I opened my mouth, but he turned away. "Look, I've got to go," he said, heading down my hallway.

For a moment, I was absolutely rooted to the floor. He was leaving? We hadn't finished our conversation. Springing into action, I hurried after Reece, finding him in my bedroom, sitting on the edge of the bed, pulling on his socks and boots.

All I could see was the rumpled sheets and comforter. The indents in the two pillows. The shirt he wore last night, the one he'd used to clean me up, a messy ball on the floor.

My heart was pounding so fast I was afraid it would burst like a balloon stretched to its limits. "You really have to leave? Right now?"

"Yes." Tying up his boots, he rose to his full height, a good two heads taller than me. "I've got to go let Colt's dog out."

I silently mouthed the words back, because I almost couldn't believe that's why he had to leave. I mean, I didn't want the doggie to go potty anywhere inappropriate, but we so needed to finish our discussion. "He can't . . . he can't wait for a little while?"

"It's a she," he replied, bending down and grabbing his used shirt. "Her name is Lacey, and no, it can't wait."

My chest clenched as he straightened once again and then stepped around me. The back of my eyes burned as he left the bedroom and I was . . . I was left staring at the bed. The morning together felt like years ago.

Wheeling around, I followed him out to the living room. He already had his duffel bag in hand and had pulled on a black baseball cap. It was pulled down low, shielding his eyes.

"Reece, I . . ." Words left me as he opened the front door. "Are we okay?"

The muscles under his white shirt rolled as if he was working out a kink in his shoulders and then he faced me. The sculpted line of his jaw was as sharp as a blade. "Yeah," he replied in that same flat tone. "We're okay."

I didn't believe him, not for one second. That ball was at the back of my mouth now and I blinked several times. I couldn't speak, because if I did, the ball would come out.

Reece looked away, jaw working. "I'll call you, Roxy." He started out the door and then stopped. In that tiny second, hope kindled to life like a match dropped on a pool of gasoline. "Make sure you lock this door."

And then he was gone.

I exhaled roughly as I gripped the door and watched as he hung a right at the sidewalk, disappearing from my view. Numb, I closed the door. I locked it. And then I stepped back. My cheeks were damp. Hands shaking, I pushed my glasses onto the top of my head and then pressed my palms against my eyes.

Oh God, this had gone as bad as it possibly could've gone. Shuffling over to the couch, I plopped down as I lowered my hands. "Oh God," I whispered.

I knew he'd be mad and I had been terrified that he'd hate me for lying. After all, that knowledge was what made it so hard for me to tell him once we started talking again, but after last night—after this morning—I didn't think he'd walk out. I got that he'd still be upset, but I . . . I don't know what I thought.

Tears tracked down my cheeks, and I dragged in a breath; it got stuck on a sob. This was so not good, and it was my fault. This was my fault.

"Stop crying," I told myself. It felt like two hundred

pounds had settled on my chest, and I replayed what he'd said as he left. "He said we were okay. He said he would call me."

And Reece didn't lie.

Not like me.

I didn't hear from Reece the rest of Tuesday.

I didn't paint—didn't even step foot in my studio. All I did was lie on my couch like a steaming pile of crap, staring at my phone, willing it to ring or for a text message to come through.

Reece didn't call or text me on Wednesday.

I didn't go into the studio at all, and the only reason I pulled my ass off the couch was because I had to go to work. I would've called in if it hadn't been for the windshield I'd broken. Yet another bad decision I'd made that I was literally and figuratively paying for.

Working at Mona's Wednesday sucked moose balls.

A steady throbbing pain moved from my temples to my eyes, and then back to my temples. My eyes were swollen, and I told myself it was allergies. I told Jax that was why I looked like crap when he asked me why I looked like shit. But that was a lie. When I woke up Wednesday morning, I could still smell Reece's cologne on my sheets and I . . . I cried like I had when I'd found out Reece was dating Alicia Mabers, a perfect blond tennis player within a handful of months of moving to town. Except then I had Charlie to ply me with chocolate and stupid horror flicks to get me through what had felt like the end of the world.

I kept telling myself the tears were for what was probably the loss of a friendship more than the potential of what we could've become. I'd never let myself truly consider a future with Reece, so the tears couldn't be because of that.

They couldn't be.

Halfway through the night, Brock "the Beast" Mitchell showed up without his usual entourage of girls or muscle-bound guys. Brock was kind of a big deal around these parts. He was an up-and-coming UFC fighter who trained out of Philly. I had no idea how he and Jax knew each other, but Jax seemed to know everyone.

Taller than Jax with a body that showed he spent hours in the gym every day, Brock was a hottie. He had dark, spiky hair and skin that reminded me of sunbaked clay. Brock had an edgy look about him that was super intimidating for people who didn't know him, but he'd always been low-key and kind every time I'd been around him.

He took a seat at the bar, giving me a wink as Jax strolled up to him. Immediately, it was bromance time between the boys. I wasn't really paying attention to them, but since it was a Wednesday night and only the regulars were in the bar and the music was off, I couldn't help overhearing their conversation. At first, it was nothing major. Just information about an upcoming cage death match and something about a sponsorship deal that Jax looked like he was going to have an orgasm over, but then the subject changed.

"Man, today has been fucking sick," Brock said, tipping the bottle back and taking a drink. "One of the girls who works in the office at the club where I train wasn't at work yesterday. Coach Simmons said she was a no call, no show but . . ." He shook his head, his dark brown eyes glinting with anger. "Some sick ass got ahold of her."

I stopped, clutching the cloth I was using to wipe down the higher end liquor bottles on display. Jax cocked his head to the side. "What happened?"

"Some fucker broke into her apartment. Messed her up pretty badly, from what I hear." His empty hand closed into a dangerous fist. "Man, I cannot even wrap my head around how a man could hurt a female. Just don't understand that."

"Jesus." Jax shook his head. "This is what, the third incident in a month or so?"

"There was that girl that disappeared at the beginning of summer." I walked over to where they were, dropping the cloth on the counter. "I think her name was Shelly or something like that."

Brock nodded. "I'm not a cop. I'm not a psychologist, but sounds like we got a psycho around here."

I folded my arms against the shiver that danced up my spine. My thoughts wandered to the strange things in my house, and I stiffened. It sounded crazy to even think what was happening there had anything to do with these poor girls. Plus it didn't make sense. How would anyone get in my house to do those things without me knowing about it? But still, I had to ask. "Do you know if the girls were stalked or anything? Like any warnings?"

"I haven't heard," Jax answered, angling his body toward mine. He arched a brow. "I bet Reece would know though."

Oh! Like a kick in the stomach, those words twisted up my insides. I didn't know how to respond to that. Last Jax knew, which was just from a few days ago, things were on the up and up between Reece and me. Now, I wasn't so sure.

"I'll tell you what, though. Whoever this guy is, he's

a dead man." Brock's lips curved into a smirk. "The girl who works in our office. She's Isaiah's cousin."

"Holy shit," muttered Jax.

My sentiments exactly. Isaiah was sort of infamous around these parts. To outsiders, he appeared like a legit businessman, but all the locals, including the police, knew he was much more than that. He ran Philadelphia and all the surrounding towns and cities. To put it simply, he was not a man to mess with, and he was smart about his under-the-table dealings, because law enforcement could never pin anything on him.

It was Isaiah who Calla's mom had stolen drugs from, to the tune of millions of dollars' worth of heroin. Because of how far reaching and powerful Isaiah was, Calla's mom wasn't even living in this time zone anymore. The only way for her to stay alive was to disappear.

But Isaiah had a code of ethics. One of his boys—Mack—had gone after Calla since he was the one who was supposed to be handling her mother. Isaiah hadn't been cool with that since Calla was innocent in all of this. No one could prove it, but when Mack's body was found on a back road with a bullet in his head, everyone knew that had Isaiah written all over it.

Even though his boys hung out in here, I'd only seen Isaiah a few times. Once every blue moon, he strolled into Mona's, and he always left amazing tips.

"Yep. So not only are the police looking for this fucker, so will Isaiah's boys, and this guy better hope the police find him first or the inside of a trunk is the last thing he's ever gonna see." Brock leaned back, crossing massive arms across his broad chest. One shoulder rose. "Then again, I kind of hope Isaiah does find him first."

Might make me a bad person but I sort of hoped the same thing.

Brock hung out to the end of the shift and the boys walked me out to my car. There was still no sign of Reece, not a single missed call or text. The hurting I'd been carrying with me during the twenty-four hours turned to bitter-tasting panic.

Before everything had gone to shit Tuesday morning, he'd told me he wanted to have lunch and when he left, he said we were okay and that he would call. A tiny part of me was holding out for Thursday afternoon.

Reece would call. We would have lunch. He wasn't a dick. Never had been, so I knew he wouldn't bail on me like that.

The street outside the Victorian was quiet and there was a chill in the night air as I walked up the pathway to the porch. I could almost feel autumn, and it wasn't too far away. After such a long and hot summer, I couldn't wait for pumpkin spice and mums.

Opening the door, I stepped inside my dark apartment and closed the door behind me. I don't know why, but as soon as the lock clicked into place, goose bumps raced over my flesh. Icy fingers trailed down my spine, and I froze as I stared in the dark recesses of my apartment.

The distinct feeling of not being alone surrounded me. Tiny hairs rose all over my body. My chest rose and fell rapidly as I stood there. Maybe I should've said something to the guys about the weird stuff happening in my apartment. If I had, they would've demanded to come home with me, but it had seemed too foolish to mention, too weird and unexplainable.

Now, I thought I might have a heart attack.

Blindly, I reached out, my fingers brushing the shade of the lamp before finding the tiny switch. I flipped the light on and a soft glow spread across the living room, but the shadows seemed to have darkened everywhere else.

Reaching into my purse, I wrapped my hand around my cell phone and pulled it out. I quietly inched forward, placing my purse on the recliner. Holding on to my phone, I went into the kitchen, turning on lights.

Nothing out of place.

As I opened up the dishwasher, half expecting to find a bra-and-panty set stuffed in there, my breath hitched in my throat as my ears strained to hear sound.

Something—something came from the back of the house, where my bedrooms were. The sound of a door shutting softly? I wasn't sure.

I spun around, heart racing. Fear tiptoed over my skin. Had I heard a door closing? Or was it just my imagination? At this point, I couldn't be sure, but I grabbed a huge-ass psycho butcher knife out of its block.

Taking a deep breath, I made my way through the entire apartment. Nothing was out of the ordinary, no doors open when they shouldn't be or vice versa, and with all the lights on, even the bathroom's, I plopped down on the bed, sighing.

I really needed to go to the local church and order an exorcism.

Glancing down at the scary knife I still held, I sat it on the bed beside me and then I looked at the phone. I could totally text Reece. Tell him I thought I heard something in my apartment. He would come over, and it wouldn't be a lie, but . . .

But it wouldn't be right.

That . . . that was like reaching a whole new level of desperation, and I wasn't to that point. Yet.

I didn't get much sleep. Weirded out by the way my apartment felt when I entered and everything else that had been going on, I woke up every hour until the sun rose and then I finally gave up.

At the butt crack of dawn, I found myself in my studio. The Jackson Square painting forgotten, I stared at a blank piece of canvas and then I grabbed my paintbrush. There wasn't any thought behind what I was doing. My hand had a mind of its own. I was on autopilot. Hours passed, and my back and neck ached from sitting so long in virtually the same position.

Rubbing the cramp in my lower back, I leaned back in the stool. I tilted my head to the side and muttered, "Fuck me."

The background of the painting was the robin's egg blue of my kitchen walls and the bright white of the cabinets. No big deal there, but it was what was in the center of the painting that made me want to get a lobotomy.

The skin tone had been hard to capture, mixing browns and pinks and yellows together until I got as close as I could to the golden tone. The shoulders had been easy to shape on the canvas, but shading the contoured muscles had been the hardest. My wrist didn't appreciate all the hard work it had taken to get the right curve of his spine, the corded muscles on either side. The black pants had been the easiest.

I'd painted Reece like I had seen him in the kitchen Tuesday morning.

Squeezing my eyes shut, it did nothing to ease the burn in my eyes or stop the tears from building. Frustration rose in me. I knew without looking at my phone that it was past ten in the morning. That knowledge made my chest ache and my stomach feel wrong, like I'd eaten too much.

I couldn't wait any longer. I'd waited two days.

Dropping the paintbrush on the stand, I hopped up and went to my phone. Without thinking too much about it, without stressing myself out any longer, I typed Reece a quick text.

I miss you.

God, that was so bizarrely true. I went almost a year not speaking to him and I had missed him during that time, but that want had been cloaked in bitterness and anger. With that gone, all that remained was how much I missed him.

I deleted that and typed *Are we still on for today?*

Then I also backspaced the mother out of that and finally settled on *Hey.*

Bringing my phone into the bedroom, I took a quick shower and blow-dried my hair. I even curled lazy waves into it and put makeup on so I'd be ready just in case . . .

Then I paced my living room and kitchen, too wired to sit down, and with each passing minute, that frustration and panic pecked away at me.

Twelve o'clock dragged into one and then two and when I had only thirty minutes left to get ready for my shift at Mona's and there was no text or call, that teeny, tiny spark of hope that I'd been holding close to my heart extinguished.

Reece had lied to me.

For the first time since I'd known him, he had lied to me. Because I knew in that moment, he wasn't going to call me. Everything between us wasn't okay.

Chapter 16

Making your bed and lying in it was probably one of the worst things ever. I hated that stupid saying with the fierceness of a thousand burning suns, but it was true. When you were disappointed or saddened by something you had no control over, it was easier to let it go, but when it was something that you did to yourself, it was so much harder to deal with.

And this mess with Reece was my fault. Sure, it took two to tango, and it took one to get plastered, but it was me who hid the truth of the night a year ago. I'd betrayed his trust. To some it might not be seen as a big deal, but it was to Reece. Honesty was everything to him.

Katie stopped by during my shift Thursday night, right before I took my break. One look at me, and she knew what was up. Or maybe it was her super-stripper powers.

Grabbing a basket of fries from the kitchen, we hid out in the office. She hoisted herself up onto Jax's desk, which made me smile in spite of how crappy I felt. Her dress, if one could call the shirt a dress, did not cover her ass when she sat down.

"Tell me everything," she ordered, holding the basket of fries.

I sat beside her and told her what went down. Trusting Katie, I gave her all the details. Well, I didn't go into that much detail about how I was gripping the headboard Tuesday morning. That wasn't a necessary part of the convo.

When I was finished, Katie had already consumed half of the fries. "Honey buns, here's the thing. There's a whole lot of could've and should've that has gone on. You can't change the past, and let's be honest, you didn't drown a kitten."

I made a face.

"Stop beating yourself up over it. You know you did wrong. You apologized and you meant it." Handing over the basket, she hopped off the desk and stood in front of me, hands on her hips. "If he can't get over that, then he's truly not worth your time. And I mean that in the most non cliché way possible."

I popped the last fry in my mouth and then placed the basket aside. "I know, but I like him—"

"You love him," she corrected, throwing herself on the leather couch against the wall.

Rolling my eyes, I waved my hand dismissively even though my heart turned over heavily. "I wouldn't go that far."

"Why else have you been crying since Tuesday if you don't love him?"

I cut her a narrowed look. "Because I like him a lot. I've liked him for a long time. And we were friends and now it's ruined. And I haven't been crying since

Tuesday." At her look of doubt, I scowled. "Not the entire time."

She arched a blond brow. "Okay. First thing you need to do is stop lying to yourself. Just admit that you've been in love with him for ages. There's nothing wrong with that." When I opened my mouth, she raised a hand. "Secondly, fuck him. Not literally, unless he comes around, but like I said, if he doesn't get over this, it's on him, not you."

Nodding, I tucked my hair back behind my ears as I slipped off the desk. I got what she was saying.

"Calla and Teresa are coming up next weekend. The four of us need to get together and get shitfaced," she announced, rising from the couch like a goddess who was summoned. "Like, we need to get stupid drunk, talk about how stupid boys are, and then wake up wishing we never see another bottle of liquor."

"Okay," I mumbled.

"Like as drunk as the night before Calla left us," she continued, and I cringed, knowing where she was heading with this. "Remember? You were convinced that one of those plastic closet organizers could hold your weight?"

"It did hold my weight," I said crossly.

She threw her head back and hooted with laughter. "Yeah, for like thirty seconds. You shoved yourself in that damn thing, with your legs touching your chest."

"You zipped me up!"

"And that thing broke and I thought you broke your ass."

I thought I broke my ass. So did Calla and Teresa, which reminded me of how grateful I was that I hadn't broken anything, because none of the girls could stop laughing long enough to make sure I was even alive.

Fucking tequila.

Katie bounced forward and hugged me, squeezing me so tight I thought I'd pop. "It'll be okay. He's going to come around."

I hugged her back. "You think this or are your superpowers telling you this?"

She giggled as she pulled away. "Call it feminine intuition."

I cocked a brow. "Really?"

"Yep." Katie flounced to the door. "I've got to go drop it like it's hot, and yes, this is hot." Smacking her ass, she laughed. "Peace out, homie homes."

A smile pulled at my lips. Katie was . . . she was different and she was awesome. Straightening my glasses, I told myself not to do it, but before I left the room, I grabbed my purse out of the cabinet and pulled out my phone.

The small smile faded from my lips. There was a missed text, but it was from Dean, and seeing it really knocked my feet out from under me. Besides the fact that the last time we spoke, I'd hung up on him, it was the same message I'd sent Reece earlier and had received no response from.

Hey.

I let out a shaky breath as sadness swelled. Holy crap, I was the female version of Dean right now, texting someone who was so not interested. Had he stressed over that text as much as I had? He'd probably gone through three different versions before settling on the innocuous greeting. Seeing that truly was a kick to the chest. My heart *ached*.

Slipping the phone into the back pocket of my jeans, I swallowed the cluster of tears that were threatening to turn me into a fat, angry baby. I needed to pull it together. I made this mess. Reece made his decision.

Contrary to what Katie believed, I wasn't in love with him.

I hadn't fallen that far for him.

I hadn't fallen for anyone *that* hard and I never would.

Friday afternoon, I wasn't thinking about Reece at all. A different kind of problem had surfaced, a far more serious one than my relationship or lack thereof.

Nurse Venter stood beside me, at the foot of Charlie's bed, her face contorted in a sympathetic expression that really did reach her tired eyes. "If you need anything, you know where to find me."

Afraid to speak, all I could do was nod. She left the room, quietly closing the door behind her, and I was stuck standing. It was like someone had pressed the pause button on life.

Charlie was back on the feeding tube.

I wanted to close my eyes, but what was the point? It didn't change what I was seeing. It wouldn't undo anything. When I opened them up, Charlie would still be in the same position. His life would not somehow rewind.

The pale lilac comforter was tucked up to Charlie's slender chest, hiding everything from the shoulders down, but I knew that his hands were restrained under the blanket, secured to the bed.

I hated that, absolutely loathed that he was tied up. It seemed too inhumane and cruel even though I knew there was a valid reason for it. The moment the feeding tube was hooked up, he'd started pulling at it. They did this for his own good, but it still hurt to see it.

I forced myself to the chair next to his bed and sat stiffly, placing the tote beside me. Reaching out, I found his hand under the blanket and folded both of mine over his. "Charlie," I whispered. "What are we going to do?"

Charlie's eyes were open, and I wished they were closed, because there was something wrong with them. They were dull, absolutely lifeless. I would've thought he was a mannequin if it wasn't for the occasional blink or tremor that coursed down his arm.

Fear clawed at me as I stared at him. Oh God, he didn't look good. I couldn't remember him ever looking this frail and sallow before.

Minutes ticked by and the only sound was the chirping of birds outside the window and the low hum of conversation from other rooms. There was a ball of cold dread sitting in the center of my chest as I sat there. This . . . this reminded me of my grandfather who'd been sick and in hospice care before passing away. I was a little girl then, but I remembered my mom sitting at a bed just like this, holding my grandfather's hand and whispering to him while he slept so deeply I couldn't remember seeing his chest move.

This felt like that, and I couldn't shake the feeling that we were not alone in this room. That there was a third entity, and it was death.

Scooting as close as I could get to the bed, I closed my eyes and rested my head on the pillow next to his. "I miss you so much," I whispered thickly. "I know you know that."

Tears leaked out of the corners of my eyes as I tightened my hold on the blanket and his hand. Who knew I could still cry so easily after the week I had? Maybe I was turning into an emotional mess. At this moment, I didn't care. The turmoil I felt over Reece was nothing in comparison to how I felt now. I wanted to crawl in bed with him, but I was afraid of disturbing his feeding tube.

I knew that I needed to act like nothing was wrong. I needed to pull out one of the paintings I brought in for him—one that I had done weeks ago, and I needed to read to him. That was the normalcy of our visits. I liked to think both of us needed that.

But as I lay there, all I could think was about the span of minutes that had changed everything for Charlie, for me. No matter how many years had passed, it still felt like yesterday.

It was Friday night, a few weeks after school had started and the only reason why I was at the football game was because Colton was playing, which meant Reece was there, in the stands, watching his older brother play.

Charlie and I made our fifth or sixth pass in front of the section of bleachers Reece was sitting at with his friends. "Man, I think you qualify as a stalker now, just so you know."

I bumped him with my hip. "It's the okay kind of stalking."

He sent me a sideways look. "When is stalking okay?"

"When it involves Reece Anders," I quipped, giggling when Charlie rolled his eyes. "Oh whatever, you think he's hot, too."

"Can't deny that." He glanced over his shoulder, back toward where Reece sat, and then quickly faced forward. "He's looking down here."

"What?" I shrieked as I stumbled over my own feet. I sent him a wide-eyed look. "You're lying."

Charlie grinned at me. "No, I'm not. Look for yourself, but try not to be so freaking obvious."

"How do you not be obvious?" I muttered, but as I took another step, I made a causal attempt at looking over my shoulder. My gaze found Reece immediately, like I was some kind of hot-boy-seeking missile.

Reece was staring down at us—at me. And he was smil-

ing. He had the best smile. Wide. Friendly. Uninhibited. My heart kicked around in my chest as I started to smile back.

"Oh," Charlie said. "My bad."

At first I didn't get what Charlie was talking about, but then a high-pitched shout whipped my head around.

One of the cheerleaders had shouted Reece's name. Rising up on the tips of her white sneakers, she blew him a kiss. My stomach dropped all the way to the tips of my toes. I looked at Charlie.

He cringed.

Reece wasn't staring at me. He wasn't smiling at me. How embarrassing. Sighing, I picked up my pace. "Are you ready to go?"

"I've been ready to leave since we got here," he retorted. "But you had to get your stalking out of your system. And look what happened? No good comes from stalking, Roxy."

"I hate you."

He laughed as he draped his arm over my shoulders, tugging me against his side. "Come on. Let's head back to my place. Parents are still at the lake house and I found the key to the liquor cabinet again."

I quickly changed my mind. "I love you."

Charlie snorted.

Ordering myself to forget about Reece, we headed out of the gated football field. He still had his arm hanging loosely over my shoulders. "I hate coming to these things," he bitched. "Every single time we have to park out in the field. We're going to be covered in ticks."

I smiled up at the starry sky as we trudged through the calf-high grass. "You probably have twelve attached to your legs right now."

"Man, that's fucked up." He dropped his arm and shoved me.

Stumbling to the side, I giggled, knowing he was going to make me check his scalp when we got to his parents' house later. "I want to watch Never Been Kissed *tonight."*

Even in the dark and without looking at him, I knew he rolled his eyes. "That movie is so old it needs to be retired."

"Never!" I yelled as I jumped over a rock someone almost parked their truck on. "That guy is hot."

"That guy is really old now in real life," he shot back.

I flipped him off. "Don't ruin it for me."

Shoving his hands into the pockets of his shorts, he shook his head. I could see Charlie's car, parked next to a van that hadn't been there when we showed up.

"Hey," a voice called out. "Where are you guys heading off to?"

I twisted at my waist, looking behind us, and swallowed a groan when I saw who it was. Henry Williams. He wasn't alone. Two friends flanked him. All three of them were in a grade higher. All three were total douche bags. Especially Henry. He was a special kind of douche bag. The kind that was good-looking and totally knew it, therefore the latter totally zeroed out the former.

"Just keep walking," Charlie said under his breath.

I didn't listen. Facing the boys, I planted my hands on my hips. "Nowhere you all are invited to."

Charlie muttered something as he stopped, turning around. I think he said something about my mouth getting me in trouble, but that wouldn't be the first or last time I'd heard that.

One of Henry's friends laughed, and the sound grated on my nerves. It was high-pitched, much like the cheerleader's voice was, but this laugh reminded me of a cat getting hit by a car.

Henry was absolutely unfazed by my greeting. He swaggered up to where Charlie and I stood, puffing out his chest like a peacock. "You're looking good tonight, Roxy."

I arched my brows at him.

Charlie sighed.

"I'm looking good every night." I crossed my arms over my chest.

He smirked as his gaze crawled over me, leaving behind a sensation of ants marching along my skin. It really was too bad he was such a pinhead, because he wasn't bad to look at. "That's true." He passed a baleful glance at Charlie, and my spine stiffened. "So, what are you doing tonight?"

"We've got—"

"I wasn't talking to you." Henry cut him off, and it truly was like I had an internal bitch switch inside me, and he'd just flipped it into the on position. "Why don't you drop this homo and hang out with—"

"Excuse me?" I saw red. "What in the fuck did you just call him?"

Charlie grabbed my arm. "Let it go. You know there's no point in arguing with stupid."

There was no way in hell I was going to let it go.

As I pulled myself out of the events of that night, I sat back and rubbed my palms along my cheeks, just below my glasses. Guilt coated my skin with clammy sweat. Lowering my hands, I stared at Charlie. His head was turned just slightly, like he was looking at me, but his gaze was focused over my shoulder, at the window.

Let it go, he had said.

If only I had listened.

Friday night was busier than usual with just Nick and me behind the bar since Jax had taken the weekend off to visit Calla in Shepherdstown. Despite the fact I looked like a hot mess with my hair pulled up in a messy bun and wearing an old tank top that was about two sizes too big, I was grateful for the fact the night was flying by. Lack of sleep was catching up with me, and my already crappy mood was somewhere between "fuck me land" and "fuck off town."

As the night progressed, my mood veered sharply into "everything sucks city." Normally Reece spent Friday nights at Mona's. Maybe not the whole night, but he usually showed up by ten. His normal buds were here, at their table, but there was no sign of Reece, and I knew it was because of me.

Dean showed up closer to eleven, and I was hiding from dealing with him on the other side of the bar. Nick was blocking him, and I don't know what was said to Dean to make him leave around midnight, and I really didn't care at the moment.

Yeah, everything sucked right now.

Keeping a smile plastered across my face was harder than it should have been as I mixed drinks and chatted with those at the bar. Staying focused on my job was the only thing getting me through the shift.

That and the knowledge there was a huge bag of nachos at home that I was so going to make my bitch when I got off. I was going to smother them in Swiss cheese, nuke the bastards, and go to town.

Sherwood, our temporary head cook in charge, had just come back from break when I turned to help the newest customer who managed to squeeze in at the bar.

My mouth dropped open. Good God, what was up with tonight?

Henry Williams stood in front of me, and he looked a little better than the last time I'd seen him. Like he might've gotten some sun. Good for him.

"I just want to talk," he said, voice barely audible over the music.

I clenched the bottle of Jack so tightly I was surprised it didn't explode. "I can't believe you're standing here," I said dumbly.

"I've been seeing Charlie." He leaned in, and heat swept down the back of my neck. "I know he's really bad and—"

"Don't talk about him. Don't even say his name." I started to fling the bottle like I had the book, but even as my hand itched to let it fly and the need to make him hurt was almost all consuming, I didn't do it.

Somehow I had learned from the last time.

A girl waved her hand, gaining my attention. Shooting Henry a hateful look, I took her order. Of course he was still there when I finished the cocktail.

"Please, Roxy," he started. "I really want—"

"Do you see how many fucks I have to give when it comes to what you want?" I spread my arms wide. "This many fucks."

Nick was suddenly there, hands planted on the bar top. "I think you really need to leave."

"I'm sorry." Henry raised his hands, looking back and forth between us. "I'm not trying to cause any problems. I just want to talk to her. That's all."

Anger swelled inside me so swiftly that when I opened my mouth, I thought I'd breathe fire. "I don't want to see your face let alone talk to you."

"You heard the lady," Nick said, raising his arm and pointing at the door. "Get out."

Henry looked like he was going to argue, but then shook his head. Reaching down, he pulled a small white square out of his pocket and placed it on the bar. He looked me dead-on. "Call me. Please."

I glanced down at what turned out to be a business card with some kind of car on it and then back at him. He'd already turned away, making his way through the crowd. Before I could stop myself, I laughed. It was kind of crazy-sounding, sort of like the noise a hyena made before it killed something.

Nick reached for the card, but for some reason unknown to me, I grabbed the card. He arched a brow, but I shook my head as I slipped the card into my pocket.

He lowered his head so he could speak into my ear. "Why?"

"I don't know," I admitted, pulling back and looking at him. "I don't know."

The rest of the shift was uneventful. Instead of seeing Reece, who I secretly kept waiting to see come through the door, all I got was Dean, Henry Williams, two drunk chicks that had puked on the floor, and a guy who offered to buy me a drink *and* let me give him head.

When I got home, I was too tired to worry about the weirdness that had been going on in my apartment. Placing my phone on the nightstand, I stripped down to my undies and unhooked the bra, leaving the tank top on since it could've doubled as a dress. Then I slinked into bed, tugging the covers up to my chin.

Today . . . today sucked.

Yesterday sucked.

Tomorrow had to be better.

That's what I kept telling myself as I lay there, utterly exhausted. Tomorrow seriously had to be better. And truthfully? When everything first happened with Charlie, it had been worse than this—the helplessness, the anger, the depression. All of it had been raw and razor sharp. I'd gotten through it. I'd get through whatever crap was happening right now, because what other option did I have? Curl up and give up? That wasn't in my nature.

I didn't realize I'd fallen asleep, but I must've, because I came awake all at once. No blinking the sleep out of my eyes. I was completely alert as I stared at the window across from my bed. I'd been dreaming. I didn't remember what the dream entailed, but someone had been calling my name.

Stretching my legs and arms, I glanced up at the nightstand. It wasn't even five o'clock. I'd been asleep for an hour and a half tops. Fail.

I was just about to flip onto my other side when I realized the backlight of my cell phone was on, like a text or a call had come through and it hadn't moved into sleep mode yet.

Jerking up, I snatched the cell phone, and with my heart in my throat, I hit the button. There was only one person who could've texted or called this late. Reece. Hope went off inside me like a cannon. Yeah, texting or calling at almost five in the morning wasn't the greatest thing, but it was *something* and it was more than nothing.

The screen came to life, I slid the little bar, unlocking it, and at first I didn't know what I was seeing. I didn't understand it, could not wrap my head around it.

It wasn't a text or a missed call.

My hand began to shake.

Unlocking the phone had taken me to the last program in use, which should've been nothing—just the home screen. Except it wasn't on the home screen. It opened to my camera roll—my pictures.

And there was a picture on the screen.

A scream exploded in my stomach and crawled up my throat, but when I opened my mouth, there was no sound. Horror had closed my throat off. There was a picture on my phone, one I could've never taken, because it was of me.

A picture of me *sleeping*.

Chapter 17

Fear and disbelief held me immobile as I stared at the picture of me sleeping. Somehow I registered that this picture was from tonight, because I could make out the dark blue straps and the pink strip that formed a bow on the straps of my tank top.

Oh my God.

The fear building inside me was like being doused with icy water. It sent my pulse racing and the only air I could get inside my lungs was in quick, shallow breaths as I launched off the bed. My bare feet slipped on the hardwood floors. I reached the bedroom door, throwing it open, and I raced down the short, narrow hall. I was at the front door when I realized whoever took that picture—because it had to be a person since I doubted a ghost could do that—could be outside.

Oh my God.

The person could still be *inside.*

Panicked, I didn't know what to do. Never in my life had I been in a situation like this. I backed away from the door and then spun around, running for the bathroom. Once inside, I locked the door and backed up until I knocked into the toilet. I sat down on the lid, struggling to breathe around the crushing pressure of the fear. I started to call the first person who came to mind.

Reece.

My finger was right over his contact when I stopped. What was the point in calling him? He wouldn't answer. Close to tears, I started to call Jax but remembered he was out of town. Part of me recognized I wasn't thinking right. I needed to call the police. Someone had been in my apartment while I *slept*. They could still be here. But my brain cells weren't communicating with one another.

I called Nick.

He answered on the second ring. "Roxy?"

"Did I wake you?" Stupid question, but that's what came out of my mouth.

"No. I haven't gone to sleep yet. Are you okay?"

Staring at the bathroom door, I pulled my legs up to my chest. A buzzing picked up in my ears, like I was sitting next to a hive of bees. "I . . . I think someone is in my place."

"What?" His voice came across as sharp as a whip.

I drew in a shuddering breath and whispered, "I woke up and there was a picture of me on my phone—a picture of me sleeping."

"Holy shit."

"I didn't take the picture." I inhaled deeply, but it got stuck. "There's been all this weird stuff happening here. My dishwasher turned on while I wasn't home. The remote in the fridge. Toilet seat left up and other stuff. I thought my place was haunted, but this—I know someone—a living, breathing someone—had to do this."

"Jesus, Roxy, are the police on their way?" he demanded.

"No. I didn't call them."

There was a nanosecond of silence. "Did you call Reece?"

"No." I straightened, putting my toes on the cool tile. "I can't call him. He—"

"Are you fucking out of your mind, girl? You need to call the police right now. Wait." He sounded like he was moving. A door slammed shut. "Where are you?"

"I'm in my bathroom." I stood, pushing my hair back from my face. "I just wasn't thinking. I woke up, saw the picture and panicked."

"I'm heading over to your place now and I'm calling Reece. He's off on Fridays, right? He'll ans—"

"Don't call him. Please don't call him." I squeezed my eyes shut. "He isn't . . . we aren't really talking right now and I don't want him . . . just don't call him." Truth was, I knew how crazy this was, how utterly bizarre it was to wake up and find a picture of myself on the phone. Someone could easily believe that I'd done it for attention, and the way things were with Reece right now, I didn't want him to think that. "Are you there?"

"Yes. I'm coming to you, but I need you to get off the phone and call the police. You need to do that right now," he said, his voice calm as I heard an engine roar to life.

"And you need to stay in that bathroom until you hear from me or the police. You understand?"

I felt stupid for not calling the police immediately. "Okay. I'm going to call them now. I'm sorry—"

"Don't apologize, Roxy. Call the police. I'll be right there."

I did what I should've done immediately. I called the police. The dispatcher didn't laugh hysterically in my ear when I told her that I'd woken up and found a picture of myself sleeping on the cell. She took my information, and stayed on the phone until Nick beeped in on the other line, letting me know he was outside.

I had no idea how he got to my place so fast. The number of laws he had to have broken astonished me.

Opening the bathroom door was the scariest thing I'd ever had to do. My entire body shook as I grabbed the doorknob. When I did, I expected to see a serial killer in a clown mask waiting for me, but the hall was empty. I ran to the door a second time.

Nick came in, dressed like he'd been earlier at the bar. He barely looked at me as he took my free hand in his and started turning on the lights throughout the apartment. "Were you in your bedroom?"

"Yes. I was in bed." My voice cracked as I followed him on shaky legs.

He steered me toward the couch. "Stay here." Reaching behind me, he tugged the quilt off the couch, draping it over my bare legs. It was then when I realized I was wandering around in my undies and tank top. "I'm going to check out your bedroom real quick, okay?"

Numb, I tucked the blanket around my legs as I clutched my phone. The next several moments were surreal. The moment he left the room, I didn't want to be alone. Getting up, I wrapped the blanket around me and found him just leaving my extra bedroom and heading into my main one.

Nick sent me a look as he checked the window.

"I don't want to be by myself," I admitted hoarsely. I didn't want to be anywhere in the house alone.

He nodded and then crossed the room, opening the closet door. I could hear hangers banging around. Then he turned to me. "Do you have some bottoms you can put on? I think the police are outside."

Flushing, I hurried to the dresser and pulled out a pair of cotton shorts. Nick started to leave the room. "Can you stay? Please?"

Running a hand through his dark hair, he turned around, giving me privacy. "Jesus, Roxy, I don't think I've ever seen you so scared."

I dropped the blanket and pulled the shorts on with shaking hands. Then I picked the blanket up once more, holding it to my chest. I didn't say anything as we went back out to the living room. I could see blue and red lights flashing outside.

The officer who Nick let inside was around Reece's age, and I vaguely recognized him. He came to the bar a couple of times with the guys. I thought he might be engaged or something. Without my glasses, I couldn't make out his name. Luckily he introduced himself, saving me the trouble of figuring it out.

Officer Hank Myers.

Ah, yes. Hankie Hank. I remembered him. That was Katie's nickname for him, and he *wasn't* engaged. On second thought, I think he had the hots for Katie, because I was pretty sure he'd let her use him as a pole a couple of times at Mona's.

None of this was important.

"I checked the apartment out," Nick said. "The window in the extra bedroom was open."

I gasped. "What?"

"I think that's how someone got into your house. Odd thing is, though, I didn't see the screen."

"I don't . . . I don't have a screen in the window right now." I watched Hank leave the room. "It was damaged a few months ago and the landlord was getting it repaired." My breath hitched. "The person . . . they came in through the window? Oh God.."

Hank did a quick search that lasted all of a minute tops before returning to the living room. "What's going on, Roxy?"

Sitting back down on the couch wrapped in a blanket burrito, I told Hankie Hank about the picture. His face was impressively blank as he made his request. "Can I see your phone?"

I handed it over, and when I looked down at my hand, the phone had left thin indentations in my palms. "You have to go into the pictures."

Nick sat on the arm of the couch. He was silent, but I appreciated his presence and that I wasn't alone dealing with this.

It pierced me in the chest when I thought that a few days ago I could've called Reece. Hell, even during the eleven months we hadn't been nice to each other, I probably wouldn't have hesitated to call him, and I believed without a doubt that Reece would be here.

The dark blue uniform stretched across his shoulders as Hank took a look at my phone, blond brows raised. He glanced up at me. "And this was on your phone when you woke up?" When I nodded, he looked at the photo again. "There was no way this happened before tonight?"

I shook my head. "No. And when I woke up, my screen was still lit up. It was just taken."

"Is there anyone who could've done this as a joke? Has access to your apartment?"

"Only my family has keys to my place and they wouldn't do this. Besides, the window was open in my other room. Obviously if someone had keys, why would they do that?"

"People do stupid shit all the time, Roxy. Shit that makes no sense," Hank explained.

Nick leaned forward. "Tell Hank what you told me was also happening."

When Hank's hazel eyes settled on me, I suddenly felt wary of what I was saying. It was like he was looking at me with suspicion, but doubt clouded his gaze. I started to tell him, but a knock at the door caused me to jump.

"Expecting anyone?" Hank asked.

Nick stood, but when I shook my head, the officer motioned for him to stay back. I was surprised when Nick listened, and even more shocked when he moved to sit next to me.

"You hanging in there?" he asked in a low voice.

I nodded. "Yeah. Thank you." My gaze flicked to where Hank was. From where I sat, I could see who it was when the door opened.

It was James and what's his name—Kip. My upstairs neighbors. "We saw the police lights," James said as he strained to see over Hank. "We wanted to make sure Roxy was okay."

The fact they got up at this time in the morning to check on me made me want to hug both of them.

"Everything's fine," Hank advised. "But I need both of you to go back to your residences. If we need anything, we know where to find you."

James didn't budge. "Roxy's okay, right?"

"Yes. I'm okay." I raised my voice to make sure both guys could hear me, and I hated the way my voice shook. I *hated* being afraid like this. "Everything's okay."

Hank managed to usher them out of the doorway, but he didn't close the door as I expected. Instead, he stepped aside and said, "I got the call handled, bud."

My heart nearly leapt out of my chest as another police officer strode into my apartment. Except it wasn't just any officer.

It was Reece.

Maybe I was hallucinating, and all of this was a nightmare.

Reece stalked into my apartment like he belonged here. Without responding to Hank, he gave Nick a cursory glance as he entered the living room. "What in the hell is going on?"

Beyond the ability of forming a response, I stared up at him.

Hank sighed as he closed the front door. "We got a call—"

"I heard the call go through," Reece cut him off. His eyes were the darkest shade of blue. "I couldn't believe it when I heard the address for a possible break-in, because all I could think was if it really was your house, you wouldn't just call the police." He thumped his hand off his chest, above the badge. "You'd call *me*."

My jaw unhinged. Okay. I was seriously hallucinating this.

"Thought you had Fridays off?" Nick commented dryly.

"I'm covering a shift tonight." Those midnight-blue eyes cut to him. "What in the hell are you doing here?"

Nick leaned back, tossing an arm over the back of the couch. "She called me."

Reece narrowed his gaze on said arm behind me. "Did she?"

Hank cleared his throat. "The window was open in

the extra bedroom, and she says there's a picture of her taken while she was sleeping."

The way he said it, with a touch of derision, snapped me out of my stupor. "That is what happened."

Reece cocked his head to the side as his broad shoulders stiffened. "What?"

"Someone took a picture of her with her phone while she was sleeping," Nick repeated, and it became obvious that Reece hadn't heard that part of the call.

Had Reece just heard my address called out and rushed over here? I didn't even know what to think of that.

He extended his hand to Hank. "Let me see it." The phone was handed over and then Reece cursed under his breath. "The window in the room was open?"

Hank nodded. "If it was locked, I have no idea how it would've gotten open. Glass wasn't broken." He looked at me. "I'm assuming you normally lock your windows. If not, you might want to start doing that."

"I lock my windows." My fingers tightened on the edge of the blanket. "I always lock my windows."

Everyone in the room exchanged doubtful looks, which I understood given the current situation. "Wait," I said, scooting forward so that my feet touched the floor. "What are you doing here, Reece?"

A muscle popped in his jaw. "I cannot even believe you'd even ask that question. Well, you know what, I'm not that surprised."

"Excuse me?" I said.

His eyes glittered as he stared down at me. "You're seriously going to ask why I'm here?"

I came off the couch, dropping the blanket and going toe to toe with him, which meant I was at eye level with his chest, but whatever. "Yeah, I'm going to ask that question and if you're surprised by that question then you're an idiot!"

"An idiot?" The large hand wrapped around my phone rose, and he pointed toward my bedroom. "You left your bedroom window unlocked knowing that there is someone in these counties—"

"I didn't leave my windows unlocked! Just like I didn't call you to come over!"

He lowered his chin, his eyes never leaving mine. "We'll talk about this later, Roxy."

Every emotion inside me boiled up and spilled over. "This is crazy," I said, my hands clenching into fists. "You've been ignoring me for days. And you—*you* lied to me."

Reece drew back, flinching.

Heedless of the fact we had an audience, I didn't stop and I knew I should've. This was no one's business and my voice was cracking on every other word, but how dare he stand here and act like he had a right to be here. "You lied too, Reece. You told me everything would be okay and that you'd call me. Yeah, well, call me an idiot, but the last I checked, you didn't do that and things aren't okay. 'Oh, let's do lunch.' Blah! You didn't even text me back, you rat bastard."

"Oh, wow, this is going in a direction I so did not expect," murmured Nick.

"Didn't text you back?" Reece's eyes widened. "I texted you back on Thursday. I told you in that text—" He cut himself off. "I texted you."

Stunned that he would tell such a bald-faced lie, I laughed harshly. "No, you didn't."

Hank glanced between the two of us as he shuffled his weight from one foot to the next. "Uh, guys, I think we need to get back—"

"Bullshit, Roxy," Reece snapped. "I did text you back."

I folded my arms. "Then your text just magically disappeared. Whatever. Don't you have another call to head to? I think Hank has this handled. Isn't that right, Hank?"

Hank raised his hands as if he was saying he wanted no part in this. A lot of help there.

"I can't believe this." Reece reached into his back pocket with his other hand and pulled out his phone. After tapping the screen, he flipped his phone around. "Look at it," he said, and when I started to look away, he stepped closer. "Look at my phone, Roxy."

Blowing out a rough breath, I reluctantly did as he asked—well, commanded. I gave his phone a quick glance and opened my mouth, ready to fire off something smartass, when I smacked my mouth shut.

What the . . . ?

I snatched the phone out of his hand, holding it close to my face so I could make out the words and time.

Hey, let's reschedule lunch for Sunday. We can talk then.

The text was time-marked. It showed delivered; probably no longer than ten minutes after I'd sent the text, while I had to have been in the shower. I stared at the text, half expecting it to vanish as a figment of my imagination.

"I swear," I whispered, looking up at him. "I never saw that text. I know it says delivered, but I never saw it."

Reece held my gaze for a long moment. "I thought you were pissed that I was rescheduling." He gently pried his phone loose from my grip. "And that's why you didn't text back. And just so you know, I was planning on showing up here on Sunday, text or no text."

"Could someone have deleted the text before you saw it?" Nick suggested.

Cold air whirled down my spine and the tiny hairs along the back of my neck stood. This . . . this was crazy creepy.

"Who would break into the house to just delete a text?" Hank asked, crossing his arms. "Not to mention, get in the house at the right moment to delete a text and only delete one from Reece? I'm not trying to be a jackass, but the likelihood of that happening is slim."

I know it sounded crazy, but that was what had to have happened. I didn't see that text. If I had, I would've responded and that text would've saved some of the heartache. Not all of it, but some. Though, right now, I couldn't wrap my head around the fact that he had texted me and he had planned on seeing me. None of that seemed to matter in this moment.

Tension had crept over Reece's striking face as he looked down at my cell phone. His knuckles were bleached white from his tight grip.

"That's not the only weird thing," Nick said, drawing Reece's unnerving stare. "Tell him what you were telling me."

I sat down on the edge of the couch, beyond unsettled. "A couple of weeks ago I came home from work and the dishwasher was running. I hadn't scheduled it to run. Honestly, I don't even know how to do that."

Hank arched a brow.

"Keep talking," Reece said quietly.

It wasn't easy, because I knew how insane all of this sounded. "One morning, I woke up and found the remote in the fridge. I thought maybe I'd done that without remembering, but I've never done anything like that before. Then there was the toilet seat thing . . ." As I spoke, Reece's empty hand curled into a fist. "I hadn't done that. I'm pretty sure of that. Then there was this other time when a new canvas had been hung on my easel. Little things like that—things I couldn't be sure if I'd done or not. I really thought my place might be haunted. I told my mom and Katie." A short laugh escaped me. "I know that sounds stupid, but then . . ."

I'd never seen Reece as still as he was, standing in front of me or his arresting face so hard, as if every feature had been carved out of marble. "Then what?"

The tips of my ears burned. This was the last thing I wanted to mention in front of Hank and Nick. "The really creepy thing—like as creepy as my picture being taken while I'm sleeping—happened a couple of days ago. Tuesday morning," I added, and Reece's gaze sharpened as his chest rose. "I was putting the dishes in the dishwasher."

"I remember that," he said.

Okay. Well, I guessed we weren't hiding anything at this point. "A pair . . ." I swallowed as the burn traveled across my cheeks. "A pair of my undies was stuffed in the utensils cubby. And yeah, I didn't do that."

"Jesus," muttered Nick as he stood, scrubbing his hand through his hair. He glanced back at the kitchen, his lip curling like he was personally disgusted by the dishwasher.

Hank didn't say anything. He just stared at me with what had to be a "what the fuck" expression if I'd ever seen one.

But it was Reece who caught and held my attention. He was as still as a statue as he continued to stare down at me. "Why didn't you say anything?" His voice was barely above a whisper.

My shoulders suddenly sagged as a wave of exhaustion rolled over me. "We were talking about . . . other *stuff* at that moment and I didn't . . ." I trailed off, shaking my head.

I knew the exact moment he realized the meaning of that. Blood pinked the hollow of his cheeks. That flush of anger was actually kind of scary, and if I hadn't known deep down that it wasn't directed at me, I would've been a wee bit frightened of him. A myriad of raw-looking emotions flickered across his face. "I was *here* and . . ." He didn't finish that line of thought. He turned toward the other officer. "I got this call, Hank."

"But—"

"I got this call," he reiterated, voice hard enough to send a shiver across my skin.

Hank stared at him a moment and then rolled his eyes. "Whatever." Hitting a button on his shoulder radio, he said "I'm ten–eight. Unit Three-oh-one is handling the possible break-in."

There was a static-filled response I barely heard, and then Hank showed himself out. Nick remained standing by the recliner. He raised a hand, rubbing his jaw. "You're okay?"

I wasn't sure I wanted Nick to leave, because that meant it would just be me and Reece, but I knew Nick had to, as exhausted as I was. I nodded. "Thank you for coming up. I owe you."

Reece cast his gaze to the window, his jaw working.

"You don't owe me anything." Nick glanced at Reece. His eyes narrowed. "You sure you're good here now?"

"Yeah," I murmured, my thoughts in a thousand different places.

Nick stopped at the door. The grin on his face warned trouble. "By the way, loved the bows on your panties."

Oh, for fuck's sake.

Reece's jaw became so hard I thought it would snap off as he watched Nick saunter out the door. Then it was just us. He stood with his back to me for several seconds and then wheeled around. Walking over to the couch, he sat on the edge of the coffee table, directly in front of me. "Are you okay?"

Yes. No. Maybe? I had no idea. I was feeling way too much. Scared wasn't even the right word for how I felt. Someone had been in here—repeatedly. I felt . . . I felt violated, like all my walls had been stripped away from my home, and I felt stupid that I'd chalked up all the weird happenings as something supernatural. Then again, why would anyone jump to the conclusion that someone was breaking into the house just to mess with things inside of it?

I shuddered as it really hit home. Someone had been in my apartment. Someone had been in here many times, even while I was here. The residual fear peaked once more. How in the hell would I feel safe in this house again? Having that taken from me angered me, and there was nothing I could do about it.

"I don't know what to feel," I said finally, leaning back against the cushion.

He rested his arms on his bent knees as he let out a weary-sounding sigh. My gaze flicked up, collided with his and held. In a second, the shields dropped, and I sucked in an unsteady breath. He looked conflicted—torn. As if he was experiencing the same wild range of emotions that I was.

"Why didn't you tell me this stuff was happening?" he asked.

I ducked my chin, shrugging. "I honestly thought my place was haunted. I mean, why would I think someone was breaking in just to move stuff around and do weird things like that? And some of the stuff I could've been responsible for without realizing or forgetting about it, like the dishwasher, the remote—stuff like that."

"Did you stick your own panties in the dishwasher?"

"No." I made a face.

"Then you knew it couldn't be you, babe." He straightened, looking around the house. "When was the last time before you found them in there that you were using the dishwasher?"

I knew what he was thinking. "I hadn't checked the dishwasher Monday."

"But you were home all day, right?"

Nodding, I pulled my legs up and wrapped my arms around my knees. He didn't need to say it out loud. I knew what he was thinking. Tonight wasn't the first time the person had gotten into my apartment while I slept. It was the only plausible explanation. Closing my eyes, I rested my forehead against my knees. My voice sounded incredibly small when I spoke. "Why would someone do this?"

"To mess with your head, Roxy. These kinds of things, what was being done around here, were minor enough that it wigged you out and you questioned it, but most importantly, you questioned yourself. Which meant you didn't tell anyone. You kept it to yourself." There was a pause. "Fuck, Roxy, I wish I knew. There was no reason for you to deal with this alone."

"You believe me?" I asked. My voice was muffled by my legs.

"Why in the hell wouldn't I believe you?"

I gave a lopsided shrug. "Hank was giving me a WTF look. I don't blame him. It all sounds highly suspect."

"Fuck Hank. He's an idiot. And when I get my hands on whoever is messing with you, I'm seriously going to fucking kill him. But that's something we'll talk about later."

My head shot up and I gaped at him. His reaction shocked me, all things considered.

Reece stood. "I don't want you staying here."

The idea of staying here, especially right now, was something I also did not want to do.

"I'm also going to need to take your phone in to see if we can get prints off it that aren't mine, yours, or Hank's. Nick hasn't touched it, right?"

I shook my head. Tonight had been a blur. "I don't think so."

"Do you have an extra phone you can switch service to in the meanwhile?"

"Yeah. I have an older one."

"Good. Why don't you pack up some stuff," he said, stepping around the couch. "I'll take you to my place. I still got a couple of hours left on my shift, but at least you'll be able to get some sleep."

I was back to thinking I was hallucinating things.

When I didn't move, Reece continued. "That works out perfectly. I need you to talk to Colton. He can come by my place. He's been investigating what's been happening around here. That's why I had to go let out his dog Tuesday morning."

It struck me then, the conversation between Brock and Jax. "The girl who works at Brock's training place?"

Reece eyes narrowed on me. "You heard?"

"Yeah, Brock was in the bar. He said . . ." I shivered. "He said she was really messed up. Was she . . . ?" I couldn't even bring myself to say it.

Cop Face appeared. All emotion gone. "I can't go

into details. Not because I don't trust that you'd keep it quiet, but it's out of respect for the vic. But we're pretty sure all the attacks recently are linked. The violence has been escalating."

"To what?" I whispered.

His gaze held mine. "It's been physical—worse than you can imagine."

A shudder of revulsion rolled through me. "Oh my God, those poor girls. I . . ." My eyes widened. "You don't think this has anything to do with what happened to them?"

He knelt down, placing a hand on my knee. "I don't know, but nothing—I swear it—nothing like that is going to happen to you. Now, come on, let's get going."

I watched him straighten and turn. "Wait. I can't go to your place."

Facing me, he cocked his head to the side. "Why not?"

"Why not? Um, I think you pretty much made it clear that you . . . that I lied and you can't deal with that. So I can't stay with you." There was no way I could put myself through that. "I can go to my parents."

His face softened by a degree. "You and I still need to talk. Now just isn't the right time for that. You're coming home with me."

My eyes narrowed. "I really don't think you have the right to be so bossy."

"Do you really want to wake up your parents? You see what time it is, and scare them like that?"

I gaped at him. "Dammit, you're right, but that's low."

"It's not low. It's just the truth," he replied. "Come on, let's get your stuff and get you the hell out of here."

Honestly, I could sit there and argue with him. I

could go to Katie's or wait until it was a more decent hour, but I could see the determination etched into his features. This wasn't a battle I'd win easily and frankly, I was exhausted and I didn't want to be there any longer than I had to.

Dragging myself up, I headed back to my bedroom with him in tow. While I grabbed some clothes, he checked out the other room. Being in my room gave me the creeps, and I didn't know if that was going to ever change.

I exhaled roughly, fighting the urge to cry.

Reece came out of my second bedroom, his face a shade or two paler. I stilled, my hand hovering over the strap on my overnight bag. "Did you find something?"

Reece blinked as he shook his head. "No. You almost ready?"

Slipping a long, thick sweater on that reached my knees, I grabbed my bag and slipped my feet into my flats. Not trusting myself to speak, I nodded.

Reece was silent as he led me out of the house and locked up. As I stepped off the porch, both upstairs apartments had lights on, and I told myself I needed to bake them cookies or something.

I got to sit in the passenger seat of a police cruiser—which, surprisingly, smelled pleasant, like fresh apples—and any other time, I'd have been excited about all the buttons and potential noise-making power, but I stared out the window, into the darkness as dawn steadily crept into the horizon.

"You hanging in there?" Reece asked.

Glancing over at him, I was struck with the urge to reach out and smooth my fingers along his jaw. To touch him. For him to touch me. "Yeah. I'm okay."

He sent me a sideways look that was a cross between

amused and worried. "It's all right not to be okay in a situation like this."

I lowered my gaze to my hands, keeping my mouth shut.

We didn't speak again as we drove to his place. He lived in a condo near Jax, a rather large apartment on the third floor. He let me in, and the crisp scent of laundry greeted me as I stepped inside.

Reece eased around me, flipping on the lights. I blinked against the brightness, wondering how exactly my night had ended up with me staying at Reece's.

He had a wide foyer that led into a large galley kitchen and dining room. The living room was neat with an exception of a basket of laundry sitting on the coffee table.

Reece frowned as he saw it.

Walking over to the basket, he picked it up. "You know where the bed is, and if I remember correctly, you thought it was really comfortable, so make yourself at home."

Surprise fluttered through me at the lack of rancor in his tone as he mentioned *that* night. I hadn't moved very far, only placing my bag near the couch, by the time he reappeared in the living room. Amused, I watched him swipe up a bag of chips that was on the end table and take them to the trash in the kitchen.

"I've got to head to the office, get your phone to Evidence to see if we can do prints," he said, running a hand through his hair. The movement caused his biceps to strain against the hem of his uniform. "I got a landline in several rooms. The number to the office is on the fridge. Call that or my cell if you need to. I should be back a little after eight or so."

I nodded.

He stopped in front of me, and I drew in a deep breath. Pulling the sides of my sweater tight, I lifted my chin. His eyes searched mine.

"I'm not really okay with what happened," I admitted in a small voice. "Any of it."

Somehow, I think he got that I wasn't just talking about what happened in my apartment. For a moment, I thought he wasn't going to say anything. That he'd just turn around and walk out of his apartment.

But then he moved forward and slowly—oh so slowly—wrapped one arm around my shoulders and then tugged me close. I hesitated for a second and then I went, pressing my cheek against his chest. The cool edge of his badge was sharp against my cheek but I didn't care. The warmth of his body, of his embrace, was worth it.

His other hand cupped the back of my neck and he lowered his chin to the top of my bowed head. He drew in a deep breath I could feel, and I closed my eyes. "I know," he replied in a rough voice. "I know, Roxy."

Reece held me for a few seconds more and then he stepped back. The hand around my neck slipped to my cheek. His eyes met mine. "Get some rest. I'll be back as soon as I can."

I didn't move until I heard the door close and lock and I still didn't move for several minutes. Reece said to take his bed, but there was no way I could sleep back there. Not with how things were left between us. Yes, he was helping me out now, but he was a good guy. That's what good guys do.

Moving two of the throw pillows to one side of his overstuffed beige couch, I dragged the quilt off the back of the couch and then stretched out. The cushions sucked me in immediately, and when I closed my eyes, I knew it wouldn't take me long to sleep. As crazy as it sounded, I felt safe here and I didn't fight the sleep that tugged at me.

I slipped into a dreamless sleep for I don't know how long. Minutes? Hours, maybe? But it was the deep kind of sleep that when I woke from it, I couldn't figure out my surroundings right off.

I was at Reece's place. Right. I remembered that, falling asleep almost immediately on his really comfy couch. He had really good taste in furniture. I started to stretch, but stilled when I realized the couch was oddly hard . . . and warm.

Confused, I moved my right hand and it slipped over something as smooth as silk stretched over marble—something also warm and very hard. And rippled. My fingers dipped. Was that a navel?

My eyes flew open.

Holy moley, I was so not where I'd fallen asleep. This was not the couch I was plastered against or currently feeling up.

It was Reece—a sleeping, shirtless Reece. I was curled up close against him, and I was in his bed.

Chapter 18

If this was a dream, I didn't want to wake up from it. For a lot of reasons, but mainly for the fact there was nothing like waking up next to this man. I'd only gotten to experience it twice before and that was not nearly enough.

Part of me was so shocked that I'd been in a deep enough sleep that he'd been able to move me without my knowledge. I tried to picture what he'd done when he returned home. Obviously he'd undressed first, and I could tell he had pajama bottoms on, because I could feel the soft, worn cotton against my bare legs. He must've scooped me up and carried me into his bedroom. I didn't know if he'd placed me as close to him as I was or if I'd snuggled up to him. Either way, there wasn't any space between us, and his hand rested on my hip.

My heart ached, and as I lay there, listening to the soft snore, I realized how badly I wanted this. Not just with anyone, but with him. Despite the messy past between us, and everything that needed to be spoken, he . . . he was still taking care of me.

That spoke of the kind of man he was. Decent and kind to his very core, and there were so very few men like that.

And Reece truly was a beautiful man.

Features relaxed in sleep, there was an openness about him that was rarely seen when awake. There was always an aura of concentrated power, and it was there even while he slept. I didn't think it was because he was a cop. It was just something innate in him, like a second skin.

Full, well-formed lips parted, I resisted the urge to run my thumb over his lower lip. It was even harder to deny the need to kiss him, because I really wanted to feel those lips against mine again.

His skin was warm and smooth under my hand, and I knew I needed to get my butt out of this bed before I did something wholly inappropriate, like slip my hand down under the band of his pajama bottoms.

Carefully, I eased away from him, and rose from the bed. Finding my sweater on the edge, I slipped it on and tugged it close, immediately missing the warmth of his body. Not wanting to wake him since it was still early and he couldn't have been asleep that long, I crept out of the bedroom, quietly closing the door behind me.

The apartment was tomb silent as I walked back out to the living room. Remembering he had a balcony, I opened the French doors and stepped outside. I dragged in the late-morning air and looked around. The balcony faced a wooded area and was rather private.

Reece gardened.

Or someone did.

Flower boxes hung off the wrought-iron railing, full of pretty pink and purple flowers. There were two green stands, and a bushy fern hung in the corner, out of the sunlight. Two wide wicker chairs were positioned close together.

I tucked my legs along the side and huddled down in the comfy chair. I couldn't believe how cool it was. When I really thought about how quickly the seasons changed, it blew the mind.

My mind wandered as I sat there. I couldn't remember if I had grabbed my glasses before I'd left my place. Didn't really matter since I didn't have my car. I'd have to go back to my place to get it before I headed into work later tonight.

Back to my place.

I shivered and it had nothing to do with the cooler temps. I almost couldn't believe it—I was being stalked. Freaking stalked. Me. I shook my head slightly. That's what was happening. I no longer could joke that it was Casper the Pervy Ghost, and barring some kind of memory disorder, it was someone sneaking into my apartment while I was there. Deleting texts while I was in the shower. Taking pictures of me. Out of everything, those were the two creepiest things ever. But even worse was the fact I really had no idea this was what was happening. I couldn't even begin to imagine that, or who it could be.

There was Dean, and while he was persistent, he didn't strike me as a psycho. Unless it was a stranger—the man responsible for what was happening to the other girls—who was doing this, and that was even more horrifying. He could be coming in the bar every night for all I knew. I could be talking to him, smiling at him.

Oh my God, that was horrifying to even imagine. It made me not want to step foot out of my apartment, except my apartment wasn't even safe. Geez. I squeezed my eyes shut. What was I going to do? I hated the idea of changing my whole life over some freak who was a virtual ghost to me.

Then again, the ghost of my past had changed my entire life. I did and didn't do things all because of what happened with Charlie. That was a sobering realization I wasn't nearly awake enough to really delve into.

A thought snuck into my head. Maybe it was someone I knew. Not Dean. Not some guy I dated. Maybe it was someone who just recently came back into my life—an unwanted recent addition.

Henry Williams.

The idea didn't make a lot of sense, but when we were in high school, he was a bit of a creeper. A handsome guy, but a creeper nonetheless. Maybe he wasn't satisfied with screwing up Charlie's life. Maybe he wanted to drive me crazy. Honestly, it sounded insane—as insane as someone breaking into my apartment and taking a picture of me.

I opened my eyes just in time to see a brown bunny rabbit bounce across the lawn below, into the tree line. Well, I guessed it was a rabbit. It was kind of a brown blur. Could've been an opossum for all I knew.

Criminy, I couldn't believe I was at Reece's place. I just couldn't let myself read too much into it. Tucking my hair back, I blew out a tired sigh. Even in the silence, surrounded by bouncing bunnies and pretty flowers, it was hard to really grasp what I felt for Reece. My feelings for him were tangled into a web of our past and our present. Lust cultivated over years and . . .

I couldn't even think it.

Where I could admit I cared for him strongly—I had

for a long time—love was scary. I learned that with Charlie. I loved that boy more than anything, and seeing him hurt had killed a part of me when I was sixteen and still was killing me. I couldn't fall for Reece, not fall that deeply. Not when going to work every day could mean he could be harmed or worse. I flinched, but that was the truth. God, these thoughts were freaking pointless, because—

The French doors opened and Reece stepped out onto the balcony, his sleepy blue gaze finding me. My tummy tumbled as I drank him in. Goodness, he was cute in the morning. Hair all messy and a shadow of brush along his jaw, he was total pinup material.

"Hey," he said, and one side of his lips quirked up in a lopsided grin.

My own lips responded. It was clear he was still half asleep. "Hey you. I didn't wake you, did I?"

"I don't think so." Lifting an arm, he dragged his fingers through his hair. My eyes got hung up on his bicep and the muscles along the side of his chest. I shifted in the chair, surprised that I could be so visibly aroused by a guy scratching his head. He moved to the seat beside me. "I mean, I woke up and you were gone." He leaned back in the chair, spreading his thighs as he tipped his head toward me. "I was worried when you weren't there. You okay?"

My lips parted as his words hummed through me. "Yeah, I just woke up and didn't want to wake you. You couldn't have been sleeping for that long."

His broad shoulders rose in a lazy roll. "I don't really sleep that much. Just a couple of hours here and there, especially when I'm working."

I thought about the night on the couch where it had seemed like a nightmare had shaken him awake. "You have to be so tired, though."

Casting the heavy-hooded eyes to me, he shrugged again. "It's the same with you, babe. You work crazy-ass hours just like me. You manage. I manage."

"True," I murmured, looking out over the lawn. "I like this—the balcony, I mean." Flushing, I mentally kicked myself. "It's very private and quiet."

"I like it, too. Try to come out here at least once a day, drink my coffee." Out of the corner of my eyes, I saw him raise his arms above his head and stretch. I had to look. I was only human, and goodness gracious, I was so glad I did. His back bowed as bones cracked. The man was pure sin. "It's a good place to think," he finished, dropping his arms.

My gaze coasted over the expanse of his chest and taut stomach, down to the fine trail of darker hair that disappeared under the band of his bottoms. "I can . . . um, understand that."

There was a pause. "I talked to Colton this morning. He's going to come by soon. I'll be here while he talks to you."

A shiver crawled along the nape of my neck, and I pulled the sweater closer. I nodded. "Does he know what happened?"

"Yes."

I watched a bird flutter past the balcony. "Does he think it's related to the other stuff?"

"I don't know. I think he wants to talk to you first before he makes that jump." He sighed softly. "Seriously, Roxy, you hanging in there?"

That wasn't an easy question to answer. So much was going on and hanging between us, and everything we needed to talk about I wasn't ready for. "Charlie's on a feeding tube," I said finally, raising my gaze to the blue, cloudless sky. The color was much like Reece's eyes. "He hated being on that before, so they have had to restrain him, and it's so hard to see him like that."

"I'm sorry to hear that." Genuine sympathy radiated from his voice.

I nodded. "The last time he wouldn't eat, he ended up having a seizure."

"I remember that," he said quietly.

Surprised, I looked at him. "You do?"

He nodded. "Yeah. I remember you talking about it, and I know how close you came to losing him."

Pain rose as I leaned back in the chair. "I'm so afraid."

"For Charlie?"

"Yeah," I whispered, and I bit down on my lip as he reached between us, curving his hand around my arm. It felt like my heart doubled in size. "I'm afraid I'm going to lose him. I really am."

He squeezed my arm gently. "I wish there was something I could say."

"I know." I swallowed the knot in my throat.

His gaze held mine for a moment and then he moved his hand. I wanted to climb into his lap and wrap myself around him like an octopus, but knew that probably wouldn't be the greatest idea. "I want to ask you something again. I'm hoping you'll answer differently than before."

Oh God, I wasn't sure I was ready for any of this. "Okay?"

"Why didn't you tell me what was happening at your place, Roxy?"

At first, I didn't know how to answer that question. "I don't know. I guess I didn't want anyone to think I was crazy for believing in ghosts or making it up, looking for attention. I mean, how many women come to the office with fears they're being stalked and it gets written off? That's the kind of fucked-up misogynistic crap that happens."

Reece shook his head. "Not when I take the call."

"You're different," I pointed out, unfolding my legs. The cement was cold under my bare feet.

"Then why didn't you say anything?"

I chewed on my lower lip as I gripped the arms of the chair. "I really didn't know what was happening, and when I found my . . . my stuff in the dishwasher, I just didn't think it was right to bring it up then when . . ." Unable to sit, I stood and walked to the railing. "I mean, you know what was happening."

His gaze held mine for a moment and then he looked away. Rubbing the heel of his palm over his heart, he frowned. "When I realized this morning I was there when you found that and had no idea, I wanted to punch myself in the nuts."

My brows flew up.

The muscle along his jaw popped. "I'm serious. What has been happening to you has to be some scary shit. Finding your panties in a dishwasher? Not knowing how that happened, wondering if your place should be on Ghost Adventures or if you need to get your head checked had to be driving you crazy. And you went through that by yourself—by yourself when I was there." He scooted to the edge of the chair and leaned forward. "I fucking loathe the idea of you going through that."

I drew in a deep breath but it got stuck. "You were angry . . . and you had every right to be angry."

"I was." He looked up at me through thick lashes. "But I should've been there for you. You should've been able to stop me and show me what happened.

That's not your fault that you didn't. I put you in that position and I'm sorry for that."

My mouth opened, but I didn't know what to say.

"It's time to have that conversation," he said, his voice brooking no argument. "And we really need to be up front with one another. Both of us. No more bullshit."

I leaned against the railing, feeling a little weak, but I didn't run or try to hide from this. I wasn't a coward. At least, I tried not to be one. "You're right," I said, but I wished he'd put a damn shirt on, because that body was super distracting.

"You know that I was pissed. You know why I'm pissed."

"You hate lying above anything else. I know it's because of your dad," I said, and I rushed on before I stopped. "Knowing that made it hard to come clean about that night. Not that I'm excusing it, but just so you know where I'm coming from."

"Lying isn't what I hate above all else, Roxy. I hate fucking predators who stalk women and people I care about. That's pretty high up there. So is murder and rape," he continued, and I think I got his point. "But yeah, I was pissed. I'm still kind of pissed."

I cringed inwardly. Here it comes . . .

"That's why I left. I wish I didn't. Gotta be honest with you, it probably was a good thing that I did, because the last thing I wanted to say was something I regretted and couldn't take back, but knowing what you were going through, I wish I was there. That I stayed and maybe you would've opened up about what was going on." He rubbed the back of his neck with one hand. "Let's take that shit and put it aside for a moment, because we'll be dealing with that when Colton gets here."

"All right," I replied, stiffening.

He lowered his head as his chest rose with a deep breath. "I needed space. I needed to clear my head of the anger I was feeling. I've learned more than once that trying to hold an important conversation when you're pissed isn't the smart thing to do. It usually fucks things up and the last thing I wanted to do was go down that road with you."

But wasn't it already fucked up?

Reece's eyes were such a deep, startling blue when they met mine. "I wasn't ready to talk to you on Thursday, but I knew then where this was heading."

My chest rose and fell sharply as I braced myself.

"I thought about it. I do get why you were upset and I know you get why I was upset. We both fucked up in this, one way or another."

"We did," I whispered, wanting to cry. I started to turn away, but his hand snaked out and caught mine. I faced him, eyes wide.

"I think we did this wrong," he said, threading his fingers through mine.

I had no idea where this was heading, but he was holding my hand, so I was going to go with him somewhere where I didn't want to pitch myself off the balcony. "We did?"

Reece nodded. "No bullshit, right? I have something I need to tell you."

"No bullshit," I repeated.

One side of his lips kicked up. "The first time I noticed you—like really noticed you—was when you just turned sixteen, and you were out in the backyard with Charlie. I had no fucking clue what you two were trying to do with a Slip'N Slide and honestly didn't care, because you were wearing the tiniest bikini I'd ever seen."

"I have no recollection of a Slip'N Slide," I murmured.

He tugged me a step forward. "I do. It was in June. It was around two in the afternoon, and I was watching you from the kitchen window. I kept telling myself you were way too young to be thinking the things I was thinking."

Interest piqued, I couldn't let that go. "What things were you thinking?"

"Things a teenage boy thinks when he sees a hot chick in a bathing suit that barely covers her ass," he replied. "I don't think I moved from that window until I couldn't take anymore, and I don't think you want to know what I did when I left the window."

My lips parted. "What did you do?"

He arched a brow. "Give you two hints. Shower. My hand."

"Oh." My skin tingled as a sharp sensation swirled through me.

"Yeah," he murmured, and tugged me another step forward. My leg pressed against his knee. "Then it was when you were seventeen and you made me a homemade birthday card. I don't know why, but when you smiled at me and handed that card over, you came onto my radar and you never left."

I totally remembered that card. I'd spent *days* on it, drawing a picture of the Statue of Liberty, because I knew he was into the whole Marines and America stuff. And I'd felt so goofy giving it to him, but *he* had smiled and he'd given me one of those awkward one-arm hugs. I'd thought he saw me as a silly kid.

"When I came back from overseas and I saw you . . ." He shook his head. "That hug you gave me. Never been hugged like that before. I didn't understand why you were the first person I really wanted to see when I got back. I didn't get it for a long-ass time why I started going to that shit hole that used to be Mona's. And when I did finally put two and two together, and came up with the fact that I wanted you, then the shit happened with the shooting."

I swallowed hard. I knew Reece had taken the officer-involved shooting hard and he'd been drinking a lot around that time, but before I could open my mouth, he went on. "My head wasn't in the right place to act on it. The reason I came to Mona's became more about getting shitfaced than seeing you, and then . . . yeah, that night happened between us." He tilted his head to the side. "That's why I regretted it. Because I was drunk and my head was in a bad place. I didn't want anyone around that, especially you."

"Reece," I whispered.

His eyes searched mine intently. "By the time I figured out what I was feeling for you, we weren't talking and as always, shit just gets out of hand."

My heart was pounding as I looked down at him. "What are you saying, Reece?"

That crooked grin appeared again as he curled his arm back. I gasped as he hauled me right into his lap, my hip cradled between his strong thighs. Still holding my hand, he wrapped his other arm around my waist as he leaned back into the chair. Having no choice, I went with him and ended up stretched out across his chest, my free hand landing on his shoulder. My body immediately warmed to being so close to him.

We were face-to-face. "And because of that—all of that, we did this wrong. Not that I regret getting in you. Fuck. No way. Looking back, I'm a hundred percent glad that was our first time." The arm around my waist shifted, and his hand slipped over my hip, to the edge of my shorts and then splayed across my bare leg. A wave of goose bumps traveled across my flesh. "But I should've done more for you. The dinner. The movie. All of that. You deserved that. I think after all this time, *we* deserve that."

"We do?" My voice squeaked. I couldn't believe what I was hearing.

"Yeah, we do." His eyes drifted over my face, settling on my mouth. "How about we start over? You want that?"

I still had no idea what to say.

He arched a brow. "The way you're rubbing my neck tells me you do, but babe, I want to hear it from that pretty mouth."

My hand? I glanced at it. Hell, I was rubbing his neck. "I didn't expect this," I admitted. "I thought you'd tell me that we'd be friends . . . or something like that."

"Roxy, I already told you I was looking for more than that."

"But—"

He tipped his chin forward, resting his forehead against mine. "I was pissed, but that hasn't changed." A heartbeat passed. "But has it changed for you?"

Part of me wished it had, because this with Reece was dangerous to my heart and common sense. I could really fall for him, but I . . . I wanted him and—and I wasn't going to finish that train of thought. "I would like that."

"Figured."

My heart flipped. "So damn cocky."

"Just truthful," he teased, plucking up the purple streak in my hair and twisting it around his finger.

I drew in a deep breath as his warm breath danced

over my lips. My mind was literally blown. So was my heart, but in a way that was both good and concerning. This really was the last thing I'd expected. I suddenly had my present and future with him altered.

"Wait," I said, drawing back. "If we're starting over, does that mean, like, no sex until the third date or something?"

"Seriously?"

I narrowed my eyes at him. "It's a valid question."

"Come on, babe." His hand slid up my leg and curved around my rear, and everything in me turned to liquid heat. "I think you know the answer to that."

"I think I'm getting the picture, but maybe I need—"

His mouth silenced me. Kissing me softly, he sent my senses spinning. Just a kiss, and my breasts already felt heavy and an ache spasmed between my thighs. Well, the hand on my rear probably also had something to do with it, especially when a finger unerringly found the center seam in my shorts. He traced that seam, sending an illicit shiver through me.

"I bet you got the picture now, right?" he said, voice rough.

Running the tip of my tongue along my tingling lower lip, I wanted to wrap my legs around his hips, press against where I really wanted him when he groaned. "Are you sure this is smart?" I asked.

The hand left the seam of my shorts and slipped under the sweater and tank top, gliding over the bare skin of my back. "Why wouldn't it be a good idea?"

I drew back, cupping his cheeks. I liked the way the bristle along his jaw tickled my palms. There was really only one good reason I could come up with. "I'm not going to fall in love with you."

Reece's grin spread into a full-fledged smile that wrapped around my heart. "Sure you're not."

Chapter 19

Colton showed up shortly after I showered and dried my hair. Dressed in jeans and a shirt that said THIS GIRL NEEDS A NAP, I dragged myself out to the living room. Seemed fitting as I plopped down on the comfy couch and watched Colton who watched his brother sit next to me.

Like sit waaay close to me.

Reece's leg was touching mine and his arm was draped along the back of my couch. If we were any closer, we'd be joined at the hip.

Colton's shrewd stare missed nothing as he sat in the chair opposite the couch, near the French doors. "What's going on, little brother?"

"What's it look like?" Reece replied.

Truth be told, I had no idea how to answer what was going on between us. Even though we'd cleared the air and we were "starting over" or something like that, I wasn't sure if we were at the stage where we were willing to announce whatever it was we were doing.

"Looks like my hand is about to do a meet and greet with the back of your head," Colton retorted.

Reece chuckled deeply, and I couldn't repress the shiver in response to the deep, rolling sound.

"Is he doing good by you?" Colton directed that question at me.

I glanced around, like someone would pop out from behind the couch and answer the question for me. "Yeah?"

"He better." His voice dropped low as he shot a warning look at Reece, who in return simply smirked. "Or I'm sure your father and either one of your brothers will kick his ass."

My lips twitched as I tried to picture my younger brother fighting anything that didn't involve a hand controller and an Xbox.

Colton reached inside his suit jacket and pulled out a small notebook and pen. He flipped the notebook open, and just like his brother, Cop Face appeared. Time to get serious. "I need you to tell me everything that has happened, skipping no details. Okay? Even if it's small, it could be something huge."

I clasped my hands together, drew in a deep breath, and I told him everything, starting with the remote in the fridge and ending with the picture of me on my phone. Through it all, Colton scribbled it all down and Reece remained silent by my side and when I got to the undies in the dishwasher part, he moved his hand from the back of the couch to my shoulder, where his fingers sought out the tense muscles there and worked them over.

"Anything else?" Colton asked, pen hovering over the notebook.

I couldn't help but feel like I'd forgotten something.

I racked my brain, but couldn't quite put a finger on what was prompting that feeling. "No," I said finally.

"Has anyone been causing you problems?" he asked.

I almost said no. "I went on a date with this guy. His name is Dean Zook. I mean, I don't think he's a psycho, but he's kind of persistent." I dared a quick peek at Reece when he stiffened. "And there's Henry Williams. He came to the bar Friday night, but Nick ran him off."

Colton scribbled down those names. "I've got Henry's info. Is Dean's on your phone?"

I nodded. "If it's not them, do you think this is related to what's been happening?"

He glanced at Reece before he answered. "Right now, there's no way to be sure. I've got to do some interviews with the vics, but as far as I know, they haven't reported anything like this."

"I'm not sure if I should be relieved by that or not," I admitted.

"No matter what, you're safe." Reece slid his hand through my hair, curving his fingers along the nape of my neck. My gaze met his. "I'll make sure of that."

"Even if it doesn't have anything to do with the serial rapist, what's happening can't be taken lightly." Colton slipped the notebook into his jacket as I sucked in a harsh breath. He'd said it. A serial rapist was here, targeting women. My stomach twisted. "Someone is obviously stalking you, Roxy. They've been doing it for a while, and taking that picture . . ."

"Means the fucker behind this is escalating." Reece withdrew his hand and rocked forward. His eyes were like chips of ice. "Before, he was doing things that didn't really alert you to his presence. Now he is."

"Agreed," said Colton. His eyes, which were so much like his brother's, met mine. "This is serious, Roxy."

"I know. Not like I don't think it is. Trust me."

Reece arched a brow. "Then you will have no problem with the fact you can't stay at your apartment. Not until we find out who is behind this."

I opened my mouth.

"The only way that apartment is safe for you is if we nail those windows shut, which would be a stupid as fuck idea," Reece explained. "And if there's a fire, you're screwed if you're in one of the bedrooms and trapped."

"What about a security system?" I asked, glancing between the brothers. "They aren't as expensive as before."

"You're right on the monthly charges, but the install and all the window and door sensors is where they get you," Colton advised.

Frustrated, I twisted toward Reece, my eyes wide. "I cannot be run out of my home, Reece. I can't deal with that."

His jaw clenched. "You're going to have to deal with it, babe. I want you safe. I'm not going to argue about it. It'll be temporary. We know a guy who can probably cut us a deal on the install."

Colton nodded. "He's a city cop down in Philadelphia. I know he'll do it. He owes us, but it may take a week or two. We'll be on his schedule and I know for sure he's got his kid next weekend."

Beggars can't be choosers. "Okay. I guess I can stay with Katie or my parents until then."

Reece tilted his head to the side. "Babe, you can stay with me. Nope, I can see your head working and your mouth is about to start working—"

My eyes narrowed.

"—You'll be safe here. No doubt about that, and I'm sure you'd rather be here than with your parents or Katie, because both of them live a hell of a lot further away from Mona's." He grinned at me. "Plus, I'm just better company."

"Debatable," muttered Colton.

That went ignored. "And I'll be more fun," Reece added.

Pink crept across my cheeks as I bit down on my lip, looking away. I totally got what he meant. Yeah, he'd be a hell of a lot more fun, but . . .

"Can you give us a moment?" Reece said to his brother.

"Sure." Colton sighed as he stood. "I've got to be going anyway. As soon as we hear anything back on your phone or learn anything else, you two will be the first to know." He started for the door, then stopped and looked at me. "You should stay with my brother. I'm not saying that because he's good company. He leaves wet towels on the floor, but I'll sleep better knowing you are with him."

As Colton left, I glanced at Reece. "You leave wet towels on the floor?"

He actually looked sheepish. "Maybe. Sometimes."

I cocked a brow.

"Okay. After every shower, but for you, I'll pick up the towels," he offered.

"I don't know. Wet towels are gross."

He chuckled, but the humor fled when his eyes met mine. "I know it seems like a huge step with you staying with me, but it's temporary, babe."

I got that, but staying with him felt like a slippery slope into . . . well, a lot of things. I was all about starting over with him. I was all about the friendship and the sex. I was even cool with dating him, but I wanted to keep all the chambers of my heart out of it, because I knew . . .

I knew I could lose him and that terrified me.

But he was right. Staying with my parents would be a major pain and staying with Katie would probably be a train wreck of crazy. The fun kind, but also the kind where you ended the night with a trip to jail.

God, I was stupid, but I found myself nodding nonetheless.

I managed to hold off on telling my parents what was going on, which was great news. I knew they'd freak, rightfully so, but I also had a long shift ahead of me and way too much going on in my head. Since I had to get to the bar and Reece needed to work, we really didn't have time for that conversation, so that meant that was how I'd be spending my Sunday. With my car still over at my apartment, Reece drove me to work in his car.

And that was different.

Not including my brothers, I'd never been driven to work by a guy before. Getting out of the car had also been a new experience for me. I'd wiggled my fingers at Reece and thanked him.

That hadn't been sufficient.

"Whoa." He'd caught my arm before I could step out of the truck. "Where do you think you're going?"

"Um? To work?"

"Not like that."

Confused, I'd opened my mouth to ask for a little more detail, but then he'd tugged me toward me. "We don't say good-bye to one another," he'd claimed. "We kiss."

And we did.

He'd tilted his head, lining up his mouth with mine. A heartbeat full of sweet anticipation had passed and then he brushed his lips across mine. Sweet and quick, I had thought that was all, but I'd been mistaken. Then he really kissed me, hot and rough. The kiss sent my blood boiling and blistered my skin. He kissed me like he thought he might never be able to do it again, and that kiss left me drowning in Reece, in his taste and in his warmth.

I'd stumbled out of that truck and walked into Mona's in a daze. Hours later, and my lips were still tingling from that scorching kiss.

Working tonight was definitely a lot different from the previous couple of days. My chatting with customers came more easily, my smiles became more sincere, and that meant my tips were through the roof.

Which was great, since it looked like I'd be adding another monthly bill to the expense list. It sucked but was necessary.

During a lull in customers, Nick pulled me to the back of the bar, in front of the displayed bottles. "Hey, I wanted to make sure you're not staying at your place tonight."

"I'm not," I assured him.

His expression was unreadable. "Reece's?"

"How did you guess?"

He shot me a bland look. Totally read that. "I'm psychic. Instead of falling off a stripper pole, I hit my head on a liquor bottle."

Laughing, I smacked his arm. "Shut up."

His lips twitched. "Seriously. I'm glad to hear you're

not staying there." He glanced at the customers sitting at the bar. "You doing okay?"

Truthfully, I wasn't allowing myself to think about the fact I had a legit stalker. If I let myself focus on it, I'd drive myself crazy. I'd end up rocking in a corner. "Yeah," I told him. "I'm okay as I can be."

He studied me for a moment. "If you need anything, you let me know, all right?"

"Okay." Affection for Nick rose, and I didn't think before I acted. Springing forward, I wrapped my arms around his waist. He stiffened like someone had dropped cement down his spine, but I squeezed him tight, ignoring the awkwardness of the hug. "Thank you for last night. Thank you . . . thanks for caring."

His arms came around me and he awkwardly patted my back. "Uh, it's no big deal."

"It's totally a biggie," I told him and then pulled back. Looking up at him, I smiled. "You're a really good guy even though you have questionable dating practices."

He grinned then, before turning to a guy who'd shimmied up against the bar. "Keep that knowledge to yourself."

The rest of the night flew by and when it came time for Reece to arrive for my pickup, there was a nervous excitement that felt like a nest of hungry butterflies had erupted in my stomach.

Reece was pulling into the parking lot as Nick and I were finishing locking up. He nodded at Nick, which earned him a weird manly nod back in greeting. I didn't get dudes sometimes. Why couldn't they just say hi to one another like normal people?

Climbing into the cruiser, I was greeted with a bag from Subway. "Roast beef for you, turkey club for me," he explained, shifting the car into drive. "Figured you'd be hungry."

"Thank you." I held the bag close. "That's really thoughtful."

I got the manly nod thing in return.

Glancing out the window, I watched the bar fade away in the night. A thought occurred to me. "Will you get in trouble for picking me up in your cruiser?" I didn't know the rules, but I figured it was a valid question.

He shrugged. "I'm on lunch, so it's really not like I'm going out of my way, and I'm in the county, so whatever."

"But you could get in trouble?" I asked again, worried.

"I won't," he assured me, grinning slightly. "How was work?"

"It went by fast. I think Clyde is coming back next week, so I'm sure Sherwood will be happy to have him back."

"That's good. No one makes old bay wings quite like Clyde does."

It was different to be talking about how my day went with someone—with Reece. It was all so very intimate. It also felt . . . real. I liked the idle, needless chat as we got back to his condo and ate our subs.

"I've never done this," I blurted out as I rolled up my wrapper.

Reece, who was sitting in the chair opposite me, leaned back. His dark blue uniform stretched across his shoulders. "Done what? Eaten subs at three in the morning?"

"Ha. I've done that more than I can count." Standing, I gathered up our trash and walked it into the kitchen. "This. I haven't really talked to a guy about what it was like at work." I was glad for the low light, because I could feel my cheeks burning. "I mean, the guys I dated—we talked, but it wasn't like this."

"It was superficial?" he asked.

I glanced over my shoulder, my gaze gliding over the smooth, angular cheeks and then my stare lingered on the handle of the gun, a frank reminder of how dangerous his life was. How incredibly short it could be. Knocking those thoughts out of my head, I dragged my gaze back to his face. "Yeah, that's the right word for it."

Turning back around, I bit down on my lip. That really was the truth. Things were truly superficial when it came down to the guys I'd dated. I searched out the trash can and disposed of the trash. When I straightened, I swallowed a gasp of surprise. Reece was behind me. I hadn't even heard him move. "Good God, can you teleport or something?"

Crowding me in the most welcome way possible, he placed his hands against the counter on either side of me. The warmth against my back sent a wave of awareness through me. He chuckled deeply. "Did you see where scientists were able to teleport an atom successfully?"

Mouth dry, I shook my head. "Nope."

"Yep." He moved one hand from the counter and brushed my hair to one side, exposing my neck. "Before you know it, we'll be beaming ourselves everywhere."

My skin heated as I felt his breath on the side of my neck, sending my pulse fluttering. "If you had a choice between teleporting and flying, what would you choose?"

"Such a weird question." He laughed again, and I grinned. "I'd teleport myself."

"Really?" I shivered when I felt his finger drift down the side of my neck. "Because if you teleported, you could end up with your arm sticking out of your head. So it's like you're choosing a ninety-nine percent chance of dying horrifically versus a one percent chance of dying."

"I hate flying." He moved his finger along the line of my jaw. "I do it when I have to, but that's about it."

My eyes drifted shut. "I love flying."

"You're not human," he murmured, pressing a kiss against my pulse point. "I still have some time left on lunch." He caught the lobe of my ear between his teeth. I gasped at the electric shock that pulsed through me. "And I want dessert."

As cliché as that sounded it was still incredibly hot.

"It's really all I've been thinking about." He slid his hand down my throat, to my breast. My nipples immediately beaded in response as he smoothed his fingers over the tip. "It's fucking distracting as hell, how bad I want you."

A hot shiver hit me. "Sorry?"

He nipped at my skin. "Oh, you should feel sorry. I've been hard as a rock all night long."

"That's got to make for some awkward traffic stops."

"Listen to you." He caught my nipple between his thumb and finger, and even through the clothes, the sharp slice of pleasure shot straight to my core. "I want you, Roxy."

"You have me," I breathed the words before I could think better of them, because they hung between us like a promise, like a key that unlocked something deep inside of Reece.

Stepping back, he gripped the hem of my shirt and lifted it up. Cool air wisped over my flushed skin as I looked over my shoulder at him. His face was shadowed, but the features were intent. Another thrill hummed through me when he reached for the button on my jeans. I kicked off my sandals as he peeled the jeans off.

He paused, kissing the spot between my shoulder blades, and then smoothed his hands up the sides of my legs as he rose, stopping long enough to press a kiss at the base of my spine.

"Reece," I whispered.

"Yes?" Those hands dragged up to my waist.

"What are you up to?"

The tips of his fingers toyed with the strap of my thong as he leaned his hips against me. I could feel the hardness against my back. "What does it feel like?" He didn't give me much of a chance to answer, because he glided one hand down my belly, under the skimpy panties. He cupped me. "In case you need a helpful hint. You said you were mine. I'm acting on that."

Oh God, he totally was acting on that. He slid a finger inside me, where I literally throbbed for him, gliding through the wetness. My hips jerked as he brushed against the spot I thought only my trusty vibrator knew the location of. His thumb circled the bundle of nerves with exquisite skill. I surged against his hand shamelessly, my body completely taking over.

He ground his hips as he continued to work me with his fingers. "I could come just with you riding my hand."

My body burned at his words. There was something truly hedonistic about this, raw and new to me. And I was so close to exploding, so much so that when he pulled his hand away, I whimpered.

Then I heard the heavy sound of his equipment belt

hitting the floor, the tinny sound of the zipper. My heart pounded. "Hurry," I urged him.

He kissed my shoulder as his arm circled my waist. "Babe, if I hurry any faster, this will be over before I get inside you."

I reached down to tug my panties off, but he stopped me. "Leave them on," he ordered. "And put those hands on the counter. Keep them there."

Surprised and turned on way too much, I placed my hands over the countertop, biting back a moan. I kind of—okay, I really did—like when he got all bossy like this.

Using his foot, he spread my legs while he blazed a path of hot kisses down the side of my neck. Then he lifted me onto the tips of my toes, pushing my front down across the counter.

"Stay right there," he said. I shuddered as I heard foil ripping. There was a pause and then he smoothed his hands over my bottom, kneading the flesh. I cried out as he yanked the thin strip of material to the side. "I wish you could see yourself right now. So fucking beautiful, Roxy."

I closed my eyes, letting the words wash over me. In this moment, I never believed the words more than I did now.

"Oh God," I panted, feeling him between my legs. His arm circled my waist again and he lifted me up until my toes barely touched the ground.

There was something irrevocably sensual about having sex still somewhat dressed and oddly, I felt more exposed than I ever did while naked. Those thoughts fled quickly as he rocked his hips against my rear, stopping as he slid in maybe an inch.

Then he slammed his hips forward, entering me

swiftly and deeply, going as far I could take him. He surged inside me, forcing a scream of unfettered pleasure out of me.

"Hell, you're so tight," he said, sealing us together. "This way isn't hurting you, is it?"

"No. No way. Not at all." I swiveled my hips just in case he missed the point, and when he groaned, I did it again. "Please, Reece, I need it."

"No." He withdrew his hips, pulling out until only the head remained in. "This isn't what you need."

"Yes, it is. Like for real."

He rocked those powerful hips, hitting that spot. "You need me. Not just my cock. Me."

I wanted to scream my denial, but those words died on my tongue like ash. He pulled me back against him, forcing my weight onto my arms. His hand balled into my hair, twisting it until my head turned to the side. The kiss was hot and aggressive, enough to get me right to the edge and he knew it.

Stretched as I was and because of the height difference, I couldn't move. Not even when he began to thrust fast and deep, setting a pace that pushed me to my limits. The hand in my hair let go and moved between my thighs.

"That's it," he urged, doing something truly shattering with his fingers at the juncture of my thighs. "Come for me."

His deep thrusts, his words, and what he was doing with his hand sent me flying over the edge. Crying out, I reached up and over, dragging my fingers through the soft brush of his hair. The release rolled through me, one tumultuous wave after another. It was like every nerve ending had fired at once. My body trembled with the force, the beauty of it.

"God, I feel you coming," he breathed. "It's fucking perfect. You're perfect."

I was boneless as he guided me down so I was bent over the counter once more. My fingers slipped over the granite as I rested my weight on my forearms. I looked over my shoulder at him. Through a mess of my hair, I saw his striking face strained, jaw locked tight.

Reece was beautiful.

"I can't hold back any longer," he said, voice strangled.

A shiver whipped its way down my spine. "Don't."

He gripped my waist and he didn't hold back. My hips hit the counter, and he was wild as he pushed into me. My muscles clenched and before I knew it, those tiny shivery aftershocks exploded into another release that wringed a sharp cry out of me.

Reece curved his body over mine, his hips pumping once more, and then he shouted hoarsely. I rested my cheek against the cool countertop, eyes closed as I panted. The roll of his hips slowed as his lips pressed against the corner of mine.

"That's the best damn dessert I've ever had," he whispered. "I'm thinking this is going to be a requirement after every meal."

"Mmm," I murmured. It was all I was capable of.

"Though I'm not sure that's a good idea." He kissed my cheek. "You might not be able to walk if we kept this up."

So true.

Reece eased out of me and disposed of the condom. I didn't move while he tucked himself away and zipped up his pants. I was just a puddle of postcoital bliss as he turned me around and gathered me close against his chest.

He kissed me softly and it was such a beautiful, tender kiss. Brushing my hair back from my face, he moved that sweet kiss to my brow. "You should get some rest. In my bed, not that damn couch. We have a big day tomorrow."

"We do?" I looked up at him.

"Yeah." His features softened, and it pulled at my heart and it made me think crazy things like forever. "Tomorrow we talk to your parents."

Chapter 20

For some reason, I hadn't really thought about the fact that Reece would be with me when I went to talk to my parents. I don't know why, but I guess it was because I don't think I ever really went to my parents' house to discuss anything with a guy tagging along.

Well, I'd brought home a guy once, and that had honestly been by accident. I was nineteen, and I'd just been at their house before a date when I realized I'd left my wallet and ID on their kitchen table. After meeting up with the guy, we had to go back and retrieve it. My entire family seemed to have been in attendance, and the poor dude never made it to another date after that.

I somehow doubted Reece would get the third degree from anyone, though. Knowing my parents, they'd roll out the red carpet for him.

We stopped at my apartment beforehand. Reece insisted that he enter first, and I waited just inside the door while he scoped things out. Returning to where I stood, he said, "Everything looks good to me. Do you need help getting anything?"

"No. Thank you."

Leaving Reece to putter around the living area, I made my way back to my bedroom. I couldn't suppress the chill that snaked down my spine when I looked around, my gaze settling on the messy bed, covers thrown to the side during my hasty departure and remaining the way I'd left them.

I started the surprisingly painful process of gathering up enough clothes and bath items to get me through a week or so. I wiped at a stupid tear that had snuck free. This was supposed to be a place of comfort and safety for me, not one of fear and paranoia.

When I left the bathroom, Reece was sitting on the edge of the bed. He took one look at me and rose smoothly. "You okay?"

"Of course." My damn voice cracked.

Doubt crossed his stunning features. He didn't say anything as I shoved my travel bag into a suitcase I'd loaded up with clothes. Forcing a smile, I zipped up the suitcase. "That should be all."

He tilted his head to the side. "Remember what I told you?"

"You tell me a lot of things. I don't always pay attention," I teased.

A brow rose. "It's okay to not feel all right about any of this."

"You're such a shrink. You sure you're in the right profession?"

"Don't give me any lip. I'll turn you over my knee." His eyes darkened to a cobalt blue. "Actually that sounds like a fantastic idea."

Yeah, it kind of did. I wondered if he'd order me to stay still when he did? That made me hot.

He groaned as he stepped forward, curving his hand around my jaw. "I can read your face like an open book." His voice dropped low, was husky. "You'd like that."

I closed my eyes, swayed by the deep timbre of his voice. "Maybe."

"There's no maybe. You would. Just like you liked it in the kitchen."

"What time is it?" I asked. "Because I think we have time to test out this theory before we go to my parents' house."

Reece tipped his head back and laughed. "Babe, the only times I've been in you have been too fast. The next time I strip you down, I want to take my time with you."

Oh, that hit me in the lady bits.

He swooped down, kissing me quickly before grabbing my suitcase. Sighing, I headed out of the room and grabbed my laptop from the living room. I didn't let myself look back as I left my apartment.

"Do you know if Colton got ahold of the guy who can hook up the security in my place?" I asked, locking the door behind us.

"What? You're done staying with me already?"

I grinned at the light tone. "Yes."

"My heart. You broke it." Waiting for me to step off the porch, he then started for where his truck was parked. "I don't know, but I'll check in with him today and see about your phone. But your spare is working, right?"

"Yep."

Reece opened the truck door for me, and took my bags, stacking them neatly in the space behind the seats.

As he stepped aside, he straightened my glasses and then dipped down, pressing his lips against my cheek. A huge part of me wanted to giggle like a little girl, because there was something so cute about being kissed on the cheek, but I managed to hold it together as he pulled away and loped around the front of his truck.

Turning around, I glanced in the back and then did a double take. At first, I didn't believe what I was seeing. Peering into the back, I froze. Tucked behind the seat, carefully stowed away, were my easel, blank canvas, and my paints, all packed up. I couldn't move as I stared at the items. I hadn't even heard him go in and out of the house, let alone into my extra bedroom, but he . . .

He packed up my paints!

Lifting my gaze, I found him behind the wheel. He was looking at me strangely, and I had no idea what the expression on my face said, but probably spelled crazy. "What?" he asked.

"You thought of my paints," I whispered.

He glanced to the back and then at me. "Yeah. I figured you'd want them. I have room in the guest bedroom for them."

I thought about what he said last night, about me needing him, and I sucked in a shallow breath. I don't even know why I thought about that, but needing him meant that I had way strong feelings for him again, which also meant that if I lost him, I'd be in a world of hurting. And connecting all of that together felt crazy, with an extra side of crazy sauce.

But he packed up my paints!

Standing outside the truck, all I could do was stare at him like a doofus until one side of his lips tipped up. "Babe, you going to get in this truck or not?"

I gripped the door, feeling my heart expand in my chest until there was a good chance it would burst from what seemed like not a big deal to Reece, but it was to me.

He chuckled that smooth, deep laugh. "Roxy?"

"I'm going to get in the truck," I told him.

A brow arched after a moment. "Anytime this year?"

"I'm taking my time." I flushed, because I knew I looked stupid. "Don't want to pull a muscle climbing into this monster. I need a freaking ladder to get into this thing."

Reece laughed while I made a face at him. Finally, I stopped acting weird and got in. As I was buckling up, he asked, "Who's that?"

I looked out the window as Kip crossed the front porch of the Victorian, the vestibule door swinging shut behind him. "Oh, that's Kip. I can't remember his last name, but he's the guy who moved in upstairs."

"Huh."

Kip looked up, and I lifted my hand, giving him a jaunty wave, which was returned with a little less enthusiasm.

Adjusting the seat belt strap so it wasn't choking me, I looked at Reece as he pulled away from the curb. His gaze flicked to the rearview mirror and then over to me. He winked. I narrowed my eyes at him. He laughed, and now my lips were twitching. Something about the way he smiled and the sound of his laugh was infectious. I leaned my head back against the seat. There was just something about him.

You need me.

The words floated through my thoughts and even though I wanted to ignore them, they didn't offend me and I didn't take them as a symbol of me being weak, a woman needing a man or any kind of crap like that. It meant something far deeper than that, something I wasn't sure I was ready to delve into.

"Thank you," I said.

He glanced at me quickly. "For what? The orgasms I gave you last night?"

I laughed. "Yeah, well, thanks for that, but that wasn't what I was referencing. It's for the paints. That was really thoughtful of you."

"That's me. Mr. Thoughtful."

Shaking my head, I fixed my glasses as they started to slip. "You're also Mr. Arrogant."

"It's called being well rounded."

I let go of a very unattractive snort. "Keep telling yourself that."

By the time we reached my parents' house I'd almost forgotten why we were going there. The insults we'd tossed back and forth on the way there had me thoroughly and happily distracted, but when we pulled in behind my older brother's black Volkswagen sedan, I wanted to crawl under the truck seat. Of course it couldn't just be my parents. Oh no, it was Murphy's Law at its finest.

Reece grinned as he glanced at me. "Want to make a bet?"

"That by the end of this visit I'm going to want to toss myself under a train?" I unbuckled myself.

Skin crinkling around his eyes, he laughed. "No. That your mom welcomes me to the family by the end of the visit."

"God," I groaned, shaking my head. "I am not making the bet, because she totally will. She'll probably start making booties for the nonexistent baby."

He laughed again, and that right there made him all kinds of awesome all over again. Most guy's would break about a dozen laws to get away from a marriage- and baby-obsessed mom. I'd never tell him that though.

Sighing, I forced myself out of the truck and we didn't even make it across all the flagstones before the front door flew open and my mom barreled out, her eyes wide as they darted from me to Reece to me and back again.

I swallowed a curse.

Mom stopped at the edge of the porch, clapping her hands together. Literally. She actually clapped. "Honey," she said, smiling so widely that I thought her face might split into two. "Are you about to make your momma proud?"

"Oh my God," I moaned.

Reece laughed under his breath as he stepped around me and climbed the steps. Before he could say or do anything, Mom enveloped him in a hug I knew could kind of be painful and dizzying, because when Mom hugged excitedly, it involved a lot of squeezing and swaying side to side.

"Mom," I said, sighing. "Reece probably can't breathe."

"Shush it," she replied. "It's not often I get to hug a good-looking young man that's not my son."

"Oh dear God," I muttered.

Reece's laughing didn't help, but when he was finally able to pull away, he glanced over his shoulder at me and winked. I shot him a look as I came up the stairs, but he spoke before I could. "I have a feeling my girl is about to make you proud."

My mouth dropped open.

"My girl? Oh!" Mom flapped her hands in front of her face as she called for my dad. "Best news I've heard all—"

"*Mom*." I was going to hurt them both. "That is not why we came here and—"

"Don't ruin this for me." She turned as I rolled my eyes. Dad was at the front door, brows raised. "Wit, you're not going to believe this! Reece called our baby girl his girl!"

"Okay," Dad drew the word out, then nodded at Reece. "It's about time, son."

As I passed Reece on the steps, I shoved my elbow into his stomach, nice and hard, too. He grunted, and that gave me a measure of satisfaction.

Mom looked close to tears as she buzzed around the porch, almost knocking off the colorful purple and orange mums. She stopped, spinning toward Reece. "I have to call your mom. We need—"

"Oh for the love of God." I threw up my hands. "Someone broke into my apartment in the middle of the night and took a picture of me while I was sleeping and I'm probably being stalked. That's why I'm here!"

Both of my parents stared at me.

"Nice way to break that to them," Reece said dryly under his breath.

Dad turned to me, letting the door swing shut with a slam behind him. "What?"

I wanted to throw myself down on the porch and flail like a toddler having an epic meltdown.

Reece placed his hand on my lower back. "Why don't we head inside and talk? We'll tell you guys what's been happening."

And that's what we did, except before we could get the story out, Gordon and his wife, who were in the kitchen making meatballs, assumed that Reece and I were moving in together tomorrow, getting married next week, and popping out a baby before Megan was even due.

Megan was sitting at the oak table, my brother standing near the island. I had no idea how they were working together like that. Gordon had the meat. Megan had the eggs and the bread. There was a good five feet or so between the island and the table. Trying to figure it out made my brain hurt.

My brother was stocky like my dad and he inherited the crappy vision from our mom. However, his wire-frame glasses seemed to never slip down his nose like mine. Gordon grinned in a way that told me he was about to say something that was going to embarrass me. "Did you know she's had a crush on you since she was fifteen?"

"Honey," said Megan, shaking her head.

Reece smiled. "Oh, I know."

"Everybody knew," Gordon tacked on. "I'm pretty sure she sketched a picture of you on the wall in her bedroom, and Dad had to paint—"

"*Gordon!* Shut up!" I screeched.

Dad entered the kitchen. "Yeah, Gordon, shut up. Someone has been messing with your baby sister."

Gordon lifted hamburger-covered hands from the bowl and his look turned serious in a nanosecond. "What?"

I plopped down at the table, across from Megan, figuring I needed to sit through this conversation. Between Reece and me, we told them everything. Well, almost everything. I left out the undies in the dishwasher thing, because seriously, I didn't need to share that with my parents, and I also didn't tell them about the wild monkey sex for obvious reasons.

As expected, my mom freaked out and then got

angry, really angry. "How dare someone do this to my daughter!" She slammed her fist on the table, rattling the little bowls of food, and then twisted toward Gordon. "You still got that shotgun? Wait." She held up a hand, glancing at Reece. "Earmuffs, boy. Because I'm about to suggest some laws be broken."

Reece clamped his mouth shut.

"Mom," I protested weakly.

That went largely ignored. "You still have that shotgun, right? You go and stay a night at her place and if someone comes in that door, you—"

"Mrs. Arks, I don't think that's a wise idea. I think Gordon wants to be home for when his first child is born," Reece interjected wisely. "Roxy is safe, and right now, that's what matters."

"What matters is you all catch this sick SOB." Dad's arms were tensed, folded across his chest as Reece explained everything that was being done. The cell phone was being searched for prints. My apartment would be wired with an alarm system. I'd be staying with Reece until that was done.

It took a while to calm down my parents and brother. Not that I blamed them for their reactions. They loved me and were worried about me, and I didn't want them to be afraid—and I didn't want to be afraid of a nameless, faceless freak.

Maybe an hour or so passed, the scent of garlic and meat filling the air, when Mom invited us to join them for their weekly Sunday spaghetti dinner, and when I glanced at Reece, he nodded and I felt that stupid fluttering in my belly, like a nest of butterflies were going to gnaw their way out. As I got up to help get the plates, I realized we were missing someone.

"Where's Thomas?" I asked, placing the stack of plates on the table.

Dad grabbed a beer out of the fridge. "Oh, he's over at a friend's, worshipping Satan or whatever it is he's doing."

My brows slowly inched up my forehead as I met Megan's gaze. Grinning, she ducked her chin. "Well, that sounds like fun."

"True." Reece grinned from where he sat. "Nothing like a little satanic worship on a Sunday."

Mom smacked Dad's arm on the way back to the table. "Thomas is with his girlfriend. And they're studying."

Gordon snorted.

"Now, see what you all made me do." She lifted her hands, clad in oven mitts. "Forgot to get the garlic bread." When she had the plate out, she spun toward me and the bread shifted precariously along the baking sheet. "Oh! I almost forgot to tell you, since I didn't get over to see you yesterday, which apparently was a good thing, because I probably would be like Dog the Bounty Hunter on someone's ass right now."

Dad sighed.

I couldn't keep a straight face and giggled as I sat down next to Reece. "I'm picturing you with a blond mullet now."

"I'd make that look good." She scooped the bread into a basket. "I ran into Miss Sponsito. Remember her? She's a curator at one of the museums in the city."

Oh no. I picked up my glass. "Yes, I remember."

Thomas brought a vat of spaghetti sauce over while Mom eyed me like a shrew. "Do you also remember how I showed her some of your work?"

"How could I forget?" I glanced at my tea, wishing

it had liquor in it. Maybe even some meth at this point. Wait. Could meth be liquid? I'd have to ask Reece. But not right now, because he was eyeballing me as Dad plopped a huge pile of noodles on his plate.

Everyone sat, but Mom was like a pit bull. "She is still very interested."

"Oh," I murmured, scooping out the biggest meatball I could find. "You make the best meatballs," I told Gordon. "Have I ever told you that before?"

Gordon smiled.

"Interested in what?" Reece asked.

"Nothing," was my immediate response.

Mom shot me a chiding look. "I showed Miss Sponsito several of Roxy's paintings a couple of months back. She's interested in commissioning pieces. You know," she said, looking at me. "You'd get paid doing something you love. Fancy idea. But Roxy hasn't taken them up on it yet."

I made a face as I twirled my spaghetti and then almost shrieked as a hand landed on my thigh. Looking at Reece, I raised my brows. He narrowed his eyes. "Why haven't you done that?"

Good question. No easy answer. I shrugged. "I haven't had time. I feel like . . . I need to give her something new, something great."

"That's why you should drop those damn classes," Dad said, stabbing at his noodles.

"Dad, I'm trying to get an education. Isn't that something every parent wants their kid to get?" I asked.

"Every parent wants their kid to be happy," he corrected. "And you're not going to be happy with some graphic design degree."

I drew in a deep breath. "I am happy."

No one looked like they believed me, and boy, was

that kind of hard to swallow. I wanted to shout that I was happy . . . as much as I could be right now. I mean, hello, I had some dude taking pictures of me while I slept, and Henry was out, running around, a total free man, and Charlie . . .

Charlie wasn't eating again.

I was no longer hungry.

Reece watched me closely, way too intently. "Everything I've seen of yours is great."

"It's true." Megan smiled. "You did that painting for the baby's room. The one with the teddy bear? Every time I go into the room, I'm blown away by how real it looks."

"Thanks," I murmured, uncomfortable. When I glanced at Reece, I could see the wheels churning in his head. I'd rather be talking about the stalker and my undies in the dishwasher.

But then, because it was my family, the convo turned even more awkward as dinner wrapped up.

"How's your father doing?" my dad asked Reece.

I stiffened as I eyeballed him. My dad was oblivious.

"He's doing okay. On Divorce Number Five Hundred," he said nonchalantly, but I knew his father's inability to be faithful and not lie was a huge issue for him. Not a hang-up, though. If it was, he wouldn't have gotten over the fact I had lied. But still bothered him nonetheless. "Same old same old stuff, basically."

Dad cleared his throat. "Well, one of these days, I hope your father finds happiness. Everyone deserves that."

Did they? I wasn't so sure about that, but my parents were seconds away from finding a tree and hugging it. It was when I was helping Mom clean up the table and Reece had disappeared into the den with Dad, my brother, and Megan, that I was completely cornered by her and the expansion of her grandmamma dreams.

"Are you two stopping by and seeing his mother before you head back?" she asked as she loaded up the dishwasher.

Wait. Were we? I hadn't even thought about that. I wasn't sure I could do Round Two. "I don't know."

She took the plates I handed her after rinsing them off. A moment passed. "What is going on between you two? And don't tell me you don't know. Last time we were chatting about your relationship status, he wasn't in the picture, and now he is."

I opened my mouth.

Mom went on. "And I know your brother was giving you a hard time." She twisted at the waist, looking me straight in the eye. "But, honey, everyone knows you've been in lov—"

"We're dating," I cut her off before she could finish. "Okay? I guess that's what we're doing. It's nothing serious. Okay? I'm not fifteen anymore."

She arched a brow.

And I wasn't drawing sketches of him on my wall. I was *painting* his face now. Ugh. Walking away from Mom, I snatched up the rest of the silverware and separated the pieces into their cubbies.

"Honey." Mom touched my arm. "I'm worried about you."

Straightening, I leaned against the sink and kept my voice low. "Because of Reece?"

She smiled, but it was a pang to the chest, because it was so sad. "Yes. Because I know you've cared strongly for him for years, and he's here, with you. That boy is here, and you're acting like it's nothing?"

"Mom—"

A hand came up, silencing me. "And you still won't try this museum thing? Now, on top of it, there's some man breaking into your apartment? That has nothing to do with the first two things and it has nothing to do with what I'm about to say to you now. It's time to have a come-to-Jesus conversation."

Oh no.

"Just because Charlie is stuck to that bed doesn't mean you don't get to live your life to the fullest."

I drew back as if she'd slapped me. "What?"

"Honey, your father and I know you are carrying a lot of guilt and that you—"

"Roxy?" Reece came into the kitchen, my father and brother right behind him. By the murderous look on all three of their faces, my heart immediately sank.

"What's wrong?" I asked.

"We need to go back to your place," he said, and as he walked toward me, his eyes never left my face. "Your apartment was broken into."

Chapter 21

On the way back to my apartment I was in a state of suspended disbelief. We'd just been there a few hours ago. How could someone break in by nightfall? Well, it didn't take a long period of time to do so, but still. I just couldn't believe it, especially after what had just happened.

Dad and my brother followed us, and when we arrived, there was a police cruiser in front of the Victorian. So was a familiar mustang—cherry red.

"Roxy!" Reece shouted as he coasted into park.

But I'd already had the truck door open and sprung out of the truck, his curse haunting my steps as I entered the courtyard of the Victorian. I caught a glimpse of Kip standing on the porch, along with James's fiancée, but I was focused on one person.

Henry Williams stood there at the steps, talking to an officer. He turned as I approached him, his eyes widening. "Roxy—

"It's you! Isn't it? You were in my place while I slept

and then you come back, and break in?" My hands balled into fists. It suddenly made so much sense to me. What was happening to me had nothing to do with the other girls. Nothing weird started happening until Henry got out of jail. "How are you getting in my place?"

He shook his head as he backed up, looking between the officer and me. "I swear I had nothing to do with this. I didn't break into your place. I don't even know what you're—"

"You're a sick fuck!" I shouted. "What is wrong with you? Why—"

"Whoa." An arm circled my waist, and the next thing I knew, I was facing the street as my dad and brother passed us. Reece spoke in my ear. "You need to calm down, Roxy. We don't know if he—"

"Who else would do it?" I shouted, wanting to swing my elbow into his stomach again. I couldn't deal if Reece defended him. To me, it was so obvious. I wiggled around so I was facing Henry again. "Why else would you be here?"

"I came over to talk to you, but when I knocked on your front door, it opened and I saw the inside of your place. I called the police."

"Oh, that's such bullshit," I spat.

"Roxy," Reece warned softly.

"He did call us," the officer confirmed. "And he claims he didn't go all the way in. We also spoke to the gentleman on the porch. He didn't hear anything suspicious, but had left the house for a few hours."

It was then when I realized my dad and brother had gone into my place and had returned. Dad came down the steps, his cheeks flushed with anger. "I don't want her seeing that."

Now, of course I *had* to see it. "Let me go." When Reece didn't, I felt that I was seconds from my head spinning right off, *Exorcist* style. "Let me go, Reece. I mean it."

"Listen to me, honey. Let Reece and me handle this," Dad reasoned with his hands planted on his hips. "Gordon will take you back to our place or to Reece's, but you really don't want to see in there. Not right now."

"What I want is to be put down and I want to see what happened inside *my* place," I said, barely in control. "I am not fifteen years old. I'm a freaking adult. Seriously."

Dad looked away, scrunching his fingers through his hair. Then he turned to my brother, who looked just as furious as I felt, and said something too low for me to hear.

"You're not going to hit anyone, are you?" Reece asked. "If I let go?"

Henry cast his gaze to the ground while I sneered. "Only if you don't let me go."

"Be nice," he ordered right before he loosened his hold.

I slipped free, stalking around my dad and dodging my brother's hand as I climbed the steps.

"You might want to wait," Kip suggested from where he stood in front of the Silvers' door. He stepped toward me, but stopped when Reece jogged up the porch steps.

I stepped inside my apartment and then came to a complete standstill. My eyes had to be messing with me. There was no way this was my place. No way was my apartment full of police taking pics and dusting for prints.

The TV had been knocked to the floor, the screen

shattered in large shards. The coffee table and end stand, both hand painted by me, looked like someone had gone Hulk on them, smashing the secondhand pieces until the legs were broken off. Both the couch and the recliner were flipped upside down. From where I stood, I could see that my small kitchen set was in one piece but also knocked over.

My heart pounded as anger pumped through me. Hands clenched, I headed down the hall. The bedroom was a mess. The comforter and sheets stripped, piled on the floor. All my bottles of lotion and perfume were scattered.

Spinning around, I almost knocked into Reece. He reached for me, but I sidestepped him and walked into my studio.

My heart broke.

"Oh my God," I whispered, pressing the palm of my hand against my chest as I stared into the room.

Thank God Reece had taken my easel and canvas earlier, along with my paints, because everything else in the room had been utterly destroyed. All of the paintings I'd done, even the ones of Reece I'd hidden in the closet, were torn into unrecognizable shreds. It was like rage had exploded in the room.

I shuddered. "My . . . all my stuff."

"I'm sorry." Reece came up behind me, wrapping an arm under my chest and drawing me to his front. His other arm came around, securing me against him. "I wish there was something I could say that could make this better for you."

Part of me wanted to pull away and start kicking stuff. "I don't understand."

His embrace tightened and for a few moments, he just held me and that . . . that helped more than I thought it could, but I thought about who was waiting outside. "It has to be Henry." Anger resurfaced, pushing away the horror and the numbness of seeing my things destroyed. I turned in his arms, meeting his gaze. "It has to be him. Who else?"

He wet his bottom lip. "Roxy—"

"Are you seriously going to defend him? For real? I mean, none of this stuff happened until he conveniently shows up. Then he's here, innocently knocks on my door and finds it already open? I mean, come on."

Reece dropped his arms. "I really don't think it's him."

Shaking my head, I stepped away. "It's obvious!"

"Why would he break into your place and then call the police?" he threw out with an even, patient voice.

"Because he's a sociopath?"

He cocked his head to the side. "Babe, the man made some shitty choices when he was a teenager and he paid for them—he's still paying for them—and I don't appreciate him showing up here unannounced, but that doesn't make him a sociopath."

My mouth dropped opened. "You're seriously defending him?"

"No. He's a jackass. Just not a sociopath."

Disbelief thundered through me.

"He's not defending what he did six years ago, honey." Dad appeared in the doorway. "He's just pointing out that it doesn't make sense for Henry to do this and then call the police."

I threw my hands up. "Did it make sense when he threw the rock and nearly killed Charlie?"

"Babe, this has nothing to do with Charlie."

I was about to spit fire. "How do you know? Maybe he—"

"I've talked to him," Reece continued, and effectively shutting me up by doing so. I gaped at him. "I've had real long talks with him."

"What?" I whispered.

Reece glanced at my dad and then his gaze settled on me. He stepped closer. Brave man, because I was pretty sure my expression said I was about to cut him. "After the first time he tried to make contact with you, I had a chat with him to make sure he wasn't going to cause you any trouble."

"Good man." My father clapped him on the shoulder, and I shot him a look. Seriously? "What?" he replied. "Reece was looking out for you."

I crossed my arms.

"By saying this, I'm not forgetting what he'd done to Charlie. Henry hasn't forgotten that either. That man is carrying around a load of guilt," Reece said, and the tone of his voice said he had a lot of experience with that. "And he isn't looking for forgiveness. He's looking to somehow make amends. Two different things, babe, and breaking into your place, messing with you like this, serves no purpose."

For a real long moment, I had no idea how to respond. Caught between fury and shock, I didn't know what to make of the sense of betrayal coursing through me. All at once I was just . . . done with it all. Exhausted to the marrow, my shoulders slumped.

I turned away, surveying the damage. "I got to clean this up."

A moment passed and Reece touched my shoulder. "We're going to talk about this later."

"Whatever," I murmured, stepping away and picking up a piece of torn canvas. Holding it close, I sucked in an unsteady breath. The blue was the same color of Reece's eyes, and I could make out the thin black lines that radiated out from the pupil. I didn't know what to think as I realized that someone had found my creepy stash of Reece paintings.

Though, whatever I felt didn't compare to how violating and scary it was knowing someone had gotten in here *again* and had done this—done something so violent and out of control.

We cleaned up as much as we could, and tomorrow, I'd have to call my insurance company. Luckily, I had renter's insurance, so it would cover what was damaged and could be replaced.

A lot of the paintings and secondhand stuff couldn't be, though, but I knew it could've been worse. Nothing had been stolen, and in the end, my place was just a mess.

Thomas offered to come back over with me tomorrow to finish up, something that Reece announced—did not ask—that he would also tag along for. I didn't protest, because the last thing I wanted was to do it by myself.

Henry had left by the time I'd stepped outside again and that was a good thing. While I'd calmed down and could see a little bit of Reece's logic, I was still fired up about the fact that he had the balls to come to my place and I wasn't entirely convinced that it hadn't been Henry. To me, it made more sense than some random guy stalking me.

It was late when we got back to Reece's condo, and I had toyed around with the idea of staying with my parents instead, but if I was going to be honest with myself—and what fun was that?—I wanted to stay with Reece.

"Want something to drink?" Reece asked, dropping

the keys on the kitchen counter. They rattled like wind chimes crashing to the floor.

"Sure."

"Tea? Soda? Beer?"

"Beer. I could use some beer."

One side of his lips turned up as he grabbed two Coronas out of the fridge and popped the tops before handing one to me. "Sorry, no lime."

"Thanks. I really don't like lime in my drinks anyway." Taking a sip, I turned away. Though it was almost midnight, I wasn't ready to sleep. Exhaling loudly, I walked over to the balcony doors. "Do you mind?"

He arched his brow. "Babe, make yourself at home."

"I always thought that was such a weird thing to say. Why would you want people to make themselves at home in your house?" I pulled the curtain back and unlocked the doors. "If people did, they'd be running around your place naked."

"If it's you, I wouldn't mind at all." He grinned over the neck of his bottle. "Actually, I'd prefer it."

"Pervert," I muttered, and then stepped out into the cool night air.

Sitting in a chair, I tucked my legs up. A couple of minutes passed before Reece joined me. He was barefoot as he kicked his legs up on the railing. I don't know why, but I thought the combination of jeans and bare feet were sexy.

There was also a good chance I just found a lot of things sexy.

We sat there in silence for a couple of moments, and I was struck by the similarity between what we were doing and what my parents did almost every night when they thought the kids were in bed.

They'd sneak outside to have a beer and some time together.

I glanced down at my bottle and toyed with the label. My heart rate kicked up a little, because this—this felt so very real and that . . . wow, that scared me.

Needing to distract myself, I asked, "Do you really think Henry has nothing to do with what's been happening?"

"Yeah, I do."

Ugh.

"I know you don't like the fact I talked to him. It wasn't like we were having drinks. I wanted to make sure you were safe from him," he explained. "And like I said, wanting to make amends doesn't make up for what he did, but isn't feeling remorse for one's own actions better than having none?"

I frowned as I mulled that over. "Yeah, I guess so."

"Guess so?"

"I mean, how do you really know if someone feels remorse? Or guilt? Or if it's just because they got caught and are in trouble?"

"You know, I saw a lot of messed-up shit when I was in the sandbox," Reece said, jarring me with the unexpected comment. "I saw what happened when someone got hit by an IED. I saw bodies of guys I considered friends riddled with bullets, some losing their legs or arms—their lives. I saw people who when it was all said and done didn't have much of anything to ship back to their families. You kind of get used to it—the anger every time your group loses someone. Doesn't make it easier, but you're at war. I guess that helps you compartmentalize the shit that's going down, what you got to do to make sure everyone survives."

He paused, taking a long swallow. "When I left the academy and started working here, I thought I could do the same. Compartmentalize the bullshit, the annoying traffic stops and the domestics at the same house every Friday, and the god-awful traffic accidents, the senseless overdoses, and dumbass-on-dumbass violence. Packed that shit away where it belongs. I was doing it. So I thought having to shoot someone would be no different from being at war or just doing my job. I was wrong."

I lowered the bottle to my lap, shocked into silence. He was talking about the shooting. Reece never talked about the shooting. I didn't dare to breathe too loudly for fear of him stopping.

"It was a normal call. A fight outside of Spades Bar and Grill. I got there at the same time as another officer did. The fight was in the parking lot, and it took us a few to make it through the crowd." He shook his head slowly. "The kid—his name was Drew Walker. Only eighteen. He was beating the shit out of an older guy. To the point that when we got there, the dude was knocked the fuck out. You know, he had a broken jaw, shattered nose, and eye. A cracked skull. That's what that kid did to him."

Reece tipped his bottle away from him, eyeing the label with a look of concentration. "He was on meth and some kind of other fucked-up drug. We yelled at him to stop and when he did . . . man, he was covered in blood. Like something straight out of a horror film. The kid had a gun. He had a gun the *entire* time. That's what he was beating the guy with. Not his fists. The handle of the Glock."

"Oh my God," I whispered. Recalling the details the press had reported on the shooting, that part had either been glossed over or never told.

He pursed his lips. "Instinct. The second he aimed that gun, it was instinct. Both of us fired, but it was my shot that killed him—my bullet from my gun that did it was what the investigation showed."

I opened my mouth, but I didn't know what to say.

"I had to go face-to-face with that boy's mom. She smacked me. Not once." He laughed, but there was no humor. "Twice. She just didn't understand. He damn near killed the guy he was beating and he was on a crazy combination of drugs. I don't blame her, though, for hating me. And she does. Still does. Always will. He was her son. I get that, but man, it's not like overseas. You don't see family members then. You aren't staring them in the eyes."

My chest ached for him—ached for the whole situation. I got the what-ifs that surrounded the incident. What if the boy hadn't been on drugs? What if he hadn't gotten into the fight? What if it had been the other officer's bullet? I'd asked myself those kinds of questions a thousand times. What if I hadn't dragged Charlie to the football game so I could catch a glimpse of Reece? What if we had decided to stay the entire game? What if I had simply walked away and not gotten into it with Henry?

"There was a lot of anger." He looked at me then and sighed. "A lot. Like why was I the one who got the call? Why was it my bullet? Did I make the right decision? Was there something else that could've been done?"

"You did what you were supposed to do," I told him, believing every single word.

A small smile appeared. "Whenever there's an officer-involved shooting, there's always an investigation. I was cleared of any wrongdoing, but that doesn't make it easier, knowing you took a life of a kid who wasn't even old enough to buy this beer I'm drinking."

He raised his bottle to that and then said, "Because doing the right thing isn't always the . . . well, the easiest thing to live with. Living with that kind of anger and guilt is a bitter combination."

Boy, didn't I know that. I took a sip of my beer. I knew there was very little I could say that would make a huge difference, but I said what I thought was true. "You are not a bad person, Reece. What you had to do was hard and he was a kid, but—"

"But it happened, babe. It was something that I had to deal with—still dealing with, so I know it when I see it."

I tensed.

"I see it when I talk to Henry. And I see it in you, but Roxy, you've got no ownership to that. You understand that?"

I nodded, mainly because it was hard to explain why I felt such guilt over Charlie. "I'm glad you talked to me about what happened," I said after a couple of moments. "I know it's not easy to talk about."

"It's not. So you know that door is two-way, right?"

I raised my brows.

"I know there's stuff you've got that isn't easy to talk about, but you need to try, and when you do, I'll be here." He pulled his feet off the railing and stood. "Want another beer?"

Blinking, I glanced down at my almost empty beer. "Sure."

As he moved to go back inside, he stopped beside me and curled his fingers under my chin. Tilting my head back, he dipped down and kissed me like he had all the time in the world. Slowly at first, just a brushing of his mouth against mine, and then deeper, parting my lips with his tongue. It wasn't just a kiss. Not when his tongue danced over mine or the way he tasted me. Reece turned kissing into an art form, and if I had to attach a color to it, to get it on canvas, it would be supple shades of reds and purples.

I was still dazed from the kiss when Reece returned with more beer. We ended up talking into the wee hours of the morning, sometimes about nothing important, and after about the third beer, the conversation got a little more serious. I might have admitted to locking my younger brother in a chest once. Then I admitted that I hated taking the design classes in college. "The guys are freaking snots to deal with," I told him. "Like you need a dick to know code or work in design, when in reality, any thirteen-year-old with a computer can design a decent website."

Reece frowned over at me. "Then why do you do it? It's a serious question."

I shrugged. "I should get a degree."

"You should do what you want."

"It is what I want."

He snorted. "Whatever."

I stuck my tongue out, and he laughed, which made me smile, because I really liked the sound of his laugh. As I watched him finish off his beer, I thought about what he shared with me tonight. It made sense why he was able to look at everything objectively when it came to Henry. Didn't mean I agreed, but I got where he was coming from.

"How did you finally let go of the anger, Reece?" I asked.

One shoulder rose. "Do you ever really let go of that? Completely? The anger and guilt? Nah. I think it cuts deep enough that it leaves scars that don't heal. You just learn how to manage before you hit rock bottom with it."

"And have . . . have you hit rock bottom with it?"

A long time passed before I realized he wasn't going to answer that question. Maybe because he didn't know the answer. Reece looked away, his jaw flexing as he stared into the woods, seemingly at nothing. Silence descended, and I knew deep down there was something he wasn't sharing with me. Something he didn't want me to know.

Chapter 22

It was a week after the break-in and I wasn't really thinking about that at the moment, because it was a little weird to be going to a cookout at Jax's place, because I felt like this was the first time Reece and I were really stepping out as . . . as something like a legit couple. I guessed that's what we actually were. We talked like we were. We had sex like we were. He had the extra key to my apartment. Mainly because if I was working when the guy wired my place, he'd be able to let him in, but whatever. We were like a couple, and that made me feel kind of stupid for being so weird about it in the first place.

But my head had been all over the place this past week. I wasn't used to being around a guy as much as I was with Reece, and I thought I'd be annoyed with the lack of space, but I wasn't. I actually missed him when he wasn't around, which was odd, because when he wasn't working, he was with me. I really liked it when Reece came home.

He was *always* very hands-on when he got off work.

And if I counted the amount of time that passed from when he hit the bed to when he was inside me, it was probably around a couple of minutes. If that. Which was also something I had a hard time wrapping my head around. With other guys, I needed foreplay, lots of foreplay. With Reece, just the feel of his skin moving against mine aroused me enough for some between-the-sheets shenanigans.

I also discovered that he hadn't been joking when he'd said he only slept a few hours here and there. There'd been a few times when he'd gotten up before me, even after falling asleep after me. On Thursday, I'd woken up to find him gone, sitting out on the balcony, his feet kicked up on the railing and his expression far away, focused on something he hadn't really been willing to share with me, but the shadows in his eyes told me it had to do with that shooting.

It still haunted him, and I hated that I had no idea how to help him with that. Or if he wanted my help. That morning, when I tried to talk to him, it had been a no-go, so I resorted to one way that I knew put that carefree smile back on his handsome face. I'd gotten on my knees between him and that balcony railing . . . and we definitely broke some public decency laws.

If my dumb nervousness was showing on the way to Jax's—which it had to be because I was as twitchy as a tweeker—Reece didn't let on that he noticed. Instead, he kept the conversation light, steering away from talk about Charlie, Henry, and the whole angry, creepy stalker dude who may or may not be Henry.

All we did know was that it wasn't Dean Zook. Colton had interviewed him after the break-in, and apparently just the sight of a detective showing up at his place had caused the guy to break out in hives. According to Colton, Dean might be persistent and rude, but he wasn't getting a stalker vibe from him and he doubted that I'd hear from Dean again.

Okay. I wasn't going to think about that—any of that. Tonight was going to be normal and fun and all things good.

When we pulled into the parking lot and Reece killed the engine, I felt my stomach drop and land on my feet as my gaze locked with a cerulean one. "Did I tell you that you look beautiful today?" he said.

My lips parted as I nodded. He had. That morning.

"Oh. I'm going to tell you again. You look beautiful."

Wordless, all I could do was stare at him. He was so handsome, but it was the openness in his steady gaze, the acceptance of me and all my crazy that really undid me.

You've fallen, an insidious voice whispered and I wanted to smack that dumb bitch upside her head, because another chirpier voice was pointing out that I probably fell when I was fifteen. It was just a long, slow-motion kind of fall at this point.

"You got the potato salad?"

"Huh?" I murmured, distracted by the warring voices in my head.

He gestured at my feet. "The potato salad that we bought at the store that you insisted on putting in another plastic container so it looked like you actually made it when I'm sure there's no one here going to believe you actually made that."

"Oh!" I bent over, scooping up the tub. "I totally made this."

"Liar."

"Shut up," I hissed, yanking on the handle, but

the door wouldn't budge. I rolled my eyes. "Can you unlock my door?"

He chuckled and hit the button. I all but fell out of the damn thing, and then was stunned that within a heartbeat, Reece was by my side, taking the potato salad out of my grasp and grabbing my hand with his.

We were holding hands.

Like boyfriend and girlfriend.

We were totally holding hands as we crossed the parking lot, and I was torn between punching myself in the lady bits and skipping like a schoolgirl.

I needed therapy.

The door to Jax's townhome was unlocked, and as soon as we stepped inside the house, we almost plowed into a beautiful redhead coming down the stairs.

"Hey!" I squealed. "Avery!" Then I frowned. "Are you okay?"

Avery looked a little green as she gave me a wobbly smile. "Hey," she replied in a much more subdued voice. "Sorry. I'm getting over a stomach bug. The stomach is still a little woozy, but I'm not contagious or anything." She glanced at where my hand was mating with Reece's, and her grin strengthened. "Hi, Reece."

He nodded. "Are you sure you're okay? Do we need to get Cam?"

Avery's laugh was airy. "Yes, I'm sure. And besides, I doubt you'll pull him away from the grill. I'm pretty sure he kicked Jax off grill duty. He does that everywhere we go. It's weird."

"Probably a good thing. Cam can cook, right?" I asked as we followed her to the kitchen and out the back door.

Her eyes got this dreamy look that was goofy and cute, and I wondered if I looked like that when people mentioned Reece. Probably not as adorable, and more whacked. "Yeah, he can cook."

Reece squeezed my hand. "I bet his omelets aren't as good as mine."

I snorted.

His eyes narrowed on me as his lips twitched. "You wait and see if I make you another omelet anytime soon."

Avery's avid gaze bounced back and forth between us. "So you guys . . . um—"

"Joined the league of the incredibly good-looking couple secret organization of annoying hotness?" Katie appeared, popping out of a wall for all I knew. Dressed down today—sort of—she was wearing hot-pink jeans and an off-the-shoulder black shirt. "Yes. The answer would be yes."

Reece raised his brows.

"What? I dare you to deny such label," she challenged. "Do it. Make my day."

I giggled.

"I wasn't going to deny it," Reece replied. "But thanks for stealing our thunder."

Unabashed, Katie rocked back on what appeared to be six-inch heels. She spun around, clapping. "Reece and Roxy, whose names link together in an incredibly cute way, are totally doing it!"

"Oh my God," I whispered, eyes wide.

"Well, that's one way of making an announcement." Reece sighed.

A whole bunch of heads turned in our direction. By the grill, Jax raised his hand and gave us a . . . he gave us a thumbs-up? Really?

"I'm so proud of our babies," Nick commented from where he sat near the grill, sprawled in a lawn chair he looked like he overgrew a few feet ago, a hoodie up over his head and rocking dark sunglasses. "They're all grown up now. What shall we ever do?"

Calla walked to us, her long blond hair swishing in a ponytail. She grinned as she took the potato salad from us. "I have so many questions," she said to me meaningfully. "But since Katie pretty much just put that all out there, I'll wait."

"Thanks," I muttered dryly.

She laughed as she plopped the container on a card table someone must've dug up from a basement or a frat house, from the looks of it. "You make this?" Her brows rose.

"Yes," I answered, not even blinking an eye.

Reece swallowed a laugh that earned him a strange look from Calla, and I pulled my hand free, shooting him a death glare over my shoulder. His grin spread.

"You totally didn't make this," she said, brows arched.

I sighed. "No."

Calla laughed again. "I was going to say I didn't know you peeled potatoes."

"Peeling potatoes is hard," I grumbled.

Avery joined Cam, who immediately draped an arm over her shoulders. "You feeling okay, shortcake?" he asked, concern evident in the way he stared at her. When she nodded, he dipped his head and kissed the tip of her nose and then looked up. "The hamburgers are almost done. Got some hot dogs on the grill, too. Wanted to grill some chicken, but Jase didn't want to wait so long."

Jase, the *extremely* good-looking one of the bunch, folded his arms. "Especially when you want to baste it like you're fucking Betty Crocker or some shit."

"Don't hate on Betty Crocker," Cam warned him.

Cam kind of made me nervous. Not in a bad way, but mainly because he was a pro soccer player—a freaking pro soccer player. I always felt out of my element when I was around him.

"They smell great." Reece glanced at Jax. "Colton's going to try to make it, but no promises."

"Understandable," he returned. He waved his hand at the numerous lawn chairs. "Help yourself."

Calla gestured at the group. "Brit and Ollie couldn't make it. He's got a big exam on Monday and Brit's staying with him in Morgantown, but I think you guys know everyone here except—"

"Me." A guy with beautiful mocha-colored skin and bright green eyes stood from one of the chairs. He was tall and lanky, and vaguely reminded me of Bruno Mars. He was wearing a gray loose-knit beanie I kind of wanted to steal. "I'm Jacob. I go to college at Shepherd. I'm a Gemini. I'm allergic to *Game of Thrones,* because I can't keep track of everyone who dies on the show. If you talk shit about *Doctor Who,* we cannot be friends, and I still want a goddamn pony and no one will let me buy one."

Teresa, who was sitting in one of the plastic chairs, ran her hand through her mane of dark hair. She looked stunning, as usual, a modern-day Snow White. "You're the only grown person who wants a pony."

"I kind of want a llama," I said.

Reece looked down at me, lips pursed thoughtfully, as if he was rethinking the whole boyfriend/girlfriend thing.

"Why would you want a llama?" Calla sounded genuinely curious.

I shrugged. "Who wouldn't want a llama?"

"Um . . ." Avery wrinkled her nose. "Don't they spit?"

Jacob shushed her and then grinned at me. "I think we're going to be great friends. We could take our pony and llama on playdates. Oh! Ollie could totally fashion leashes for them. I want one with Swarovski crystals."

Another man I hadn't met before groaned from where he stood. "That is not going to happen."

Jacob then shushed him. "Mr. Dream Crusher, also known as Marcus, is my boyfriend. He doesn't understand the need for an obscenely large four-legged friend."

I grinned at what had to be the greatest introduction of all time.

Marcus was equally handsome, even more so, and nicely tanned. "Out of college," he said, standing and offering a hand to Reece and then me. "I don't know any of these people."

"That's probably a good thing," Jacob said. "Half of them are insane."

"Hey!" shouted Teresa from her seat. "We're not insane. We are eccentric."

"Speaking of insane"—Katie returned to our huddle, holding a bottle of Corona—"have you thought anymore about trying out that pole?"

Jacob choked on the beer he was drinking and turned sideways quickly, waving a hand in front of his face. Before he could say anything, Jase's head swiveled around so fast I thought it might spin right off. "What?" he demanded.

Teresa grinned as she bit down on her lip. "Nothing, honey."

"No. Seriously. That's not a 'nothing.' I don't ever want to hear my sister's name and the word *pole* in the same sentence that involves dancing." Cam glanced at Katie, wielding a slotted spatula, causing Jacob to side-step a spittle of grease. "No offense."

She shrugged a shoulder. "None taken. Only the few and the proud can handle it."

I scrunched my nose. "Isn't that the Marines' motto?"

"Yes," sighed Reece.

Jase eyed his girlfriend and then shook his head. Giggling, Teresa rose from her seat and went to his side. Stretching up, she clasped his cheeks and whispered something in his ear. Whatever it was turned the frown upside down. She returned to the seat, cheeks flushed.

Before I could do anything, Reece dipped his head and kissed my cheek and then wandered off to where all the boys were converged around the grill.

"Sit." Teresa patted the chair next to her. "Sit down, girl who's dating a hot cop."

My heart did a happy little twirl at that as I sat next to her. Calla and Avery joined in while Katie remained standing, nursing her beer. "Cops are hot," she said, eyes squinting. "Well, any guy in a uniform is hot. Wait. Not any uniform, but you get what I'm saying."

I had to agree with her.

"Have you heard anything more about the stalker?" Avery asked in a quiet voice.

Calla leaned forward, expression serious. "Your place was broken into, right?"

I nodded. "Yeah, last weekend, but nothing else has happened since then. I know Reece's friend is coming out on Monday or Tuesday after he gets off to go ahead and wire the place, so hopefully that helps."

"That's so frightening," Avery said, shaking her head. "Yeah, I know that makes me Captain Obvious, but God, that's just crazy. I'm glad you're staying with Reece."

Teresa shuddered. "So am I. If I were you, even with a security system, I wouldn't want to be alone until they found the freak."

"Have you thought about just staying with him until they find out who's doing this?" Calla asked, glancing to where the guys were laughing over something Jacob had said. "I doubt he'd be against that."

Crossing my legs, I couldn't even try to hide the grin that pulled at my lips. "I don't think he would either, but I don't want to impose on him any more than I am."

Teresa cocked a dark brow. "I so doubt you are doing any imposing."

"True, but . . ." I shook my head, unsure of how to put it in words I didn't want overheard. I didn't have to worry long, because Katie did it for me.

Voice low, she said, "Roxy is stupid. No offense," she said to me, and I glared at her. "She thinks she's not in love. Or she doesn't want to be in love, and probably has no idea that he's already willingly taken that leap, so she's trying to protect her whittle heart."

Avery tucked a strand of strawberry-colored hair back behind her ear. "I'm pretty sure most of us have been there."

"Yep," commented Calla as she raised her glass of tea. "Been there, done that, and got the T-shirt."

I arched my brows at them.

"Am I the only one who went after a guy?" Teresa asked, her expression puzzled. "Because I totally knew I wanted to make sweet, sweet loving to Jase from like before day one."

"That's because you have lady balls," announced Katie. "The rest of them just have ovaries."

"Do I want to even know what you all are talking about?" Jacob asked, appearing behind Avery. He gripped the back of her chair and leaned over her.

Calla laughed. "Probably not. So how much longer till we eat?"

He glanced over at the grill. "Another five minutes, I guess? What the fuck do I know though."

Teresa stretched her legs out in front of her, sighing as she smiled. "I'm glad we all were able to get away and hang out."

"Yeah, this is probably going to be the last time for a while," Avery said, smacking at Jacob as he picked up a strand of her hair and tossed it in her face.

"Why?" I asked.

"After this semester, I'm moving back here," Calla said, a sad smile on her face as she looked at me. "You will be stuck with me, but I'm going to miss seeing Avery and Teresa."

"With Cam's schedule, he's got a lot of traveling coming up. I try to go with him when I can, but it's not always possible," Avery said. "But we got a wedding to plan, so don't forget that." She grinned at Teresa. "I'm totally leaving that all up to you and Brit, by the way."

"Fine with me. You'll be wearing red instead of white."

Avery rolled her eyes. "Yeah, because that will go great with my hair. Thanks."

Jacob patted her head sympathetically.

"Weekends are going to be hard for Jase and me to get away. With his new job at the agriculture center, he's working all week and our weekends are pretty packed right now since Jack will be staying with us during the weekends for now," Teresa continued.

"Isn't Jack his brother?" I asked, hoping something wasn't going on with his parents that meant they couldn't care for him.

"Uh . . ." Jacob straightened. "I don't think Roxy knows, Tess."

"Crap. You're right." Teresa scooted forward on the plastic chair. "Well, it's kind of a complicated, long story, but the short version is that Jack's not his brother. He's Jase's son."

My mouth dropped open, and I couldn't help it. I glanced over at Jase, who was holding a plate Cam was heaping burgers onto. I knew that Jack wasn't a small child and Jase wasn't much older than me, so . . .

"He was dating a girl in high school and she got pregnant," Teresa explained when I turned back around. "Instead of putting Jack up for adoption, Jase's parents legally adopted him and they raised Jack as Jase's brother. Jase finally told Jack the truth a couple of weekends ago."

"Wow," I said. "How'd that go?"

Teresa smiled sadly. "Jack understands, but in a way, he doesn't. He's old enough to get what Jase is telling him, but he's looked at him as an older brother since he was born. It's going to take a while to get used to the fact that he's his father. The great thing though is that Jase's parents have been really supportive, and since Jase just closed on a house, it's a good place for Jack once he's ready." She shrugged. "And hey, it's like a practice run for me."

Avery shot her a look. "Oh dear God, don't let Cam hear you say that."

"He needs to get over the fact I have sex. Lots of sex," she replied dryly. "Look at Jase. Who wouldn't?"

"That boy would never leave my bed," Katie said.

"Mine either," murmured Jacob. "Hell, I'd take all these boys."

Part of me couldn't believe that Jase had a son, but the guy had *awesome* genes so I guessed it was great that they were being passed down.

"What about the mom?" Katie asked.

Teresa cringed. "She passed away years ago in a car accident."

"Oh. Wow. That sucks." Katie took a long gulp of her beer. "I think it's time for food." She wandered over to the grill.

Reece was the man.

He pulled over a chair next to mine, asked what I wanted and returned with a plate full of food and a fresh beer. I could get used to that kind of service. And as corny as it felt, I could also get used to coupledom.

Katie left shortly after she finished eating, stating she had a hot date to get ready for, and I wished her luck. There were a lot of laughs and insults flying once the food was done and the chairs were moved around a fire pit that kept the cold chill of the September air at bay. When I came back from using the bathroom and helping put the cold stuff away in the fridge, Reece snagged me around the waist and pulled me into his lap.

I let out a soft squeal. "We're going to break the chair!"

He straightened my glasses and then looped his arms around me. "We'll be fine." Light from the fire flickered across his face. "Want to know a secret?"

"Sure," I whispered back.

One side of his lips kicked up and he rested his forehead against mine. "I'm glad we're here. I'm enjoying this."

My heart expanded in my chest and I admitted, "Me, too."

"Good." He reached up with one hand, smoothing my hair back from my face. "Because I can see us doing this again. And again. What do you think?"

I closed my eyes, secretly thrilled to hear what he was saying.

"I think it's kind of weird seeing you two be nice to each other," Jax said as he walked past us, joining Calla on a thick blanket.

Reece lifted his head from mine. "I think it's kind of weird that you're paying that close attention to us."

I laughed as I rested my cheek on his shoulder. There was no denying I was happy where I was at the moment, and yeah, I could really see us doing this. I could see us together, seriously together. And maybe I could even get over myself—over the fear of getting hurt again.

For him—for this—wasn't it worth it?

My breath caught as I placed my hand above his heart and he immediately folded his over mine. I opened my eyes and stared at our joined hands.

Katie was so right.

And it was so stupid, because I wasn't even sure why I was fighting this anymore. What I felt for Reece when I was fifteen was nothing like what I felt for him now. Back then, I thought I knew what it was like being in love with someone. Maybe I did, but now I truly knew how it felt. Because this was like flying and drowning all at once, like wrapping yourself in your favorite sweater and running naked through a sprinkler. It was a thousand conflicting emotions all rolled into a ball.

I loved Reece.

A knot formed in the back of my throat as I lifted my head. I really did love him. I was *in* love with him.

There was no more playing around with how I felt, no more lying.

Reece looked at me, his brows knitting. "You okay?"

I opened my mouth to tell him yes. No! To tell him the truth, and I didn't care that people surrounded us, because I was going to scream it—scream it right in Reece's face.

But my butt vibrated.

"Oh." Drawing back, I pulled my cell out of my jean pocket. My stomach dropped the moment I saw the caller ID. "It's Charlie's parents," I mumbled.

Reece stiffened.

Going cold, I sat up straight as I answered the phone. "Hello?"

"Roxanne?" Charlie's mother never called me Roxy. Never in my whole life had she ever used my nickname. And never in my whole life had I heard her sound as hoarse and shaken as she did now.

Hands shaking as knots formed in my belly, I slipped out of Reece's embrace and stood. I stepped over Jax's legs, giving myself space as I walked away from the fire. "Yes. This is Roxy. What's going on?"

I don't even know why I asked the question. I knew what she was going to say. Deep down I already knew, and everything inside me started to unravel like a loose thread that had been tugged.

"I'm sorry," she said into the phone.

"No," I whispered, turning around. I saw Reece standing a few feet behind me. Concern poured into his expression and so did realization. He stepped toward me, and I stumbled back.

Charlie's mother let out a broken sound—a sound I didn't even know she was capable of making until that moment. "It's over. He . . . Charlie passed away this evening."

Chapter 23

I never knew pain could hurt so bad that it made you numb. That the pain could cut so deep it took every bit of emotion out of you, just sucked it right out. That was what I was feeling. Empty. Bottomless.

I didn't cry that night.

Not when Reece took me back to his place. Not when he helped me undress or when he got me in bed. Not even when he wrapped his arms around me and held me until I fell asleep.

The weekend and the days coming after that phone call were a blur. Jax gave me the week off from the bar, and I hadn't even pretended to fight his decision. My head wasn't in the right place to be working with the public. My head wasn't anywhere it needed to be.

I didn't cry when I went to the facility on Tuesday to get all the paintings and the little personal mementos I'd loaded Charlie's room up with. Three large boxes went out, placed side by side in the back of Reece's truck. I didn't cry, not even when I saw his empty bed. Not even when I learned that he'd gone in his sleep from an aneurysm. Not when I discovered that he'd died alone.

There would be no autopsy and the funeral was scheduled for Thursday. I couldn't believe it was going to happen so soon, as if his parents were waiting for this to happen, as if the grave had been dug all those years ago and was just waiting to be filled.

I didn't cry when Reece took me to my apartment or when I stacked the paintings I'd done for Charlie in the corner of my studio. Nor did I really notice that my place had been wired for security, all the windows and doors. Actually, I did notice but I just didn't care.

It was Thursday morning, as I slipped on the only pair of black dress pants that I owned and were now a little too loose, that I noticed Reece hadn't gone to work at all this week. Smoothing my hair back into a low ponytail, I squinted at my reflection. The purple streak had faded, becoming barely noticeable. What was glaringly visible were the dark shadows under my eyes.

Slipping my glasses on, I left Reece's bathroom. He was in the kitchen, fixing his black tie. Freshly shaven and shoulders broad in his suit, he looked good. Real good. I guessed that even though I felt so incredibly hollow, all my lady bits were still functioning.

He looked up, his head tilting to the side as he studied me. We really hadn't talked much since Saturday. It wasn't for lack of him trying. Obviously, he'd been here this entire time without me even asking. The same with the funeral. Not once did I ask him to go, but he was ready before me, and I lo—I appreciated him for that.

I stopped at the edge of the kitchen counter. "You've been taking off time from work."

Reece nodded slowly as he fixed the cuffs on his suit. "Yeah. I didn't want you to be alone."

The burn in my chest was renewed. "You didn't have to do that."

"I have the time. Plus everyone is understanding." He came around the counter, stopping in front of him. His eyes searched mine intently. "I go back to my shift next week."

I swallowed—swallowed hard. "Thank you. You've been . . . you've been so good about everything."

Reece cupped my cheeks with both hands. "Babe, that's just what someone does in this situation." His thumbs trailed along my cheekbones, a gesture I looked forward to. "I'm here for you."

My gaze flicked away and then I squeezed my eyes shut as he hauled me against his chest, wrapping his arms around me. I was stiff for a moment. I wasn't even sure why, but then I clung to him, my fingers clawing through the clothes to get a piece of him—to hold a piece of him.

"It's not fair," I murmured against his chest.

He pressed a kiss against the top of my head. "No, it's not."

Chest aching, I pulled away from him and drew in a deep breath that didn't seem to loosen the pressure wrapping around me. "I'm ready," I told him.

That was a lie.

I think he knew that.

The service was held at a funeral home situated in the middle of a cemetery the size of a small town. With its winding roads and tall, graceful oaks that still had all their leaves, it truly was a calm place. Peaceful. Beautiful in a morbid way.

Mom and Dad were already there, waiting outside,

along with Gordon and Thomas. Megan stood next to her husband, her hand resting lightly on her swollen belly. All of them, even Gordon, hugged me, and I wished they wouldn't. I wished they'd greeted me like they'd greeted Reece, with a handshake or a nod. I could deal with that.

"Honey," Mom murmured, kissing my forehead. Tears gathered in her eyes. "There really isn't anything I can say right now to make this better."

"I know," I whispered, pulling away and squinting up at the cloudless sky. Too pretty of a day for a funeral, I thought. I glanced at my dad, who looked as uncomfortable in dress pants and shirt as Gordon did.

Dad caught my stare, and I saw the bone-deep sadness in his otherwise steady gaze. Charlie had been like a third son to him, to both of my parents. I knew this was hurting them, too.

"Walk with me, baby," he urged, and I went over to my dad's side. He draped an arm over my shoulder as he guided me through the double doors.

Reece stayed close behind me as I tried not to breathe too deeply. I hated the smell of funeral homes. The mixture of floral and something else I really didn't want to think about.

I was surprised when I recognized the two people signing the guest book. Jax and Calla were here. "Hey," I said, voice low as I stepped ahead of my father. "Guys, I . . ."

Calla approached me, smiling sadly. "The rest of the gang couldn't make it, but I was able to skip class today."

"You didn't have to come," I told them.

"We know," replied Jax. He placed a hand on my shoulder and squeezed.

I was literally moved beyond words. Never knew

what that felt like before. Totally got it now. They didn't know Charlie, never had the pleasure of knowing him, but they were here, for me.

All of us piled into the large room where the service was being held, and I sat between my dad and Reece, staring straight ahead. The casket was closed, and Charlie's parents were sitting up front, their backs straight through the whole shebang. Part of me knew that I should make an attempt to go talk to them, but so much festered inside me. I was never close to them, never comfortable in their sterile and rigid home. I remembered how they treated Charlie, like he was something to be ashamed of.

That wasn't fair either, because Charlie knew how they felt.

When the service finally drew to a close, tears streaked my mother's face and my father's eyes were glassy. I couldn't cry. My eyes were broken. That frustrated me as I rose from the uncomfortable pew. The burning was there, in my chest and throat, and had been there since the phone call, but it was like something had broken off deep inside me.

Reece's hand landed on the small of my back and moved in a slow, comforting circle as we waited our turn to step into the center aisle. The urge to turn and wrap my arms around him was hard to ignore.

On our way out, I thought I caught a glimpse of Henry slipping out one of the side doors. That pressure thickened in me as I stared at where I thought he'd been. I wasn't sure how to feel about Henry coming to Charlie's funeral. A few weeks ago I would've been spitting mad, like puking green vomit and head-spinning level of rage, but now? I almost wanted to laugh—the hysterical never-ending kind of laugh. I wanted to sit down in the middle of the funeral home and laugh.

"Babe, you okay?" Reece asked.

I nodded slowly, realizing I was probably rocking one hell of a crazy face.

He took my hand in his and squeezed gently. "We can take a couple of minutes if you want."

God, he was . . . so good to me.

"I'm okay," I said, and I think everyone within a ten-mile radius knew that wasn't the case at all, but Reece held my hand tight as we started out of the funeral home.

The walk out to the gravesite was as quiet as one would expect such a thing to be. Our group stood near the back, and when I saw the hearse arrive, I looked away hastily. My gaze landed on the grave.

I sucked in a sharp breath, and all I got was the suffocating scent of rich soil. This was really happening. This was it. No more trips on Friday. No more hope that one day Charlie would get better, that he'd look at me and say my name.

That he'd tell me that all of this wasn't my fault.

Oh God. A slight tremble rocked my body, starting in my toes pinched due to the too-tight black heels, coursing all the way up the tips of my fingers.

Reece let go of my hand and slipped his arm over my shoulder. He bowed his head, pressing his lips against my temple, and my heart squeezed even more, clenched to the point I wondered if I was having a heart attack.

Instead of standing at Charlie's funeral, I saw myself standing at Reece's. Might've sounded crazy, but because of his line of work, it was believable. One day I could be standing right here and saying good-bye to him.

I couldn't get enough air in my lungs.

Pain sliced through me. I couldn't do this anymore. I turned to Reece, saying just that.

"Okay. I'm going to get you out of here," he said, and I knew he didn't get it. He couldn't get it. He turned to my father, speaking too low for me to hear. My dad nodded, and then without saying a word, Reece steered me away from the graveside service.

I was walking fast, my hands balled into tight fists by the time we reached his truck. When we were both inside, I stared out the windshield as Reece drove and once we were back at his condo, I wasn't feeling empty. I was feeling *wild*, like an animal snared in a trap.

I knew what I needed to do.

Being with Reece could easily end up with me being utterly destroyed, beyond the point of repair. For a sweet, brief time I convinced myself that I could deal with that. I could let myself fall for him and it would be worth that risk. Standing there at Charlie's grave was a brutal wake up call.

I had to have the strength to walk away.

Sliding past Reece, I headed straight to his bedroom, where my suitcase and tote were next to the dresser. I took my glasses off, placing them atop the dresser and then pulled my hair up into a quick bun.

"Roxy?"

Not turning around, I kicked off my heels. "Yes?"

"You're not okay right now."

I opened my mouth, and a harsh laugh slipped out. "I'm fine." I picked up my shoes, placing them in the bottom of my suitcase.

"Babe, you just walked out of your best friend's funeral service," he countered gently. "You're not fine."

Hands shaking, I grabbed the neat stack of jeans I

know my ass didn't fold. It had to have been Reece. I placed them in the suitcase.

"What are you doing?" His voice was closer.

I shook my head as I reached down, unhooking the silver button on my pants. I let them fall to the floor and then I carelessly tossed them in the suitcase. The blouse went next, leaving me in my undies and a black cami.

"Roxy," his voice snapped. "Look at me."

Against my will, I slowly turned around. Reece had gotten rid of the jacket and his tie. His dress shirt was unbuttoned, flashing golden skin. I dragged my gaze up to his stunning blue eyes. "I'm looking at you."

His jaw flexed. "What do you think you're doing?"

"I'm packing my stuff." My voice shook as I waved toward my suitcase. "Seems pretty obvious, right?"

"Yeah, it does seem obvious, but what I don't get is why are you doing it?"

Turning from him, I walked over to my shirts and picked them up, dropping the pile into the suitcase. "My place has security. I don't need to impose on you any longer."

"You can stay here as long as you want to, and you damn well know that, Roxy."

"I know, but I'm sure you want your space." Finding my yoga pants under my tote bag, I started to pick them up, but Reece grabbed my arm, spinning me back around. My breath caught.

His lips were thin as he spoke. "If I wanted my space, I would've told you. That's something else you damn well already know. So don't play this game with me and put this on me. You're leaving because of—"

I didn't want to hear him finish the sentence, and I wasn't sure what happened next other than I lost it. All my control snapped like a band pulled tight. I yanked my arm free and then I planted my hands in his chest, shoving him.

Caught off guard, he stumbled a step, the backs of his legs bumping into the bed. His brows flew up. "Did you seriously just push me?"

I couldn't tell by his tone if he wanted to laugh or push me back, and that pissed me off. I was no longer empty that was for sure. I was brimming to the top—full of anger, helplessness, and a million other things. So I pushed him again, and this time he sat down. I was breathing heavy as I stared at him.

"Did that make you feel better?" he asked, voice deceptively even.

"Maybe it did."

Tipping his chin up, he raised his arms. "Babe, if pushing me around gets you to slow the fuck down and think about what you're actually doing right now, then have at it."

My jaw dropped. "You want me to push you?"

"Not really."

I hesitated and then started to turn back for my pants, but his hand shot out and the next thing I knew he'd hauled me into his lap. "Oh no, you don't. You're going to tell me why you want to go back to your place. The real reason."

"I already told you." I pulled back, and he yanked me forward. We were chest to chest, my knees on either side of his legs, and he had an iron grip on my wrists. My heart was racing as our gazes locked. "Let me go."

"That's not the real reason."

My fingers curled helplessly. "What? Are you also psychic? Did you hit your head on your gun belt?"

One side of his lips curved up. "No. I'm just not

blind. Man, this wasn't how I imagined today was going to go," he said. "I know you got a lot going on in your head, but we need to talk it out."

"There's nothing we need to talk about." His hold loosened enough that I was able to push off his shoulders to stand. Or try to. The moment my hands connected with his shoulders, he muttered a curse and held me tight.

"That's such utter bullshit and you know it. There's one thing I never thought you were, and that's a coward. But you are acting like one now."

"What?" I drew back as far as I could. Leaving him would require every ounce of strength I had. That wasn't weak.

"Don't do this," he said again. "Stop acting like a coward."

"I'm not being a coward! I just don't want to do this anymore with you. It was fun, but that's it. I want to go home. I want to move on with my life—"

"Oh, for fuck's sake, you can lie better than this. You've wanted me since you were fifteen and now that you have me you aren't willing to risk getting hurt for me? What kind of shit is that?"

Whoa. He just called me right on that. "W-what do you mean getting hurt?"

"You think I don't know?" He shook his head. "You are afraid, Roxy. Afraid of getting hurt—ever since what happened to Charlie. You don't want to feel that kind of pain again. I get that. But you can't live your whole life like that, throwing everything away—throwing *this* away—just because you think you are going to get hurt. And it's not just with me. It's with everything."

I didn't know what to say to that.

Reece kept going. "What? You leave today, are you going to go back to dating a string of losers who aren't worth breathing the same fucking air as you, because when it comes down to it, you really don't care about them? Your heart isn't in it, so you're safe? But with me, it's different."

"You don't understand," I whispered, stunned.

"I don't understand?" He looked like he wanted to shake me. "Babe, I know what it's like to be afraid. I watched friends die overseas. I come home and every day I go to work knowing it could be my last. I think about my brother, knowing he faces the same shit I do. I'm afraid of losing *you*."

I gasped. "Me?"

"Yeah, you. You, Roxy. You have a fucking stalker. I'm scared shitless for you." Now he really looked like he wanted to throttle me. A little. "It goes beyond that. You could get into the car and crash. I've seen the way you drive."

"Ha," I muttered.

"Anything can happen to you at any moment, but you don't see me running away from what we have—what we could have. You've got to deal with what happened to Charlie. That doesn't mean you have to deal with that alone."

"What do you know about dealing with this?" I snapped.

He pinned me with a look.

"You barely talk about the shooting! You have nightmares because of it!" I shouted, throat stinging. "It's not like you know how to deal either, Mr. Fucking Perfect."

"I'm not saying I know how to deal. Fuck, Roxy. You and I both know I had a hell of time handling that and

I still do!" he yelled back, and for a second, I thought he might pitch me across the room. I'd kind of deserve that. "I drank myself into a fucking stupor by not dealing with the fact I shot and killed an eighteen-year-old kid."

I flinched. "Reece, I—"

"No. You're going to hear me out on this. For almost a year, I dealt with what I *had* to do by drinking instead of talking to someone—anyone about it. If it weren't for Jax, I probably would've swallowed a goddamn bullet, because let me tell you something, I had to make that choice between life and death enough times in the fucking sandbox to know making that call fucking sucks. I still chose to be a cop knowing I could face that again. Didn't make it a goddamn bit easier when I had to."

This was what he hadn't shared with me the night on the balcony, how bad the guilt and the anger had really gotten for him. Oh my God, I didn't want to hear this as terrible as it sounded. I didn't want to even think of him being in that kind of pain. It slaughtered me.

"But Jax got me to talk about it. He got me to take the damn counseling the department required I take seriously. And you're right. I still don't deal all that well with it, but at least I'm fucking trying. I'm not pushing you away. I'm trying to deal. But you haven't tried once, not in six years."

Unable to stand to hear any of this, I tried again to pull free, but he wasn't letting me get anywhere.

"You're going to college for a degree you don't want, because you're too afraid to admit and accept that you like working at Mona's. Not because you don't have any drive, but because it gives you time to do what you love—paint. But you won't even take that risk. You'll continue on, just to stay safe. To not take any risks."

"Shut up," I seethed, wishing I never told him about

how much I hated taking those classes. It was a good thing he was still holding my wrists, because I probably would've smacked him upside the head.

"Yeah, the truth is a fucking bitch, right?" His eyes glinted. "What I don't understand is how what happened with Charlie made you so afraid to do anything, but you want to know what I do know?" His eyes flashed blue fire. "I love you, Roxy. Charlie's death isn't going to change that. *This* isn't going to change that. And I know you feel the same way."

He—he *what*?

He—he said I feel *what*?

Yep, it was time for me to roll on out of here. Using all my strength, I jerked away from him, which got me nowhere.

"Roxy, stop it," he commanded.

Frustration rose sharply but so did something else. We were pressed together in all the places that matter, and despite the fact I was trying to leave him and we were arguing, the longer I sat on him, the more I could feel him hardening underneath me, and my blood was simmering from the contact.

And he said he *loved* me.

I twisted in his lap, which only succeeded in me grinding down on him. The red-hot sensation licked through me, and I saw the exact moment he felt the same thing I did.

His features tightened. "Jesus . . ."

My breath was coming in short pants as I zeroed in on his expressive lips. I was still trying to pull my arms free, and it was probably a good thing he hadn't let go, because I'd probably fly backwards. I rocked forward, hoping to knock him off balance, and his answering groan set my body on fire.

I stopped thinking. Or maybe I was thinking so

much that I couldn't grasp and hold any one thought in particular, other than I needed this—I needed him. Just one more time. It took nothing to reach his mouth, and when our lips met, he jerked back a little.

"Roxy—"

I didn't want to hear it, especially if he was going to introduce logic into what was happening. Pressing my lips against his, I kissed him harder, and when he didn't kiss me back, I bit down on his lower lip.

Reece gasped, and I took advantage, slipping my tongue into his mouth, twisting mine with his as I rocked my hips again, but this time I didn't stop. I moved in his lap, moaning into the kiss as pleasure spiraled so brightly I thought I saw white behind my eyes.

He let go of my wrists, dropping his hands to my hips, and I wrapped an arm around his neck, running my fingers along the hair as I slid the other down his throat and further, over his chest and his taut stomach. My fingers reached the top button and I unhooked it with ease.

"Shit," he hissed, eyes clouded with need. "We haven't settled anything—" He groaned as I palmed him through his trousers. "Fuck, Roxy . . . you're not playing fair."

"I'm not playing." My lips felt swollen as I brought my mouth back to his and rubbed him through his pants. When he didn't stop me, I quickly pulled down the zipper and eased the hot, pulsing length out from his boxers.

Reece leaned back, his gaze gliding down to where I held him in my hand. His voice was like smoke when he spoke. "This isn't what you need right now."

"Yes it is." I rested my forehead against his. "This is what I want right now."

"Roxy," he said my name like it was a curse and a prayer.

I dragged my hand up his length, running my thumb over the head of his cock. "Touch me," I implored, begged. "Please. Reece, touch me."

He made that sound that drove me crazy, the deep growl that was so raw and masculine it curled my toes and caused the muscles low in my belly to tighten. Then he lifted one of his hands. Finally. He tugged the front of my cami down and then tugged the cups of my bra aside, baring my breasts.

Reece touched me.

He did more than just touch me. His hands were greedy and so were his kisses. We were flushed and panting as I worked him to the point he pulled my hand away and all but tore my panties off. There was no more waiting. On my knees, I lowered myself on him, skin against skin. I cried out at the feeling, at how he stretched me, and how I burned around his length, and how I was scorched every place he touched and kissed me.

Letting me set the rhythm, Reece gave me complete control as I moved over him, rising and lowering myself slowly at first and then more frantically as my muscles contracted around him. As the pleasure built, spun tighter and tighter, and the release I sought began to whip out through me, he moved then, taking over. Gripping my hip with one hand and the back of my head with the other, his hips powered up, thrusting into me, setting me off. The release was so powerful, so explosive it was almost painful, almost too much. I wasn't sure I could take it, but I didn't want to escape. Not when I felt him start to lose control, when he grunted my name in my ear. I knew he was close.

His hold on my hip tightened, and he started to lift me off him. I didn't want him to pull out. This . . . this was going to be our last time, and I wanted to feel him so very alive inside me. I trusted him, and I hadn't missed any more of the pills.

I bore down on him, holding him just as tightly as he held me, and he knew what I wanted, because I felt him start to shake.

"Roxy," he growled my name, his large body stilling against mine as his arms surrounded me in a powerful embrace.

It took a while to move after that. I could feel his heart pounding just as fiercely as mine, and I felt each flex of his body throughout every cell in me. Neither of us spoke as I rested in his lap. We . . . we just held each other quietly, in a silence that was filled with a thousand unspoken words. It was only when we were no longer joined that I knew it was time.

"I need to clean up." My voice sounded strange to me. Too low. Too empty.

He eased his arms away from me, and I climbed off, snatching my panties off the floor. Our gazes met briefly, and I tried to ignore the question in them as I fixed my bra and top. Then I turned, hurrying into his bathroom. I didn't take long, because I knew that if I delayed this, I wouldn't leave. After cleaning myself up, I pulled on my undies.

I needed to leave, right? I couldn't stay here and I couldn't be with him, because I'd . . .

I already loved him.

I'd been in love with him for so long.

The burn rekindled in the center of my chest. I backed away from the door, struggling to clear my thoughts, but there was so much sparking back and forth. The backs of my legs hit the tub and I sat down. The undies were no protection against the cold ceramic.

What was I doing?

I was running. I was scared. Nothing he said was truly new to me. Fuck, I knew a lot of it already, but hearing it come from him shattered walls I didn't even know I had erected around myself.

"Roxy?" Reece's deep voice shook me.

My eyes glued to the door, I tried to take a deep breath, but it went nowhere. The pressure was back, and it was too much.

"Are you okay?" he demanded.

My lower lip trembled as I balled my hands into fists. Walking away from Reece wasn't strength. This was me being *weak*, me doing what I always did when it came to fucking everything. But it wasn't just born out of fear. Oh no, it ran deeper than that.

The bathroom door swung open and Reece's body filled it. His shirt was askew and he hadn't fastened the top button on his pants. He took one look at me, and everything I'd been thinking must've been written on my face. His expression softened as he stared at me.

Emotion crawled up my throat. "It's my . . . it's my fault."

Reece stepped into the bathroom slowly, as if he was afraid of startling me. "What's your fault, baby?"

"What happened to Charlie." My voice cracked. I fissured straight down the middle.

His brows knitted as he knelt in front of me, keeping his hands on his thighs. "Honey, what happened to him is not your fault."

"Yes it is," I whispered, because saying it too loudly

was too much. "You don't understand. You weren't there. I antagonized the situation."

His eyes widened. "Roxy—"

"He was hitting on me. Henry was."

"You did nothing wrong, Roxy." Anger flooded Reece's face, mixing with sadness. "You're allowed to tell a guy no, you're not interested, and not be worried about retaliation. It's not your fault."

I shook my head. "He always hit on me, and I could deal with that, but he insulted Charlie. He called him a homo." I started trembling as I wrapped my arms around my waist. "I started yelling at Henry. Then he called Charlie worse names. Charlie kept asking me to just leave it alone, but I couldn't, because I knew how much that bothered him. He *hated* that kind of stuff, and it *hurt* him. Henry then asked if I was a 'dyke' and if that was why I hung out with a 'faggot' all the time. I lost it. I pushed Henry. Like I pushed you." I bent over, staring at my toes as the night replayed itself in vivid detail. "Charlie had grabbed me and we were walking away. So was Henry. Then I . . . I turned around and said . . . I told him to go fuck himself because that was the only way white trash like him would get any action."

Reece closed his eyes.

"That's when he picked up the rock and threw it." I rocked slowly, shaking my head. "If I had just kept my mouth shut, we all would've walked away and *everything* would've been different. I am scared. You're right about that. I'm so scared of losing you and feeling that kind of pain again, but it's more than that. Why do I deserve to get to do whatever I want when Charlie never will? I ran my mouth. I took the situation to the next level. Haven't they put people in jail for that kind of thing? Accessory to assault—to murder? Why do I deserve you? Why do I deserve to do what I love for the rest of my life?"

When Reece opened his eyes, they weren't full of censure or judgment, just so much pain. "Words," he said quietly. "You threw out some words. Just like Henry did. And you know that words can do a lot of damage. I'm not saying they don't. Sometimes they can cut deeper than a knife, but you did not pick up that rock. You did not throw it. Henry made that decision. It's one that he seems like he regrets more than anything and I doubt he ever truly thought he'd hurt Charlie the way he did, but he can't change that. And you can't change what you said, but Roxy . . ." He dropped down on his knees in front of me and slowly, carefully, cradled my face in his hands. "What happened to Charlie was not your fault. You did not hurt him. Henry did. And I know it's going to take more than just my words for you to really accept that, but I'm going to be here for you every day to remind you that you so deserve every fucking thing this life has to offer."

My voice hitched on a sob. The backs of my eyes burned. His face blurred and my cheeks were damp.

"Remember everything I said in the bedroom? I'm scared, too. And there are times I question what I deserve, but we're in this together. So fall with me," he said, smoothing his thumbs along my cheekbones. "Let yourself go and fall with me, and baby, I will catch you. I will get you through this. You just got to take that risk."

I broke then, split wide open. I cried the deep, ugly kind of tears that no one looked good doing. Those tears came and they were for all that Charlie had lost. They were for Reece and everything he had to do.

They were even for Henry, because a tiny part of me had woken up in that moment, had opened my eyes, and realized that Henry . . . he'd thrown his life away when he threw that rock and that sucked too, because maybe Reece was right. Maybe he never meant to do that. I cried because I was no longer numb. I *hurt*. I was *afraid*. I'd started the process of losing my best friend six years ago, and I hadn't even begun to let go of any of that pain or hate and all the other toxic emotions.

I didn't even remember sliding off the rim of the tub and into Reece's arms, but like he had promised, he was there to catch me when I fell apart.

Chapter 24

"My head hurts."

Reece's fingers sifted through my hair, gently massaging my scalp. "The ibuprofen will kick in soon."

It felt like it was taking forever. My temples throbbed, as did the somewhat useless space behind my eyes. There was a good chance that I'd cried myself into a brain meltdown. Once I had started crying, it was like a levy had broken inside me. I had no idea how long we stayed in the bathroom, Reece planted on his ass and me in his arms, soaking his dress shirt. I'd only been vaguely aware of him picking me up and carrying me to his bed. He'd held me for hours, only leaving me not too long ago to grab some water and ibuprofen. He'd removed his shirt then and changed into a pair of nylon running pants before climbing back in bed. I was still in my cami and undies, and there was absolutely nothing sexy about that right now.

I was sprawled across his chest like one of those marionette dolls. My cheek rested above his heart and his legs cradled my thigh as he kept his fingers moving against my scalp. Night had fallen hours ago and while neither of us had eaten a thing since that morning, I think both of us were too exhausted to get out of bed and scrounge up something to eat.

"I'm sorry I cried all over you," I said.

"That's what I'm here for. I'm your personal tissue. Among other, more fun things, but I'm multipurpose."

I cracked a grin as I stared into nothing. "I like those more fun things."

"I know."

Curling my fingers against his taut stomach, I drew in a breath and was surprised that it felt steady and didn't hurt. It would be a long time before I fully accepted my role in Charlie's fate. Maybe I would never absolve myself of guilt completely, but I wanted to try. I really, honestly, wanted to try for the first time.

"Can I tell you something?" Reece asked.

"You can tell me anything."

"I'm going to hold you to that statement in the future," he said dryly. "I don't like to ever say good-bye."

My brows knitted. "I . . . I remember you saying that once."

"I did. I told you we never say good-bye. We kiss instead. Hell, we can say anything to each other, but not good-bye."

"Why?" I whispered, but I thought I already had a good idea to why.

There was a pause. "It's too permanent, especially in my line of work, the last thing I ever want you to hear from me is good-bye. And that sure as hell will never be the last thing I say to you."

I shivered as I thought about one day facing a phone

call or a knock on the door from—I pushed those thoughts out of my head. That wasn't trying to take a risk. I would not, could not allow myself to think about the possibility of him not coming home one day.

"There's something I want you to know, Roxy. I'm a stubborn motherfucker. You know that. I'm not going to disappear on you without one hell of a fight. I can promise you that."

My eyes burned, and I thought there was a good chance I might start crying again.

With my head somewhat clear, a huge part of me now recognized how . . . how weak it was to keep someone away from you just because you might lose them one day. How silly it was. But there was still a little piece of me that wanted to retreat and not take that risk. I just couldn't give in to that fear.

"Do you think I'm crazy now?" I asked in a quiet voice.

He chuckled and I liked how the sound rumbled under my cheek. "Babe, I've always thought you were a little crazy. That's what I love about you."

Hearing him say that now, when my head was sort of screwed on right, stole my breath. "Can you say that again?"

He slipped his hand down my jaw and tilted my head back. Our eyes met, and his chest rose deeply. "I saw them," he said.

I frowned. "Saw what?"

He took a deep breath as he eyed me. "The paintings."

For a moment, I didn't get where he was going with this. Not when he traced the curve of my cheek with his thumb and not when a soft smile curved his lips. And then it hit me.

"The paintings?" I swallowed and started to sit up, but he didn't let me get very far. "The paintings at my place?" When he nodded, I felt my face heat like I was out under the summer sun. "The ones that are . . . ?"

"Of me?" he supplied.

I squeezed my eyes shut. "Oh my God. Seriously?"

"Yes."

Mortified, I didn't know what to say. "They were in my closet. Why were you in my closet?"

"Looking for a psycho stalker," he answered.

My eyes popped opened. "That . . . that was like two weeks ago! You saw them back then and didn't say anything."

Reece sat up, bringing me with him. Somehow my body ended up between his legs and we were face-to-face. "I didn't say anything, because I figured you'd respond this way."

"Of course I'd respond this way! It's embarrassing. You probably think I'm some kind of freak. A stalker—a creepy stalker who paints pictures of you when you're not around."

"I don't think you're a stalker, babe." His voice was dry.

I screwed up my face. "I can't believe you saw them."

He chuckled, and my eyes narrowed on him. "Honestly? I really didn't know how you truly felt about me until I saw them."

My brows flew up. "I thought you were all-knowing."

Reece smirked. "I had my suspicions that you were in love with me from the first time you laid eyes on me."

"Oh dear baby Jesus in a manger," I muttered.

"But I don't think I was a hundred percent until I saw those paintings, especially the one of me in the kitchen. You painted that after . . . after I left." His brows lowered as he gave a little shake of his head. "It's nothing to be embarrassed about. I think it's sweet."

I still thought it was a little creepy.

"But you know what's important? The first thing I thought when I saw them is how much talent you have. It was like looking in the mirror."

That went a little way to making me feel better about this.

"I wish you'd put your focus there, babe. You have something real."

Leaning against him, I blew out a soft breath. My mind was churning over a lot today, I wasn't sure I was ready to look too closely at the whole college thing. "Getting a degree couldn't hurt."

"You're right." He smoothed his hand up my arm. "It's smart. Just like doing what you love, no matter what it is, is right."

I smiled as I thought about that. "I really do love working at Mona's."

"And like I said before, there isn't a damn thing wrong about that."

Reece was right. Jax was happy as a monkey with a banana owning and working at Mona's. So was Nick. Well, I guessed Nick was happy. I never really asked him and he sure as heck never volunteered the info.

"You think you can eat something?" he asked, and when I nodded, he smacked my behind. "Come on, let's get some cheese and crackers."

I climbed out of bed and was out into the hallway when Reece caught me around the waist and spun me around. He pulled me to his chest as he cupped my cheek with one hand, tilting my head back.

"I love you, Roxy." He dipped his head, kissing

me softly, and I suddenly understood the emotion behind those sweet, tender kisses. It was that four-letter word. Love. "You wanted to hear me say it again. I'm going to say it so much that you get tired of hearing it."

Smiling against his lips, I placed my hands on his chest, inhaling deeply and catching the faint scent of his cologne. "I don't think I can ever get tired of hearing that."

The next couple of days were a blur for a different reason. I wasn't numb anymore, which meant when I woke up Friday morning, I had another crying fit, because I realized I wouldn't be seeing Charlie on Friday like I had for the last six years. That was hard, and I honestly don't know what I would've done if Reece hadn't been there. Not only had he let me have my tear fest, when I finally stopped crying, he hadn't treated me like something was wrong with me or like he was over the emotional outbursts.

Reece had simply ordered Chinese and we ate a late lunch, spending the entire day on the couch, watching really bad zombie movies. That carried into Saturday and then I had another crying jag, because I was so frustrated with myself, with how I'd tried to push Reece away and how Charlie would've smacked me upside the head if he was around and knew that, and how I wasn't being strong enough to just . . . to just fucking let it all go.

It was Sunday, as I sat on the bed, while he—in all his shirtless and pajama-bottom-wearing glory—fiddled with his duty belt and attached the numerous things on his uniform, that I told him what I planned to do tomorrow.

"I'm going to go to my apartment tomorrow."

His head had been bowed as he hooked his badge into his shirt, but his fingers stilled as he lifted his chin, both dark brows raised. "Why?"

I scooted to the end of the bed and looked down at where he sat on the floor. "I want—no, I need—to go through the stuff I brought back from . . . from Charlie's room. I just dropped them in my living room."

He finished hooking the badge in. "Can you wait until I can be there with you?"

I smiled a little. "I appreciate you wanting to be there, but I think . . . I need to do this alone." In other words, I knew I was going to break down again, especially seeing all those paintings and little things I'd brought with me whenever I visited Charlie. After all the time spent crying on Reece, I really didn't think he needed to see that again. I needed to start letting all of this go and that was something I needed to try to do on my own first. "My place is safe now."

"It *should* be safe now." Setting the shirt aside, he started messing with the clips on his belt. Getting his uniform ready was a freaking complicated process, I was learning. "You know I want you staying with me until we find this guy."

"I know." I folded my legs under me. "But with the security system, I'm pretty safe. That was the point of putting that in there, right? Plus, what if they don't even find the guy?"

"You can stay here forever," he replied.

I shot him a bland look. "Reece, I . . . don't think I could. I mean, we just started dating and most people—"

"I don't give a fuck what most people do. I love you. You love me, even though I haven't heard those words yet." He stretched his belt out on the floor while

I arched a brow. "So if we want to move in together now, we move in together. What-the-fuck-ever."

My lips twitched. "I'd like to see you explaining it like that, with so much grace, to my parents."

Reece stood swiftly. "What do you think your parents are thinking we're doing while you're staying with me now?"

"They think we're playing cards and knitting blankets."

He chuckled as he placed his hands on either side of me and leaned over the bed. "They know we're fucking each other's brains out whenever we get the chance."

"Ew." I wrinkled my nose. "They think we're doing pure and wholesome things."

"Your parents?" He snorted. "They're probably hoping we give them a grandbaby by next summer."

"No way, no . . ." I groaned. "You're probably right."

Grinning, he kissed the tip of my nose and then pulled back so he could look me straight in the eye. "You planning on going over during the day?" When I nodded, he sighed. "Please tell me that if you notice anything suspicious, you'll get your ass out of there and call me. I'll be working, but I will drop anything."

I smiled and then rocked forward, kissing the tip of *his* nose. "I'll be fine. I just need to . . ."

"You need your privacy. I get that. I really do."

And that . . . that was so Reece. Yeah, he could be bossy and demanding, in and out of the bedroom, but he was also considerate and compassionate. He was strong-willed, but the softer side of him dug deep into my marrow. I loved every side of Reece, no matter how incredibly annoying he could be sometimes.

I thought about what he'd said about how he dealt

with the shooting—how he was still dealing. My chest ached. "Are you okay?"

"Perfect," he mused.

"That you are, but that's not what I meant." I took a deep breath. "Everything with the shooting? I knew it had gotten bad, but I didn't know *how* bad, and I . . . I just want you to know that you can always talk to me. Okay?"

A small smile appeared. "I know."

"Don't forget that," I demanded softly.

That smile spread. "I won't."

Placing my hands on his biceps, I closed the tiny distance between us and kissed his parted lips. The way he sucked the air between his teeth stirred desire deep inside me. Kissing him again, I pulled back just enough so we were eye to eye once more.

I drew in a deep breath. "I love you, Reece."

His eyes deepened to magnetic blue as he stared at me. For a moment, he didn't say anything, didn't move, and I wasn't even sure if he breathed. Then he sprang into action, clasping my hips. He lifted me up and placed me on my back as he came over me, his body blocking out the entire world.

"I already knew that, babe, but nothing is as good as hearing you say that."

I started to say it again, but his mouth claimed mine with a blazing kiss that rocked me. There was nothing angry about the way we went at each other, and we really *went* at each other. Neither was it a slow, seductive joining. We were frantic, but this time because there was nothing between us, no words left unspoken, no walls, and most important, no fear holding us back.

Our clothes came off in a rush, and our hands were everywhere. Reece *was* everywhere, and what he felt for me, which was something I could not doubt, was in every sweep of his hand and brush of his lips. He worshiped what we had together, and as minutes ticked by and with every kiss and caress, I knew I deserved this with him.

I knew *he* deserved this.

Reece worked his way down my body, his head between my thighs, his mouth on me, his tongue in me. God, he knew what to do. With every lick, he drew me into him. When his mouth moved to the bundle of nerves and he slid a finger inside, finding that ultrasensitive spot, the sensation was too much. I came, head thrown back and my fingers clenching the short strands of his hair. Those tiny kisses and sweet nips of his teeth eased off as my legs fell to the side, boneless. I was barely aware of him moving to the nightstand, but the rip of the foil drew my eyes open. With a heavy-lidded gaze, I watched him roll the condom on and then he was above me, his hand curving around my jaw as he guided himself into me with one quick, shattering thrust. His mouth silenced my cry, and I could taste me on him, the combination highly erotic. I curled my legs around his waist, relishing in the deep, powerful strokes.

Reece lifted his head, his lips glossy and cheeks flushed. Before he could say a word, I told him again. "I love you," and I said it over and over, until whatever semblance of control and rhythm were lost, until I threw my arms back and planted the palms of my hands against the headboard, anchoring myself as he slammed into me, hitting every nerve and sending pleasure racing through me. I flew apart again, shattering into a million happy, messy little pieces, but this time, he was right with me, with his head kicked back and my name nothing more than a sexy, throaty growl as he spent himself.

He collapsed when he was done, his breathing erratic. "I can't move," he murmured, face buried in my neck.

"That's okay."

"I'm going to crush you."

"That's also okay."

Reece chuckled. "I don't like flat and squishy Roxy."

I grinned. "I'm pretty flat as it is."

"You're fucking perfect." He rolled off me, flat on his back. "Fuck, babe . . ."

Prying my eyes open, I turned my head toward him. One arm was tossed over his eyes and his other hand was on my thigh, as if he couldn't stand the idea of us not touching. Maybe that was me just having an orgasm-induced romantic fantasy, but whatever.

"You know," I said, sighing as I reached down, placing my hand over his. I got a little giddy when he immediately flipped his palm up and threaded his fingers through mine. "I would like to paint you."

"With me knowing?" he teased.

"With you being naked," I corrected.

He moved his arm and snapped his head toward mine. Those lips curved up at the corners. "I'm so fucking down for that."

I left for my place about an hour after Reece headed out to work. It was weird parking in front of my apartment and walking inside. Not because I had to hit a button on my new key fob that disarmed the alarm system and clicked it again to arm it once I was inside or because I was freaked out about being in my place after the break-in.

I wasn't even thinking about Mr. Friendly Neighborhood Stalker.

No. It was the boxes next to my couch. It was the stack of paintings I knew were in there. It was the reminder that Charlie really was gone.

Setting my keys on the end table, I shuffled over to the boxes, feeling a burn in the back of my throat. A huge part of me wanted to turn around, run back to Reece's place, and hide under the covers, but I needed to deal with this.

But that wasn't trying—that wasn't moving past this.

Running my hands down the sides of my shirt, which read I'M A SPECIAL SNOWFLAKE, I pulled out the first painting like I was reaching into a box of venomous snakes.

Of course it was a painting I'd done of Charlie and me sitting together on a bench, our backs visible and the trees full of golden and red leaves.

My face started to crumble and my hand shook, rattling the canvas. What happened was so not fair, but it *had* happened and there was nothing I could do to change that.

Tears still fell as I dragged the box to the couch and sat down. Each painting cataloged either an event with Charlie or where I was mentally while I painted it. It was strange, seeing all the beautiful landscapes and memories of Charlie and me, and realizing that even though I held on to a lot of bad stuff, there'd been rays of sunshine in there. Like the way I saw Charlie. After the incident, I didn't see him in a different light. He was still the most beautiful person inside and out that I knew.

It was hard going through those paintings, even worse when I placed them in my studio and then moved on to the box, picking out the framed photos of us.

I didn't ever want to let go of Charlie. I didn't need to. I just had to get to a place where thinking of him made me happy.

But I needed . . . God, I needed to start letting go of this ugly ball of hate, sadness, and frustration that had festered inside of me for far too long. Instead of learning from what happened to Charlie and living my life to the fullest, I'd nurtured all those nasty feelings. It was like a rotten growth that tarnished everything it came into contact with, an infection that I had to cut out.

Placing the framed photo on the table near where my easel normally was, I glanced at the open door to the hall. Before I knew what I was doing, I'd retrieved my cell phone and then walked into my bedroom, stopping in front of my closet door.

I thought about what Reece had said all those days ago when he'd talked about how hard it was to let go of everything surrounding the shooting. I knew from what he'd said to me the night of the funeral that he was still struggling with truly letting it go, but he was trying.

I knew what I needed to do to really begin the whole process of letting it go, and it would be one of the hardest things I'd ever done.

Opening the closet door, I dropped down on my knees, placing my cell next to me, and started rooting around in the clothes that I had a habit of just tossing on the floor instead of folding neatly like Reece did. I grinned as I picked up a pair of jeans and tossed them aside, thinking that if Reece and I did make that step to live together permanently, I'd have my own personal clothing folder.

Couldn't beat that.

It took me a few minutes to find the jeans I was looking for. I had to push all the shirts hanging to the sides to clear a path to the back of the closet to locate the pair I'd worn the night Henry had come into Mona's. Plucking them from the floor, I wondered how in the world they'd gotten all the way to the back of the deep closet.

I sat back on my butt and dug into the pocket, my fingers easily finding the business card. I pulled it out as cool air washed over my hand. Frowning, I glanced up and eyed the closet. Till this day, I could not figure out why the closet was so drafty.

My gaze flicked to the business card. Shaking my head, I couldn't believe he had one. Really? Like, "Hi, I'm out of prison. Here's my card!" But it was some kind of car-detailing business card, a business, I thought, if I remembered correctly, his father ran while we were in high school.

I don't think he really meant to hurt Charlie.

Reece's words floated through my thoughts, and for the first time in like forever, I thought about his parole hearings, I thought about his trial and everything since that night until now. It killed me to acknowledge it, but never once did Henry make excuses for what he did. Never once did he not show remorse, and not the kind when you get caught doing something bad. I remembered him crying at the trial. Not when the guilty verdict was handed down or at sentencing, but when I took the stand and recounted the events.

Henry had cried.

And back then I had hated him so much for that. I didn't want to see his tears, couldn't even understand how he could cry when he was the one who hurt Charlie. But now I knew it was more than that. All this time

I also blamed myself and I had cried an ocean's worth of tears. When I thought of Henry, I always thought of my role in things.

I squeezed my eyes shut for a moment and tried to picture Charlie's reaction to what I was thinking about doing. Would he be upset? Or would he turn to me and say *finally*? I let out a shaky sigh. My throat felt thick. My eyes burned when I reopened them.

Then I dialed the number on the card.

My stomach twisted until I thought I'd hurl all over the clothes as the phone rang once, twice, and then five times before voice mail picked up. I didn't leave a message, because seriously, what would I say? I didn't even know what I was going to say if he did answer. I started to stand up when I felt the cold air again, this time stronger and steady, as if a hard gust of wind blew out of the closet.

So freaking weird.

Placing the phone on the floor, I scooted forward on my knees, pushing the hanging clothes even further back as I scanned the closet. The air couldn't be coming from outside, because the closet butted up to where the steps used to go upstairs. Could it be from the main door opening? Stretching, I placed my hand against the wall. The surface was cool, as expected, but the wall didn't feel . . . *solid*. Not like the rest of the closet. It almost felt like fake wood, the kind cheap bookshelves were made out of and would fall apart if it got wet. Upon closer inspection, I could actually see a crack, a separation between whatever kind of wood this was and the actual wall. Almost running the length of the back wall, it was about two feet wide and five feet in height.

Which probably explained why drafts were getting through.

Pushing on the section of the wall, I gasped as it shifted, swinging open into a space behind the wall without so much as a whisper.

"Holy crap," I murmured, thinking of the hidden doors and pathways the Silvers mentioned when I first moved in, but I hadn't really believed them. Or at least figured they'd be closed up by this point.

Curiosity got the best of me. So did the mad need for a distraction. The wall shifted far enough that anyone could really squeeze through, just by dipping and turning sideways. I shimmied through, entering a dark and musty-smelling space that was only lit from the light spilling in through my bedroom.

I was almost able to straighten to my full height. Reece would barely be able to stand bent over in here. There was so much dust in the air as I glanced up, I didn't want to breathe too deeply. I think I really was under the stairs.

Oh my God.

Totally reminded me of that way old movie—*The People Under the Stairs*. I shivered. Creepy. Slowly moving to the left, I realized there was a flight of stairs inside the cramped space. Placing my hands on either side of the wall, I carefully climbed the steps. They turned out to be steep and narrow, and I couldn't imagine anyone climbing up and down them without breaking their neck unless they seriously knew the layout.

At the top of the stairs was another hidden door like the one in my closet—same dimensions—and when I pressed on the panel it popped open without a sound.

I was in another closet, but it wasn't a normal closet by any means. There were no clothes, no hangers, and there were also no doors. There was nothing stopping me from seeing the room. In a dumbfounded trance, I moved forward.

Daylight spilled in through the large bay window and tiny flecks of dust danced in the beams. The room should be warm, but my skin was chilled to the bone as I stepped out of the closet. My eyes squinted behind my glasses.

Oh my God.

My stomach dropped as my gaze crawled over the walls. Not a square inch of paint was exposed. Photos were hung everywhere, some taped, some tacked up.

I couldn't be seeing this.

Pictures of women I'd never seen before were all over the walls—walking outside of businesses, outside of homes, and other normal, everyday things, but some—*oh my God*—some were close-ups of wrists and ankles bound, but that . . .

My gaze moved over the left wall and then darted back. I turned to it, clamping a hand over my mouth.

There were pictures of me.

Photos of me inside *my* apartment—me sleeping on the couch and in my bed. There were photos of me walking through my bedroom, wearing nothing but a towel, and then photos where I was wearing *nothing* at all. Photos of me naked, from almost every possible conceivable angle known to freaking man. There were so many of them, and I wasn't alone in some of them.

There were pictures of Reece and me.

Cuddled up on the couch together. Him sitting on my bed and me standing in front of him. Photos of us kissing. And photos . . . photos of us making love.

Horror dug razor-sharp claws in me as I stared at the photos. I couldn't get enough air in my lungs. In the back of my head, I knew I needed to get out of here.

I needed to call the police, but when I took a step back it was like I was walking in quicksand.

Floorboards creaked, the sound clapping through the room like thunder.

Tiny hairs rose all over my body. Ice drenched my veins.

"I really wish you hadn't seen this."

Chapter 25

Terror seized me at the sound of his voice, the shock of realizing I was so not alone making me a little dizzy for a moment. The photos on the wall blurred as I spun around.

He stood in the doorway of the room, his blond hair messy, like he'd run his fingers through it several times. Those sharp, dark eyes appeared to miss nothing, and his arms were loose at his sides, but his hands opened and closed, grasping air over and over.

Kip. It was Kip.

He was the one who'd been breaking into my house and it obviously went further than that. The photos of the other women . . .

Kip tilted his head to the side like he could hear what I was thinking. "You shouldn't have seen this. You wouldn't understand."

Fear had my throat seized up and I croaked out, "What is there to understand?"

One shoulder rose as he glanced toward the closet. "Probably should've made sure you couldn't find your way up here, but I honestly didn't think you'd find it." He took a step forward and to the side, putting himself between the closet and the door. My muscles locked up. "I mean, you hadn't discovered it this whole time. Figured you weren't smart enough."

Any other day I'd be insulted for not being "smart enough," however, today I honestly didn't care what he thought about my level of intelligence. I had to get out of there. My frantic gaze moved to the doorway. I'd been in James and Miriam's apartment before, and if the layout was anything like theirs, I knew this room led to a hall and then to the door.

"I know what you're thinking," he said gently.

I looked at him sharply. "That you're a freak?"

His eyes narrowed. "And you're a whore." He spat the words out. Drawing back, I stared at him as a muscle flickered along his jaw. "You're just like all the rest of them—just like Shelly."

"Shelly?" I whispered.

"When it came to her, I was relegated to the friend zone for years, but I loved her. I *loved* her, Roxy." His dark eyes flashed. "But she spread her legs for just about any guy who crossed her path. I wasn't good enough for her, I guess." He barked out a short, harsh laugh. "Well, I showed her just how good I was."

When it hit me who Shelly was—the girl that had gone missing at the beginning of the summer—my knees went weak. I doubted showing her how good he was had anything to do with something I wanted to be a part of.

I thought about the other women—the ones in the photos on these walls. "You . . . you hurt them because of Shelly?"

His lips curled up in a mockery of a smile. "I don't think I hurt them."

The guy was insane, absolutely crazy-pants insane. I opened my mouth, but then I heard what felt like a lifeline. The distant ring of my cell phone. I'd left it in my closet. I had no idea who could be calling, but I prayed that it was Reece, because I had to think he'd check on me if I didn't answer. He knew the passcode to the security system and he had a key.

Kip didn't acknowledge the sound of my phone. He was studying me like one would look at an insect through a microscope. "I sent you flowers."

I blinked. "What?"

"I sent you the flowers," he repeated, taking another slow, measured step forward. "I sent them after I heard you talking with your mother," he continued, sending a shiver of repulsion through me. "I told you things would be better."

The man was seriously deranged.

"You never brought them home. That upset me." He shrugged again and then he reached out, brushing his fingers along a photo. "I wanted you to know I was here with you." A real smile appeared and somehow that was creepier than anything else. "I loved how you thought the place was haunted. Cute."

Those dark eyes settled on mine. They were bottomless, wholly frightening. I heard the phone ringing again downstairs, and as my heart pounded in my chest, he lowered his arm. His hand opened and closed. "I never got to do that with the rest of them. Only Shelly. I knew where she kept her spare key."

My arms were shaking so bad I wrapped them around my waist as I took a sideways step, moving closer to the door. I had to keep him talking. That much I knew.

"You really pissed me off when you brought him home," he said. "I thought you were different.

You were different from the rest of them—artistic, funny."

"You messed up my apartment."

"Of course I did. How else was I to get you back here?" He inclined his head again. "Sometimes I would watch you at Mona's. I'd be there and you'd have no idea. Just like I've laid beside you and you've had no idea."

My stomach knotted with disgust and horror. I couldn't even wrap my head around that, couldn't even allow myself to truly think about it.

"What . . . what are you going to do?"

"That's such a repetitious question," he replied, the grin slipping from his face. "I don't know what I'm going to do. I didn't plan this. You weren't supposed to come up here. I was supposed to come to you, when the time was right."

When the time was right? Dear God, I was staring into the face of someone truly unhinged. I heard my phone start ringing again, and this time Kip's eyes narrowed. His hands closed once more, and I sprang into action, my flats slipping on the wooden floor as I took off toward the door. My stomach was in my throat, and all I could let myself think about was making it to that door—making it outside.

I didn't make it very far.

Tackled from behind, I went down hard, my glasses flying off, my knees smacking the floor, and my palms scraping across a rough board. Pain flared, but I didn't cave in to it. I wiggled and twisted, trying to loosen the arms circled tight around my waist.

Kip grunted as he flipped me on my back, and I swung out. His round cheeks flushed, he shifted, pushing his knee into my stomach with enough force to knock the air out of my lungs. "Knock it off," he ordered, jerking back as I swung again. This time he wasn't fast enough. My fist connected with his jaw, and I hit him like my brothers taught me to. Hard and fast. Dull pain danced over my knuckles, but I swung again, screaming as loud as I could.

"Scream all you want, Roxy." He caught my hand and slammed it down, pinning it to the floor with bruising force. "James and his girl aren't home and you know the Silvers can't hear shit."

That didn't stop me from screaming.

He hauled me up by one arm and slammed me back down. My head cracked against the floor, and for a second, bright lights flashed in back of my eyes, dotting my vision. I was stunned as pain whipped around along the side of my head and down my neck.

Fear rose inside me, insidious as choking, thick smoke, but so did a fury that was far stronger. This would *not* happen. Not after everything. I wasn't stupid. The other women obviously hadn't been able to identify him, and Shelly—that poor girl didn't sound like she was still walking this earth. I knew the chances of me walking out of there were slim. I was not going to go down like this. There was no way.

I was going to fight.

Rolling my hips, I succeeded in knocking him to the side. Once his weight came off my stomach, I didn't hesitate. I rolled onto my knees, scrambling to put space between us. "Help!" I screamed until my throat felt raw. "Help!"

Kip snatched my ankle, yanking hard enough that I cried out as sharp pain flew up my leg. I didn't stop. On my hands and knees, I crawled across the floor, toward the bedroom door.

"I don't know where you think you're going." He grunted as he got a hand on my upper leg and pulled.

I went down, my chin banging against the floor. The walls whirled as he flipped me onto my back once more. This time his body settled on mine, and the weight, heavy and consuming—terrifying and repulsive—drove me crazy. I clawed at his face, screaming as my fingernails dug into his cheek. Pink welts appeared, quickly spilling blood as I dragged my hand down.

He threw his head back, howling as he lifted his arm. I didn't even see his fist coming. Pain exploded along my cheek and eye. A fiery sensation stole my breath as the pain burst along my mouth. I tasted something metallic. Dazed, it took me a second to realize that he'd hit me twice. Twice. A man had never hit me in my entire life. Not counting my brothers when we were younger and used to beat the snot out of one another.

I opened my eyes—or one eye. My left didn't seem to want to work right. I saw him raising his fist again, and as my heart dropped, I brought my leg up as hard as I could. He anticipated the move, shifting so my knee connected with the inside of his thigh.

Cursing under his breath, he wrapped his hand around my throat and squeezed—squeezed tight enough that I hadn't realized I'd taken my last breath until it was too late. "For such a little thing, you sure as hell—"

"Roxy!"

Hope kindled to life at the sound of Reece's voice floating up from my apartment. He was here—oh my God, he was here. I couldn't believe it. I opened my mouth to yell back, but Kip slammed his hand down on my mouth, muffling my scream. The grip was brutal, smashing my lips against my teeth. He moved so quickly, his other hand reaching around to his back. There was a quick glimmer of something shiny and the cool metal pressed against the base of my throat.

He had a *knife*.

"Say one word, and I'll give you a different kind of smile," he whispered. "Do you understand me?"

My chest clenched as I stared into his cold, piercing eyes. I really couldn't nod, but he seemed to see the understanding in my face. "Up," he ordered.

As Kip hauled me onto my feet, I heard Reece down below, shouting out my name again. He sounded closer, as if he were near the closet. My heart pounded as Kip kept the knife against my throat, pushing me toward the bedroom door. Reece was smart. He would see the open door inside the closet, the stairwell, and he would come looking for me. Kip had to have realized that too.

Kip cursed again as he turned so I was facing the closet door. Heavy steps thundered throughout the apartment, matching the tempo of my racing heart. We were almost out of the room when Reece burst out of the closet, gun drawn and pointed straight at where we stood.

Time appeared to have frozen.

Terror and hope warred inside me as my gaze briefly met Reece's. For the tiniest moment, I saw what he was feeling when he saw me. It was in those beautiful, sea-colored eyes of his. Panic. Fear. A rage I knew could be deadly, that promised retribution. I couldn't imagine what he was thinking when he came through that door and saw this. I had no idea how I started off the day waking up with resolve and determination to really start the process of moving on with my life and then this, God, this *was* happening.

But I should know by now that none of life could

truly be planned. My life—our lives—were about to be thrown off course yet again.

Kip slipped his hand off my mouth and wrapped his arm around my waist as he kept the knife against my throat.

In a split second, Reece's jaw locked down and his lips thinned. Everything about his face went emotionless.

"I'm sorry," I whispered, my words coming out a little mushed-sounding.

Reece's eyes were like chips of blue diamonds. "Babe, none of this is your fault."

I knew that, but I didn't want Reece to see any of this, and I didn't want him to get hurt. Those were the last two things I wanted.

"You're right," Kip spat back. "If it's anyone's fault, it's yours. She was fine before you came along. You made her into a whore."

The man was legit crazy.

"You really are making me want to put a bullet between your eyes," Reece countered, his voice threaded with barely controlled anger.

"And you really want me to finish this?"

The muscle flexed along Reece's jaw. "Bud, all I want you to do is really think about—"

"Don't come any closer." Kip pushed the knife into my skin, causing me to yelp. A thin trickle of wet warmth ran down my throat as he stepped to the side, bringing me with him. "I swear to God, I will end her!"

"I'm not coming any closer." Reece kept the gun level. "But I want to know what you're thinking. How you're planning for this to go down."

"Does that really fucking matter?" Kip stepped again, and Reece didn't move toward him, but he mirrored his movements until we'd switched positions. Our backs were to the closet now. "There's no way out of this. I'm not fucking stupid. I know what needs to be done."

My pulse skyrocketed as Kip's fingers flexed around the handle of the knife. My mind raced into scary places, one where my throat ended up slit and Kip got away with everything he'd done by doing one thing. Committing suicide via police officer. Kip knew he was done. I doubted he would just put the knife down and surrender.

I saw Reece's gaze slide to the left, behind us for just a fraction of a second, but I could've been imagining it or seeing things, because my vision wasn't the greatest without my glasses and one open eye.

"We can talk this out," Reece said, lowering his gun. "You and me. We talk this through. Let Roxy go, and it will be just you and me."

I could feel Kip shaking his head behind me, and I drew in a shallow breath. Any move I made would most likely result in the knife cutting into my skin, but I couldn't just sit here and do nothing. My head spun. What could I do that wasn't virtual suicide?

If this was going to be my last couple of minutes on Earth, I wished I could kiss him just one more time, feel his hands on me.

My voice was shaky when I spoke. "Reece, I . . . I love you."

"Babe, you're going to tell me that again for a long time coming, you understand?" Reece didn't look at me since he was trained on Kip. "But Kip and me are going to talk this out. He's going to let you go, and we're going to chat about this."

"You think I'm going to let her go? That there's

something to say?" Kip replied, his voice cracking. "This is—"

There was a sickening thudding sound that jolted Kip and then me. The knife slipped, glancing over my skin and then Kip let go. Dazed, I stumbled forward as he dropped to the floor behind me.

A second later, I was in Reece's arms and he was saying something to me, pushing my hair back and gently pressing his hand against my neck, but I wiggled around to see what happened, because I hadn't heard a gun fire. I hadn't seen Reece pull the trigger. I didn't understand.

But then I did.

Henry . . . Henry Williams stood behind the crumpled body.

Chapter 26

Staring out the window across from Reece's bed, I absently ran my finger along the bottom of my lip. The swelling had gone down, but the cut just off the center was still rough and the inside of my mouth was still tender, especially if I wasn't careful and ate something with irregular edges. I couldn't stop messing with it. Sort of like when I had chickenpox as a kid, and couldn't stop itching. My self-control hadn't improved.

I didn't know what time it was. I'd been awake for a while. Sometime in the early morning, I guessed, since I couldn't make out the time on the nightstand clock. At some point I needed to get my glasses replaced. Unbeknownst to me at the time, they'd been broken when they'd hit the floor in . . . in that apartment.

It had been four days since I'd found that hidden door in my closet. Four days since I stumbled into a room that reminded me of something straight out of nightmares. Four days of my stomach aching and my face throbbing, a painful reminder of how close I'd come to not walking out of that room. Four days filled with a lot of introspection.

I guessed near-death experiences at the hands of a blossoming serial killer did that. Made you rethink a lot of your choices and plans.

Come to find out, Henry had tried to call me back after I'd called him. When I hadn't answered, he'd called Reece and when he'd found out that I was at my apartment he'd made the decision to come, apparently not wanting to miss his chance to talk to me, and having no idea what he was walking into. When Henry had called Reece to tell him that I hadn't answered when he returned my call, Reece had tried calling me. He knew I would've answered with everything going on. Instinct had led him to my place, and when Henry showed, finding the front door unlocked, he'd grabbed a crowbar from his car and made his way to my bedroom, then he'd heard Reece talking to Kip.

The rest was history.

Funny how one decision, the choice to start letting go, had literally been what had saved my life.

In more ways than the obvious, I was beginning to realize.

Kip had been taken to the hospital for a rather minor head injury and then released into the custody of the county jail. That's where he was now, and from what I'd been told, he hadn't confessed to anything, but from what he'd said to me and all those horrific photos on his wall, there was enough evidence to charge him with multiple accounts of assault, plus Colton had explained that Kip would most likely be charged with the disappearance of Shelly Winters even though no body had been recovered. I'd also been told there was a good chance that the district attorney would try to strike some kind of deal if they could get Kip to tell them where Shelly was.

A few weeks ago that would've infuriated me. How dare someone like him get a chance to receive a better sentencing—life in prison versus a needle in the arm—when he'd done such terrible things? He'd obviously murdered someone and terrorized innocent women—scared me and violated every definition of privacy—and deserved capital punishment.

But Shelly's family also deserved closure and she deserved to be found, to be laid to rest by her loved ones. And I was done with holding on to so much hate. For the last six years, I'd let hatred and guilt shape me in more ways than I ever realized. Nothing against those who sought lethal punishment, but for me, I just wanted to move on. To look toward a future where a part of me wasn't wrapped up in hating someone. I wanted to see Kip pay for his crimes, but I wouldn't stand in the way if it meant they could locate that poor girl.

So yeah, I'd done a lot of thinking about a lot of things these past four days. College. Painting. The bar. Reece. Henry. Charlie. As corny as it sounded, I felt like I was finally waking up and getting a second chance.

The bed shifted and a hard body curled around me, a warm and bare chest against my back, legs pressed against the backs of mine. An arm carefully settled around my waist.

A second chance when it came to a lot of things.

"Stop messing with your lip," Reece ordered, voice gruff from sleep. His hand flattened against my lower stomach.

My finger stilled. "I'm not."

He chuckled softly, stirring the hair around my neck. "Uh-huh. You been awake long?"

I lowered my hand to where his rested, placing mine atop his. His hand was so much larger than mine. "A couple of hours, I think."

Reece didn't say anything for a long moment. "Talk to me, babe."

Wiggling my fingers in between his, I held his hand. Reece had been great the last four days. Staying with me while I'd been checked over at the hospital. Talking my parents and brothers off the cliff when they arrived. Being there for me when I finally freaked out and had a wee mental breakdown the night after the attack. Distracting me when I closed my eyes and saw those photos of me—of us—because those photos had been creepy and nothing like the portraits I'd done of Reece. Oh man, nothing like that at all. He'd been my raft in a churning ocean, but I knew it hadn't been easy for him. None of this had been.

Easing onto my back, I turned my head and met his gaze. "I'm okay, honestly. Just been thinking." With my free hand, I reached up and placed my hand on his cheek. Stubble grazed my palm. "What about you?"

"Just woke up."

I would've rolled my eyes if my right eye still didn't feel funky. I had one hell of a shiner. "That's not what I meant."

He held my gaze for a moment and then closed his eyes. Under my palm, his jaw tensed, and concern pinged around inside me. He hadn't really talked about himself during these four days. It had been the twenty-four-hour Roxy channel.

I was about to straddle him and force him to speak when he finally did. "I saw that bastard yesterday."

I didn't have to guess who he was referring to. "You went to the jail?" Reece had to work since he'd taken time off when Charlie had passed away.

"I had to take someone in, and they had him in general lockup." His eyes opened and they were a bright, angry blue. "I wanted to go into that cell and kick his fucking head in. I almost did. He was at the front of the cell, eyeballing me, and I was coming at him, about to grab him through the bars and knock his ass out, but one of the COs must've seen what I was about to do and stepped in."

"Got to say, I'm happy to hear that." I ran my thumb along the curve of his high cheekbone. "It would suck if you ended up in jail."

"Yeah, that could be problematic, but damn, babe, for a moment, whatever repercussion I faced would've been worth it." His gaze drifted over my face. "Because when I see you right now, I'm reminded of what the fucker did to you, what he wanted to do to you."

My breath hitched. "Reece—"

"I know you're as okay as you can be. And I know you're going to be a hundred percent, because Roxy, you are strong. I know that, but I think about what he'd been doing. The fact that he was there when you and I were *together.*" Fury laced his words, forming a bitter edge. "He was there when you were alone. The sick fuck got close to you. He *touched* you. It's going to take a little bit for me to get past the point where I want to beat his face in."

I searched his eyes, afraid I'd find a shadow of guilt somewhere in there. "You know there was nothing you could do, right? No one suspected that it was him or that was how someone was getting into my place."

"I. Was. There. He stood in the fucking closet and

watched us. All the training I've had, and I had no idea it was him." He rolled onto his back, causing my fingers to slip off his face. He lifted his hands, scrubbing them over his face. "Fuck, I didn't even remember his name."

My stomach twisted as I sat up, and I ignored the twinge of pain just below my ribs. I reached out, grabbing his wrists. I tried to pull his hands away from his face, but he resisted. Not to be deterred, I let go and yanked the comforter off him.

"What are you doing?" His voice was muffled behind his hands.

I swung one leg over his narrow hips and then straddled him. Grabbing his wrists, I yanked on his arms again. This time he let me pull them away. He arched a brow at me as his gaze dipped. "Have I ever told you how much I like it when you wear my shirts and nothing else?"

I ignored that, because as crazy as it sounded, I thought his eyes held a certain sheen to them as I stared down at him. And that made my heart ache something fierce, because I didn't want him to take on the heavy weight of responsibility for someone else's actions. That wasn't fair, and it hurt to watch him carry that.

It struck me then, like being hit by a ton of flying monkeys—flying monkey asses, actually. That piercing pain in the chest must've become something all too familiar to my parents after watching me blame myself for what happened to Charlie. Yeah, what was going on with Kip was totally different, but in a way it was still the same, and it had to be what Reece felt when he heard me talk about the way I felt.

What a hell of a wakeup call.

"None of this was your fault," I told him. "Please tell me you understand that, because I cannot deal with you blaming yourself when you had nothing to do with this."

His brows furrowed together. "You were hurt—you *are* hurt."

"But you didn't hurt me. You *saved* me. So did Henry." The last words were something I never thought I'd ever utter in my entire life. "And you've been here for me. You've been there for me when Charlie passed away and before that. And if I'd given you the chance, you would've been there for me a hell of a lot longer." Tears pricked at my eyes, stinging my right one. "You did what you needed to do, Reece."

A moment passed and then he exhaled roughly. Slipping his hands free from mine, he cupped my cheeks, drawing my face down toward his. "I'm going to be real with you, Roxy. I would not know what to do if something happened to you," he said, his voice thick. "The very thought of losing you kills me. And knowing how close I came to doing just that isn't something I can easily forget."

"I know," I whispered, blinking back tears.

He let out another raw, shaky-sounding breath. "But I'm going to try, because that's what I asked you to do with everything, and I know that's what you're going to do."

My smile was wobbly but wide and then he lifted his head off the pillow, kissing me gently, mindful of the cut in my lip. "I love you," he said against my mouth, his words barely above a whisper but packing an emotional punch. "Baby, I love you."

I could spend the rest of my life hearing those words over and over again, and never grow tired of hearing them. Not only that, I wanted to *feel* them. I wanted to be wrapped around Reece until we didn't know where each of us began or ended.

Kissing him softly, I shifted so I was able to slide one hand down his bare, hard stomach. When I reached the band on his sleep pants, he pulled his head back, resting against the pillow as he stared up at me. His cheeks heightened in color as I held his gaze and glided my hand under the band. Unsurprisingly, he was already hard when I wrapped my fingers around him.

A deep sound came from the back of Reece's throat. His eyes remained latched to mine as I worked my hand over him. Just touching him like this made me damp and achy between the thighs. It had never been like that with anyone else and I knew there would never be anyone else.

Reece was for me.

I was for him.

One hand found its way up my borrowed shirt, settling on my hip. Concern clouded the arousal building in his eyes. "Do you think—?"

"I think it's the smartest idea ever," I cut him off.

His hips rose slightly. "Babe, I want you. I always want you, but we don't have to do this right now. We got time. Lots of time." His eyes glimmered as I got his bottoms down, exposing him. "And you also had those toys I'm so going to break out one of these days."

The idea of him using those on me made me all kinds of happy, but unless he had a vibrator stashed somewhere, that fantasy would have to be lived out on a different day. "I want to do this. A lot."

His lips parted. "Roxy—"

I cupped him as I squeezed his hard length.

"Fuck," he grunted out, kicking his head back.

"Okay. Perfect idea. Completely. One hundred percent behind whatever you want to do."

I giggled, but that sound died in a moan as his hand traveled to my breast. It wasn't long before my undies ended up off, the shirt was lying on the bed next to us and we were joined together. With his hands on my hips and mine pressed against his chest, he let me set the pace and *we* took our time. This wasn't about screwing each other's brains out or doing so to just get off. No. This was all about showing each other how we felt and there was something restorative in that, beautiful and consuming as we moved together. No rush. Just that moment. And when the building pleasure finally peaked, he was right there with me, our bodies shattering and coming back together.

I didn't move afterward, sprawled out on top of him, my good cheek resting on his chest while he toyed with my hair. "What happened to the streak in your hair?" he asked.

"What?" I was feeling way too lazy and sated to think about his question.

"The purple streak. It's gone."

I laughed, because the way he said it made it sound like it took some kind of voodoo magic to make that happen. "It faded out."

"Huh." He continued to play with my hair and I liked that. "You should do the pink again."

"The pink?" I frowned. "I haven't had the pink for like almost a year."

"I know, but I liked it. It was you."

My frown turned into a grin. He remembered I had a pink streak that long ago? God, I loved this man. For realsies. "Well, maybe I'll go pink next time."

"Well, maybe you should," he teased.

"Bossy," I murmured, still grinning. We lay there for a few minutes, my mind wandering over all the things I'd been thinking about. I was ready to give voice to one of those thoughts. "I've been thinking."

His hand dropped to my back. "Should I be worried?"

"Maybe?" I laughed softly. "It's about what I . . . what I want to do with my future."

He started to rub a slow circle along my lower back. "Okay. What do you want to do?"

For some bizarre reason, it was easier to say this than I thought it would be while lying on Reece naked. Odd. "I was thinking about maybe . . . stepping back from classes. I mean, I know getting a degree is smart, but it's not my passion. Not right now. And college will always be there, but you know, if I learned anything from everything that has happened, who knows what tomorrow or next week will bring. I don't want to . . . live my life doing something I honestly don't care about. Maybe that will change one day."

"Babe, you don't need to convince me." He kept moving his hand, and I wanted to arch my back like a cat. "I think it's a great idea. It will give you more time to paint and to work on web design if you still want to do that."

"I do." My stomach dipped with excitement. "I like doing them, and I can keep working at Mona's." I paused, lifting my head so I could see his face. "You don't think it makes me . . . I don't know, a loser for dropping out of college?"

His eyes narrowed. "First off, you're not dropping out. You're stepping away for a while. Maybe forever, but it's not like you're doing it because you can't cut it. Secondly, college isn't always the fucking answer, babe. Choosing not to go down that route doesn't make you a loser. I'd *love* to hear someone say that to you."

"Simmer down." I patted his chest, but secretly I was super pleased. I took a deep breath and, yeah, it felt lighter, better. "I want to take painting seriously. Who knows? Maybe I could follow up on what Mom told me about the art dealer in the city. She liked my stuff. I have more. I can give her more."

"As long as you don't give her any you've done of me."

Flushing, I rested my forehead against his chest and groaned. "You suck."

He chuckled as he looped his arms around my waist. "Especially the ones you do of me naked. Yeah, I haven't forgotten that request."

I sighed.

"But seriously, I think it's a great thing," he said. When I lifted my head, he smiled up at me, tugging at my heart. "I'm proud of you."

"Really?" My voice squeaked.

He shook his head. "Yes, really."

I opened my mouth, but his cell went off. I climbed off him, reclining on my side as he sat up and grabbed his phone.

"Yo," he answered.

Based on the way he answered, I assumed it was not business. He twisted at his waist, glancing down at me. His gaze tracked over the length of my bare body and the look on his face said he wished he wasn't on the phone, but then he turned away. "Yeah. Okay."

"Is everything okay?" I asked when he hung up.

"It was Colton." Reece frowned as he placed his cell back on the nightstand. "He's outside. I'll be right back."

Before he swung his legs off the bed, he kissed my

cheek and then my temple. The act was both sweet and tender, and really made me want to flail around the room like a broken ballet dancer.

Reece closed the door behind him and for a moment I lay there, and then I grabbed my shirt, because knowing my luck, I'd get caught naked in his bedroom. Pulling the shirt over my head, I let it pool around me and then worked on getting all the huge knots out of my hair while I resisted the urge to go out and see what Colton was doing here. I didn't have to resist for too long.

Less than five minutes later, Reece came back in, leaving the door open behind him. I grabbed for the comforter to cover my bare legs. "Is Colton still here?"

He stopped a few steps from the bed. "No. He had to head back out."

"Okay." I cocked my head to the side, eyeing him closely. Something was definitely off about him as he dragged his hand across his chest. "Did something happen?"

Reece nodded. "Yeah, something did."

Now I was starting to get anxious. A lead ball formed in my belly. "What?"

"Kip's dead."

I blinked once and then twice. "Come again?"

His throat worked. "He was found dead in lockup this morning. A few hours ago, actually. Fucking bizarre."

All I could do was stare at him.

"The thing is, he choked himself with his shirt by tying it to the bar and letting his weight drop. Doable. But really unlikely considering who would do that to themselves, plus he wasn't alone. Colton said there were eight other guys in lockup."

I still hadn't found any words.

He shook his head slowly as he stared over my shoulder. "He left a suicide message, supposedly."

"Supposedly?" There. I could speak. Well, I could parrot Reece.

"He told one of the guys locked up with him where Shelly Winters' body could be found, and then, according to the witnesses, he proceeded to hang himself. No one stopped him." He paused, confounded just like me. "There's a unit heading out there now, since the location is in our jurisdiction."

All right, I was bowled over by surprise. "No one tried at all to stop him? They—eight people—just watched him choke himself to death by tying his shirt around his neck and to the bars?"

"Yeah," he replied. "But here's the thing." He stepped closer to the bed. "News broke about him by Monday night, right? When we were in the hospital, it was on the evening news. Word got out fast that he was suspected of assaulting all the other women and that he was incarcerated."

"Okay."

"Colton tells me that about a day and a half ago, a guy was brought in for robbing a liquor store. Strange situation. The dude walked in, grabbed a bottle of whiskey off the shelf and then sat outside and drank it. Sat there until the cops showed up. He was arrested and has been in jail. Still is. City cops say the guy they brought in has a history, but guess who he's also tied to."

I shook my head. "Who?"

"Isaiah."

My eyes widened. "Holy shit. Wasn't it Isaiah's cousin that was attacked?" When Reece nodded, it all started to come together. "Oh my God, do you guys think this guy was ordered by Isaiah to get arrested, then end up in the same jail to take out Kip?"

"Remember Mack? The guy who was threatening Calla over the money her mom owed? He ended up with a bullet in his head, and we all know Isaiah is capable of it, especially when someone has fucked with someone in his family. Even more convenient is the fact the camera on the cell went down during the early-morning hours."

Holy . . . "So one of the officers was in on it, too?"

"We've known for years that he had people on the police force. God knows how much he paid this guy to do this and whoever fucked with the camera. Probably more than enough to take a man's life and risk getting caught. The department is launching an investigation into it."

"But no one has ever been able to pin anything on Isaiah. Ever. Like in the history of ever and ever."

"Yep."

I didn't know what to think or how to feel when it came to discovering that Kip was dead. That he'd either taken his own life or Isaiah had someone take him out. Either way, there would be no life in prison or deals being made. If what the guy in the cell was saying was true, Shelly's body would be found and that was the only light at the end of this messy tunnel. I searched through my emotions for something, but I was kind of like . . . *meh.* And didn't that make me the crappiest person ever? It wasn't that I didn't care. I just didn't want to waste any more time or energy on that monster. I couldn't.

Reece sat on the bed, scrubbing his fingers through his hair. I watched him in silence. As he lowered his hand to his knee, he shook his head. "Does it make me a shit person to say I'm not too torn up about what just happened?"

Crawling over to him, I plopped down so my knees were pressed against his legs. "I think it doesn't . . . I mean . . ." Sighing, I raised my hands. "You know, I could lie and say it sucks that someone died, but I'm not sure if that's the truth. And lying is a sin, right? I mean, is being glad someone is dead a sin? You know, I really don't know if that is. We need to find someone who's super familiar with the Bible or something."

His lips twitched.

"I bet Melvin would know."

He arched a brow. "Melvin? The old guy who's usually drunk at the bar?"

I nodded. "Yep. Melvin kind of knows everything. Actually, I bet Katie would know. She's another one who kind of knows everything. It's weird. Oh!" I clapped my hands. "I never told you what Katie told me once about you."

Both brows flew up this time. "Should I be worried?"

"No," I laughed. "She told me once, about two years ago, that I'd already met and fallen in love with the person who I'd spend my entire life with. I didn't believe her, even when she said it was you."

His eyes widened. "For real?"

"She did. And I didn't want to believe her, but I think I knew in the back of my mind that she was right, because I already knew you and I've loved you a lot longer than even I wanted to admit."

He stared at me, a mixture of amusement and disbelief written across his face.

I grinned. "She also told me once she was drinking moonshine a relative brought her from the South and she ended up in the woods and talked to fairies all night. And then this other time, she told Nick that he already met the chick he was going to be with, and he looked like he wanted to run for the hills. So maybe that's just her M.O.? Wait! She also said—"

"Back to the you loving me part," he corralled me back in. "She really said that to you *years* ago?"

"Yes, she did."

"Oh, babe." He leaned in, resting his forehead against mine as he curved a hand around the back of my neck. He kissed me, and I melted like an ice cube in the sun. "Katie really does have psychic powers."

Chapter 27

I supposed it was a good thing that my stomach had stopped hurting, because I was on my fourth or so death grip hug, and I was sure all the excess air had been squeezed right out of me.

It was Friday night, almost two weeks after what I was now referring to as Monday Suckday. I'd returned to Mona's that past Thursday even though Jax insisted I could take off as much time as I needed, even a month, but I needed to get back to my life and I needed the money. The whole gang was there, hanging out at Mona's for the night before heading back Sunday morning. They were staying at Jax's house, camped out in the guest bedroom and the couch.

"I think you kind of look badass with the black eye," Katie said as she hitched up her neon-blue halter top. "Like I should be afraid that you could kick my ass."

Calla leaned against the bar beside me, folding her arms along the top. Her blond hair was pulled up in a high ponytail. "She could probably kick all of our asses. The skinny ones are always the scrappy ones."

My black eye had all but faded to a pale bluish purple and it probably should've been completely gone by now, but there were some broken blood vessels. But it was barely visible. I wasn't worried. "It's true," I told the girls. "Watch out."

Avery laughed as she held a refilled glass of Coke. "I took Teresa out last weekend."

My brows flew up as I looked at the stunning dark-haired girl. "I feel like I need details on this."

Teresa laughed as she swiveled around on the bar stool. "I found these boxing gloves of Jase's and we had a match. I was going easy on her, though, only popping her in the arm."

"Whatever." Avery glanced over to where Cam stood with Jase and Jax. They were fanboying over Brock. "I thought Cam was going to have a heart attack when we started."

"Yeah, I thought we were going to have to call nine-one-one." Teresa snorted. "It was funny, because I'm pretty sure Jase thought it was like watching some kind of pervy fantasy come true. Two girls with boxing gloves."

Calla laughed as she poured a shot. "Poor Cam. Gotta suck when one of those girls is your sister."

"You know, I think that would be a great show to do at the club. The girls could be in bikinis. Or topless." Katie took the shot and downed it in an impressive swallow. Smacking her lips and sighing happily, she placed the glass back on the bar. "I'm totally going to pitch that to Larry. He liiiiikes my ideas." Katie shimmied her hips.

I arched my brow as I looked at the two girls. "What have you guys done?"

Avery giggled.

"Anyway guys, I've got to get back and make some mon-nay! Peace out—oh wait!" She spun to where Nick appeared behind the bar. A bushel of fresh limes was in his hands and his dark brows rose as he met Katie's wide stare. "You!" she shouted, hopping forward, her breasts defying gravity and the halter top.

He set the limes on the bar. "Me?"

I grinned as Calla pushed back, curiosity settling into her features.

"Yes. You!" She pointed at him with blue nail polish that matched her top. "I have something to tell you."

"Oh no," murmured Calla while I barely refrained from hopping with excitement.

Katie wiggled her fingers like she was about to break into a jazz hand routine. "She's coming tonight."

Nick arched a brow. "I don't know who the lucky lady is, but I sure hope so."

I snorted.

Undeterred, Katie waved her hand. "It's her. The one you're going to fall for and fall hard. Oh, boy, you have so met your match. Totally." Beaming at a now silent Nick, she spun toward us and laughed. "Toodles, my bitches."

We watched Katie strut her way out of the bar in five-inch platform heels, then I turned to Nick, tapping him on his arm. "Oh, snap. She's totally right about these things."

Nick paled. "Shut up."

"No. She was right when it came to Jax and me," Calla confirmed. "She's like the stripper love psychic or something."

He looked horrified. "Both of you shut up."

I giggled gleefully. "I cannot wait for this."

Nick scowled.

The door to the bar swung open and all of us whirled toward it. A laugh burst out of me, a high-pitched cackle when I saw who it was. "Oh my God."

Aimee with two e's Grant walked in, frowning in our direction. Her golden-blond hair was styled in pretty waves and her uber-tanned midriff was on full display. The girl was hot, but she also had no concept of personal space, plus she'd been a total bitch to Calla, and I was so not okay with that. But the idea that Nick would fall for her? I about died. Laughing so hard, my stomach hurt as I smacked my hands down on the bar top. "Oh my God, it's her!"

Calla folded her arms when Aimee started toward the guys and then grinned like the cat that ate an entire cage full of canaries when the girl veered off at the last minute. "That's sick," Calla said to Nick. "I don't know if I can be friends with you now."

Nick rolled his eyes. "I can tell you right now that Katie's juju is broke as shit because no part of my body is getting near that."

"Whatever," I sung loudly. "It's true love."

The look he shot me was dark, but it didn't wipe my grin off my face. Eventually Avery and Teresa joined the guys, and when we had a down moment behind the bar, Calla got all serious-face with me.

"Are you really okay?" she asked. "I mean, I know what you've gone through is crazy, and I've been through some crazy myself, so I know it can be hard."

I nodded as I started to cut up a lime. "I am. Well, I think I am, if that makes any sense. There are a couple of moments where I'm still freaked out about it. I'm not going to lie. What Kip did, I just don't want to really dwell on it, you know? He's gone. And they found that girl's body, and that's what matters now. At least her family will have some kind of closure."

"Yeah," she replied, eyeing me closely. "And everything with Charlie?"

Cutting through another lime, I smiled. It was a little sad, but it was real. "I miss him. I miss not seeing him every Friday, but I'll get through this and it's getting easier."

"I'm happy to hear that. By the way, I love the new glasses. Pink frames look great on you—what in the world?"

I looked up, following her gaze. A girl had just walked into the bar. I'd never seen her before, but good Lord, she was absolutely stunning. With shiny black hair and a body I'd probably give away an ovary or two for, she was tall and looked like she belonged on the cover of a fashion magazine.

The newcomer was headed toward the bar, but she stopped, her mouth dropping open as she spotted the crew over by the pool tables. I looked at them.

It was Teresa who saw her first, and she drew back, surprised and obviously recognizing the girl. Then she smiled as she glanced over at Cam and Avery—a tentative smile that grew. "Steph?" she called out. "What in the hell are you doing here?"

The girl named Steph recovered enough to walk over toward them. I couldn't hear what she said over the noise, so I glanced up at Calla. "You guys know her?"

"Yeah. She went to Shepherd. Graduated with Jase. Remember what I told you happened to Teresa's roommate before she moved out of the dorm?"

"The girl that was killed?"

Calla nodded. "When Teresa found her body, she freaked, and it was Steph who took care of her and called the police. Turned out, she lived in the other suite, but Teresa never saw her. I don't know her that well, but she's really hot."

"Like if Angelina Jolie and Megan Fox were joined together kind of hot."

She laughed. "So true. Wow. Okay. I got to go see what she's doing here. You good back here?"

"Yep." I waved her off. "Go get me some gossip."

Things got pretty busy, and when Calla returned to help run orders out of the kitchen, there wasn't any time to find out why the girl who used to go to Shepherd was up here, but I couldn't help but think of what Katie had said to Nick when I saw him grinning at her when she came up to the bar to get a rum and coke.

I knew that grin.

Since Calla was here for the weekend, she was closing down the bar with Jax and Nick and that meant I didn't have to hang around. After saying good-bye to everyone and getting a hug from Jax that lifted me clear off my feet, I pulled on my cardigan and headed outside.

A cruiser waited for me in the parking lot.

Grinning, I headed toward it as the window rolled down and revealed one hot-as-hell cop. "Lunch break?" I asked.

He bit down on his lower lip. "My favorite kind of lunch break."

Heat simmered low in my belly. I totally knew what kind of lunch break he was thinking of. "Mine, too." Hoping I wasn't breaking some kind of cop in a cruiser rule, I bent down and kissed him through the window. "Meet me back at your place?"

One side of his lips kicked up. "See you then."

At some point, I was going to move back into my apartment, sooner rather than later. Not because I didn't love staying with Reece. I did, especially on nights like this when it took only a handful of minutes to get from Mona's to his condo and we could engage in some freak-a-deak.

I hadn't told Calla, but the idea of sleeping in my apartment gave me the sweats, and the only way I could overcome that was by doing it. Obviously, I wouldn't do it alone. Reece would be there with me, but getting back into my apartment was one way to get back to normal.

When we got to Reece's condo, there was no time for fooling around and pretending we were going to actually eat something. He wrapped his strong arms around me and kissed me like he was a man dying of thirst, and I was dizzy and breathless from it. We went at each other, ending up on the couch with me on my knees grasping the back of the couch with his body behind mine, one hand on my hip and the other between my thighs. *This* really was the best kind of lunch break.

My muscles were jelly and I stayed where he left me, curled over the back of the couch as Reece fixed his uniform, secured his duty belt, and then rooted through my clothing. I watched him, my cheek resting on my hands, and as he straightened, he smacked my butt.

"Pervert," I murmured.

He winked. "You like it."

"Maybe."

Laughing, he picked up my cardigan. "Let me help."

I raised my brows at him, but lifted one arm with a sigh. Dressing me in the cardigan was like herding wildcats, but he stuck with it, securing each button. "I want to come home in the morning and find you in my bed wearing just this."

"You really are a pervert."

Reece brushed his lips over mine. "And I really wish I didn't have to head back out."

"Me, too." I fixed the collar on his uniform. "But I'll be here."

He kissed me again, curling his arm around my waist and lifting me off the couch. Placing me on my feet, he drew me up against him. "Walk me to the door?"

Since the door was a whopping ten feet away, I could manage. Following him, I contented myself with the knowledge of a pint of double-fudge ice cream in the freezer just for me. I was going to make that pint my bitch as soon as I closed the door.

Reece turned, his gaze moving over me with enough intensity that it felt like a physical caress. "We're still on for Sunday?"

Ah, Sunday. Phase two of moving on from . . . well, from everything, began on Sunday. It was going to be a rough day, but I was ready. Stretching up on the tips of my toes, I kissed the corner of his lips. "Yeah, we're still on."

"Good," he replied and then started out the door.

"Reece."

He looked at me over his shoulder, and I said, "I love you."

His face transformed from striking to stunning with a broad smile that had my heart spinning around in a happy dance. "I love you, babe."

As I closed the door and threw the lock, I had to admit that was much better than saying good-bye.

A soft breeze rattled the limbs lining the road as we stepped out of Reece's truck, and I walked around to the driver's side. Lifting my chin, I squinted as I stared out over the cemetery, my gaze drifting over the marble tombstones and large tombs. It was a sunny day. The sky was the perfect shade of blue, the scarce clouds fluffy and white. My mind churned with the watercolors I'd have to mix to capture that right color of blue and clouds, well, clouds were easy and fun to paint. I tugged on the hem of my light sweater and then reached up, tucking the streak of pink hair back behind my ear.

Reece walked to where I stood, with the tips of my flats just brushing the manicured grass. "You ready?"

Pressing my lips together, I nodded and so we started out, following the paved walkway. There was a ball in my throat, a mixture of nerves and a sadness that would linger probably for a long time. I knew that one day I would think of Charlie and there wouldn't be sadness. There would just be warmth and happiness that cuddled the memories of him I would always have and cherish.

Neither of us spoke as we crested the small hill and we could see Charlie's final resting place for the first time since I'd left the funeral. My step stumbled and my heart pounded. His parents had, as expected, spared no expense when it came to marking their son's grave. It was weird to me since they'd barely been there for him the last six years, but who was I to judge? Maybe this was their way of showing him how much they did love him, how much they missed him.

A pearly white angel had been erected behind a rather simple headstone, wings spread wide and head bowed. In her arms was a small child, held close to her breast. I don't know why, but seeing the statue made me want to plop down in the grass and weep like I'd never cried before.

But we weren't the only ones in the cemetery. Nor was Charlie's resting place empty. Not that I was expecting it to be.

Standing off to the side, with his hands shoved into the pockets of his jeans and his head tipped up as if he too was caught up in the angel's mournful expression, was Henry Williams.

The breath I took was shaky. When I'd told Reece the second thing I wanted to do was finally talk to Henry, he'd been 100 percent behind it, just like he was when it came to my college plans. And that's why we were here, at the cemetery on a breezy Sunday afternoon.

Henry lowered his head and turned toward us. A small, unsure smile appeared as he pulled one hand out of his pocket and ran it over the buzz of blond hair that had grown since the last time I'd seen him, which had been in Kip's apartment.

I had to be honest with myself. Henry and I were never going to be friends. I didn't even think that was what he wanted, and it would be too strained, too painful, and that was asking a lot out of both of us. But to really, truly, forgive myself, I had to forgive Henry first.

For a moment, I let myself picture Charlie somewhere up in that beautiful sky, looking down on all of us, and I imagined him smiling. I imagined him being happy about this. Most of all, I imagined him being proud of me—of all of us. And God, that felt good.

Reece's hand found mine and he squeezed reassuringly. "You want to try to do this?"

"No." I looked up at him and our gazes met. Love was spelled out in every flicker of emotion on Reece's striking face. God, I was such a lucky girl and I was so in love with him that it could lift me right off my feet. I squeezed his hand back and said, "I'm not going to *try*. I'm *going* to do this."

Secrets of

YOGA

Secrets of YOGA

CONSULTANT

JENNIE BITTLESTON

A Dorling Kindersley Book

LONDON, NEW YORK, SYDNEY, DELHI, PARIS,
MUNICH, and JOHANNESBURG

Art director *Peter Bridgewater*
Editorial director *Sophie Collins*
Designers *Kevin Knight, Jane Lanaway*
Project editor *Caroline Earle*
Picture researcher *Liz Eddison*
Photography *Guy Ryecart*
Illustrations *Coral Mula, Michael Courtney, Andrew Milne*
Three-dimensional models *Mark Jamieson*

First published in The United States of America in 2000 by
DORLING KINDERSLEY PUBLISHING, INC.
95 Madison Avenue, New York, New York 10016

Natural Health ® is a registered trademark of Weider Publications, Inc. *Natural Health* magazine is the leading publication in the field of natural self-care. For subscription information call 800–526–8440 or visit www.naturalhealthmag.com

Published in Great Britain by Dorling Kindersley Limited.

A CIP catalog record for this book is available from the US Library of Congress

ISBN 0-7894-6781-X

Note from the publisher

Information given in this book is not intended to be taken as a replacement for medical advice. Any person with a condition requiring medical attention should consult a qualified medical practitioner or therapist.

Originated and printed by
Hong Kong Graphic and Printing Limited, China

CONTENTS

Yoga styles

Secrets of Yoga *presents 50 classic asanas or poses taught to beginners in most modern yoga styles.*

HOW TO USE THIS BOOK

Secrets of Yoga is a startup guide for anyone just beginning yoga, and a useful handbook for teachers and for more experienced students who wish to practice between classes. Chapter 1 traces the evolution of yoga, Chapter 2 looks at the basics, and Chapter 3 takes you through your very first practice. Chapter 4 presents 40 classic poses roughly in the order in which you would normally learn them and Chapter 5 completes your introduction to yoga by explaining how to create a program for home practice.

Levels of Difficulty

Within each category the poses appear in order of increasing complexity, and each has an icon

BEGINNERS for complete beginners

INTERMEDIATE slightly more advanced—you have worked through Chapter 3 at least once

ADVANCED more advanced poses to use when your body has gained some flexibility

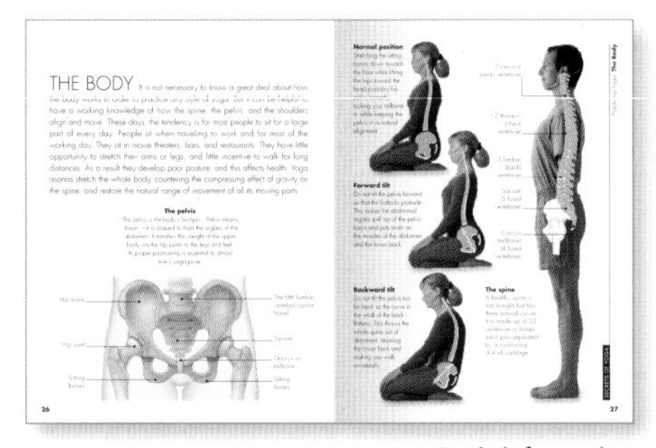

THE BODY It is not necessary to know a great deal about how the body works in order to practice any style of yoga. But it can be helpful to have a working knowledge of how the spine, the pelvis, and the shoulders align and move. These days, the tendency is for most people to sit for a large part of every day. People sit when traveling to work and for most of the working day. They sit in movie theaters, bars, and restaurants. They have little opportunity to stretch their arms or legs, and little incentive to walk for long distances. As a result they develop poor posture, and this affects health. Yoga asanas stretch the whole body, countering the compressing effect of gravity on the spine, and restore the natural range of movement of all its moving parts.

The pelvis

Normal position

Forward tilt

Backward tilt

The spine

26

27

Basic information

The first part looks at what you need to begin, the body and breathing, and how to approach the poses.

GATE POSE In this pose, called **parighasana**, your body makes a shape rather like a gate with a crossbar formed by your trunk and outstretched arms. Like the triangle pose it stretches the sides of the body, but because you kneel and extend your trunk to the side, it is a little more demanding than the triangle.

Poses

Full-color pages show each pose in detail, with a clear introduction explaining the name and the purpose of the pose and its health-giving benefits. Numbered illustrations and captions show how to achieve the pose step by step.

The gate pose is a sideways stretch that bends and extends the hips and abdomen in one movement, making it an excellent exercise for keeping the stomach and waist trim. Although this is a kneeling pose, stretching up at the beginning is the key to achieving the sideways extension, so pause in a kneeling position, press your legs firmly into the floor, and stretch from your knees all the way up the front of your body to the crown of your head, lifting your hip bones, and stretching your sitting bones down.

Working on the pose
If it is hard to rest the toes of your outstretched foot on the mat and keep your shin facing up, rest the foot on a foam block or a folded blanket.

Sideways extension
Be conscious of your shoulders as you raise your arms. Broaden across the collar bones while keeping your shoulder blades flattened against your ribs. As you bend your trunk, take care not to allow your shoulders and hips to roll forward. Instead, keep them in line, as if both buttocks and both shoulders were touching a wall. Keep your tailbone tucked in and your outstretched foot in line with your bent knee. Bend from the hips, keeping your trunk facing forward. Extend your whole body from your hips as far to the side as you can, breathing normally and feeling the stretch from your thigh to your hip joint, and up both sides of your trunk.

Keep both arms straight, and bring them as close together above your head as you can. If at first you find it uncomfortable or difficult to narrow the gap between them, simply keep your upper arm vertical. As you practice, your hip and shoulder joints become more elastic, enabling you to bend further to the side until eventually the palms of your hands meet and the back of the lower hand rests on your foot.

136

Analysis

Black-and-white pages analyze each pose. The main text explores the pose, while the correct positioning of each body part is pinpointed with annotation and arrows show direction of stretching.

A THIRD-LEVEL PROGRAM This program includes some of the basic poses from Chapter 3, such as the triangle and the kneeling forward bend. One of the reasons for this is that the body, especially the legs, needs to be strong for the more complex poses, and the standing poses at the beginning of the program are chosen to give essential preparatory stretches. The program concentrates on energizing: the standing poses at the beginning wake the body up, and the backbends stimulate the mind and body. It focuses on backbends, which mobilize the spine, giving it an extreme stretch. The sequence should take about 75 minutes, although it is important not to hurry. Repeat the program at least once a week.

Home practice

The book finishes with three sample programs based on the 50 classic poses presented in Chapters 3 and 4.

Why Yoga?

Of the many fitness systems popular today, yoga is the oldest, yet the multiplicity of classes and courses available all over the world testify to the 21st-century relevance of this ancient art. Its roots are buried more than 4,000 years deep in the soil of southern Asia, and as it has grown, the great tree of yoga has developed many branches. Yoga is meditation and it is philosophy, it is chanting and deep, rhythmic breathing, and it is healing through exercise.

Contemporary teachers
The popularity of Iyengar yoga, founded in the 20th century by the Indian teacher, B.K.S. Iyengar, testifies to yoga's importance to the modern world.

Restoring harmony

"Union" is the meaning of the word "yoga," and in this increasingly fragmented age yoga offers a way of restoring harmony. It teaches how to unite body and mind, and mind and spirit. It brings physical fitness and increased energy, and a feeling of well-being. It offers relaxation and calm to counter the anxiety and mental stress of 21st-century living. It replaces mood swings and emotional strain with a balanced mind and clear thinking.

This book is for newcomers to yoga, for anyone—from teenagers to the over-nineties—who is interested in learning yoga or just beginning. It has been written for anyone intending to learn alone at home, and as a useful handbook for practice between classes. As well as explaining the basics—the classic and modern styles, when, where, and how to practice—it focuses on 50 classic poses practiced in the traditional schools of yoga and in the modern styles which derive from them.

Caution

If you are taking medication, have recently had an operation, have a chronic complaint or a recent injury, or if your mobility is restricted, check with a doctor or a physical therapist before beginning. Always learn with an experienced instructor who knows about your condition.

• Do not practice standing poses if you have high blood pressure or heart disease.

• Do not practice sitting poses if you have had a hip replacement.

• Do not practice forward bends, side bending, or twisting movements of the trunk if you have a back injury or a prolapsed intervertebral disk.

• Do not practice shoulder stands or inverted poses if you are menstruating or have dizzy spells; eye, ear or sinus problems; a head, neck, or back injury; high blood pressure; or migraines.

• Never adopt a position that causes any pain or undue discomfort since you risk injury.

• Do not practice backbends if you have heart disease or high blood pressure, or a slipped disk or other back problems.

• If you have a knee injury, do not practice kneeling poses or backbends.

• If you have osteoporosis or a stiff back, ease very gently into stretches and twists and do not attempt backbends, inverted poses, or the boat or half-boat.

• Do not begin yoga during pregnancy.

STYLES AND SCHOOLS

The evolution of yoga is believed to span almost 4,000 years, and during this long development it has branched into many different schools. Some concentrate on the mind and meditation, some on exercise and breathing. This chapter maps the story of yoga, from its origins in the Indian subcontinent some 4,000 years ago to its spread worldwide during the 20th century. It introduces some yoga luminaries of the past whose writings and observations inspired the great classic schools. And it ends by focusing on some key 20th-century teachers, founders of styles and schools that are carrying yoga forward into its fifth millennium.

The Philosophy of Yoga

In the West, most people think of yoga as a system of exercises designed to maintain health and prevent illness. But although physical exercise is indeed important, yoga practice synthesizes body, mind, and spirit. Thought is a major component of yoga practice.

Yoga evolved primarily as a philosophy; the exercises or "asanas" developed later as a way of concentrating the mind in order to be able to meditate more deeply. The ultimate aim of yoga has always been to achieve oneness with what some call universal thought or consciousness, and others call God. Today, meditation is still an integral part of practice in many schools and styles of yoga, while in others it is considered an advanced technique and not taught to beginners.

The way of yoga

Yoga is not a religion, but its development has been influenced by the ideas of many great thinkers and teachers. Their writings provide a set of commonsense principles by which to live a peaceful and healthy life. Foremost among their collective beliefs is the principle of nonviolence. Yoga works to establish inner peace and mental and physical harmony.

The path of yoga is a personal search for deeper self-knowledge through the asanas or poses, and through breathing, relaxation, and learning to quiet and focus the mind. The way of yoga is a spiritual journey into the self and beyond.

Awareness

Yoga emphasizes opening oneself up to the influences of nature and the natural world.

Rules for Right Living

The sage Patañjali who lived some 2,000 years ago left a collection of writings called the *Yoga Sutras* (a sutra is a short saying, packed with meaning). They contain simple advice for living a useful and fulfilling life. Here are ten of his best-known guidelines:

THE FIVE YAMAS
—or how to be kind to others

1 Refrain from violence in thought, word, and deed.

2 Do not steal.

3 Do not covet the possessions and achievements of others.

4 Speak and live the truth.

5 Practice self-restraint and refrain from indulging in excess and sexual depravity.

THE FIVE NIYAMAS
—or how to be kind to yourself

1 Maintain mental purity and physical cleanliness.

2 Rise above objects of desire.

3 Accept your situation in life.

4 Repeat the sacred words of the great teachers.

5 Devote yourself to a personal deity—or the universal consciousness.

Buddha
Gautama Buddha is sometimes described as the first yogi.

ANCIENT ART

The origins of yoga are buried in ancient history. Historians think that the ideas from which it evolved may have emerged in southwestern Asia more than 3,000 years ago, and been carried southward through the Indian subcontinent by migrating tribes. Artifacts unearthed in excavations of the ancient Indus Valley civilizations, which flourished around 1500 BCE, show people meditating. The Upanishads, written between 900 and 400 BCE, are the oldest known writings on yoga.

Karma yoga
The Bhagavad Gita (Song of the Lord)*, a gripping epic tale of a battle between two clans, was written around 300 BCE. It presented karma yoga, a new yoga of selfless action that explores ways of dealing with life's many problems.*

Buddha's birthplace
The Himalayan foothills were the birthplace of Gautama Buddha around 550 BCE, a time of religious and intellectual ferment in the East. He became a wandering sage who followed the path of raja yoga to attain enlightenment.

Lotus pose
The ancient sages were often depicted meditating in the cross-legged lotus pose or padmasana, a passive sitting position which, once mastered, is comfortable and frees the mind to concentrate.

Raja Yoga

The earliest form of yoga was meditation. In the art of the ancient East the Buddha was often depicted meditating, his knees crossed in one of the classic cross-legged sitting positions. These were the first asanas or yoga postures, developed by the sages because they enabled them to sit in meditation without moving for long periods. The ancient form of yoga Buddha practiced survives today as raja yoga—"the king of yogas"—because all yoga pathways are said to lead to it. Raja yoga is the way of deep meditation. Through it, dedicated individuals and communities of yogis explore the realm of abstract thought, seeking to tap into universal consciousness, to attain spiritual unity with the universe through a life dedicated to yoga.

Classic Schools

The tree of yoga has many great branches, for along with the countless thousands of people who practice the exercise-based styles of modern yoga, there are numerous followers of the great classic schools that arose in ancient times. Most of these evolved during the first millennium BCE, when freethinkers broke away from the religious establishment of the Indian subcontinent to develop new philosophies and ascetic ways of living.

Kapila

This sage, who lived about 2,750 years ago, founded the samkhya philosophy, which contributed concepts such as life force and life energy to yoga.

BEFORE 1000 BCE

RAJA YOGA

The practice of meditating sitting in a cross-legged position reaches the Indian subcontinent from Persia, and is carried southward by Dravidian-speaking people. Raja yoga, "the king of yoga," is practiced by philosophers seeking spiritual unity with universal knowledge or consciousness.

C.900 BCE

JNANA YOGA

Philosophers exploring intuitive knowledge develop the yoga of wisdom or jnana ("geeyana") yoga. Their ideas appear in the Upanishads, a set of innovative scriptures that contain the first written accounts of yogic practice and experience. Jnana yoga develops intuitive knowledge through meditation.

C.500 BCE

Gautama Buddha and his followers practice the ancient meditation techniques of raja yoga, and achieve the state of nirvana or loss of the Self in a universal oneness.

BUDDHA

C.300 BCE

KARMA YOGA

The sage Vyasa writes the *Bhagavad Gita (Song of the Lord)*, introducing a yoga of action, karma yoga, as a conversation on the eve of the battle between Arjuna, a warrior chief, and his charioteer, the god Krishna. Karma yoga emphasizes taking the right action at the right time to avoid future unhappiness.

The last great classic school

The first millennium CE saw the development of new meditational practices, including chanting incantations or mantras, such as "om," and contemplating geometric patterns called mandalas. From this new wave of breakaway thinking emerged hatha yoga (pronounced "hatta"), the last great classic yoga school. "Ha" means "sun" and "tha" means "moon" and the name refers to breathing exercises called pranayama, which are practiced as a way of linking mind and body. Hatha yoga was the first school that combined physical exercises and deep breathing to help concentrate the mind for meditation. During the 1400s, a sage called Svatmarama produced a work known as the *Hathapradipika* (*The Compendium of Hatha Yoga*), the first written guide to hatha yoga.

c.200 BCE

The sage Patañjali writes the *Yoga Sutras*, giving guidelines on meditation and the practice of yoga—the first yoga manual.

PATAÑJALI

c. 300s CE

TANTRIC YOGA

Asanga, a Buddhist philosopher, initiates tantric philosophy, incorporating yoga ideas and practices, in which the senses and the imagination are harnessed to attain ecstatic states, which may lead to enlightenment. It encourages mantra yoga—chanting sacred words—to aid meditation.

c. 1000–1200 CE

BHAKTI YOGA

The sage Ramanuja initiates bhakti yoga, the yoga of devotion to a personal god. He teaches devotion to a supreme Brahman, creator of the universe, a loving and understanding presence. Through service to God or to other people, through prayer, and through faith, one achieves enlightenment.

c. 1000 CE

HATHA YOGA

The development of physical exercises during the tantric era paved the way for hatha yoga. It was the first school to recognize asanas, breathing and cleansing exercises, and visualization techniques as valid aids to attaining union with universal consciousness through meditation.

Yoga reaches out

During the 20th century the tree of yoga spread its canopy across the Western world.

CONTEMPORARY STYLES

The latest chapter in the story of yoga began in the 1800s, when explorers, academics, soldiers, and administrators from the West who resided in India translated the ancient yoga texts and studied the asanas. By 1900, yogis from India were touring the West and in the mid-1900s, Paramahansa Yogananda, author of the well-known *Autobiography of a Yogi*, settled in the US. Hatha yoga was the classic school destined to influence the modern world, since its emphasis on asanas, breathing, and healing appealed to the Western mind. After World War II many Westerners visited India to study hatha yoga, and respected Indian teachers, most notably B.K.S. Iyengar, taught in the West.

Iyengar

B.K.S. Iyengar married classic hatha yoga with detailed Western knowledge of the body to establish a new yoga style based on accurate positioning and movement.

Pioneer

The teaching of yoga to mixed groups of men and women students in India was pioneered by B.K.S. Iyengar during the 1940s. Iyengar developed his own style of yoga and founded the Iyengar Institute in Poona. Today it has branches in many Western countries.

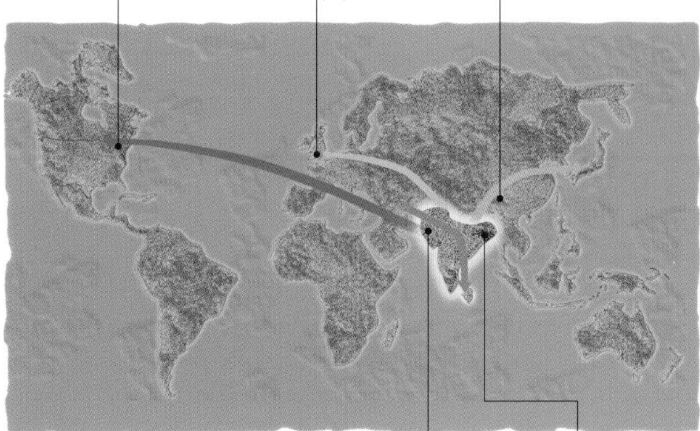

The spread of yoga

In modern times yoga has spread eastward beyond the Indian subcontinent, and out to the West. Today, its popularity worldwide proves its relevance to pressurized 21st-century living.

Yoga for the 21st Century

Yoga originated as a healing art, whose purpose was to dispel disharmonies of mind and body that might impede an individual's journey along the path to universal wholeness and understanding. Such disharmonies might express themselves in rigidities of the body or in physical illness, and in discontent or anxiety. Over the centuries, yoga sages discovered how to calm and overcome them by gentle stretching and exercise, by slow, rhythmic breathing, which gradually quiets the mind, and by techniques such as visualization and meditation, which concentrate the mind.

Mental healing

Yoga gently erodes the mental turmoil of 21st-century living, bringing peace and personal fulfillment.

Modern appeal

Today, just as in ancient times, people neglect their bodies, injure themselves, and develop illnesses. They become dissatisfied, agitated, and unhappy. Yoga continues to be relevant because it provides some answers to the difficulties of living in the modern world. The styles and schools of yoga that are popular today are those which, like Iyengar yoga, focus on stretching and movement. We sit for most of the day when traveling, at work, as well as when relaxing, yet if bones, joints, and muscles are not stretched and moved, the body deteriorates. Yoga restores natural flexibility to stiff backs, necks, and limbs. It helps the body heal after strain and trauma, and practiced regularly, it promotes health and prevents illness.

People everywhere react against the speed of contemporary living, against the unquestioning acceptance of competition in everyday life, and against the effects of overcrowding. Many people turn to yoga as a remedy for the effects of stress on mind and body. Experiments in the US at the Menninger Institute and at other respected medical research centers have shown that by a combination of breathing, visualization, and concentration, yogis can reduce their heart rate and blood pressure.

Yoga is a holistic practice, not just an exercise system. When you begin yoga, you harness the powers of the body and the mind to soothe the nerves and calm the body systems, reducing stress and allowing the body to restore normal function. Rhythmic breathing, called pranayama, and meditation techniques enhance this healing process. They are an important part of hatha yoga, and in Iyengar yoga, pranayama and concentration techniques are taught to advanced students.

PRACTICING YOGA

In contrast with most of the exercise systems that have become fashionable in recent years, yoga is a minimalist art, requiring almost no expense or preparation. Your own body is all the equipment you really need. There is no special clothing to buy or equipment to use, and you can practice almost anywhere. This chapter explains the basics: when to practice, how often, and for how long; the parts of the body that need special attention, and the essentials of breathing and relaxation. But yoga is a holistic art, involving the mind as much as the body, and the chapter ends by explaining how yoga might deepen your understanding of your mind and your personality, and lead you to explore its hidden spiritual dimension.

Preparation

If you are just beginning yoga, learning alone at home, or needing a place to work on poses between classes, your first consideration must be to find a place where you will be able to stretch with a minimum of interruption. It may be tempting to practice outdoors if the weather is warm, but it is not advisable to practice yoga in the hot sun, and there can be distractions from traffic and building work. In the modern family home it can be hard to find a place where you can be undisturbed by telephones, doorbells, or family members, but think of using your bedroom, a bathroom, a utility room, an office, or a den. Put a "do not disturb" notice on the door.

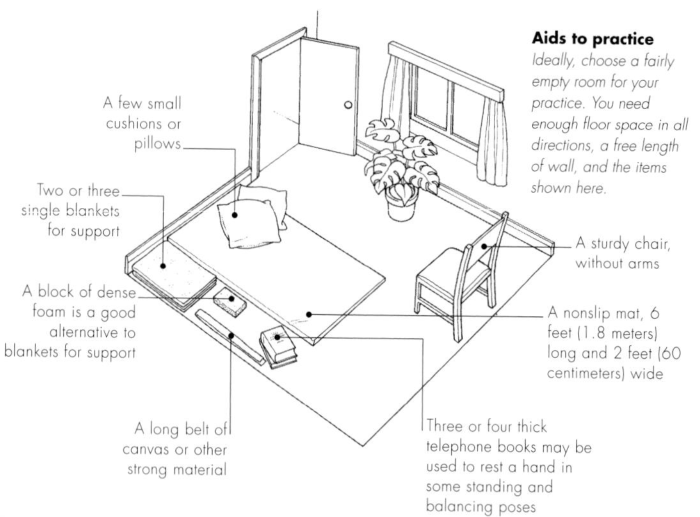

Aids to practice

Ideally, choose a fairly empty room for your practice. You need enough floor space in all directions, a free length of wall, and the items shown here.

Making time

Practice as often as you like, but practice regularly. Do not be overambitious at first. It is best to set aside a certain time on a certain day a week to practice and be disciplined about keeping that weekly date. Allow for half an hour at first, working up to longer sessions as you are able. Some people like to practice for a short time every day, early in the morning, or before bed, and to have one longer session once a week.

Yoga imposes very few rules, and some poses aid digestion—for example, you can practice the hero floor pose straight after eating a meal. This is not true of most poses, however, so as a rule of thumb, do not practice for four hours after a large meal or two hours after a snack.

For yoga, wear comfortable clothes that stretch easily, such as a t-shirt and leggings, a leotard, or jogging pants and a sweatshirt. Practice barefoot. If your hair is long it is best to fasten it up so it cannot obscure your vision.

THE BODY

It is not necessary to know a great deal about how the body works in order to practice any style of yoga. But it can be helpful to have a working knowledge of how the spine, the pelvis, and the shoulders align and move. These days, the tendency is for most people to sit for a large part of every day. People sit when traveling to work and for most of the working day. They sit in movie theaters, bars, and restaurants. They have little opportunity to stretch their arms or legs, and little incentive to walk for long distances. As a result they develop poor posture, and this affects health. Yoga asanas stretch the whole body, countering the compressing effect of gravity on the spine, and restore the natural range of movement of all its moving parts.

The pelvis

The pelvis is the body's linchpin. "Pelvis"means "basin"—it is shaped to hold the organs of the abdomen. It transfers the weight of the upper body via the hip joints to the legs and feet. Its proper positioning is essential to almost every yoga pose.

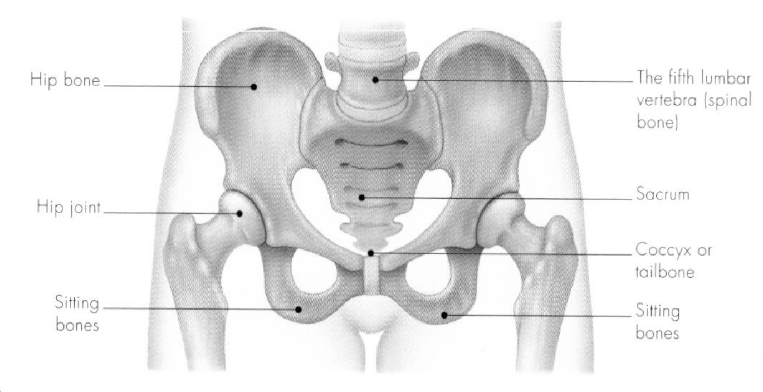

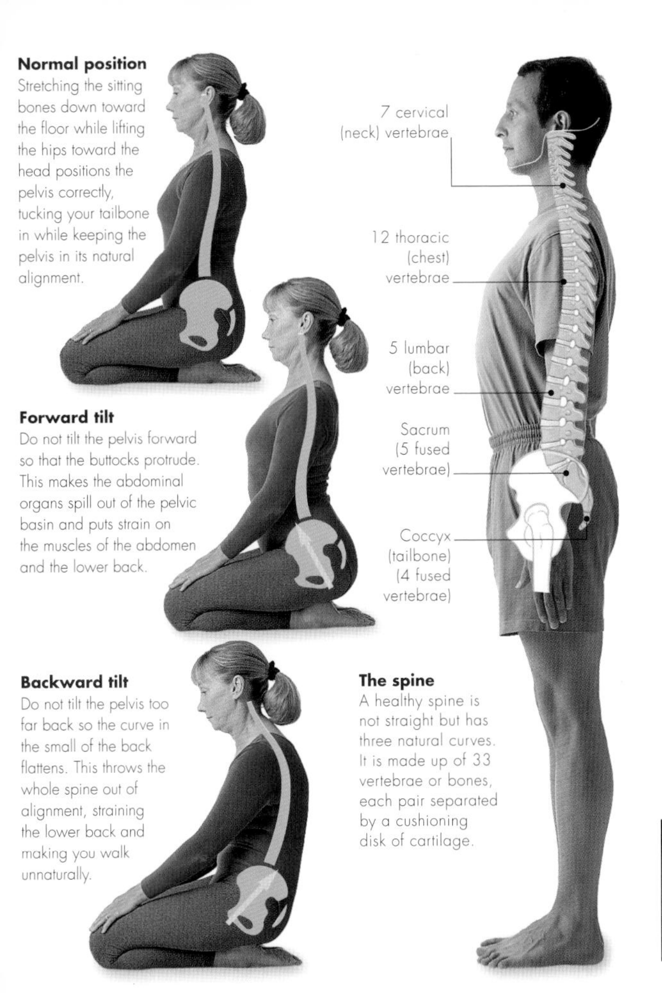

Normal position

Stretching the sitting bones down toward the floor while lifting the hips toward the head positions the pelvis correctly, tucking your tailbone in while keeping the pelvis in its natural alignment.

Forward tilt

Do not tilt the pelvis forward so that the buttocks protrude. This makes the abdominal organs spill out of the pelvic basin and puts strain on the muscles of the abdomen and the lower back.

Backward tilt

Do not tilt the pelvis too far back so the curve in the small of the back flattens. This throws the whole spine out of alignment, straining the lower back and making you walk unnaturally.

The spine

A healthy spine is not straight but has three natural curves. It is made up of 33 vertebrae or bones, each pair separated by a cushioning disk of cartilage.

Breathing and Relaxation

Breathing is both a physical and a mental process, a link between body and mind. Breathing at a normal pace supplies the blood with oxygen and other nutrients, and these keep the body and brain functioning. Rapid breathing or hyperventilation reduces the supply of oxygen to the brain, causing dizziness and abnormal heart rhythm, tension, panic, and black-outs. Slowing the breathing and restoring its natural rhythm restores calm and normal functioning.

Good breathing habits

Remembering to breathe properly is an important part of every yoga pose. In the early stages, the focus is on developing good breathing habits. People living a pressured existence often develop shallow breathing habits as a stress response. Yoga discourages that tendency, helping to reestablish normal breathing patterns.

The guidelines on how to perform the asanas contain frequent reminders to "breathe normally." This may seem obvious, but when trying to concentrate on a movement it can seem almost natural to hold your breath, and you need to watch for those moments. If your nasal passages are blocked because of a cold or other sinus problem you will have to breathe through the mouth, but normally, you should breathe through the nose.

Some instructions about when to breathe in and when to breathe out are given in the captions explaining each pose. In general, you breathe out on an

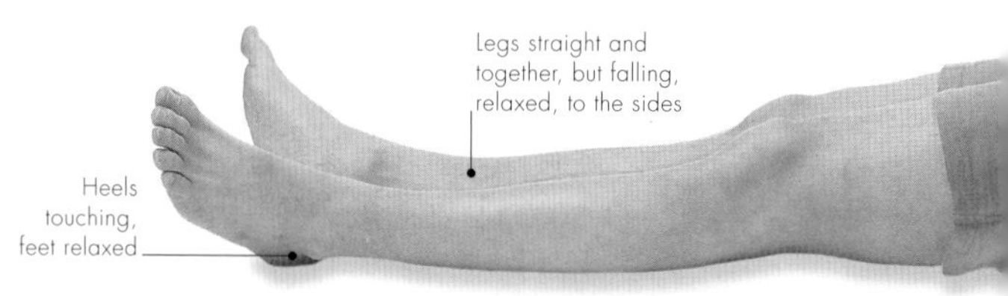

exertion—as you lift or bend forward, for example. Breathe in, breathe out as you execute the movement, then breathe normally again.

Breathing and relaxation

Stretching and rhythmic breathing relax body and mind. Relaxation is an essential part of yoga. A practice session should begin with a few moments of repose in a restful posture—sitting in a simple cross-legged pose, for example, and the more demanding poses should be followed by a few brief moments of rest just standing, kneeling, or lying down.

Corpse pose

Savasana I, analyzed in detail on pages 64–65, helps relax body and mind during moments of particular stress and tension.

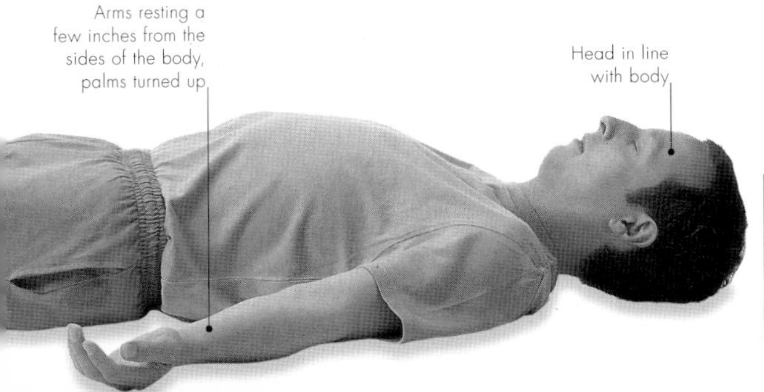

Spiritual union
The word "yoga" signifies spiritual union between the individual and the world beyond the self.

MIND AND SPIRIT

Learning to perform the asanas and regulate your breathing are ways of learning to calm and focus your mind. Mastering these skills helps you progress. Concentration is the ability to focus on a particular thought or action. Yoga directs your attention to something physical: a posture, and for a short time this holds your attention. In this way you exercise and improve your concentration. One of the greatest problems people have in everyday life is being able to concentrate, and yoga can be a great help. Moreover, achieving the ability to concentrate is the first step on the path to exploring the spiritual dimension of yoga by bringing meditation into your life. Meditation is total concentration.

Free spirit
The ultimate aim of yoga is to release the mind from the restrictions of the physical body and allow the spirit to explore new levels of consciousness.

Practicing concentration

When you practice yoga, you involve your whole being in the actions your body is making. That is why yoga is said to be a form of meditation through action. A restful pose such as this cross-legged sitting pose is ideal for encouraging concentration. Although it looks simple, the mind needs to focus on the many small details of the posture, such as positioning the knees and maintaining an upward stretch.

Holding the head erect facilitates blood flow to the brain and efficient breathing

Rhythmic breathing through both nostrils encourages concentration

Palms pressing together

Emotion and Control

To practice yoga is to make some quiet space in your life, a little time to let negative emotions subside, and allow the natural rhythms of mind and body to reassert themselves. Rather than give inner turmoil opportunities to express itself in sudden or violent outbursts, yoga gives strong emotions gentle physical release through intense stretching, and deflects the mind away from them by directing the attention on precise movement and accurate positioning. The result is the diffusion of anger and resentment, the lifting of heavy spirits, and the calming and containing of hurt and mental discomfort. At the end of a concentrated yoga practice, feelings of ease and tranquillity saturate body and mind.

Enrichment

Yoga enriches your inner life, teaching you to be less dependent on outside events for happiness.

Tranquillity

The ability to restore tranquillity is a major gift of yoga to an increasingly turbulent world. People have to deal with mounting stress in all aspects of their lives. In time, many succumb to the emotional turmoil this causes, and this can result in clinical depression, the breakdown of relationships, and, more and more frequently, aggressive outbursts, such as road rage, and rising crime rates. A tranquil person radiating inner harmony benefits others by transmitting calm and reassurance in tense situations.

Practicing asanas is a way of learning to exercise self-control. Yoga begins this process by teaching control of the body, then control of the breath.

Through this you learn concentration—control of your thought patterns—and this helps bring about emotional control. In the long term, yoga has a leveling effect on your whole emotional life. People who practice yoga do not cease to feel, but they become less negatively affected by life's disappointments, less anxiety-ridden, and less dependent for happiness on outside factors such as wealth, success, and luck. The perpetual need for excitement, gratification, and thrills is replaced by inner peace and contentment.

Reaching this stage of emotional development is to achieve pratyahara or release from the dominance of the senses—the fifth stage on the path of yoga as described by the sage Patañjali. Achieving the state of pratyahara signifies that you are ready for the serious practice of dhyana or meditation, through which you may achieve the state of samadhi or oneness with the universal consciousness or spirit. This is the aim of every branch and school of yoga.

A FIRST PRACTICE

This first chapter illustrates and describes ten poses which, carried out in the order shown, make a good introduction to yoga. Together, these ten poses form a complete practice taking perhaps 20 minutes to half an hour—please read the caution note on page 9 before beginning. Working through this program two or three times a week, carrying out the steps in the order given, and concentrating on the accurate positioning of the feet, the arms, and various other parts of the body, will strengthen your muscles, make your joints more flexible, and give you confidence. Like every yoga practice, this one ends with a welcome five to ten minutes of complete relaxation in the corpse pose.

Beginning Yoga

The following pages introduce ten basic yoga poses. They start with sitting and lying down, and go on to analyze standing in tadasana—the mountain pose. Learning to stand properly improves posture, and this can eliminate the often debilitating aches and pains caused by slumping. The standing poses that follow tadasana stretch the legs and spine and, in time, strengthen the whole body.

Resting between poses
After an intense stretch, rest briefly in a different position. You might do a standing or a kneeling forward bend, or stand in tadasana for a few seconds.

Step by step

These first ten poses, carried out in the given sequence, make a good first class for beginners. Work through each one step by step. The instructions in the captions help you achieve the pose without strain, so follow them as closely as you can, holding the stretch at the end for as long as is comfortable.

Triangle, extended side angle, and tree (see pages 46–53 and 58–61) are carried out first on one side of the body, then on the other side. For example, in triangle you bend first to the right, then to the left. And in cross-legged sitting on page 38 you cross the right shin over the left, then the left shin over the right. Do not rush through the poses. Make each movement deliberately, working at your own speed. If you find it hard to stretch into the full pose, do not try to force your body into the unaccustomed position. Joints and muscles that have long been inactive may well feel stiff at first, but if any movement or body position is painful, stop immediately.

The rule is: always work to your own potential; stretch as far as you can comfortably, then rest. Next time, you may be able to stretch a little further.

Finishing a pose

To leave a pose, move through the steps in reverse order until you return to the start position. The sequence of poses in this chapter ends with a few minutes of total relaxation in the corpse pose or savasana. This resting pose should make an enjoyable end to every future practice.

Tips on Breathing

Breathe normally while performing all yoga poses, and remember:

- Do not hold your breath while concentrating on the movements.
- Breathe in before a stretch or other exertion and execute the movement on the out-breath.
- Always breathe through the nose unless you have hay fever, a cold, or other sinus problem.
- When relaxing in the corpse pose at the end of the practice, concentrate on quieting the breath, focusing on its rhythm.

SITTING AND LYING POSES

The simple cross-legged sitting pose, **sukhasana**, shown on these pages is the basis for many sitting postures. Practiced regularly, it strengthens the back and makes the hips more flexible. The name of the pose at right, **supta tadasana**, or "the lying-down mountain pose" sounds like a contradiction, but this is the basic standing posture performed lying on the mat. It gives a good stretch and relaxes the lower back.

Cross-legged sitting

1 *Sit upright, hands beside your hips, legs stretched out in front, toes turned up. Press your legs and hands down, lift your spine, and bend your left leg and then your right leg, crossing the right shin across the left.*

2 *Let your legs relax down to the floor, stretch your spine up, and rest your hands on your thighs. Sit stretching up for up to 20 seconds, then repeat the pose, crossing the left shin over the right.*

Lying-down stretch

1 *Lie with the your legs straight, the soles of your feet against a wall, and your arms, palms down, by your sides.*

2 *Bend your legs, and adjust the position of your pelvis by bending your knees and raising them to your chest. Then straighten your legs until your heels touch the floor and the soles of your feet press against the wall.*

3 *Lift your arms up and back over your head until the backs of your hands touch the floor behind. Pressing your legs down, stretch from your groins to your fingertips, and from your lower back to your feet. Stretch for up to 20 seconds, then relax.*

Introducing Floor Poses

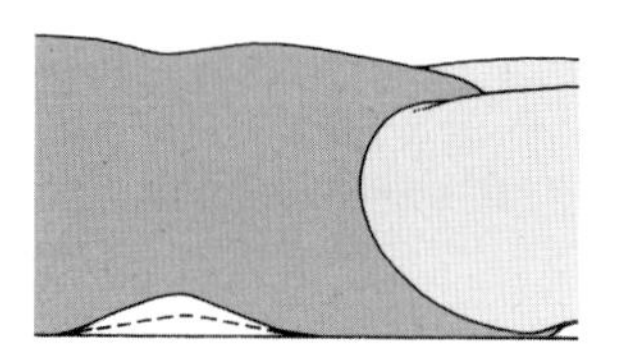

Aligning the spine

If your lower back arches when you lie down, exercising may strain it. To reduce the curve, raise your knees to your chest, then straighten your legs.

The Buddha is often depicted sitting meditating in the lotus pose —each foot placed on the opposite thigh. However, the lotus position is one of many sitting poses and, like the simple cross-legged sitting position on page 38, the alternatives are easier for most people to perform. In this, as in all sitting poses, the lower spine needs to be straight and stretching up. If at first you find it hard to lift your lower back, sit on a blanket folded three or four times, or on a foam block. This supports your back muscles while you work on strengthening them.

Aligning the knees

Sitting on a foam block or a blanket folded two or three times also raises the level of your pelvis, which helps you align your knees. When you cross your legs, your knees need to be the same distance as your hip bones from the mat, but this can be hard to achieve at first. Sitting on a raised level makes it easier to lower the knees. If your knees are stiff, support them on a folded blanket.

Lying-down poses

Many yoga poses are performed lying on the mat. Supta tadasana, the lying-down stretch on page 39, is a

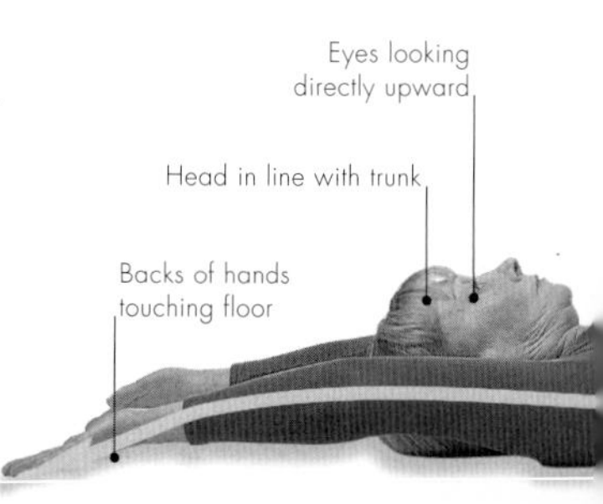

wonderful whole-body stretch. Press the sitting bones (see pages 26–27) toward your feet, and your legs and heels down, and stretch from your hips to your head, along your arms to your fingertips, and along your legs, pressing your feet into the wall.

Lying-down stretch analyzed

Just lying on the floor seems too simple to need analysis, but attention to the details shown below is the secret of a satisfying stretch.

Points to Watch

- When you stretch toward your hands while sitting or lying, keep your rib cage in its natural alignment so that the lower ribs do not protrude.
- Keep your sitting bones stretching down to the floor in the sitting pose and toward your feet in the lying-down stretch, while lifting your hip bones toward your head.
- While stretching your spine up, keep your shoulders broad but relaxed downward so your shoulder blades remain flat against your ribs.

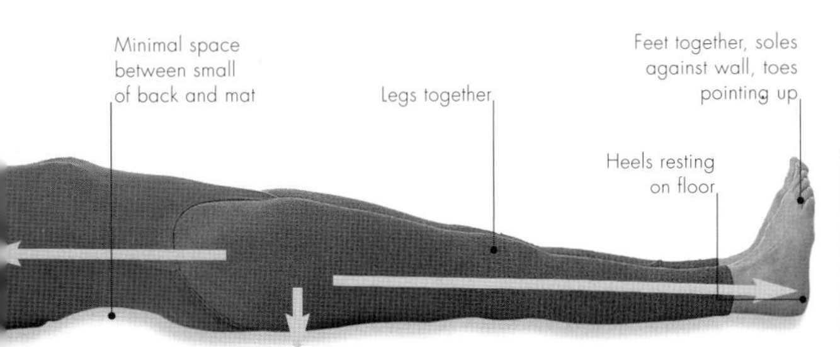

Mountain pose

The basic standing pose in yoga is called tadasana or mountain pose because you stand as upright and immobile as a mountain.

STANDING

Tadasana, the standing mountain pose, can be practiced indoors or out, waiting for a train, for instance, or standing in a line. It is the basis of good posture and consequently of good health. Making a habit of standing in tadasana corrects poor posture and can make back and joint pains disappear so that your whole body feels healthier and lighter. It also deepens your understanding of every other yoga pose.

Balancing points

Spread each foot, broadening and lengthening it, stretching the toes forward, and balancing the weight of your body evenly on each of the four key balancing points on the sole of the foot, shown in this diagram.

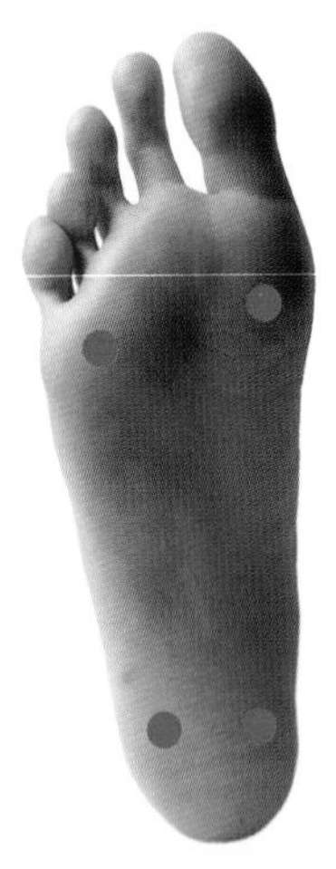

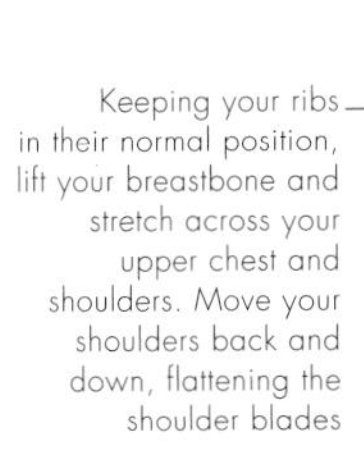

Keeping your ribs in their normal position, lift your breastbone and stretch across your upper chest and shoulders. Move your shoulders back and down, flattening the shoulder blades

Straighten your neck to align your head with your spine and position your chin parallel to the floor, and direct your gaze forward. Hold the position for about 20 seconds, breathing gently

Stretch your legs up, lift your trunk from your hips, and stretch your sitting bones downward. Tighten your thigh muscles to press your thighs back

Stand with your feet together, distributing your weight evenly on the balls and heels of both feet, big toes, heels, ankles, and knees touching, arms relaxed by your sides

Feet first

Begin tadasana by thinking about the positioning of your feet and the fall of your weight down to the floor. Then work up your body, positioning your legs, hips, trunk, shoulders, and, finally, your head. As you hold the position, you should be standing as erect and steady as a mountain.

Improving Posture

An erect spine is the basis of good posture, but this does not mean that the spine should be ramrod-straight. A spine that is correctly aligned lifts from the sacrum—the shield-shaped bone at its base which forms the back of the pelvis—and stretches up, falling into its three natural curves (shown on pages 26–27).

Aligning the pelvis

Clearly, the key to this upright posture is the correct positioning of the pelvis. To lift your spine from the sacrum, your pelvis must be properly aligned, so the best way to start all yoga poses is by checking and adjusting it. Do this in the mountain pose on pages 42–43 by stretching your sitting bones toward the floor, and lifting the front of your body from the hip bones.

If your back muscles are weak, the pelvis tends to tilt forward and you lift from the waist instead of from the hips. In time, simply practicing the mountain pose—tadasana—will correct this defect by strengthening the spine's supporting muscles. This will enable you to lift from the hips without support in standing and sitting poses.

Achieving stability

Beginning the pose by distributing your body weight equally between the key points on the heel and forefoot (see page 42) gives you stability. Lift the arches of your feet without disturbing your balance and maintain your stability as you stretch your legs up, lift your trunk from the pelvis, raise your breastbone, and align your lower back. Make this pose part of your daily routine and any back pain you experience will soon disappear.

Points to Watch

- Straighten your legs without locking your knees by lifting the kneecaps and stretching the leg muscles up.
- Keep your hips back, in line with your ankle bones.
- Do not pull your abdomen in. Lift the front of your pelvis and your abdomen will move back toward your spine.

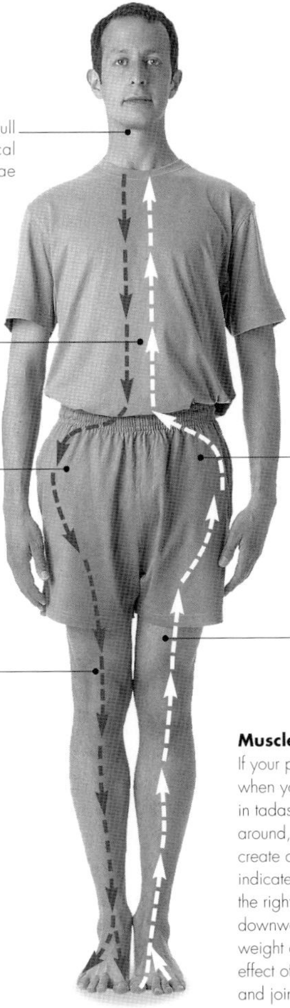

Weight of skull descends to cervical or neck vertebrae

Spine carries weight of upper body to pelvis

Trunk lifts from hips, spine stretches up from sacrum to skull

Pelvis transfers weight of upper body to legs and feet

Legs and feet transmit body weight to ground

Legs stretch up from arches of feet to hip joints

Your body weight

The body is designed to transmit its own weight efficiently to the ground—indicated by the arrows on the left. The spine transmits the weight of the upper body to the sacrum at its base, which transfers it around the pelvic girdle to the hip bones. From there it travels down the legs to the feet.

Muscle action

If your posture is erect when you stand correctly in tadasana, sit, and move around, your muscles naturally create an upward thrust, indicated by the arrows on the right, which counters the downward force of your weight and the compressing effect of gravity on the spine and joints.

TRIANGLE

Utthita trikonasana—the triangle pose—starts you working on improving the flexibility of your hips and legs. Like all the standing poses, you begin in the mountain pose and go on to make a series of triangle shapes with your body, legs, and arms.

1 *Stand in mountain pose (page 43) and jump your feet about 3½–4 feet (1 meter) apart, raising your arms to shoulder height as you do so. Turn the palms of your hands down, and straighten your feet so they are parallel.*

2 *Stretch from feet to head and from breastbone to fingertips. Turn your left foot slightly inward and your right foot and leg out at right angles to your trunk, aligning the right heel with the left instep.*

Breathing

Breathe in before jumping your feet apart in step 1, and together again when finishing, breathe out as you extend your trunk left or right in step 3, and breathe normally through the nose as you hold the pose.

3 *Breathe in and stretch up, then breathe out and bend from the hips to the right until your right hand touches the floor beside and slightly behind your right calf. Align your trunk with your legs, stretch your left arm up in line with your right arm, and turn your head to look up at your left hand. Hold, breathing normally, for 10–15 seconds.*

Using a Wall

Practicing the pose with your back against a wall—represented by the tinted frame of this box—makes it easier to keep your shoulders back, in line with your hips and leg, and your legs and trunk aligned.

Repeat and finish

At the end of step 3, turn your head and raise your trunk to face forward. Reverse the positions of your feet and repeat steps 2 and 3, this time stretching to the left.

To finish, face forward and stand up, turn your feet forward, breathe in, and jump them together, lower your arms, and stand in tadasana.

Focus on Alignment

Good alignment of all the body parts is the key to triangle pose, and that alignment depends on whole-body stretching. The pose begins with a stretch: a good tadasana (see pages 42–45) lifting all the way up from the arches of the feet to the crown of the head. Then after you jump your legs astride, pause, feet parallel, to stretch your legs, lift your breastbone, and extend your arms out to the fingertips while keeping your shoulders back and down.

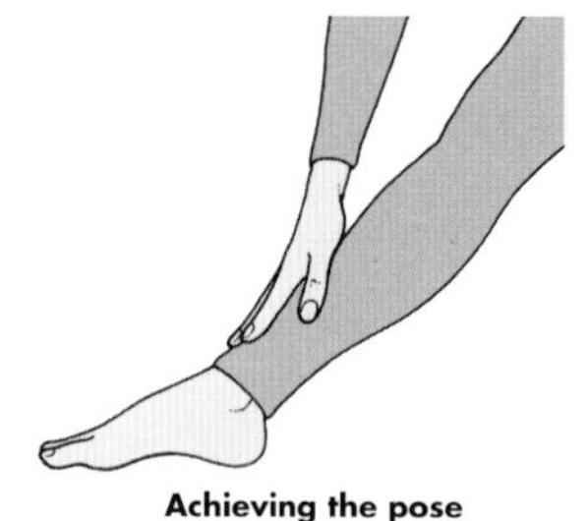

Achieving the pose

If when bending from the hips in step 3 you can reach only your calf at first, rest your hand on your leg, then work lower until you can reach the floor.

Extending the stretch

Before bending from the hips it is important to continue the stretch, lifting up from the groins and opening the chest. Keep your legs stretching up, your sitting bones (see pages 26–27) extending down toward the floor, and lift along both sides of the trunk, and you can be confident you are achieving the pose even if you are unable to reach the floor with your hand. Rest the hand on your leg, a chair seat, or a pile of books instead, and concentrate on stretching while keeping your legs and back aligned. The stiffness in your hips will soon ease, enabling you to lower your hand a little more each time you practice triangle pose.

Points to Watch

- Do not allow the side of the trunk that is uppermost to roll forward. Revolve it back as if pressing it against a wall.
- Keep your thighs pressing back.
- Turn your right leg out to the right and keep your left shin facing forward.

Triangle pose analyzed

Once you have learned the basic steps for the triangle pose on pages 46–47, you need to work on the details. It is easy to allow the trunk to roll forward or the legs to turn in. The details make all the difference in every yoga pose, so concentrating on the points in the diagram below and stretching in the direction shown by the arrows will help you improve and benefit.

EXTENDED SIDE ANGLE

Triangles continue to be the theme of **utthita parsvakonasana** illustrated here, in which you stretch from your feet, along your sides to your fingertips, forming a triangle with your whole body. This pose tones and aligns ankles, calves, knees, and thighs, and it is said to slim the waist and hips.

2 *Turn your left foot in about 15°, move your right foot 90° to the right, turning the leg out from the hip, and stretch up. Breathe in, then bend your right leg until it forms a right angle.*

1 *Stand in tadasana (see page 43), stretch up, inhale, and jump your feet about 4–4½ feet (1.5 meters) apart, depending on your stride. Raise your arms to shoulder height, palms facing down, and stand with your feet parallel, heels aligned.*

3 *Keeping your trunk facing forward and your arms extended out at shoulder level, stretch up, bend your trunk to the right, and place your right hand beside your right ankle. Your left arm extends vertically upward.*

Your Stride

Several standing poses require you to jump your feet between 3 and 4½ feet (1–1.5 meters) apart, but how far you can jump your feet apart depends on your leg length—3–3½ feet (90–110 centimeters) may be right for a short person, 4–4½ feet (120–140 centimeters) for a long-legged person.

4 *Rotate your left arm to the right and move it toward your head until the arm almost touches your ear and the left side of your body forms a straight line from foot to fingers. Look up, and hold for up to 10–15 seconds.*

Repeat and finish

Turn to face forward, raise your trunk, straighten your right leg, and turn your feet to the front. Repeat steps 2 and 3, bending to the left, and stretching your right arm up.

Side-stretches

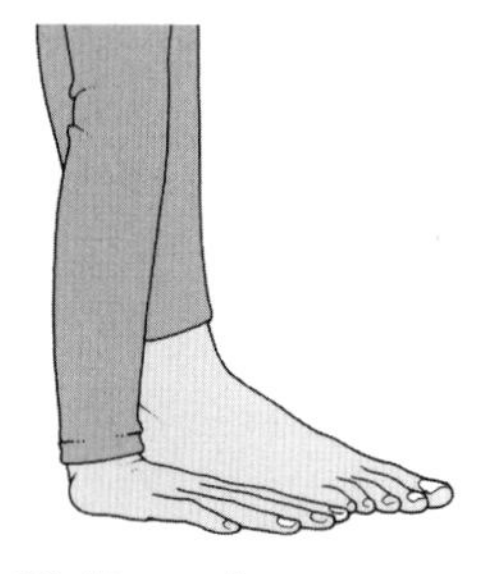

Working on the pose

When you bend your knee in step 2, your shin must make a 90° angle to the floor. As you bend to the side in step 3, place your right hand beside your right ankle, in line with the foot.

The extended side-angle pose on pages 50–51 gives both sides of the body a stretch, and to benefit fully you should maintain the stretch from step 1, when you inhale and stretch up from the groins and out from your breastbone to your fingertips.

Think about the position of your feet when you turn them in step 2. Move the toes of your left foot in slightly, pressing the outside of the foot into the floor and lifting the arch, stretching the left leg up and turning it out from the hip to face forward. Press your thigh muscles back, then rotate your right leg out from the hip joint, turning the right foot at right angles to the trunk, and aligning it with the left instep.

Bending to the side

Maintain the upward stretch and keep both legs turned out at the hip as you bend from the hips to the right. Keep your trunk facing forward as you extend your right side along your right thigh, and place your right hand beside the ankle directly beneath your right shoulder. If you find it difficult to reach the floor, rest your elbow on your thigh, or your right hand on a block or a thick book placed on the floor beside your right foot. Then, as you straighten your left arm, turn it to the right and stretch it up and to the right. At this point the left side of your body forms a straight line from the outer edge of the left foot, along the line of the straightened left leg, to the hip, up the left side of the trunk, and along the left arm.

Points to Watch

- Keep your head, shoulders, trunk, and hips in line. Do not let your shoulders and trunk roll forward.
- As you turn your feet, rotate your leg in the same direction from the hip joint. Feet, leg, and knee should all face the same way.

Extended side angle analyzed

Work on the details to improve in step 4 of extended side-angle pose on page 51.

Shoulder kept back, in line with hip

Trunk facing forward

Knee directly above ankle, pressing back to upper arm

Hips facing forward

Left leg turned out at hip joint and straight

Right thigh parallel to floor, in line with left leg

Body weight placed evenly on both feet

Toes relaxed, arches lifting

FORWARD BENDS

Something relaxing is needed after the exertion of the last two poses, and these forward bends are particularly good for resting the back. They are the first of several classic forward bends in this book, some performed while sitting, others while standing. All can be very restful.

Kneeling forward bend

1 *Kneel on the mat with your feet together and your knees about 12 inches (30 centimeters) apart, and sit back on your heels. Rest your hands on the floor beside your hips.*

2 *Keeping your buttocks touching your heels and bending from the hips, stretch your arms forward, and rest your chest on your thighs, your forehead on the mat, and your hands, palms down, on the mat in front of your head. Relax your arms. Hold the pose for 20 seconds or more, breathing normally. Then raise your trunk and your arms until you are kneeling.*

Standing forward bend

1 *Stand about 3 feet (1 meter) from a chair back, your feet 12 inches (30 centimeters) apart, your weight evenly balanced on the balls and heels of both feet. Stretch your legs up, inhale, and raise your arms above your head, lifting from hips to fingertips.*

2 *On an out-breath bend forward from your hips, placing your hands shoulder-width apart on the chair back. Stretch your legs up, move your hips back in line with your heels, and lower your head level with your shoulders. Breathe in and stretch your trunk forward for up to 20 seconds, breathing normally. Then raise your arms and trunk and stand briefly in tadasana* *(see page 43).*

Introducing Forward Bends

Forward bends calm the mind and rest the body. They position the head level with or lower than the trunk, and this is said to refresh the nerves. They counter the compressing effects of gravity on the spine by stretching it, separating the vertebrae. A kneeling forward bend can be an antidote to backaches caused by spending most of the day on your feet.

If at first it is difficult to kneel, rest your knees on a folded blanket. You can perform this pose with knees and feet together, but bending forward with your knees apart makes it easier to keep your heels touching your buttocks *and* your forehead on the mat. If you do not achieve this at first, rest your head on a blanket folded two or three times, or a foam block, and, if necessary, place one on your heels to sit back onto. Stiffness in your knees, hips, and spine will soon ease, allowing you to dispense with these aids.

Kneeling forward bend analyzed

Once you have learned the basic steps for the kneeling forward bend on page 54, work on improving these details.

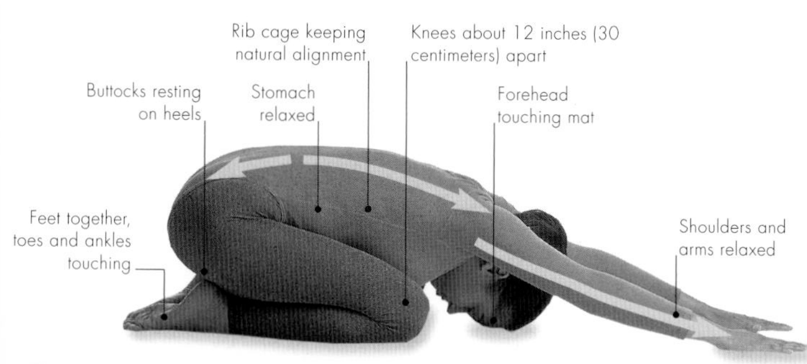

Bending from the hips

The standing forward bend on page 55 will loosen the muscles and tendons at the back of your thighs, but because you bend only to hip level you will not stretch them too far, too quickly. It is essential to bend from the hips, so choose a chair (or a stool or a table) that reaches roughly to hip level. If it is higher, the tendons will not be well stretched, and if it is too low for your height, you will tend to bend from the waist. Straighten your legs only as far as you can without feeling pain.

Standing forward bend analyzed

Working on the points shown below will help you improve the standing forward bend on page 55.

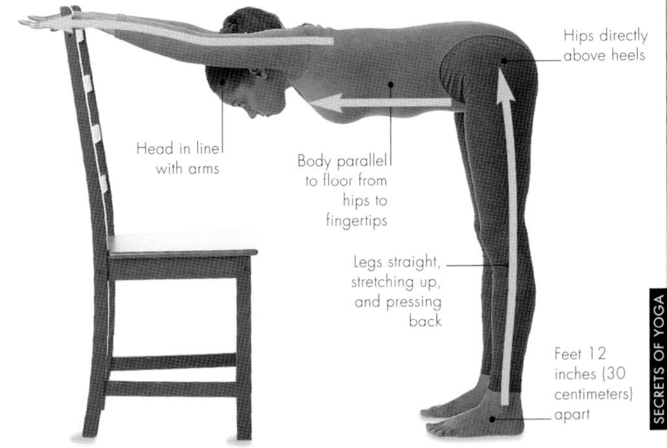

Inspiration from nature
In tree pose your joined hands stretch skyward like the topmost branches of a mountain pine.

TREE

Striving to achieve perfect balance is fundamental to all aspects of yoga. You may wobble when you first try **vrksasana**, the tree pose, but with perseverance you quickly find your ankles and legs strengthen and your balance improves. Having greater confidence in your balance gives you more poise. The tree pose also stretches your body from your toes to your head and arms, toning the muscles of your legs, lifting your spine, and straightening your back.

1 *Stand in tadasana (see page 43) stretching up. Move your weight to your left leg, turn your right leg out at the hip, and bend the knee, grasping the ankle with your right hand.*

2 *Place the right foot against your left thigh, close to the groin. Keeping your left leg straight, press foot against thigh, and thigh against foot. Extend your arms out at shoulder level.*

Aligning the Legs

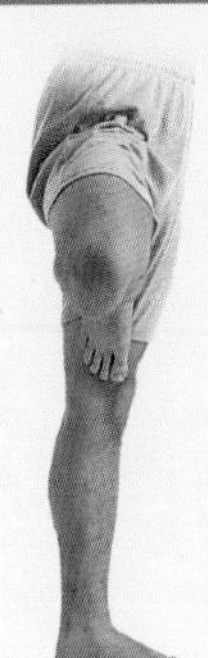

When you have positioned the sole of your right foot against your left thigh, stretch your left leg up and move your right knee and thigh back in line with your hips.

3 *Turn your palms up, inhale, and as you exhale, stretch the arms up, bringing your hands as close together as you can above your head. Hold for 10–15 seconds.*

Repeat and finish

Lower your arms, release your right leg, and stand in tadasana. Transfer your weight to your right leg and repeat steps 1–3, this time pressing your left foot against your right thigh. Then lower your arms and leg, and rest.

Improving Balance

Balancing in the tree pose on pages 58–59 depends on beginning by stretching up in a good tadasana. As you transfer your weight to the leg you are going to stand on, stretch that leg up still more strongly. Your hip joints may be stiff at first, making it hard to raise the foot to the top of the opposite thigh, but you can raise your foot and keep it lifted with a belt around the ankle. In time the joints ease. Although the belt prevents you from raising both arms, it enables you to stand upright while stretching.

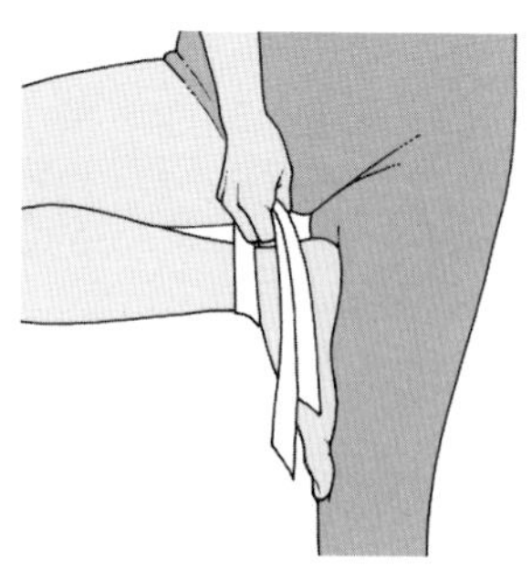

Working on the pose

If you have trouble keeping the foot in position against the thigh, or if your arms are short and you cannot reach your ankle, wind a belt around the ankle and hold the belt in the same hand.

The key to balance

Keeping the raised foot pressing into the thigh of the standing leg, close to the groin, and the thigh pressing into the heel and sole of the foot is the key to balancing in this posture. Imagine your foot and the inside of your thigh acting like a magnet, pressing into each other. Extending your sitting bones toward the mat and focusing your gaze on some object at eye level also makes it easier to maintain your balance.

Making the most of the stretch

Once you feel balanced, slowly raise both arms level with your shoulders, palms facing down. (If one hand is holding a belt, place your free hand on your hip.) Keeping your head up, rotate your arms to turn your palms up. On an out-breath, raise your arms above your head. Breathe normally as you hold the pose, and really stretch up from your feet to your fingertips. Enjoy the stretch.

Points to Watch

- Keep the thigh and knee of your bent leg back in line with your trunk.
- Keep your hips level and aligned.
- Keep your sitting bones stretching downward.
- As you stretch your arms up, lift your breastbone, but do not push your rib cage forward.

Tree pose analyzed
Learning to balance in the tree pose on page 59 involves careful attention to the details pinpointed here.

LEG-STRETCH

Urdhva prasarita padasana is a wonderful pick-me-up if you feel fatigued or if your feet or legs ache, and a restful posture to insert briefly between some of the more complex poses in Chapter 4. Some authorities recommend it for relief of gas. Do it without the support of a wall if you want to tighten your stomach muscles and slim your abdomen.

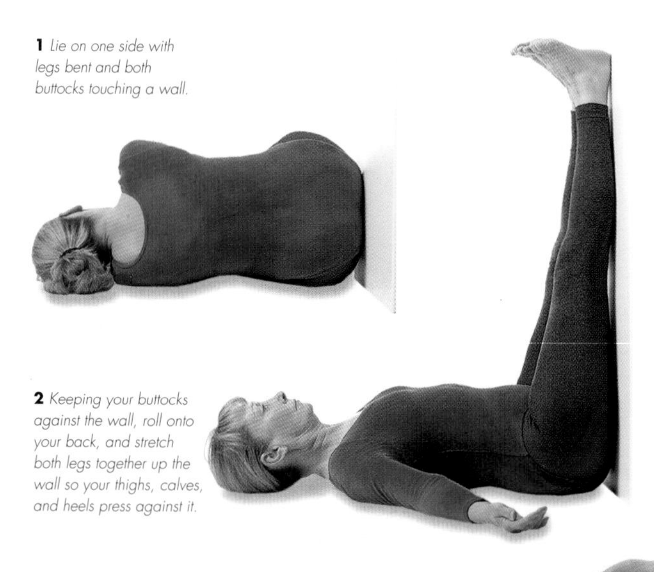

1 *Lie on one side with legs bent and both buttocks touching a wall.*

2 *Keeping your buttocks against the wall, roll onto your back, and stretch both legs together up the wall so your thighs, calves, and heels press against it.*

Working on the Pose

Your whole spine should rest on the mat, and there should be no space between your buttocks, the mat, and the wall. If your hamstrings are tight, your buttocks may lift off the mat when you straighten your legs. To close the gap, move your buttocks back from the wall a little, increasing the angle between your legs and trunk. As your hamstrings stretch you will be able to reduce any space between your buttocks, the mat, and the wall.

3 *Stretch your legs up, and raising your arms, stretch them out on the floor behind your head. There should be no gap in the angle between wall and thighs, buttocks, and floor. Hold the pose for 15–20 seconds.*

Finish and rest

Move your arms to the floor by your sides, bend your knees, and roll onto your side before getting up.

Ending with Relaxation

The most relaxing pose of all is the corpse pose, **savasana I**. It relaxes your muscles after stretching and rests your mind, which has been concentrating on movement. You begin by stretching your back, your legs and feet, and your arms and hands, then close your eyes and focus your mind on each part of the body in turn—relax the muscles in each limb, and in the joints, release any tension in your stomach muscles and your spine, soften your jaw, and eradicate any tension in the muscles of your face and around your eyes. Focusing on each part of the body in turn and on slow, rhythmic breathing helps keep your mind free of encroaching thoughts that may make you tense up.

Antidote to stress

Your first practice should end with a few minutes of complete relaxation of mind and body in savasana I. This completes the practice, preparing you physically and mentally to rejoin your everyday life. These poses can be a useful antidote to stress and tension outside practice time. Spending five to ten minutes alone in savasana clears the mind and makes difficult situations easier to handle.

Corpse pose analyzed

Follow the steps for savasana I opposite, check these details, then focus your mind on your breathing and on relaxing each part of your body.

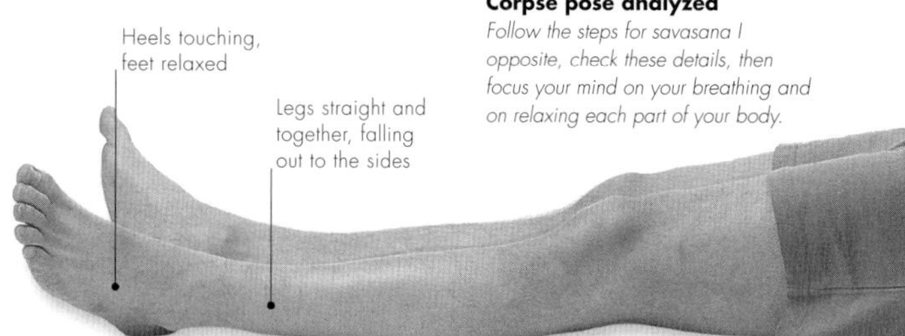

1 *Sit with your legs together, knees bent, and hands on the floor beside your hips. Lie back, gently lowering your spine until your head touches the mat. Stretching your sitting bones toward your feet, slowly straighten your legs and draw them together until your feet touch.*

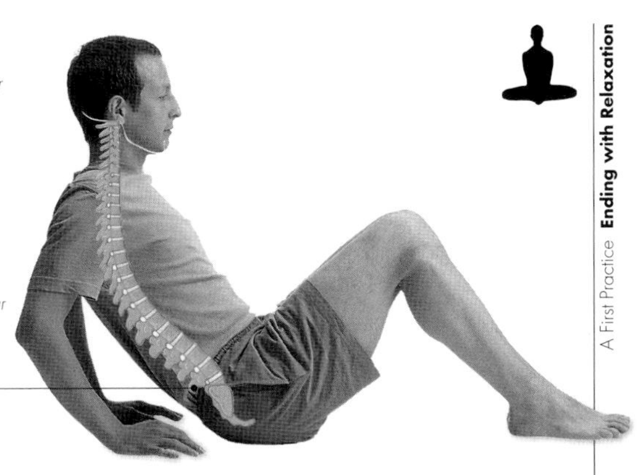

2 *Lift your head to check your legs and body are aligned, then lower it in line with your trunk. Draw your legs together so your feet touch, and stretch your legs, pushing your heels away from your head and your toes toward it, then let your legs fall apart. Rotate your arms from the shoulders until your palms face up. Stretch from shoulders to fingertips, then relax them, close your eyes, and slowly relax your whole body.*

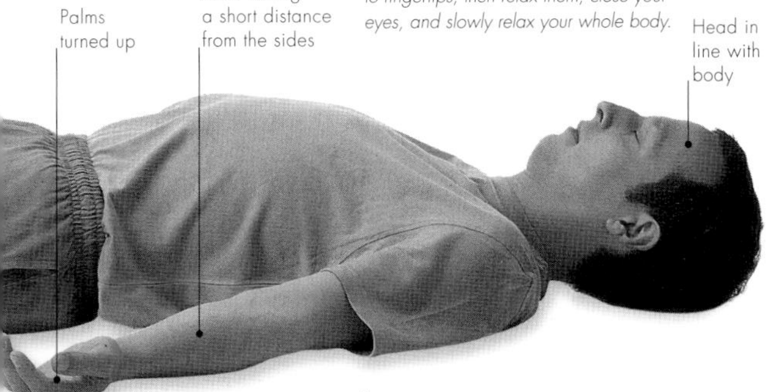

CLASSIC POSES

When you feel familiar with the ten basic poses in Chapter 3, you may wish to learn some new ones. This chapter illustrates and gives you step-by-step instructions showing how to perform some 40 classic poses. The six major categories: standing and sitting poses, floor poses, sitting twists, backbends, and inverted poses, follow on from each other, and the chapter ends with a few fun exercises for the shoulders and hands.

Making Progress

The ten poses in Chapter 3 are the foundation of many asanas. As you progress, you learn new ones, yet you never stop practicing those you learned first. People who have studied yoga for years continue to work on improving tadasana. Every pose is a lifelong learning experience.

Standing poses

You need not work through every pose in this chapter in the order given, but beginners should start with some of the standing postures on pages 70–105 because they build stamina and improve flexibility. Practicing the less demanding standing poses (indicated by a light blue icon in the top right-hand corner of the page), with a wall behind you for support, will help you regain strength after illness. But it is unwise to work on holding stretches for longer and longer periods. The best approach is to hold a pose for five to ten seconds, then rest and repeat it. You are sure to see a steady improvement.

Holistic practice

All yoga poses work on the whole body, so if, for example, your shoulders feel tense, you should not spend all your practice time repeating shoulder exercises. Standing, sitting, and floor poses will also help loosen them.

The more vigorous sitting and floor postures that follow the standing poses may need more effort at first. But do not try so hard that you strain your body. Give it time to gain flexibility and strength, and be satisfied to achieve your personal best. There are no goals to score in yoga. Work at stretching and gradual extension, and if a pose seems to stress any part of your body, stop, and work on less demanding postures until your flexibility improves.

Support and protection

Learn each pose by following the steps shown in the color photographs. The black-and-white pages that follow analyze the pose. They help you achieve it by using foam blocks, folded blankets, or piles of telephone books to support your back or rest your weight, and belts to help you stretch. Always use folded blankets or foam blocks for support during the inverted poses on pages 186–93. And when getting to your feet from a lying position after any floor pose, roll onto one side before getting up, to protect your back from strain. Keep these warnings in mind, but do not limit yourself to a narrow range of poses. Be adventurous and you may be surprised at how much you can achieve.

Exploring the poses

Be willing to try out a new pose, however difficult it seems. Some poses will seem astonishingly simple, and you will need to work to achieve others.

EXTENDED LEG-STRETCHES

These two poses work on extending the limbs to their fullest extent in order to improve the balance and strengthen the legs. They are assisted versions of the pose for beginners, for which you need a piece of solid furniture or perhaps a ledge the right height for you to rest your heel on with your leg straightened.

Utthita hasta padangusthasana I

1 *Stand in tadasana (see page 43), about 3 feet (1 meter) from the ledge or chair, stretch your legs and spine up, then bend your right leg and place your right heel on the chair or ledge.*

2 *Wind a belt around your right foot, and holding it with both hands, stand upright, arms straight. Stretch your left leg up, and stretch your right leg by pressing your foot against the belt. Hold the pose for about 20 seconds.*

Repeat and finish

Remove the belt and lower your right foot to the floor. Stretch up for a few seconds, then repeat steps 1 and 2, this time raising your left leg.

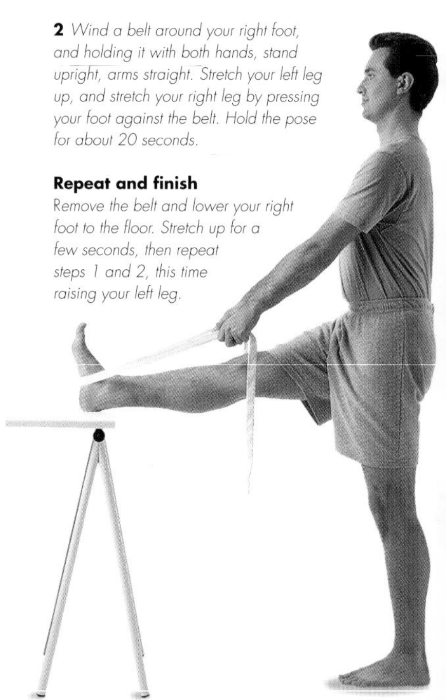

Utthita hasta padangusthasana II

1 *Stand about 3 feet (1 meter) from the chair or ledge and facing it, turn left and stretch up. Move your weight to your left leg, bend your right leg, turning it out from the hip, and place the heel on the surface.*

2 *Wind a belt around your right foot and hold both ends in your right hand. Now stand upright, facing forward, straightening your right arm and lifting your left arm to shoulder level. Hold for 10–15 seconds.*

Repeat and finish

Remove the belt and lower your right foot to the floor, stretch up, and repeat steps 1 and 2, raising your left leg. Rest and repeat the whole pose, first on the right, then on the left.

Exercising the Legs

For padangusthasana I and II on pages 70–71 you need to find a heavy piece of furniture or a ledge at the right level to rest your foot—high enough to make you stretch your legs, keeping your hips level, but not so high that you cannot straighten them. Some people can lift their legs quite high, so check first by standing about 3 feet (1 meter) away, steady yourself, lift one foot, and bending at the knee, place your heel on it. Now try to straighten your raised leg. If you cannot, the ledge or chair is too high. As you practice you will find you need to raise the height gradually by placing a foam block or books on it and resting your foot on top. If you use a chair back, place the chair seat against a wall for stability.

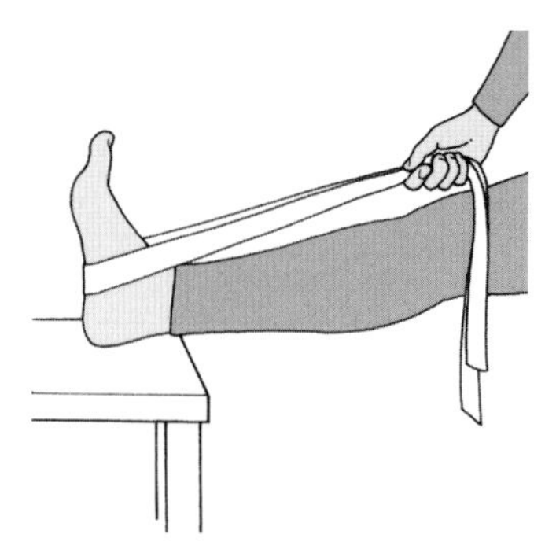

Achieving the pose

Winding a belt around the arch of your raised foot will help you stretch the leg by pressing the foot against the belt with your toes facing up.

Points to Watch

- Keep the leg you are standing on straight and stretching up, foot pointing forward.
- Keep your trunk and hips facing forward, and your hip bones level.
- Stretch your sitting bones down toward the mat and lift up from the groins.

Moving on

You can take these two poses to progressively more advanced levels. As your legs gain flexibility, you will be able to lift your leg high without the help of a chair or a belt. Eventually, you will be able to raise your foot to shoulder height and keep your leg straight while holding the big toe with the hand on the same side of the body. But that can take years to achieve.

Extended leg-stretches analyzed

Although this diagram shows the leg-stretch on page 71—utthita hasta padangusthasana II—these details will also help you keep your balance in utthita hasta padangusthasana I, shown on page 70.

EXERCISING THE BACK

These poses turn and extend the spine to make it more flexible. The standing pose introduces the twists, which rotate the vertebrae, and **uttanasana I**, at right, bends the spine forward from the hips (please read the caution note on page 9 before attempting these poses). Together these poses give the spine an intense and satisfying stretch.

Standing chair twist

1 *Stand beside the chair with your right side close to the wall, feet together, hands by your sides. Place your right foot on the chair, and stretch up.*

2 *Put your left hand on your right knee and pull on it to turn your left side toward the wall.*

3 *Place your right hand on the wall and press with the fingertips to push your right side away and your left side toward it. Twist for 10–15 seconds.*

Repeat and finish

Lower your hands, turn to face forward, and stand in tadasana, then repeat the pose, turning the chair and twisting to the left side.

Marichyasana Twist

The pose shown on this page, called **Marichyasana** because it is based on an exercise devised by a sage, Marichi, exercises the spine by twisting it. Position a chair so its seat touches a wall, and place two foam blocks or telephone books on the seat and also touching the wall, and place your foot on the blocks.

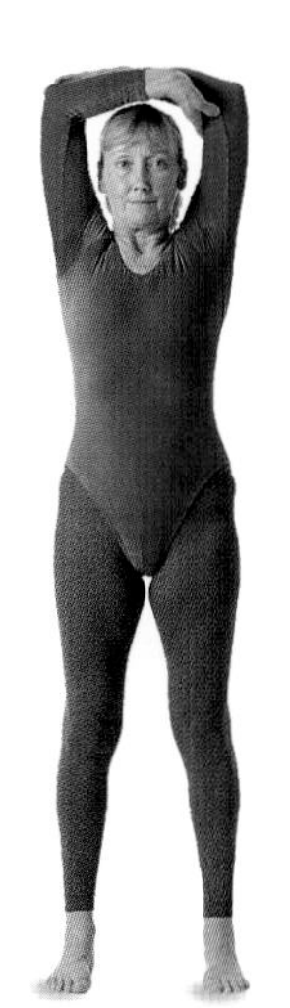

2 *Lift your elbows, then bend forward from your hips. Stretch your legs up, let your body relax down, head hanging, and lower your elbows toward the floor. Hold for 10–15 seconds, then inhale, place your hands on your legs, lift your head and your elbows, and sliding your hands up your legs, raise your spine from your hips until you are standing upright in tadasana.*

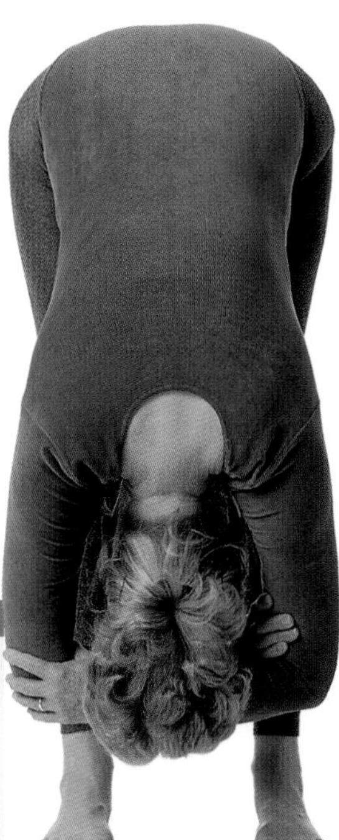

Standing forward bend

1 *Stand with your feet parallel, hip-width apart, your weight evenly balanced. Stretch up from your feet, and lifting from your hips, raise your arms above your head. Bending your elbows, catch hold of the upper arms just above the elbows.*

Uttanasana I

When you feel you can do the simplified standing forward bend in Chapter 3 easily, move to **uttanasana I**, the slightly more advanced version shown here. This pose stretches the whole spine, yet it is perfect for resting between more complex poses.

Achieving a Supple Spine

The secret of twisting is to lift and stretch, so begin the simple twist on page 74 by standing erect, the crown of your head facing the ceiling. Stretch the leg on which you stand strongly up, pressing it firmly back at the same time. Stretch your sitting bones toward the floor and your spine up, and exhale as you turn. Your arm acts as a fulcrum as the hand pressing against the wall levers one side of your body away from the wall, and the hand pulling against your knee draws the other side closer to it. This combined action helps you turn a degree or two further.

Making a forward bend

Stretch your legs strongly upward before bending forward in uttanasana I on page 75, lift from the hip bones, and extend the trunk upward. Stretch your arms as you raise them, and with your hands keeping hold of your upper arms, lift your elbows high, then breathe out as you bend forward—from the hips, not from the waist. This is a relaxing pose, for the body hangs from the hips while the legs do the hard work.

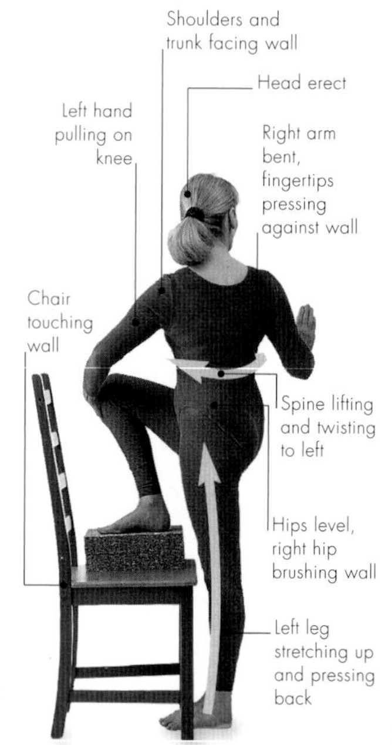

Standing chair twist

Think about the details shown in the diagram, right, to achieve the Marichyasana twist on page 74.

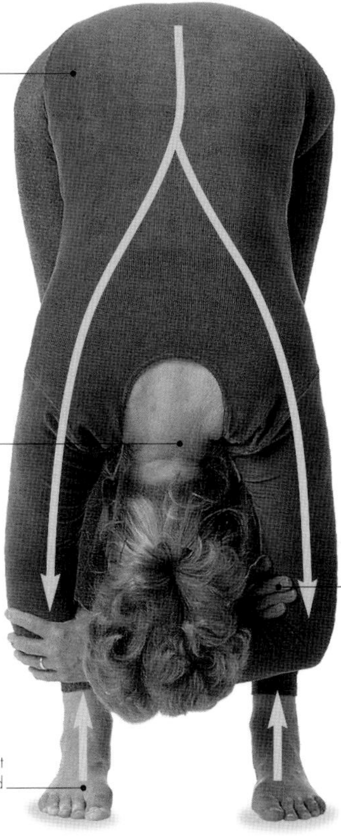

Trunk bending from hips, left and right hips aligned

Neck relaxed, head hanging

Opposite hands holding upper arms, elbows relaxed downward

Feet apart, weight evenly distributed

Standing forward bend analyzed

The key to achieving the standing forward bend on page 75 is to think about stretching the legs strongly up, while concentrating on the points shown here. If you have a slipped disk or other back problem, you should not attempt this pose. Instead, continue to practice the version shown on page 55.

WARRIOR II

Virabhadrasana is the name of a great warrior in an epic poem by the fifth-century Indian dramatist, Kalidasa. There are several warrior poses. **Virabhadrasana II**, the first and simplest, develops the muscles of the calves and thighs and is a good preparation for the more advanced standing poses, especially the forward bends.

1 *Stand in tadasana (see page 43), inhale, and jump your feet about 4–4½ feet (1.5 meters) apart (depending on your stride) stretching your arms out at shoulder level. Adjust your feet until they are parallel, and stretch up.*

2 *Keeping your trunk facing forward, move your left foot slightly inward and rotate your right foot to the right, aligning the heel with your left instep.*

3 *Stretch your trunk up from the hips, breathe out, and keeping your left leg straight, bend your right leg to form a right angle. Keeping your left and right arms in a line, turn your head to the right, and stretch strongly upward from the groins and across the upper body, from breastbone to fingertips. Hold the stretch for 10–15 seconds.*

Repeat and finish

Straighten your right leg and turn to face forward, reverse the positioning of your feet, and repeat steps 2 and 3, this time bending your left knee. Then repeat the whole pose before resting.

Lifting and Stretching

If you have worked through the ten poses in Chapter 3 once or twice, your legs should be stronger and your stance will be firmer. The two warrior poses—virabhadrasana II on pages 78–79, and the slightly more advanced virabhadrasana I on pages 82–85—work on strengthening the lower body. Focus your attention on maintaining an upward stretch and on the changing alignments of the different parts of your body. After jumping your legs apart in step 1, your feet must be parallel and the toes aligned so that your leg and foot face the same way.

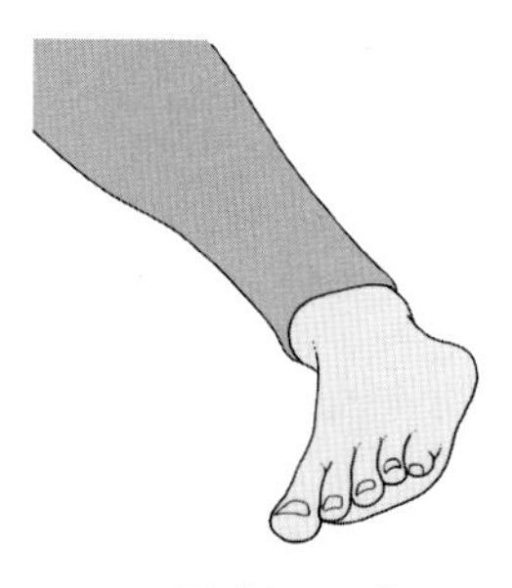

Working on the pose

Your stance needs to be firmly based, so when you turn your feet in step 2 the outer edge of the back foot must not lift, as shown above. If your weight is distributed evenly on both feet, the outer edge of the sole and heel rest firmly on the floor.

Your stance

At all stages of this pose keep your whole body lifted. Stand erect before you jump your legs apart, and pause before you rotate your feet to stretch your legs up from the arch of each foot to the hips. Turn each leg out at the hip joint, and lift your trunk from your groins. Keep your trunk erect as you bend your knee, and your head up. If possible, check your stance at this stage in front of a mirror. The thigh of your bent leg should be parallel to the floor, and the shin needs to be at a 90° angle to the floor. Feel the stretch across your groins. While holding the pose, lift your breastbone and stretch out from the center of your chest. Extend your left arm to the left and your right arm to the right, keeping your shoulders down, then level your arms until they form a horizontal line across your body.

Points to Watch

- When your right knee is bent do not allow your left hip, the left side of your trunk, or your left shoulder to roll forward and down—and vice versa. Revolve them back as if pressing them against a wall.
- Keep your shoulders and your raised arm pressing back, so your arms and shoulders form a ruler-straight line.
- Keep your tailbone tucked in and your sitting bones stretching down.

Warrior II analyzed

To perfect your stance in step 3 of warrior II on page 79, check the details pinpointed on this image.

WARRIOR I

Virabhadrasana I is a strengthening pose, a dynamic posture in which you turn the trunk to the side. It stretches the joints between the vertebrae, working at restoring the spine's natural flexibility. It is recommended for its efficacy in relieving stiffness in the back, shoulders, and neck.

1 *Stand in tadasana, then inhale and jump your feet about 4–4½ feet (1.5 meters) apart depending on your stride, while stretching your arms out to shoulder level. Stretch upward and from fingertips to fingertips.*

2 *Rotate your arms from the shoulder joints so your palms turn up, inhale, and raise your arms, keeping them straight, until your palms touch above your head.*

Stretching the Arms

When you raise your arms in step 2, stretch them up and back so your upper arms touch your ears or the sides of your head behind them.

3 *Turn your left foot in 50–60°, rotate your right foot to the right, your right leg out from the hip joint, and turn your trunk to the right.*

4 *Stretch back to the left heel, then exhale and bend your right leg until it forms a right angle. Lift up from the groins and look up at your fingertips. Hold for 10–15 seconds.*

Repeat and finish

Breathe in, straighten your right leg, turn to face forward, exhale, then lower your arms and rest. Repeat steps 2–4, this time turning to the left, then repeat the whole pose.

Arm Lifts

Warrior I is one of many poses that encourage you to flex, extend, and rotate your arms further than you thought they could go. You start the pose by extending your arms out at shoulder level, and stretching them. This stretch should be a powerful one, starting at the breastbone and flowing outward via the shoulder and the armpit, along each arm to the fingertips. In this pose you go further, however, rotating your outstretched arms backward through 180° from the shoulder joint until the palms face the ceiling, before raising your arms above your head.

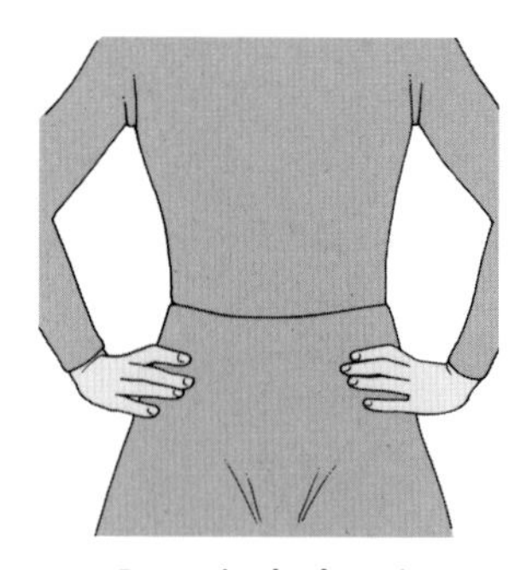

Preventing back strain

If you have a slipped disk or other more serious problem you should practice the pose without raising your arms above your head. If you keep your hands on your hips, you can work on your spine's flexibility without straining your back.

A powerful lift

The arm lift is a powerful movement that involves stretching more than the arms. It begins at the sides of the ribs, an action that lifts the rib cage, and stretches the armpits, the upper arms, the elbow joints, the forearms, and the hands. Work at stretching your upper arms back to your ears—or even behind your ears—and bring your hands as close together as you can above your head, palms touching. This arm lift should be the culmination of a lifting movement that begins at the arch of the back foot, stretches up the inner back leg to the groins, rising to the hip bones and up the trunk to the neck and crown of the head. Finally, raise your head to look up at your outstretched fingertips.

Points to Watch

- Your weight should remain distributed evenly on the key points of both feet (see page 42) throughout the pose.
- From the moment you raise your arms, keep them straight.
- Press your tailbone firmly in and stretch your sitting bones downward, but broaden across the sacrum at the back of the pelvis, and lift up from your hip bones.

Warrior I analyzed

To perfect your stance in step 4 of warrior I on page 83, check the details pinpointed on this image.

HALF MOON

The graceful **ardha chandrasana** pose is thought to resemble the half moon, hence its name. It radiates harmony, and it develops balance and coordination. All the standing poses strengthen the legs, but practiced regularly over time, this pose is especially beneficial for anyone with weak knees or ankles.

1 *Begin by repeating steps 1–3 of triangle pose on pages 46–47. Pause, looking up at your hand and breathing normally.*

2 *Turn your head to face forward, rest your left arm along your side, exhale, bend your right leg, and move your left foot closer to your right foot.*

3 *Lower your right hand to the floor about 12 inches (30 centimeters) ahead of your right foot and slightly behind it. On an out-breath, lift the left leg to hip level, straightening your right leg. Raise your left arm, palm facing forward, in line with your right arm, then look up at your fingers. Hold for 10–15 seconds, breathing normally, then turn your head to face forward, bend your right knee again, and return to triangle pose.*

Checking your Alignment

Practicing this pose against a wall—represented by the tinted frame of this box – is a good way of learning since it aligns your shoulders, trunk, hips, and legs, and helps you balance.

Repeat and finish

Repeat steps 1–3, lowering your left hand and raising your right leg. Then inhale, raise your trunk, jump your feet together, and rest.

Balance and Poise

Half moon is a second-level asana which you begin in triangle pose (see pages 46–47), then balance on one hand and leg. Pause in triangle pose and concentrate on stretching and alignment. Breathe normally throughout, keeping both legs and both sides of your trunk stretching up.

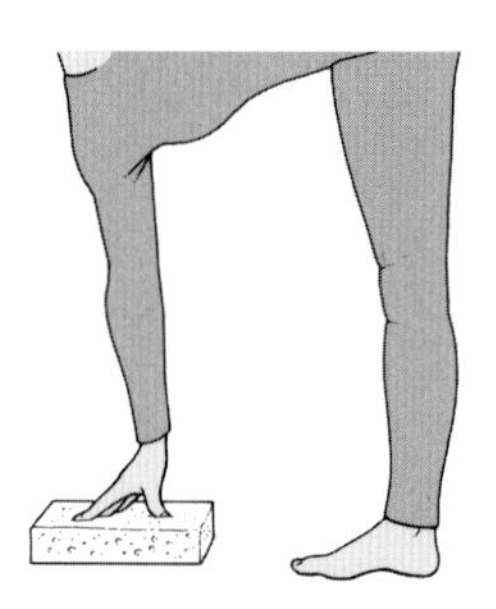

Working on the pose

If you cannot lower one hand right down to the floor, rest it on a foam block or a pile of telephone books.

Transferring your weight

Shifting your weight from two legs to one marks the transition from triangle to half moon in step 2. Make this transition smoothly, distributing your weight evenly onto the four key points on the sole of the foot (see page 42). As your left leg rises, you make another weight transfer onto your right leg. Turn your leg out from the hip as you raise it to hip level, so the knee faces forward.

Focus on balance

At this point, pause to balance yourself by stretching your standing leg strongly upward and your raised leg leftward, toward the outstretched foot. Fixing your gaze on your raised hand also helps you maintain your balance. The angle that is formed by your lower body is mirrored by the upper body as you stretch your upper arm vertically in line with the downstretched arm. Here, pause to turn the entire upper side of your trunk up and back, and to press your tailbone in, then stretch your trunk from the groins to the crown of your head. Follow this movement by turning your head to look up, aligning it with your trunk.

Half moon analyzed

Step 3 of half moon pose on page 87 is detailed below. If you can, perform the pose in front of a mirror, checking each point shown.

Points to Watch

- Keep your shoulders and your raised arm back, forming a ruler-straight line with the lower arm on which you are balancing.
- Do not allow the side of the trunk that is uppermost to roll forward. Revolve it back as if pressing it against a wall.
- Keep your tailbone tucked well in throughout the pose—do not allow your buttocks to protrude.

Left arm straight, palm turned to face the front

Left hip lying vertically above right hip

Left leg straight

Gaze directed up to left hand

Right arm straight, forming 90° angle to floor

Right leg straight, forming 90° angle to floor

CHAIR

Utkatasana is an antidote to the effects of poor posture, because you sit in the air, balanced on your two feet and using your own muscles for support. Literally translated, the Sanskrit word "utkatasana" means "powerful pose" and this is an apt description because it gives power to the calves, the ankles, and the large muscles of the buttocks and thighs.

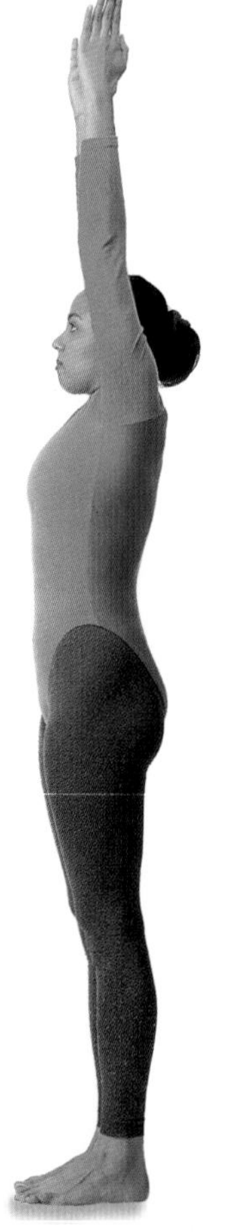

1 *Stand in tadasana (see page 43) with your feet together, inhale, raise your arms above your head, and stretch up.*

Head and Arms

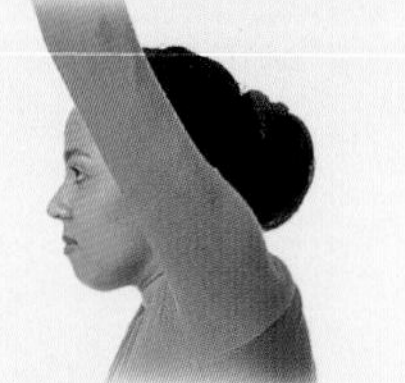

Work on keeping your arms stretching up,and your elbows back in line with your ears. Keep your gaze level and directed forward.

2 *On an out-breath, bend your ankles, your knees, and your hips, and lower your seat as if you were sitting on a chair, while keeping your heels on the floor. Hold for 10–15 seconds, stretching up from your hips.*

Hands and Arms

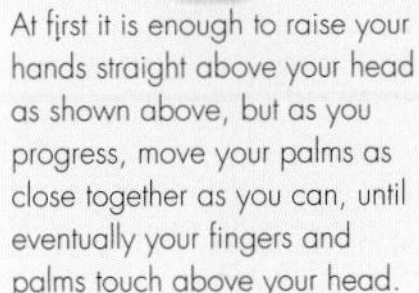

At first it is enough to raise your hands straight above your head as shown above, but as you progress, move your palms as close together as you can, until eventually your fingers and palms touch above your head.

Repeat and finish

Straighten your legs and lower your arms to your sides. Stand briefly in tadasana, then repeat the pose.

Strengthening the Legs

The unusual positioning of the spine and pelvis in the chair pose on page 91 makes the muscles of the thighs, calves, and feet bear the weight of the upper body. It exercises the powerful, four-headed quadriceps muscle of the thigh, and exercises the calf muscles. Although we use these muscles when we sit, stand, run, and climb stairs, many of us neglect to stretch and exercise them, and our legs are often weaker than we think—as people often discover, painfully, after skiing practice. Chair pose is a great exercise for skiers and also for horse riders. It builds on the toning and strengthening you have already achieved by practicing standing poses.

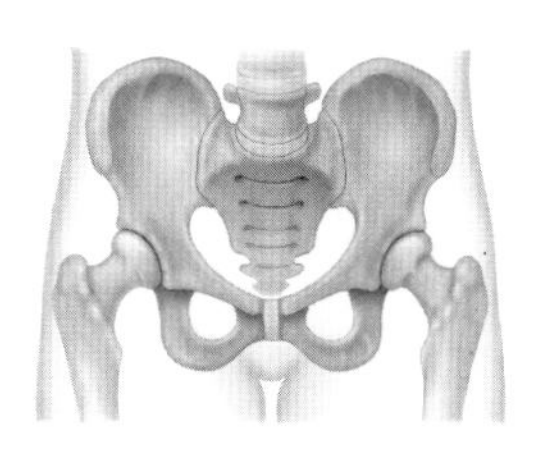

Aligning the pelvis

Do not tuck your tailbone under but imagine you are stretching the sacrum and sitting bones at the base of the pelvis down to the floor. Simultaneously lift the hip bones at the front.

Forming diagonals

In this pose, the arms, trunk, thighs, and calves form a succession of diagonals. Because the body is bent into a sitting position, the trunk inclines along a diagonal, but in fact the spine is straight. The chair depends on the correct alignment of the pelvic girdle, which must not be tucked right in and under, nor pushed out behind. If you find your lower body is stiff when you try the pose, move your feet about 12 inches (30 centimeters) apart at the beginning of step 1. The stretching action of the raised arms is an excellent exercise for the shoulders, an area of the body that is often found to be stiff.

Points to Watch

- Keep your shoulders and hips in horizontal alignment.
- Let the trunk incline forward from the hips, but keep your back straight and stretching up.

Chair pose analyzed

To perfect the chair pose on page 91, check each of the details pinpointed on this image.

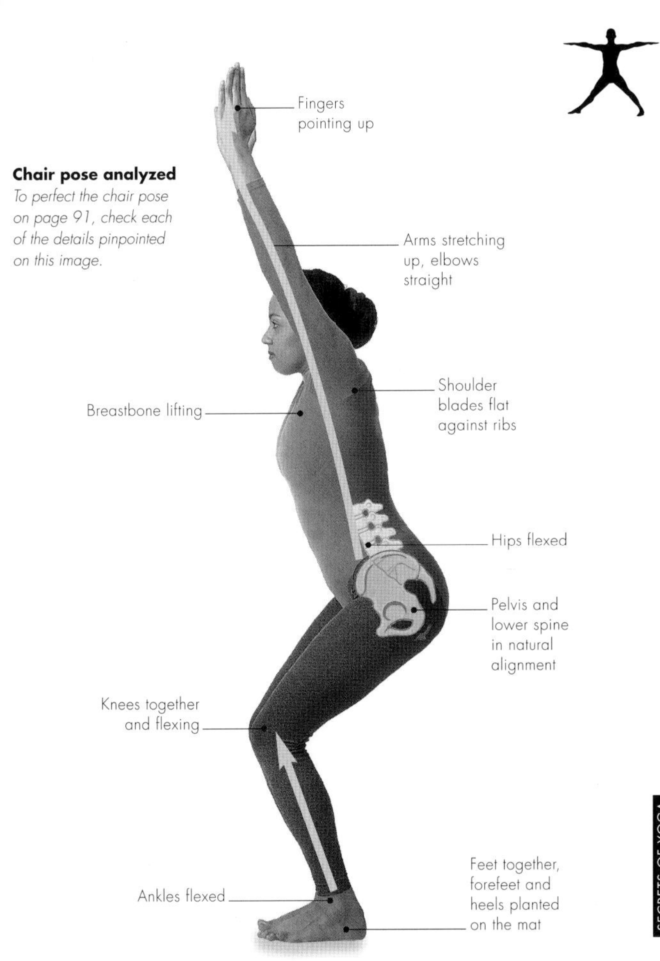

SIDE-STRETCH

A forward bend that extends the legs is a good pose to follow the bent-legged chair pose on the preceding pages. In **parsvottanasana** the body extends over one forward-striding leg. This pose is really two exercises in one, since the arms join behind the back in **namaste**, the prayer pose.

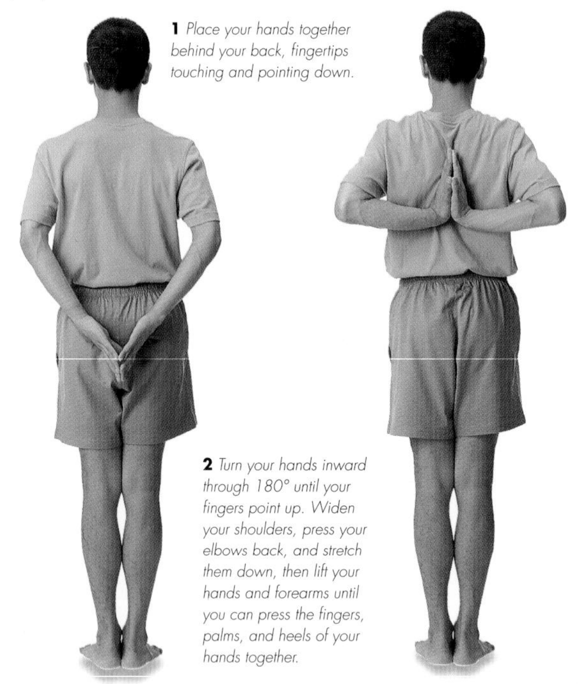

1 *Place your hands together behind your back, fingertips touching and pointing down.*

2 *Turn your hands inward through 180° until your fingers point up. Widen your shoulders, press your elbows back, and stretch them down, then lift your hands and forearms until you can press the fingers, palms, and heels of your hands together.*

3 *With your hands in namaste, inhale and jump your feet about 3½–4 feet (1 meter) apart depending on your stride.*

4 *Turn your left foot in and your right leg and foot out to the right, aligned with your left instep. Press your left heel down, stretch both legs up from the feet, and turn your hips and trunk to the right. Stretch your trunk up from the hips, lift your breastbone, and look up.*

5 *Bend forward from the hips until your head touches your shin. Hold the pose for 10–15 seconds.*

Repeat and finish

Inhale, and pressing your tailbone in, lift your trunk from the hips, stand erect, and, with your arms still in namaste, turn your hips and trunk and both feet to face the front. Turn your feet to the left and repeat steps 1, 2, and 3, turning to the left. Rest briefly and repeat the whole pose.

Intensive Stretching

This pose gives the body a strong stretch—its Sanskrit name means "intensive stretching". As you bend to the right, you stretch the muscles and joints of the legs, the knee and hip joints, and sides of the abdomen and chest. At the same time the prayer position of the hands activates the pectoral muscles of the upper chest and arms and the muscles that move the shoulders and the collar bone.

Hand position

This pose incorporates a special hand position—namaste, the prayer pose, which is more familiar when performed at the front rather than the back of the body. You may need to practice rotating the wrist to turn the downward-pointing hands, fingertips touching behind your back, inward and up. With your fingers pointing to the ceiling, widen your shoulders and press your forearms back, stretching the elbows down. This will help you raise your forearms and joined hands behind your back—and you will find that the higher you raise them, stretching up as you do so, the more your chest opens. With practice you will be able to press not only your fingers together but also the palms, the thumbs, and the heels of your hands.

Upward stretch

Strong legs are the foundation of forward bends, so before bending forward, pause to stretch from feet to head. Lift the arches of your feet and feel an upward stretch in both legs—but more of a stretch in the back leg because you press the outer edge of the heel firmly down. Check that one hip is not higher or further forward than the other, and keep the wings of your arms stretching firmly back. Lift your trunk up from your hip bones, raising your breastbone as you look up.

As you bend forward, extend your trunk away from your legs. Feel the intense stretch from your legs along your sides. This mobilizes the hip joints, and, incidentally, has the effect of flattening the lower abdomen, and it gives the lungs more breathing space.

Points to Watch

- Keep your shoulders pulled back, your upper arms stretching toward your hips, and your hands pressed together throughout, to open your chest as fully as possible.
- Do not allow your right hip to project outward when your right leg is forward, or vice versa. Your hips need to be perfectly level and in the same plane throughout the pose.

Side-stretches analyzed

When you have mastered the hand position, work on the points shown here to perfect the side-stretch on page 95.

WIDE LEG-STRETCH

Stretching the legs very wide apart exercises the abductor muscles of the hips. These rotate the legs outward from the center of the body and are often underused. **Prasarita padottanasana** increases blood circulation through the trunk and to the head, and it is said to help if you are trying to slim your hips.

1 *Stand in tadasana (see page 43), stretch your arms out to shoulder level, inhale, and jump the feet about 4½–5 feet (1.5 meters) apart, or as wide as your stride allows. Align your toes and turn both feet in slightly.*

2 *Stretching your legs and trunk up, put your hands on your hips and incline your trunk forward. Put your hands on the floor, shoulder-width apart and in line with your feet, and look up.*

3 *Stretch your spine forward, breathe out, bend your elbows, and keeping them parallel, lower the crown of your head to the mat between your hands. Hold the pose for 10–15 seconds, keeping your elbows in.*

Repeat and finish

Raise your head, straighten your arms, breathe in, straighten your back, and stand up. Breathe out, jump your feet together, rest, and repeat the pose.

Downward Stretch

Lift your trunk from the hips before bending forward in step 2, and bend from the hips. Straighten your spine and lift your breastbone before stretching down in step 3.

Loosening the Hamstrings

Like many people, you may find your hips bend easily when you try the wide leg-stretch on pages 98–99, but that you need to work on your legs. Most dancers will find this pose easy because the hips incline forward readily if the hamstrings are flexible. Try the pose and if you cannot reach the floor, rest your hands on a pile of foam blocks or telephone books, or on the seat of a chair with its back against a wall.

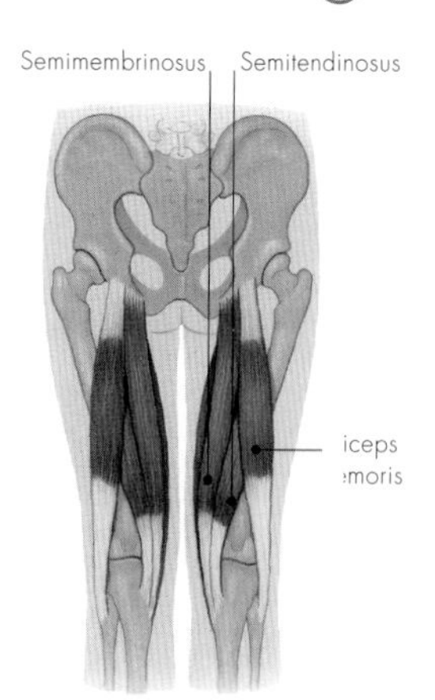

The hamstrings

Three muscles with long names stretch down the back of the thigh. They straighten it and bend and rotate the knee. Two have long sheaths and tendons (the "hamstrings"), which attach them to the bones of the pelvis.

Preparation

As you jump your feet apart at the start, distribute your body weight evenly on the four key points of both feet, then lift your arches and your ankles so they do not sag outward, and stretch your legs up. Keep your legs stretching up, your arms and your spine straight, and your breastbone lifting as you lift your head and look up in step 2.

Working on the hamstrings

Your legs need to be pressing back as well as lifting throughout this pose, and you should feel a strong stretch from feet to hips. If your hamstrings are tight they will quickly loosen with practice and you can gradually reduce the number of telephone books or other thick books you are using for support. Eventually, your legs will be flexible enough to allow you to lower your hands, and eventually your head, to the mat.

Points to Watch

- Do not curve your back into a hump when you bend from the hips in step 2. Your spine should be slightly concave (inward-curving).
- In step 3 keep your elbows parallel and drawn in toward your chest. Do not let them stick out like wings.
- When you lower your head to the floor, keep your weight on your feet by stretching your legs up and keeping your hips and heels in line.

Wide leg-stretch analyzed

Achieving the full wide leg-stretch in step 3 on page 99 takes regular practice and careful attention to the details shown here.

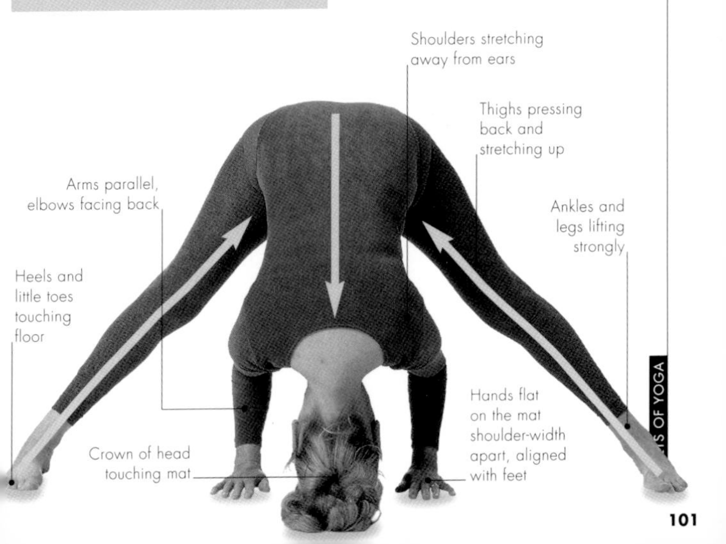

REVOLVED TRIANGLE

Parivrtta trikonasana is a standing twist in which you begin with your trunk facing forward and you end up with it facing the opposite direction—so it is often called "reverse triangle." It is the last of the sequence of standing poses which begin this chapter.

2 *Turn your left foot in at a 50°–60° angle, and your right foot out at a 90° angle, then on an out-breath swing your trunk to the right from your left hip until you face the same direction as your right foot, your arms still stretching out.*

1 *Stand in tadasana, then jump your feet about 3½–4 feet (1 meter) apart, and raise your arms to shoulder level.*

3 *Continuing to revolve your trunk to the right, and bending from the hips, place your left hand on the floor beside your right foot. Your head and trunk now face the opposite direction to step 1. Stretch your right arm up in line with your left arm, align your left hand parallel to your right foot, and press your left palm and your left heel onto the ground. Look up at your fingertips. Hold for 10–15 seconds.*

Repeat and finish

Raise your trunk and turn to face forward, arms still stretching out. Repeat steps 1–3, turning your feet and trunk to the left, and revolving to place your right hand beside your left foot. Rest, then repeat the pose.

Turning the Trunk

For the triangle pose on pages 46–49 your trunk remains facing forward while you bend to left or right, placing one hand on the floor beside the front foot. In the revolved triangle on pages 102–103 you turn the trunk through a half circle before you bend it and rest your hand on the mat. The pose gives the spine a satisfying twist.

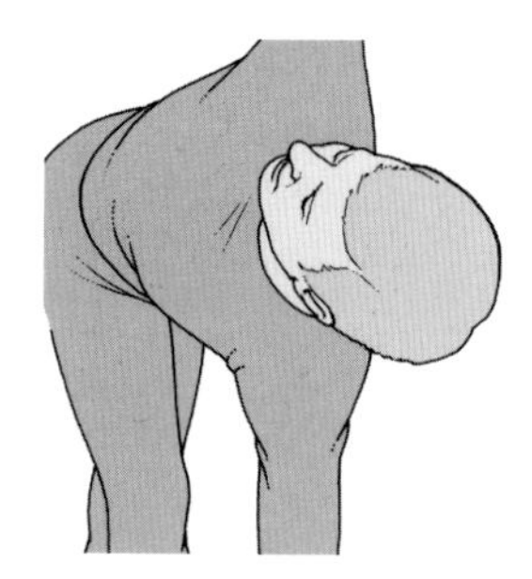

Head and shoulders

Keep your shoulders back and your shoulder blades flat against your ribs. Straighten your spine and align your head with it so that neck and head lie at right angles to your shoulders.

Which way to turn?

You began facing forward, but as you revolve your trunk, your head turns with it, so you look backward. Practicing close to a wall makes it easier to work out which way to turn. Begin facing the wall, and turn your trunk until you face into the room. Stretch your legs up and your arms out before twisting your trunk, and breathe in. Turn on the out-breath, rotating the hips, the abdomen, the waist, and the chest.

Stretching your spine away from your legs helps you turn and bend further. If your spine needs more flexibility, lower your hand onto a chair seat, then progress down to a pile of telephone books placed beside your little toe. Pause to equalize your weight on the four key points on each foot. Stretch both legs up from the arches of your feet, and press the palm and heel of your downward-stretching hand flat on the floor beside what is now your front foot. As you turn your face up, check that your upward-stretching arm rises vertically from your shoulders, so your outstretched arms form a straight line. Breathe normally as you hold the pose.

Points to Watch

- Bend and rotate the trunk from the hips, not from the waist.
- Keep your spine straight and stretching toward your head.
- Your hips need to be in line with your legs and trunk, your sitting bones stretching away from your shoulders.
- Do not allow your neck and shoulders to tense up.

Revolved triangle analyzed

Once you have worked out the correct alignment for step 3 of revolved triangle on pages 102–103, check the details shown here.

SITTING AND KNEELING

This page begins a sequence of sitting poses, starting with rod pose or **dandasana**, which is the foundation of most sitting asanas, and hero pose, **virasana**, which underlies all kneeling postures. These asanas rest the heart, quiet the mind, and calm the nerves. They are an antidote to stress and encourage a good night's sleep.

Rod pose

Sit on a mat, stretch your legs out, and place your hands on the floor either side of your hips. Press your hands and legs down and stretch up from your hips. Hold the stretch for 15–20 seconds, then rest.

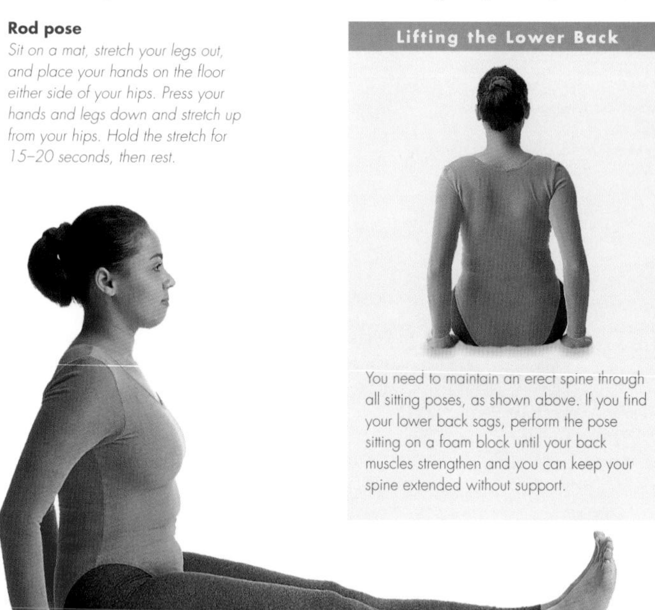

Lifting the Lower Back

You need to maintain an erect spine through all sitting poses, as shown above. If you find your lower back sags, perform the pose sitting on a foam block until your back muscles strengthen and you can keep your spine extended without support.

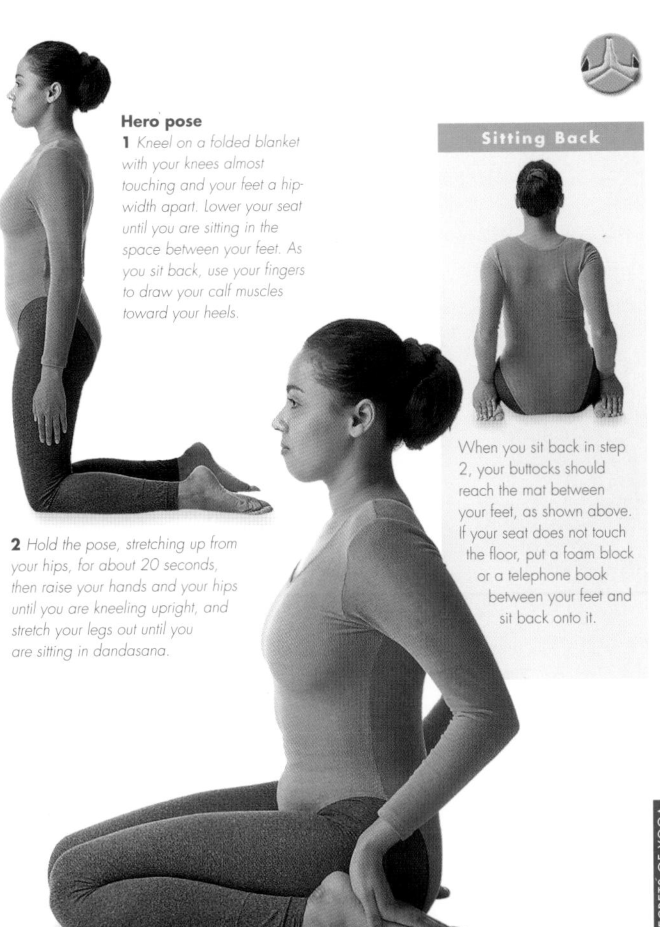

Hero pose

1 *Kneel on a folded blanket with your knees almost touching and your feet a hip-width apart. Lower your seat until you are sitting in the space between your feet. As you sit back, use your fingers to draw your calf muscles toward your heels.*

2 *Hold the pose, stretching up from your hips, for about 20 seconds, then raise your hands and your hips until you are kneeling upright, and stretch your legs out until you are sitting in dandasana.*

Sitting Back

When you sit back in step 2, your buttocks should reach the mat between your feet, as shown above. If your seat does not touch the floor, put a foam block or a telephone book between your feet and sit back onto it.

Basic Floor Work

Dandasana is called rod pose because the back must be rod-straight and stretching up. Sitting on a foam block or a blanket folded two or three times will help, and as you lower your buttocks to the floor pull the large gluteal muscles that form the fleshy buttocks out to the sides. Then, to help yourself lift your trunk you need to press your legs into the floor and use the rebound to stretch up from the hips.

Kneeling

In virasana, the hero pose, you kneel, but sit between widely parted feet. It is good for stiff knees, but if when you sit back your buttocks do not reach the

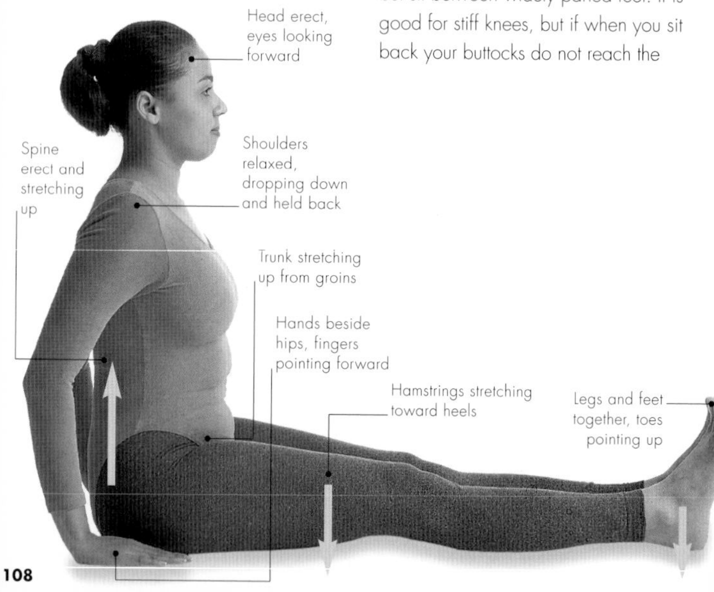

floor your legs tend to roll inward. This stretches the knees unevenly, causing discomfort. Placing a foam block between your feet will help you to keep your thighs aligned and to maintain an erect back while stretching up from the hips. If your knees or your feet are painful at first, place a small folded towel or blanket at the back of each knee, or beneath your ankles and feet.

Hero pose analyzed

Checking the details shown in the illustration on the right will help you perfect the hero pose or virasana on page 107.

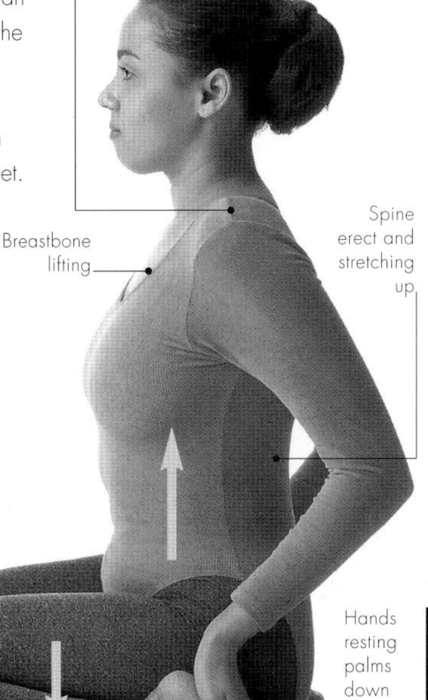

ANGLED LEG POSES

Baddha konasana is often called cobbler pose because in India cobblers traditionally work sitting with their knees wide apart and their feet together. Sitting with the legs widely angled, as in cobbler pose and the angled leg-stretch, **upavistha konasana**, gives a good stretch across the groins. They are believed to be effective in preventing urinary disorders and relieving menstrual pains.

Using a Belt

To keep your back straight while holding your feet, you may need to wind a belt around your feet and pull on it so that you do not bend from the waist.

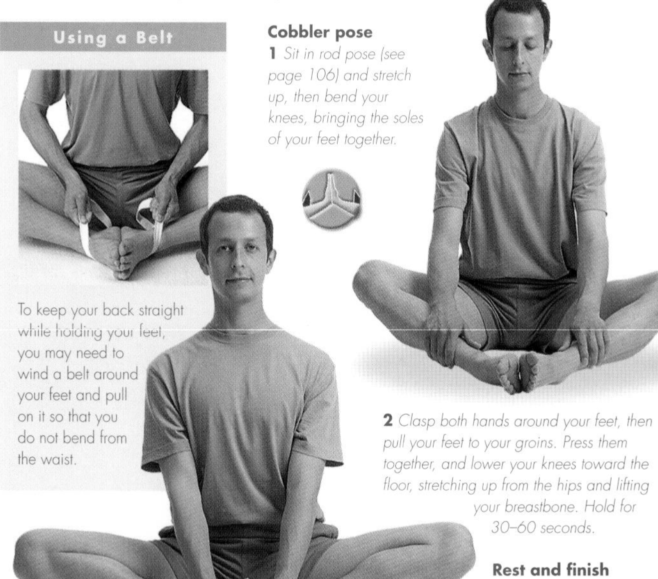

Cobbler pose

1 *Sit in rod pose (see page 106) and stretch up, then bend your knees, bringing the soles of your feet together.*

2 *Clasp both hands around your feet, then pull your feet to your groins. Press them together, and lower your knees toward the floor, stretching up from the hips and lifting your breastbone. Hold for 30–60 seconds.*

Rest and finish

Place your hands on the floor beside your hips, straighten your legs, and rest.

Angled leg-stretch

1 *Sit in rod pose and stretch up, then keeping your back straight and your toes pointing up, move your legs out as far as you comfortably can so they form a wide angle. Press your hands and legs into the floor and stretch up, then, on an out-breath, bend your trunk forward from the hips, stretching your arms out, and catch hold of your big toes. Hold for 5–10 seconds.*

2 *On an out-breath, pull on your toes, and stretch forward and as far down as you can—if possible, until your forehead touches the floor. Hold the stretch for 5–10 seconds.*

Rest and finish

Breathe in, raise your head and your trunk, place your hands on the mat beside your hips, move your legs together, and rest.

Warning

If your legs feel strained when you catch hold of your toes in step 1, do not go on to step 2. Instead, breathe in, move your legs together, and rest. Return to this pose later, when your back and hips have become more flexible.

Stretching the Hip Joints

The two leg-stretches on pages 110–11 involve flexing the hips as well as stretching across the groins. In the angled leg-stretch you incline the spine forward as far as you can without bending from the waist. This movement exercises the lumbar spine, the hip joints, and the muscles and tendons of the buttocks and thighs. And in the cobbler pose you lower your bent knees to the floor while keeping your back straight.

Cobbler pose analyzed

The diagram on the right shows a number of important details to check in step 2 of the cobbler pose on page 110.

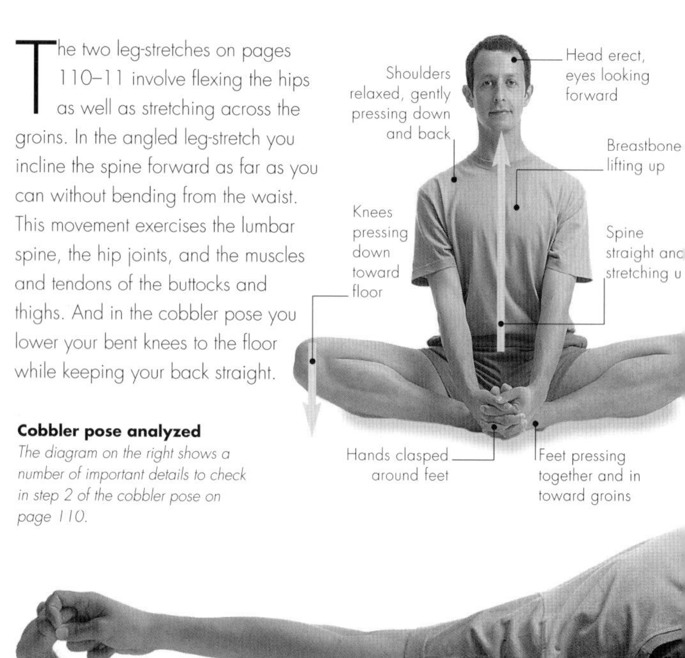

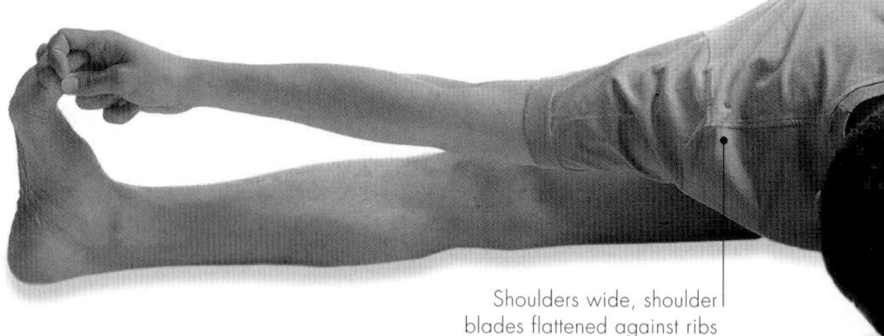

Aids to stretching

Begin both poses sitting on a folded blanket or a foam block. This makes it easier to lift the lower back, and in the cobbler pose helps you lower your knees to the floor. If your knees are high off the floor at first, sit on three folded blankets or two foam blocks.

If when you bend forward in the angled leg-stretch your hands do not reach your toes, do not allow yourself to bend from the waist, but work on your hip flexion by holding your calves. And if at first you cannot stretch down far enough to touch your forehead to the mat, rest it on a foam block, or on the seat of a chair positioned in front of you. Eventually, with practice, you will be able to extend your trunk further forward and rest your forehead on the mat in the full pose.

Angled leg-stretch analyzed

Check you have the details shown below correct when you practice the full angled leg-stretch on page 111.

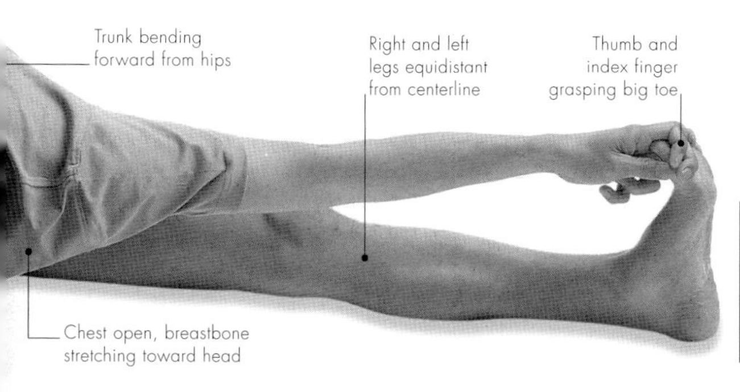

HEAD TO KNEE

The head-to-knee pose or **janu sirsasana** is a forward bend from a sitting position. It stimulates the organs of digestion, particularly the liver and kidneys, and is said to be particularly helpful to men with prostate disorders. Like all forward bends, it is a restful, calming posture.

1 *Sit in the rod pose, your hands on the floor beside your hips. Bend your left knee and, keeping it touching the floor, draw it to the left until it forms a 90° angle to your right leg. Press the foot against your right thigh.*

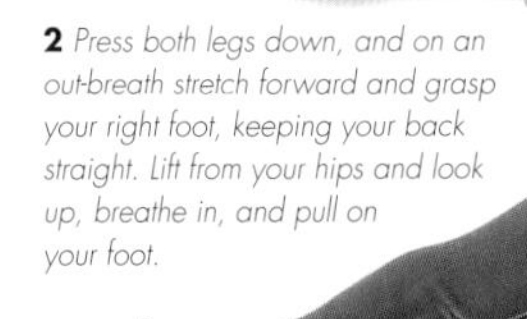

2 *Press both legs down, and on an out-breath stretch forward and grasp your right foot, keeping your back straight. Lift from your hips and look up, breathe in, and pull on your foot.*

Relaxing into the Pose

If your bent knee is uncomfortable, rest it on a foam block or a folded blanket. Your head and neck need to be relaxed, so if your forehead does not reach your shin, rest it on a blanket folded three or four times, or on a foam block.

3 *On the out-breath, extend your trunk along your right leg, resting your forehead on the shin. Hold the extension for 10–15 seconds, breathing normally.*

Repeat and finish

Release your foot, stretch out your left leg, inhale, and raise your head and trunk until you are sitting in the rod pose. Then repeat steps 1–3, bending your right leg.

Straightening the Spine

All the sitting forward bends begin in the rod pose, and they depend on stretching the back until it is as straight as possible. Even when bending forward to touch your knee with your head in janu sirsasana on pages 114–15 you need to elongate your trunk, lifting from your hips, and extending forward from the groins. If you bend from your waist you will find it hard to straighten your trunk, so your hands may not reach your feet. Use each opportunity the pose provides to stretch your spine from your fifth lumbar vertebra to the atlas on which your skull rests, and your trunk from groins to breastbone.

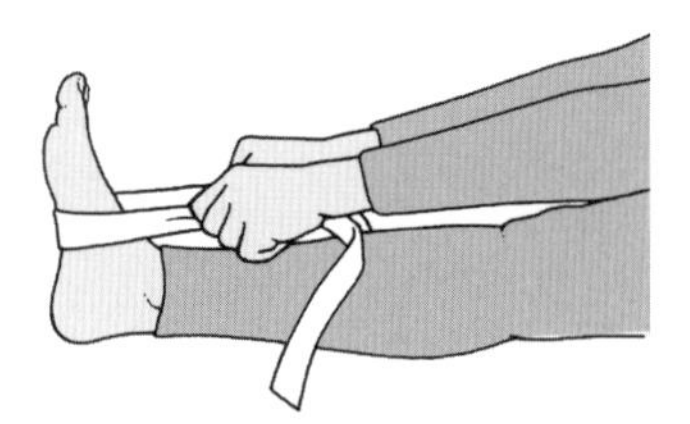

Working on the pose

Work on bending from the hips by winding a belt round your outstretched foot, holding one side of the belt in each hand, and pulling on it. Press your foot into the belt as you walk your hands down it, right, then left, then right.

Achieving the stretch

In step 2, press your legs down in order to stretch up further before lowering your head to your outstretched leg in step 3. If you can reach your foot, hold it in both hands, and pull on it to lever your trunk forward, but do not strain your body in trying to reach it. Instead, use a belt to pull your trunk forward as shown in the illustration above, while keeping your spine straight and stretching, and inclining your trunk a little further forward each time a hand moves forward. If at first your head does not reach your leg, place a folded blanket or a foam block on your shin and rest it on that—and put one under your bent knee if it feels uncomfortable. As you practice, your body becomes more flexible, until eventually you can clasp your hands around your foot and relax down into the full pose, resting your forehead on your leg.

Points to Watch

- When you bend your leg in step 1, draw the foot toward the opposite leg until it just rests against the groin and the top of the thigh. Be careful not to push it under the outstretched leg or beneath the thigh.
- Stretch your trunk toward your head, keeping your chest parallel with the floor and your breastbone in line with your straight leg.

Head-to-knee pose analyzed

Observing each of the details pinpointed on the image below will help you achieve the full head-to-knee pose on page 115.

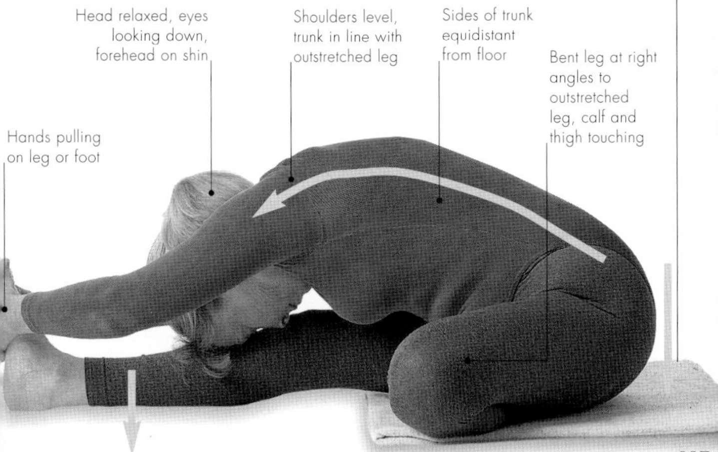

THREE-LIMBED POSE

The body is said to have three limbs in this pose: the feet, the knees, and the buttocks. Its lengthy Sanskrit name—**triang mukhaikapada paschimottanasana**—indicates that in this forward bend the head touches one leg. This pose stimulates the digestive system and relaxes the heart and brain, and is said to relieve pain and swelling in the legs and feet.

Aligning your Legs

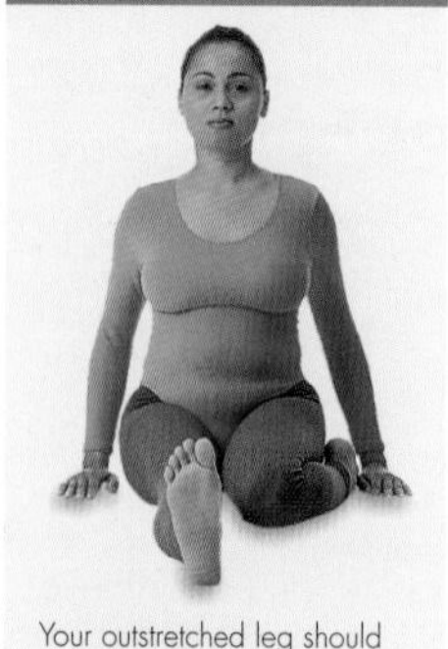

Your outstretched leg should remain straight and stretching away from your hips, the knee and toes pointing up. Without disturbing this alignment, draw the bent leg toward it until the thighs touch and the inside heel of the foot touches the buttock behind it.

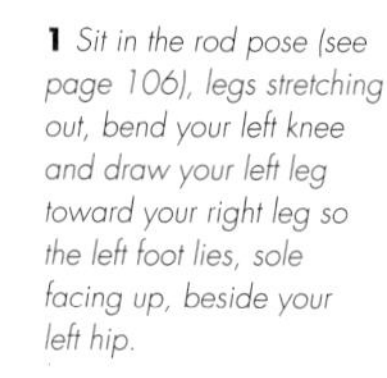

1 *Sit in the rod pose (see page 106), legs stretching out, bend your left knee and draw your left leg toward your right leg so the left foot lies, sole facing up, beside your left hip.*

2 *Press both legs down, lift your spine, and on an out-breath stretch forward and catch hold of your foot. Extend your trunk forward from the hips along the outstretched leg until your forehead touches the shin. Hold for about 20 seconds.*

Leveling your Pelvis

Keep your pelvis level. Your hip bones should remain aligned when you bend your leg in step 1, and both sitting bones should press down to the floor through the pose.

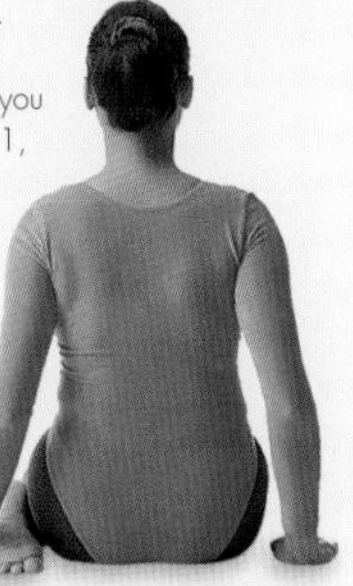

Repeat and finish

Lift your head, stretch and straighten your spine, release your hands, and raise your trunk until you sit in the rod pose. Then repeat steps 1 and 2, this time bending your right leg.

Working the Legs and Feet

The legs and feet are often over-used but underexercised, and the three-limbed pose on pages 118–19 helps to redress the balance. Each leg is bent and stretched in turn, exercising the knee joint, stretching and flexing the ankle joint, and strengthening the arches of the feet. Stretching each extended leg toward the foot while pressing it down exercises the hamstrings and the quadriceps muscles of the thighs, and the calf muscles.

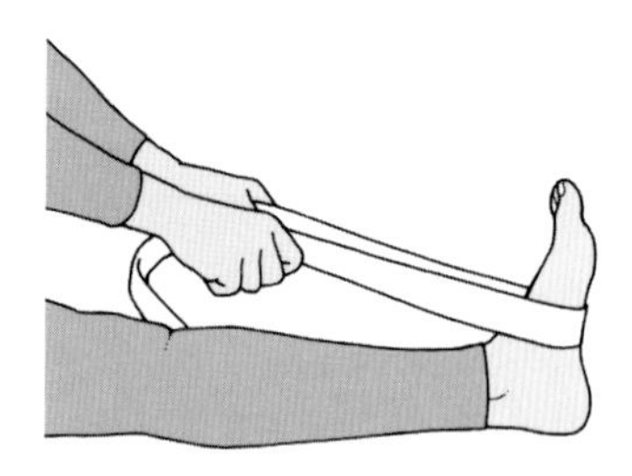

Using a belt

Wind a belt around the sole of your foot, hold one end in each hand, stretch your spine up, and pull on the belt with your hands while pressing into it with your foot to bend forward from the hips.

Three limbs

The third limb in this three-limbed pose is held to be the seat, and this stresses the active role of the hips in forward bends. Begin this posture sitting in the rod pose, with your hips level, and press equally down on both sitting bones as you bend your leg and incline your trunk forward. If you find that it is difficult to keep your hips level during this action, raise the level of your pelvis by sitting on a folded blanket or a foam block.

While the head-to-knee pose on pages 114–15 works the abductors—the muscles that turn the leg out at the hip—this pose exercises the adductors. These muscles turn the leg in toward the body's midline. Use them to keep your thighs parallel and pressing down, the centerline of both pointing up.

Press your hips and both legs down and lift your trunk before stretching forward. If your hands only reach your outstretched calf, use a belt as

illustrated. And if your head does not reach your shin, rest it on a pillow or even on a chair seat.

Persevering with the three-limbed pose improves the mobility of your hip joints, and with practice you will soon be able to clasp your hands behind your foot without difficulty.

Points to Watch

- Keep your balance—the center of each thigh needs to face the ceiling throughout.
- Pull on your foot to lever your body forward, bending your elbows and keeping them the same distance from the floor.
- Stretch the front of your body, from pelvis to breastbone, as well as your back.

Three-limbed pose analyzed

It is essential to position the parts of the body accurately in yoga, so check the details pinpointed below for step 2 of the three-limbed pose on page 119.

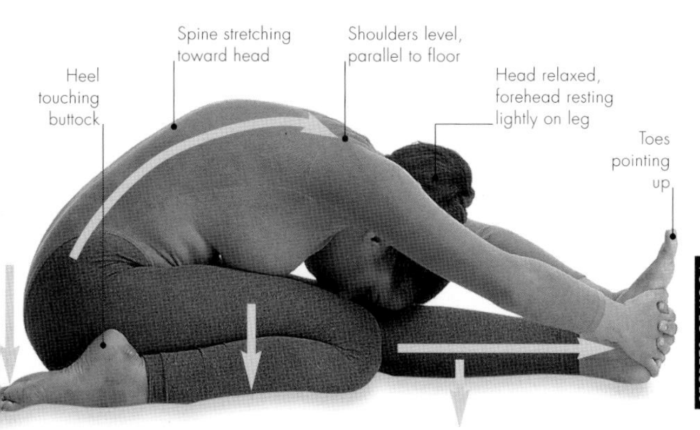

SITTING FORWARD BEND

In this forward bend, called **paschimottanasana**, you extend your whole body forward from the hips as if you were folding yourself in half. By positioning the heart below the spine, it reduces the heart's workload and stretches the spine, increasing the circulation to the lower body, so it calms, relaxes, refreshes, and revitalizes.

1 *Sit in the rod pose (see page 106), press your hands and legs down, and stretch up.*

Warning

In this as in all forward bends, do not attempt the full forward stretch if you suffer from back problems. You will benefit from this pose if you raise the level of your pelvis and stop at step 2.

2 *On an out-breath and bending from the hips, stretch your arms forward and catch hold of the sides of your feet, straightening your spine.*

Working on the Pose

Do not bend at the waist in the effort to reach your feet. Instead, wind a belt around the soles of your feet and walk your hands down it as far as you can, stretching a little further forward from the hips each time you move your hands along the belt.

3 *Extend your trunk along your legs. Bend your elbows out to the sides as you pull on your feet, and lower your head until your forehead rests on your shins. Hold for up to 20 seconds.*

Finish and rest

Raise your head, release your hands, and keeping your back straight, raise your trunk until you are sitting in the rod pose, then rest.

An Extreme Stretch

The sitting forward bend on pages 122–23 ends a sequence of three forward bends, giving the body the most intense stretch of all. Unless your back is very supple and your hip joints flexible, you may need to work on the pose for some time before you can achieve it without using aids. If you can reach forward only as far as your knees or calves, begin by sitting on a foam block or folded blankets and use a belt to pull your trunk forward while keeping your back as straight as you can. You might begin practicing by placing a low chair over your outstretched legs and resting your forehead on the seat, or placing one or more foam blocks on your knees. As your body develops flexibility, the forward bend will become easier.

The impetus to stretch

Stretching up from the hips makes it easier to bend from the hips. It also elongates the spine, enabling you to reach further. It is easy in a demanding pose to let your trunk sag backward, so pause from time to time and press your sitting bones, your legs, and your feet down onto the floor firmly, to give yourself the impetus to stretch your spine and breastbone toward your head. Grasp your feet, stretching your elbows out to either side—or pull on the belt—as you move your trunk forward. Eventually, you will be able to clasp your hands around your feet and rest your trunk and your forehead on your legs. Breathe normally and rhythmically as you hold this calm, restful position.

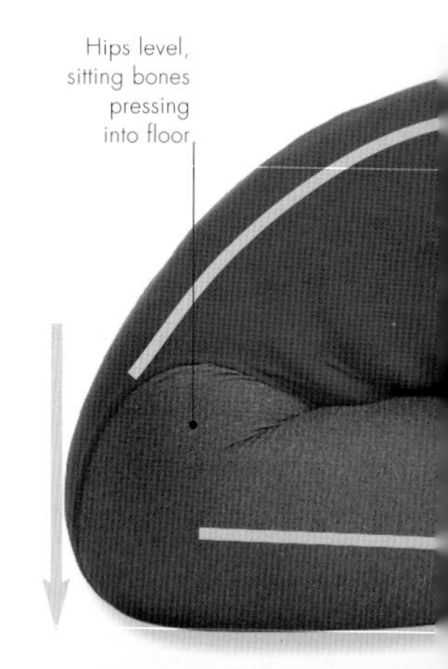

Points to Watch

- Remember to breathe in before you stretch, and to reach forward on an out-breath.
- Keep your shoulders relaxed and your shoulder blades flat against your ribs.
- As you lean your trunk forward, imagine that your spine is straightening and lengthening.

Sitting forward bend analyzed

To achieve the full forward stretch in step 3 of the sitting forward bend on page 123, check the details pinpointed on the image below.

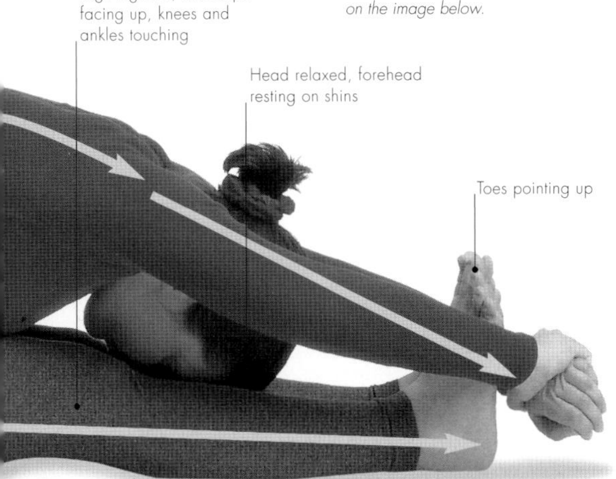

COBBLER FLOOR POSE

This lying-down version of the cobbler pose, **supta baddha konasana**, is a passive pose and a restful position. It provides a deep stretch across the groins, boosting the circulation to and from the pelvic area, and toning the muscles of the legs and hips.

1 *Sit in cobbler pose with the tips of your toes just touching a wall and your hands on the floor on either side of your hips.*

2 *Pressing down with your hands, lift your hips just clear of the mat and move your seat as close to your heels as you can, then use your hands to lower your trunk to the mat.*

3 *Raise your hips clear of the mat, move your seat closer to your heels, then lower your seat, rest your head on the mat, and relax your arms over your head. Hold this position for 1–2 minutes.*

Finish and rest

Place your arms on the mat by your sides, turn onto your side with your legs bent, then sit upright, straighten your legs, and rest.

A Resting Pose

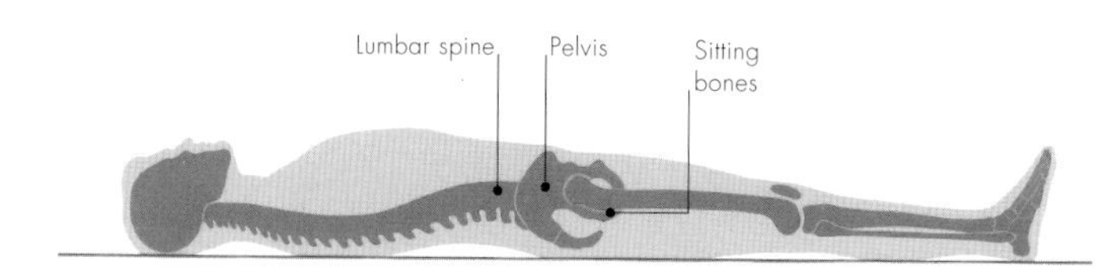

In some ways floor poses may seem harder work than standing poses, simply because a floor is hard, while the air gives readily. Looked at another way, however, floor poses are more restful than standing poses, because it is easier to relax when lying down. The cobbler floor pose is a perfect example. It is a passive pose—one in which you stretch, but do not change position—so it is more restful to perform lying on the floor than the sitting cobbler pose on page 110. But, like every lying-down pose, it will be restful only if the arch that forms in your lower back when you lie down is reduced by stretching the lumbar spine. Lifting your hips and moving your seat toward your heels in step 2 is designed to achieve this.

Avoiding strain

If you align your pelvis properly before lying back, your lumbar spine will be closer to the mat and more comfortable.

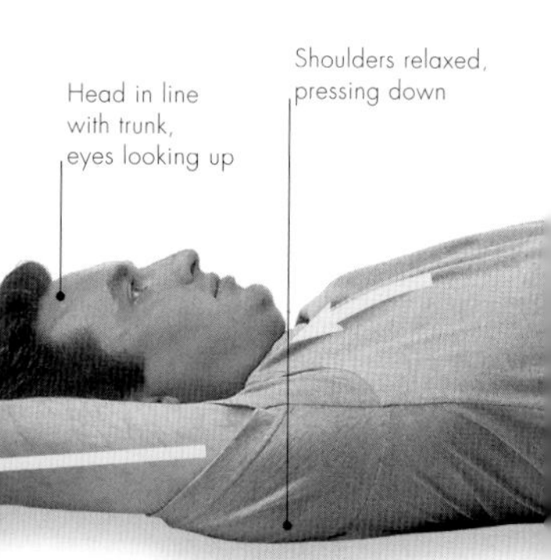

Supporting the upper body

Before you start, place a blanket folded into a square on the floor between the points where your waist and head will be when you lie back, so that your upper back is supported. Your groins need to be as close as possible to your feet to get a good stretch across thighs and groins, but if your knees are stiff, leave more space between your groins and your feet. Lie squarely on the blanket and concentrate on stretching your lower back and your sitting bones away from your waist, toward the wall.

Points to Watch

- Start the pose with your toes touching a wall so that your feet do not creep steadily further away from your groins as you lie back and stretch.
- Keep your hip bones stretching toward your head and your sitting bones stretching toward your feet.

Cobbler floor pose analyzed

To achieve a good stretch in step 3 of the cobbler floor pose on page 127, check the details shown below.

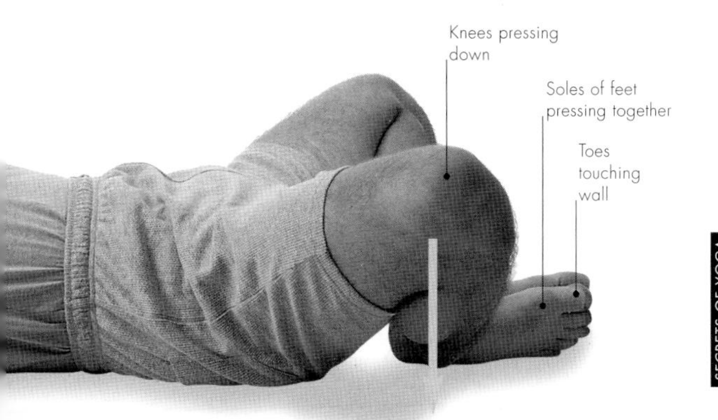

DOWNWARD-FACING DOG

This pose, called **adho mukha svanasana**, imitates a dog stretching with its rump in the air. It is a healing pose, capable of relieving stiffness in the shoulders and strain and tiredness in the legs and heels. It also relieves fatigue, since it slows the heartbeat and invigorates the brain and nervous system.

1 *Lie face down on a nonslip surface, with your elbows bent, your hands on the mat palms down, fingers spread out, fingertips just below your shoulders, your feet about 12 inches (30 centimeters) apart.*

2 *On an out-breath, press your hands and feet down and raise yourself into a kneeling position. Adjust your hands so the two middle fingers lie parallel, and stretch your fingers forward. Tuck your toes under, and breathe in.*

Toes and Heels

Your feet remain 12 inches (30 centimeters) apart throughout the pose. In step 3, lower your heels as close to the floor as you comfortably can. Press them down to the mat as you stretch your legs up toward your hips.

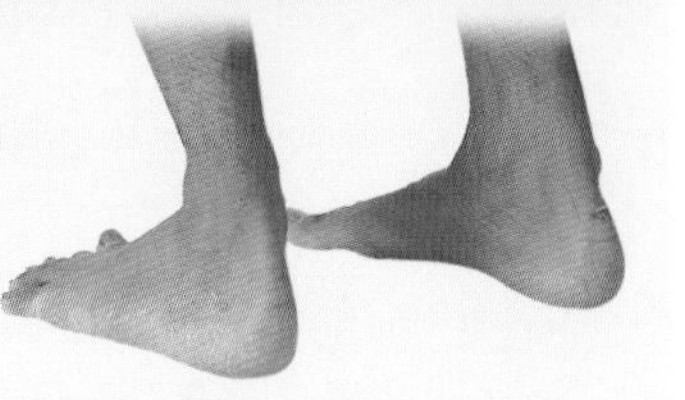

3 *Breathing out, lift your hips so your body forms an upside-down V-shape. Stretch your arms and trunk, and your legs, up toward your hips, pressing your hands and heels to the floor. Drop your head between your shoulders. Hold the stretch for 15–20 seconds.*

Finish and rest

Raise your head, bend your legs into a kneeling position, and rest in a kneeling forward bend.

Gathering Energy

The downward-facing dog pose stretches the whole body, boosting the circulation, so it is an excellent antidote to fatigue. To achieve the full stretch, pay attention to the alignment of all parts of your body. Start by positioning your hands carefully, fingers spread out, middle fingers parallel, fingertips level with your shoulders. Start stretching from the moment you raise your hips. Press down on your feet and hands, and stretch your arms up, continuing the stretch along your sides.

Working on the pose

If you can, check your reflection in a mirror to be sure that your body is making an inverted V. Your legs and back should be straighter than in the illustration above, and your heels lower. Stretch your trunk and legs up, away from your hands and feet.

Inverted V-shape

Your straight legs should form one side of an inverted V-shape, with your hips at the apex and your trunk and arms the other side. Do not walk your feet further forward to enable yourself to touch your heels to the floor while keeping your legs straight. The more you stretch up, the further down your heels will go, so instead, stretch up hard and work your heels further down. Press your feet into the floor,

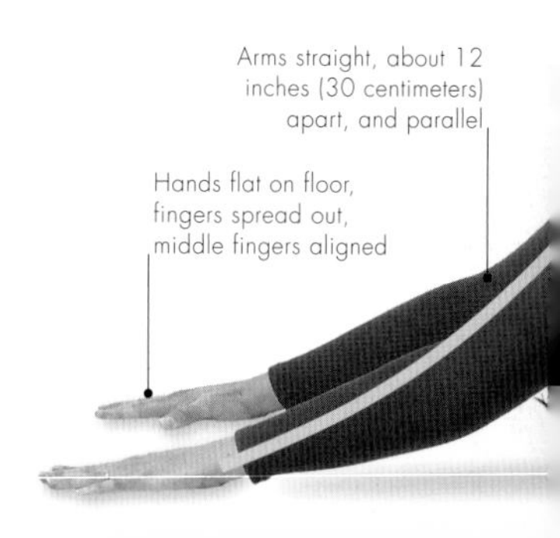

and stretch your thighs up to your hips at the apex of the V. At the same time, stretch your arms and trunk up toward your hips. Your neck is relaxed and your head hangs, the crown touching the floor. Your feet, legs, and hands create a stretch all along the back of your body, while your abdomen remains relaxed.

Points to Watch

- Take care not to practice this pose on a rug or a slippery floor. Instead, practice on a mat with a nonslip undersurface, a wall-to-wall carpet, or other nonslip surface.
- Do not change the positions of your hands and feet while performing the pose. At the beginning of the pose you place your hands and feet in the right places for your body. If you move them, the pose will not be as effective.

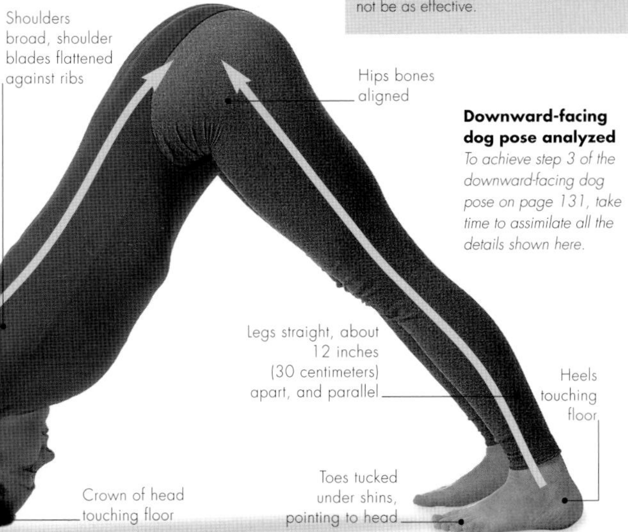

Downward-facing dog pose analyzed

To achieve step 3 of the downward-facing dog pose on page 131, take time to assimilate all the details shown here.

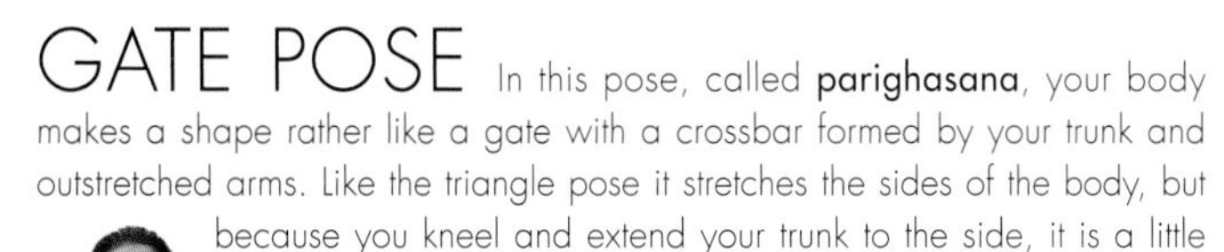

GATE POSE

In this pose, called **parighasana**, your body makes a shape rather like a gate with a crossbar formed by your trunk and outstretched arms. Like the triangle pose it stretches the sides of the body, but because you kneel and extend your trunk to the side, it is a little more demanding than the triangle.

1 *Kneel on a folded blanket with your knees together and your arms by your sides. Press your legs into the floor, stretch the front of your body up, and your sitting bones toward the floor.*

2 *Breathe in and as you breathe out raise your arms to shoulder level, palms facing down, and stretch them to the sides, while turning your right leg out extending it to the right, pointing the foot.*

3 *Keeping your arms straight and your trunk facing directly forward, breathe in, and as you breathe out bend your trunk to the right from the hips until the back of your right hand touches your leg.*

4 *Move your left arm to the right until the upper arm lies over your left ear. Hold the stretch for up to 10 seconds.*

Repeat and finish

Repeat steps 1–4, bending to the left and stretching your left leg to the left. Return to step 1, sit back, and rest.

Raising your Arm

Keep your trunk facing forward and your shoulders level and broad so your upper arm lies along the side of your head. Work at stretching it back behind your ear.

Sideways Extension

The gate pose is a sideways stretch that bends and extends the hips and abdomen in one movement, making it an excellent exercise for keeping the stomach and waist trim. Although this is a kneeling pose, stretching up at the beginning is the key to achieving the sideways extension, so pause in a kneeling position, press your legs firmly into the floor, and stretch from your knees all the way up the front of your body to the crown of your head, lifting your hip bones, and stretching your sitting bones down.

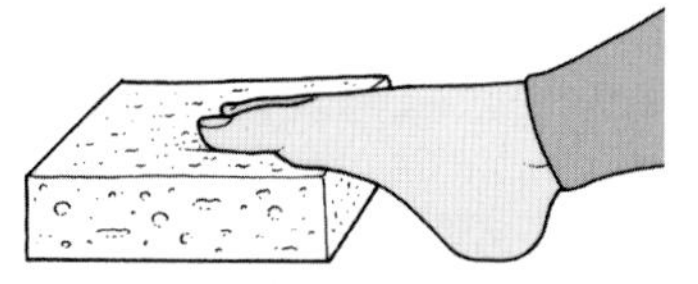

Working on the pose
If it is hard to rest the toes of your outstretched foot on the mat and keep your shin facing up, rest the foot on a foam block or a folded blanket.

Sideways extension

Be conscious of your shoulders as you raise your arms. Broaden across the collar bones while keeping your shoulder blades flattened against your ribs. As you bend your trunk, take care not to allow your shoulders and hips to roll forward. Instead, keep them in line, as if both buttocks and both shoulders were touching a wall. Keep your tailbone tucked in and your outstretched foot in line with your bent knee. Bend from the hips, keeping your trunk facing forward. Extend your whole body from your hips as far to the side as you can, breathing normally and feeling the stretch from your thigh to your hip joint, and up both sides of your trunk.

Keep both arms straight, and bring them as close together above your head as you can. If at first you find it uncomfortable or difficult to narrow the gap between them, simply keep your upper arm vertical. As you practice, your hip and shoulder joints become more elastic, enabling you to bend further to the side until eventually the palms of your hands meet and the back of the lower hand rests on your foot.

Points to Watch

- As you stretch your leg to one side, turn it out from the hip so your kneecap and shin bone face upward throughout the pose.
- As you bend your trunk to the right or the left, turn your face toward your upper arm and look up.

Gate pose analyzed

Stretching effectively in step 4 of the gate pose on page 135 depends on the details shown below. Note that your right shin and foot rest on the mat.

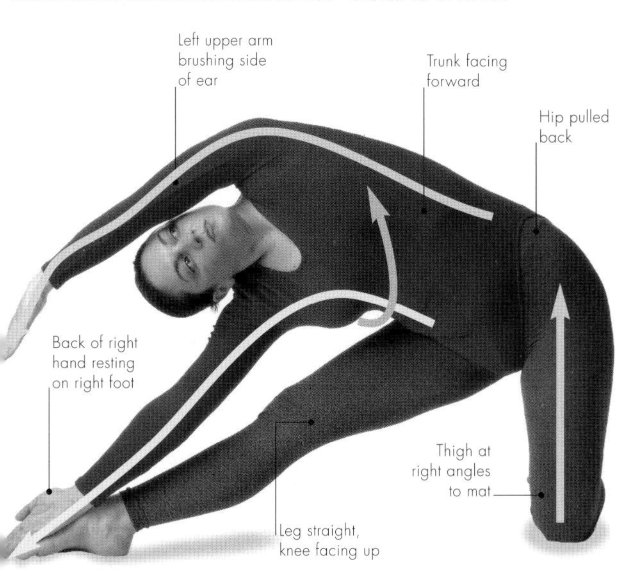

REVOLVING ABDOMEN

The ultimate posture for toning flabby abdominal muscles, **jathara parivartanasana** is an exercise that also improves the functioning of the liver, the spleen, the pancreas, and the intestines. It is said to be a good slimming exercise, and to relieve backache. The legs follow a half-circle as they swing from one side of the body to the other, giving the waist an invigorating stretch.

1 *Lie on your back on the mat, bend your legs, and stretch your arms out to the sides, palms facing up.*

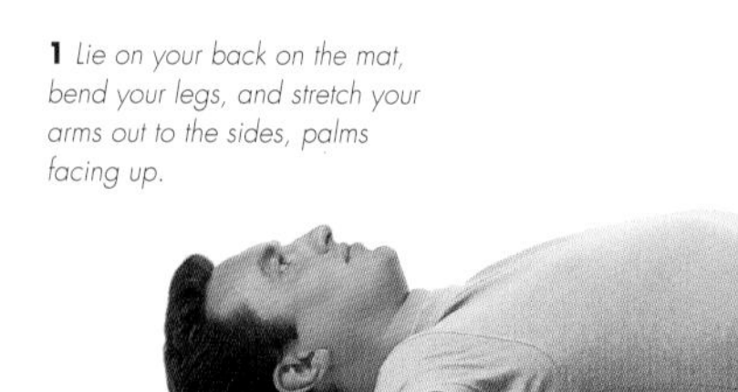

2 *Pressing your shoulders down, raise your legs and draw your knees inward, toward your chest.*

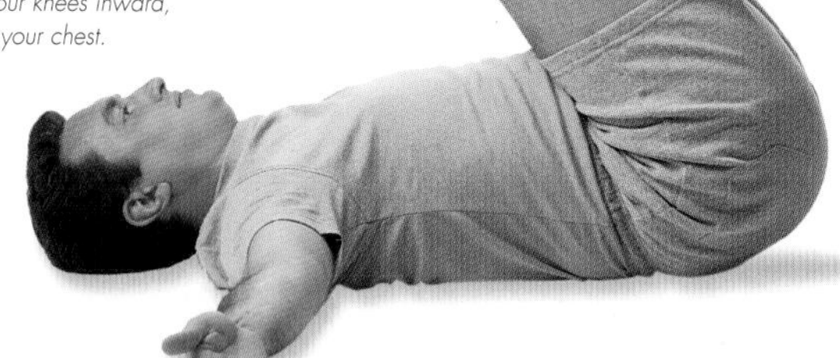

Aligning your Shoulders

As you lower your knees to the right, do not lift your left shoulder. Both shoulders should remain aligned, touching the mat, through the pose.

3 *Keeping your left shoulder on the mat, swing your knees over to the right while turning your abdomen (the part of the body between the diaphragm and pelvis) over to the left. Hold the position for 10–15 seconds.*

Repeat and finish

Raise your knees to your chest, then repeat step 3, this time swinging your knees over to the left and your abdomen to the right. Return to step 1, straighten your legs, and rest.

Massage Through Exercise

Swinging the legs slowly from side to side while keeping the upper back and shoulders on the floor twists the spine, and massages and stimulates the lower back, relieving backache. Raising the knees to the chest at the beginning of the pose stretches the lower back, so the spine can turn without strain. Raise your knees high up on your chest, then pause to extend your sitting bones away from your head, and to stretch from your hip bones to the top of your breastbone, and horizontally from your breastbone out to the fingertips of each hand.

Revolving the abdomen

Do not drop your legs to the floor, but lower them gently and deliberately on a slow out-breath, keeping your hips and trunk in line so as not to jar the spine. As you move your legs to the side, turn your abdomen in the opposite direction. If you keep your knees close to your chest and turn from the hips, this will stretch your back and waist.

Revolving abdomen analyzed

To achieve a massaging effect while moving your lower body right and left in the revolving abdomen pose on page 139, check the details shown here.

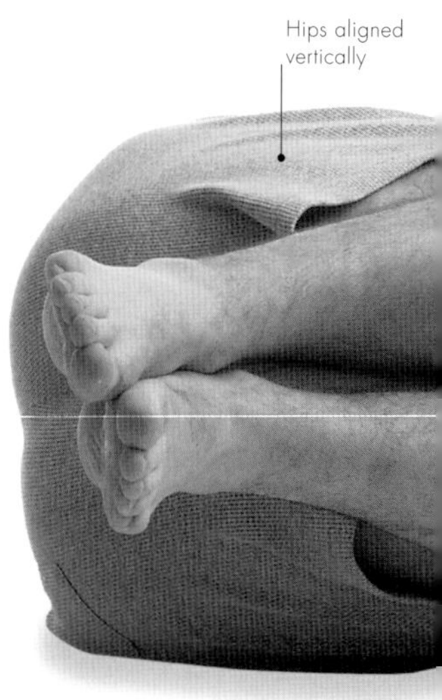

Points to Watch

- Keep your hips in vertical alignment throughout the pose. Do not allow the uppermost hip and the trunk to follow the movement of the legs and roll over.
- Keep both shoulders and as much of your back on the floor as you can when swinging your knees to right or left.

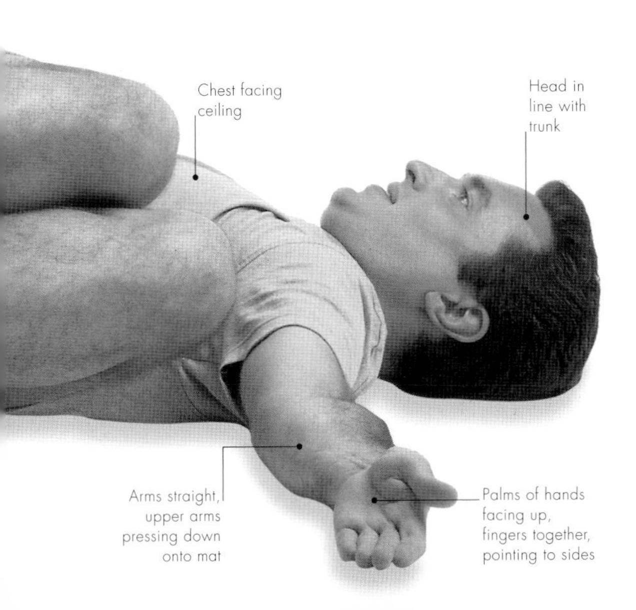

BOAT POSES

These two poses strengthen the muscles of the back and the stomach. Both are graded at the second level of difficulty, but half boat, **ardha navasana**, demands more of the abdominal muscles than boat with oars, **paripurna navasana**. They vitalize the back and benefit the organs of digestion: the liver, gallbladder, spleen, and intestines.

Boat with oars

1 *Sit in the rod pose (see page 106), press your sitting bones down, and lift your spine and trunk. On an out-breath, incline your trunk back and raise your legs until your feet are higher than your head.*

2 *As your trunk drops back, lift your arms, stretching them forward, parallel to the floor. Hold the pose for 10–15 seconds, breathing normally.*

Half boat

1 *Sit in the rod pose, and clasp your hands behind your head, fingers interlocking, upper arms parallel and lifting. Press your sitting bones down to the floor, lift your spine, and raise your trunk.*

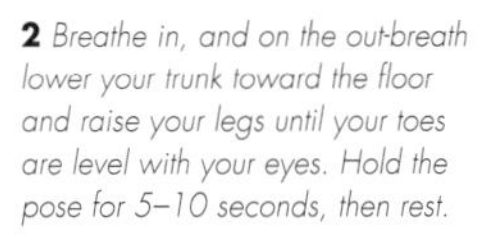

2 *Breathe in, and on the out-breath lower your trunk toward the floor and raise your legs until your toes are level with your eyes. Hold the pose for 5–10 seconds, then rest.*

Maintaining Balance

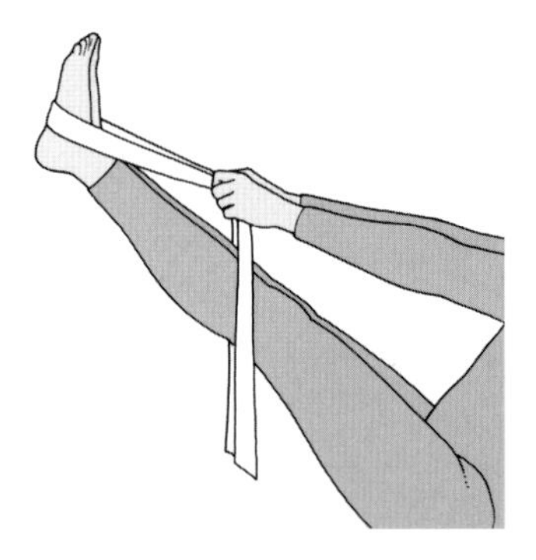

In the two boat poses on pages 142–43, you lower your back and raise your legs, so you balance on your buttocks. In boat with oars, the trunk and legs are raised at a 60° angle to the mat, so your body forms an almost perfect V-shape, but in the half-boat pose your back and legs are raised at a more oblique angle.

Keeping your balance

Stretching is the key to balancing in these poses: keep your spine and trunk lifting, press your sitting bones toward the floor, and keep your legs rod-straight, pressing together, and stretching toward your heels. Inhale as you stretch, exhale as you lift your legs and arms, then continue breathing normally to the end of the pose.

Rock back onto your sitting bones as you lift your legs. In boat with oars, place your hands on the floor beside your hips to balance until you have lifted your legs, then stretch your arms forward. If you find it hard to balance, bend your legs, clasp your hands around the backs of your knees, and pull on your legs, stretching your trunk up as you do so. Alternatively, place your feet against a wall to steady them, or rest your legs on a chair seat, holding the chair legs with your hands.

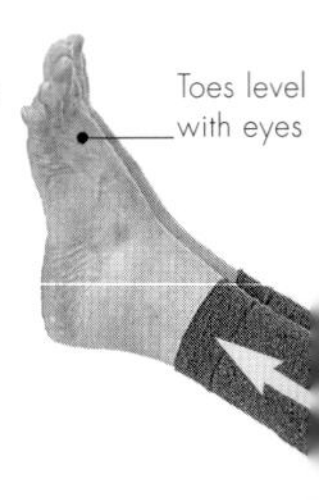

Boat with oars
If you find it difficult to hold the boat-with-oars pose, work on strengthening the muscles of your back and abdomen. One way is to loop a belt around your feet, hold an end in either hand, and pull on it, lifting and straightening your back.

Points to Watch

- Do not hold your breath while holding the pose.
- If the muscles of your abdomen start to shake, ignore the shaking as long as there is no pain. It is a sign that the muscles are working.
- Keep your shoulders down and relaxed throughout, so your shoulder blades lie flat against your ribs. If tension mounts in your neck and shoulders, rest and work on the pose again later.

Half-boat pose analyzed

Sustaining your balance in the half-boat pose requires practice. Pay attention to each of the details shown here to help maintain the pose.

Head and neck upright, eyes looking forward

Upper arms lifting

Shoulders back, shoulder blades flattened against ribs

Trunk stretching up

Legs straight and stretching up at 30° angle

Lower back pressing in

FLOOR LEG-STRETCHES

The sequence of floor movements called **supta padangusthasana** stretches the legs and works the hips. Two movements are shown here. They boost the blood circulation in the lower body, so they are a good warming exercise for the legs and feet in cold weather. They also improve the flexibility of the hip joints.

Supta padangusthasana I

1 *Lie in supta tadasana, bend your knees and raise them to your chest, then slide your feet along the floor until your legs are straight.*

2 *Press your left leg into the floor and lift your right leg, bending the knee to catch hold of the big toe with the fingers and thumb of your right hand.*

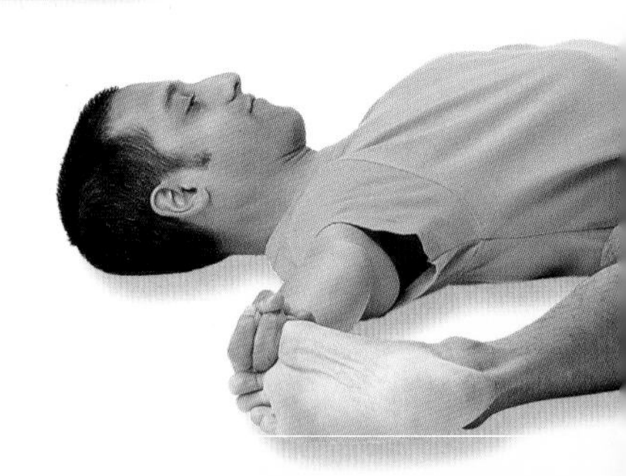

3 *Still holding your toe, straighten your right leg, and, keeping it straight, draw it as far toward your head as you can. Hold this stretch for up to 10 seconds.*

Repeat and rest

Release your toe and lower leg and arm to the mat, then repeat steps 2 and 3 lifting your left leg and arm, and rest briefly.

Supta padangusthasana II

4 *Repeat steps 1–3 of supta padangusthasana I, then put your left hand on your left thigh and press down hard, turn your right leg out from the hip, and lower your right leg and arm together to the floor. Hold this pose for up to 10 seconds.*

Repeat and finish

Rest in supta tadasana, then repeat step 4, grasping your left big toe with your left fingers and thumb, and lowering leg and arm to the left.

Holding the Toe

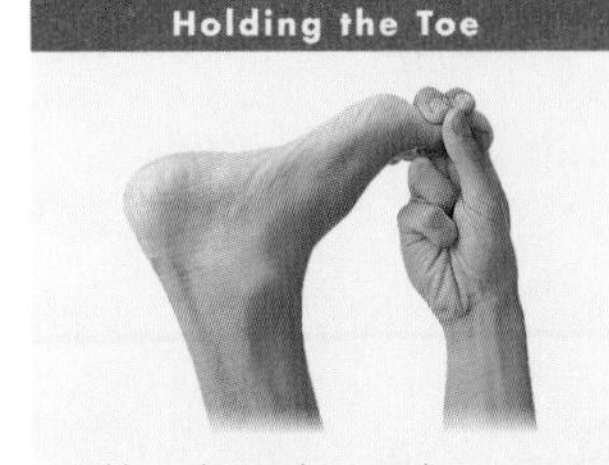

Hold your big toe between the thumb and index and middle fingers of your hand.

Working the Hip Joints

Keeping your legs straight through the leg-stretches on pages 146–47 will mobilize your hips and legs. At the beginning of each pose your knees, ankles, and big toes need to be touching, and when you raise one leg, do not disturb the alignment of the other. It remains pressing down on the mat and stretching toward the upturned toes through the remaining steps.

In step 3, stretch your right leg up and gradually draw it toward your head, feeling the stretch from hip to heel. Keep your foot at right angles to the leg, as it was when it left the floor. When you grasp your toe or pull on a belt, do not pull your toes down toward you, nor point them upward.

Second movement

The second movement in this sequence—padangusthasana II—is shown as step 4 on page 147. For this you need to turn your raised leg out a little at the hip joint before pulling it down to the floor to the right, pressing your left hip firmly down. Keep it straight and moving toward your head as you lower it, so that when it rests, your arm is in line with your shoulder. Lower it just as far as you can at first. If necessary, rest it on books or foam blocks by your trunk. In time you will be able to take it down to the floor.

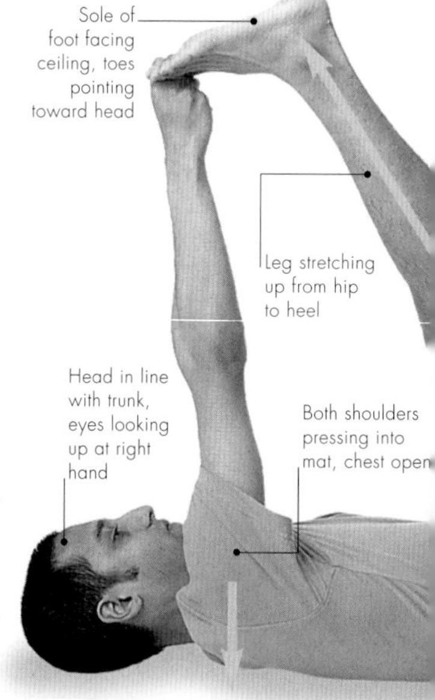

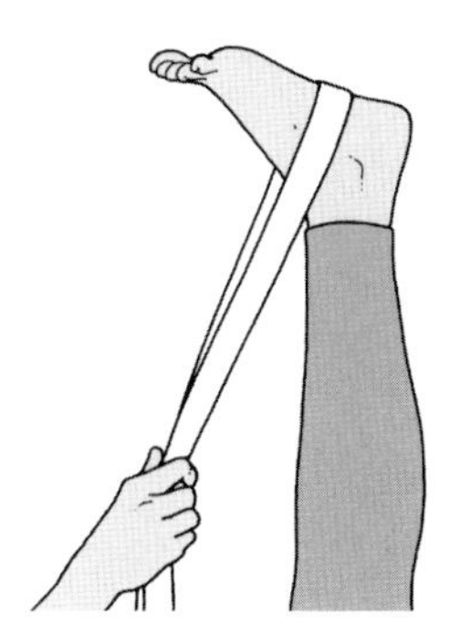

Working on the pose

If you cannot straighten your leg while holding your big toe, wind a belt around your foot in step 1 of padangusthasana I, and hold both ends in your raised hand, as close to your foot as you can.

Points to Watch

- Do lower your legs to the floor before straightening them in step 1. If you straighten them in the air, their weight will pull your pelvis up, arching your lower back. This can cause your back to strain.
- Do not let either leg roll out. Your knees, shin bones, and toes point directly up in steps 1 and 2, and the raised leg and foot point toward your head in step 3.
- If you use a belt in either pose, hold it in one hand while keeping your leg stretching up and your foot pressing into it.

Supta padangusthasana I analyzed

Follow the details shown in the diagram below to achieve step 3 of padangusthasana I on page 147.

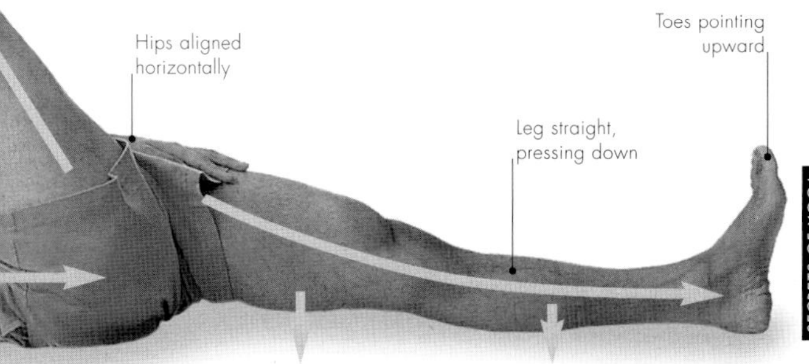

HERO FLOOR POSE

Supta virasana is similar to hero pose shown on page 106, but performed lying on the floor with the arms extended over the head. This is a pose that stretches the entire front of the body, from the thighs to the neck, and it is a sure cure for leg ache for people who have to be on their feet all day.

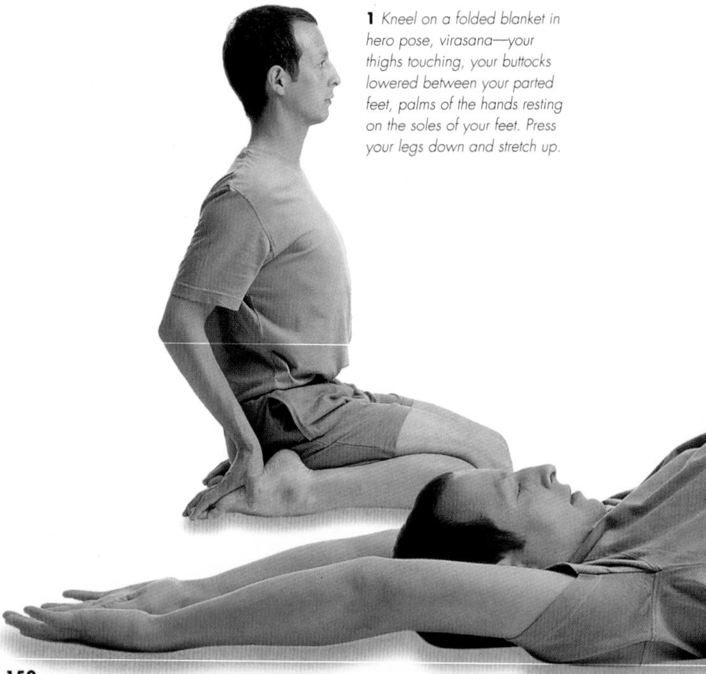

1 *Kneel on a folded blanket in hero pose, virasana—your thighs touching, your buttocks lowered between your parted feet, palms of the hands resting on the soles of your feet. Press your legs down and stretch up.*

2 *On an out-breath, bend back from the hips until your trunk rests on your elbows, your hands still holding the soles of your feet. Stretch your trunk toward your head and straighten your back by lifting your sitting bones off the floor, stretching them toward your feet, then lowering them.*

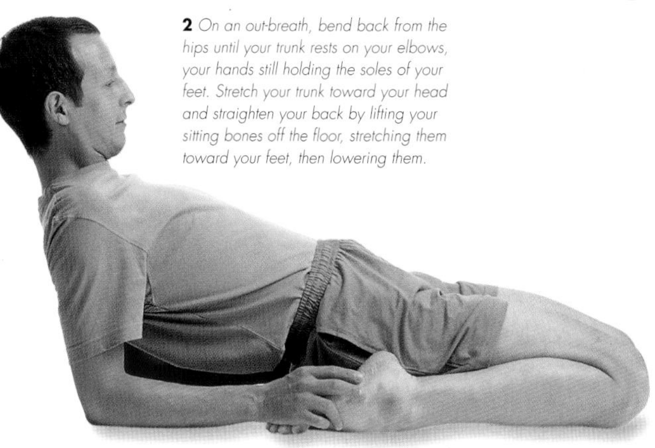

3 *Lower your back until your head rests on the mat. Release your hands, stretch your arms up and rest them, palms facing up, on the floor behind your head. Hold for 20 seconds or longer.*

Finish and rest

Lift your arms over your head and place your hands on your feet, raise your trunk onto your elbows as in step 2, sit up in hero pose, and rest.

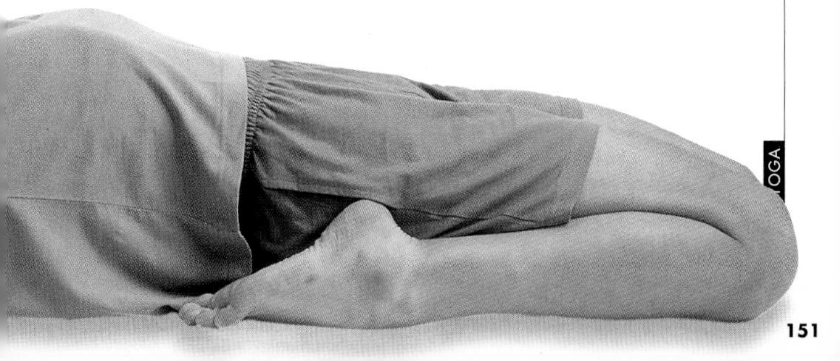

Relieving Aching Legs

Stretching any part of the body has an invigorating effect. We tend to stretch our upper body when we feel tired. This pose is effective for aching legs because it stretches the lower body—the thighs, knees, ankles, and feet, as well as the abdomen and trunk—resting muscles and improving circulation within the whole area.

Before moving back onto your elbows, stretch your spine from your pelvis to the crown of your head, press your sitting bones down, and level your hips. Lifting your buttocks just clear of the floor and stretching your sitting bones toward your knees in step 2 prevents strain when you lie back, so continue stretching as you lie, pulling up from your hips. Keep your thighs touching, but when you stretch your arms back over your head, rest your hands on the floor about 12 inches (30 centimeters) apart. Relax your abdomen. Do not push it out or up.

Using supports

If your seat does not reach the mat when you kneel in virasana in step 1, place one or two folded blankets behind you, so when you lie back your

Hero floor pose analyzed

This illustration pinpoints the many details to think about in step 3 of the hero floor pose on page 151.

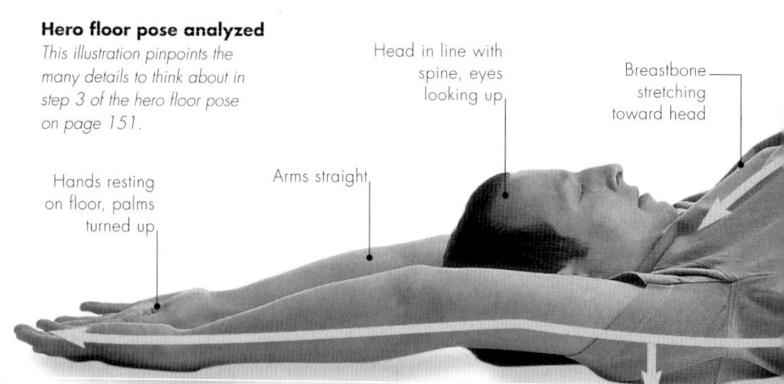

upper body rests on them. If your knees are stiff, kneel on a blanket; and if you find you resist dropping back onto the floor, accustom yourself by lowering your back onto a pile of cushions or a row of foam blocks placed so that they support you from just above your waist up to your head.

Points to Watch

- Stretch upward from the groins to the fingertips and downward from the sitting bones to the knees.
- Keep the tops of your thighs facing up. Do not let them roll in toward each other.

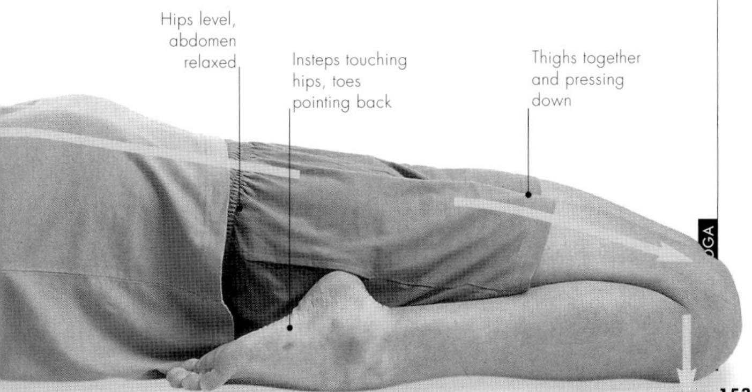

FOUR-LIMBED POSES

The four-limbed rod or **chaturanga dandasana** is a strengthening exercise, the Eastern version of press-ups, with the difference that you push up once, then hold. In contrast, the eternal pose, **anantasana**, is a reclining pose. It relieves back strain and tones the pelvic area.

Eternal pose

1 *Lie on your mat on your left side, with your legs straight and stretching toward your feet, your right arm along your right side, palm resting on your thigh.*

2 *Move your left arm over the floor to align with your head, bend the elbow, and rest your head in your hand. Lift your right foot and arm, bend the knee, and catch hold of your big toe.*

3 *Now straighten the leg and move it back in line with your trunk. Hold for up to 20 seconds.*

Repeat and finish

Bend your knee and lower your leg, letting go of your toe and dropping your arm to the floor, and rest briefly in supta tadasana. Repeat steps 1–3, lying on your right side and lifting your left leg.

Four-limbed rod pose

1 *Lie face down with your feet about 12 inches (30 centimeters) apart, your heels raised, your elbows bent, and your hands palms down on the floor beside your chest. Spread your fingers, move your elbows toward each other, and stretch them toward your feet.*

2 *Raise your head and look forward. Breathe in, stretch your legs toward your heels and your breastbone toward your head and press your toes and hands down. Breathe out, and lift your thighs and trunk to align with your heels. Hold for up to 10 seconds, breathing normally. On an out-breath, lower your trunk to the floor, turn onto your back, and lie with your knees bent.*

Using the Floor

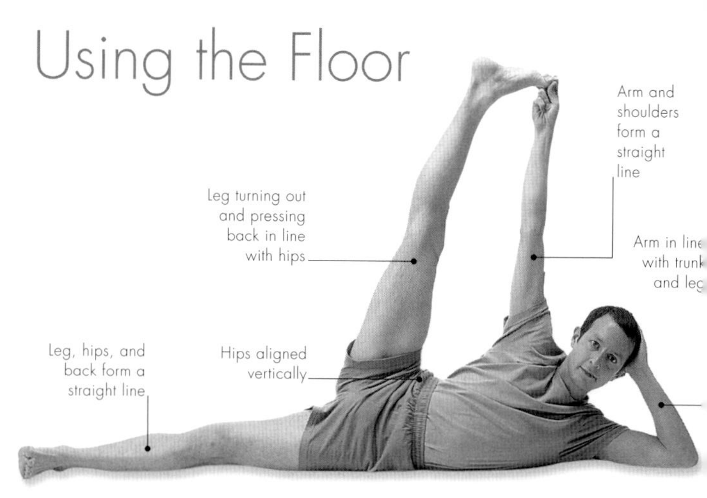

Eternal pose analyzed

The image above analyzes step 3 of the eternal pose on page 154. To perfect the pose, check the details in your reflection in a mirror.

Anantasana, the Sanskrit name for the eternal pose on page 154, is the name of the serpent whose coils formed the couch on which reclined the Hindu god, Vishnu, and it is a fundamentally restful pose. It demands attention to alignment, so begin by checking that your ankles, legs, trunk, and shoulders are in line. Keep your sitting bones stretching toward your feet, your hip bones lifting toward your head, and your tailbone pressing in. Your raised leg should be pressed back in line with your hips.

If you find you cannot straighten your leg while holding your toe, do not pull it forward. Instead, wind a belt around your foot and hold the two ends as you lift your leg vertically above your hips, pressing your foot into the belt. Finally, do not allow the upper side of your trunk to roll forward. Shoulders and trunk should align vertically.

Pressing up

The four-limbed rod pose strengthens the wrists and the muscles of the shoulders, arms, and abdomen. You need to make your legs as stiff as a rod or staff, so before lifting, tighten the muscles at the sides of your thighs, press your tailbone in, and stretch from hips to breastbone. Press your hands and feet down to the floor to raise your trunk and legs. If you find this difficult, lie with the soles of your feet against a wall and press them into it. Use this technique if you find it hard to balance in the eternal pose.

Four-limbed rod pose analyzed

If you find it hard to lift from the floor in step 2 of the four-limbed rod pose on page 155, check each of the details shown here. Placing each hand on a foam block or a thick book also helps you lift.

Head raised, neck relaxed, eyes looking forward

Upper arms stretching toward feet

Forearms at right angles to floor, close to chest

Spine aligned with legs

Legs rod-straight, thighs pressing up

Toes tucked under heels

Fingers spread out

CROSS-LEGGED TWIST

Here, the cross-legged sitting pose or **sukhasana** is transformed into a twist: sitting upright and keeping the spine stretching up, you rotate it right and then left. Not only does this pose make the spine more flexible but it also feels good. Before attempting the exercises on pages 158–92, please read carefully the caution note on page 9.

1 *Sit in the rod pose (see page 106) and cross your right leg over your left leg as shown on page 38. Place your hands on the mat beside your hips, and stretch your spine up.*

Crossing Your Legs

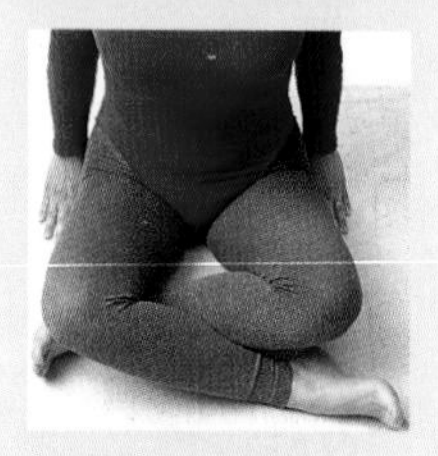

Do not cross your legs too tightly or you will pull your spine out of its natural alignment and you will not be able to stretch it up. There should be a sizeable gap between your calves and your groins.

Working on the Pose

Sit on a foam block or a blanket folded two or three times, and place another close behind you. Pressing your hand onto it while you turn keeps your spine upright. To twist further, walk your hand as far around as you can.

2 *Turn your trunk to the right and place your left hand on the outside of your right leg and your right hand close behind you. Press that hand down and pull with your left hand to rotate further. Look over your right shoulder and twist for10–15 seconds.*

Repeat and finish

Return to step 1, then repeat step 2, this time crossing your left leg over your right and twisting to the left. Rest, and repeat the pose.

Introducing Sitting Twists

Many a back problem starts with an abrupt turn to reach something behind the back. If the muscles that rotate the spine are well exercised they respond easily to a sudden turn, but if they are tight through lack of exercise an awkward movement can strain them. The next few pages concentrate on the twists, which gently exercise the many small muscles that rotate the spine. The standing chair twist on page 74 introduced the twists; the three twists in this chapter are performed sitting down.

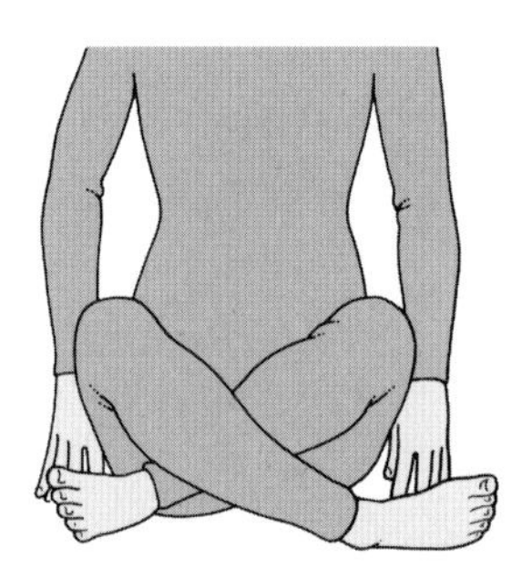

Positioning the knees

When you cross your legs, your knees should lie close to the floor. If you find it difficult to lower them, cross them at the shins, then move them toward each other before pressing them down.

Helping your spine turn

A twist will only be effective if your back is straight when you rotate it. Sitting on a foam block or a blanket folded two or three times will help you lift your back. When you sit down, roll or pull the large buttock muscles out to the sides. Then with your trunk facing forward and your legs pressing down, stretch your spine up. Use your hands to help yourself turn. The hand pressing down behind you keeps you upright, and pulling on your knee with the other twists you further around. Never let your spine collapse—keep it stretching up, even when you turn to the front.

Points to Watch

- Lift and open your upper chest, pressing your shoulders down and back.
- As you turn, level your shoulders so that one side of your chest does not rise higher than the other side.

Cross-legged twist analyzed

Turn your spine further around each time you practice the cross-legged twist on pages 158–159 by checking the main points, summarized here.

MERMAID I

In this pose your legs, bent to the side of you, look like a mermaid's tail. But its Sanskrit name, Bharadvajasana, commemorates the warrior Bharadvaja, a mythical figure from the Hindu epic, *Mahabharata*. This pose, **Bharadvajasana I**, rotates the spine, exercising the middle and upper spine particularly, dispelling stiffness and making your back feel supple.

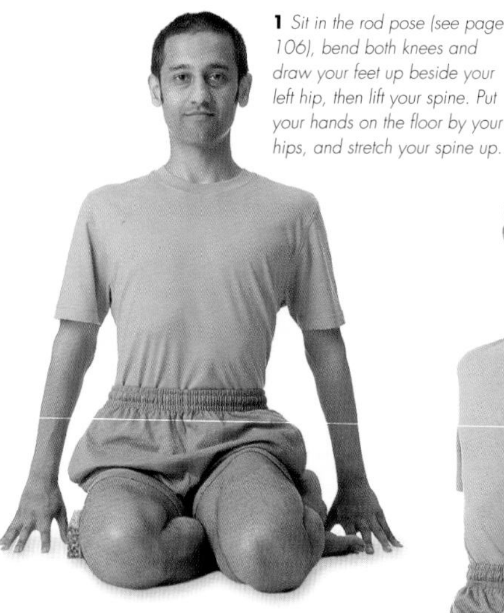

1 *Sit in the rod pose (see page 106), bend both knees and draw your feet up beside your left hip, then lift your spine. Put your hands on the floor by your hips, and stretch your spine up.*

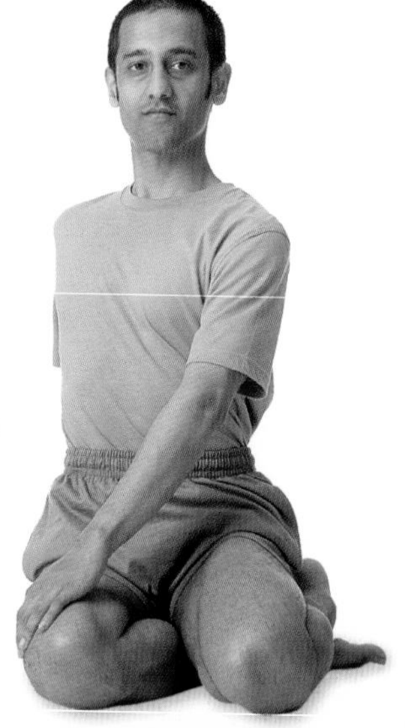

2 *Breathing out, turn your trunk from the hips to the right. Place your left hand on your right thigh and pull gently to rotate to the right, and press your right hand down behind you to lift and rotate further.*

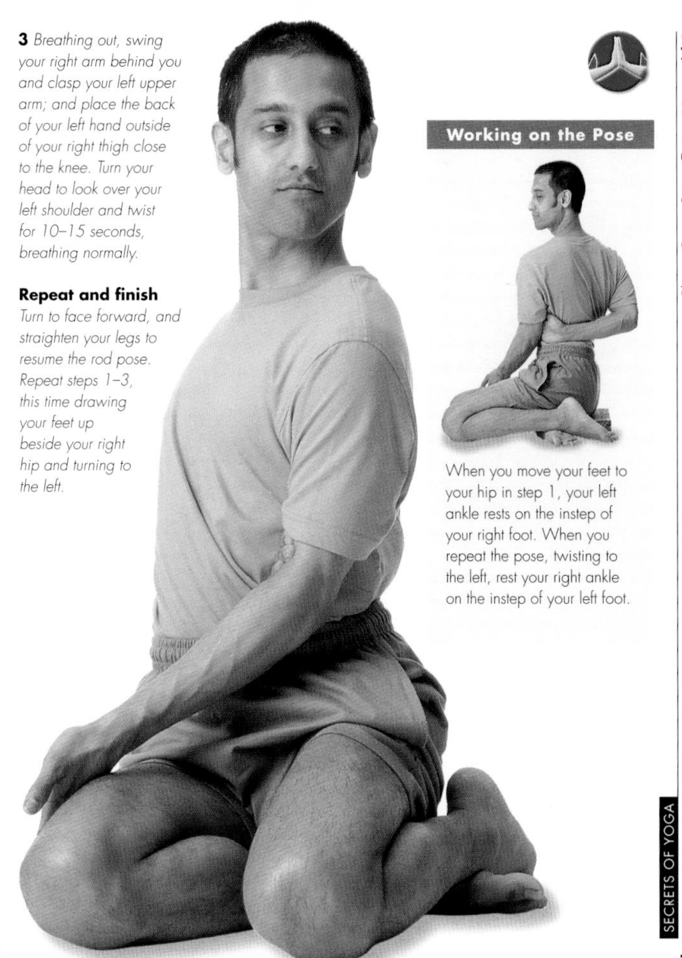

3 *Breathing out, swing your right arm behind you and clasp your left upper arm; and place the back of your left hand outside of your right thigh close to the knee. Turn your head to look over your left shoulder and twist for 10–15 seconds, breathing normally.*

Repeat and finish

Turn to face forward, and straighten your legs to resume the rod pose. Repeat steps 1–3, this time drawing your feet up beside your right hip and turning to the left.

Working on the Pose

When you move your feet to your hip in step 1, your left ankle rests on the instep of your right foot. When you repeat the pose, twisting to the left, rest your right ankle on the instep of your left foot.

Spiraling

To be effective, twists need to be performed as gently and precisely as any other movement in yoga. The idea is to rotate the spine as far as it will comfortably go, not to wrench it around. Rotation takes place mainly in the upper back—the thoracic area of the spine (see pages 26–27). Here, the joints between the 12 thoracic vertebrae, the ligaments that bind them, and the muscles that move them respond to stretching and exercise. If you practice this twist regularly and gently, you find that your spine will twist a little further around each time.

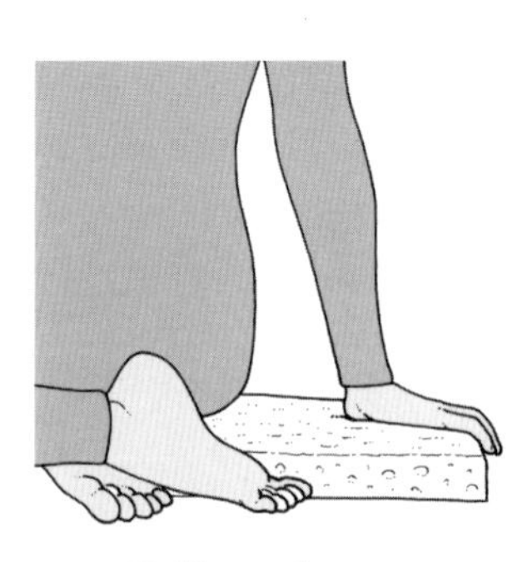

Working on the pose

Press your hand down into a foam block or a blanket folded two or three times and placed behind you. This helps you lever your trunk further around during the twist.

Learning to spiral

From the beginning of step 1, every movement in the mermaid pose contributes to helping the spine spiral. You start by sitting in the rod pose and lifting your whole trunk from the hips. Lifting your trunk strengthens the upward stretch, making it easier to turn the trunk from the hips. Start turning on an out-breath, and keep up the momentum by stretching your sitting bones down, and pressing one hand firmly down and the other against your thigh to rotate your body further right or left. Finally, the actions of swinging one hand behind your back to clasp the other arm, and turning your head to look over your shoulder, cause your body to spiral just that little further. Holding the pose for a few seconds, still stretching up, accustoms your trunk to turning, making the pose easier next time.

Points to Watch

- Do not disturb the balance of your hips when you move your feet, or when you turn. Keep both sitting bones pressing down and your hip bones level. If this is difficult, raise your pelvis on two folded blankets or on a foam block with a folded blanket laid on top.
- Keep your shoulders in line—do not allow one to rise higher than the other when you twist your trunk.

Mermaid 1 analyzed

Check the details shown in the illustration on the right to achieve a good twist in step 3 of the mermaid 1 pose shown on page 163.

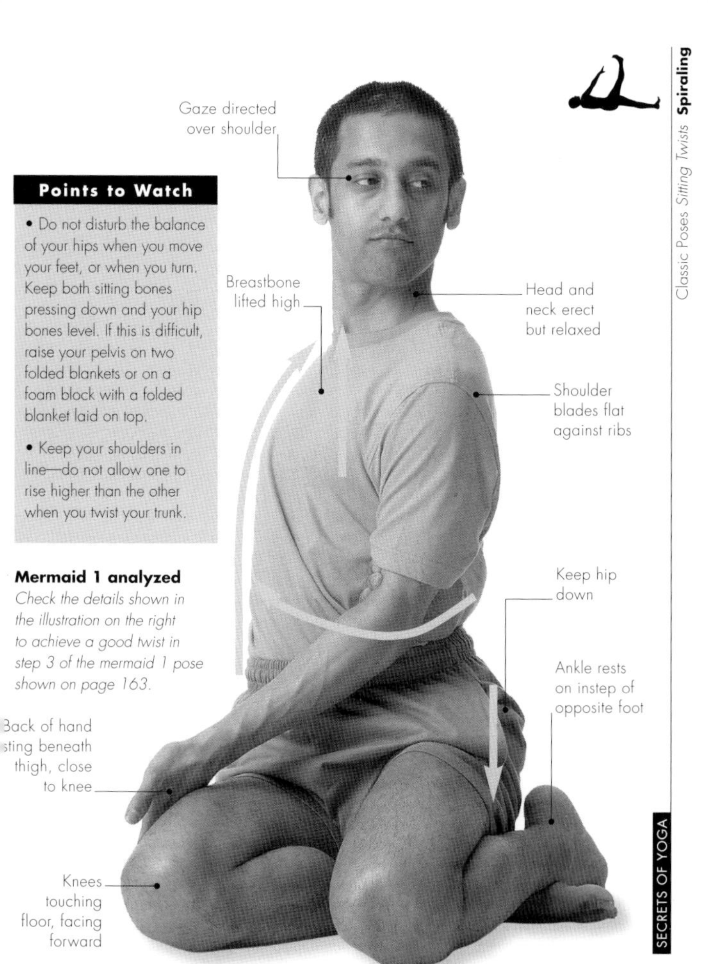

SAGE POSES

These two twists and the standing chair twist on page 74 are dedicated to a mythical sage from the Hindu pantheon, Marichi, grandfather of the sun god. The versions of the two sage poses shown here are suitable for beginners. They strengthen the muscles of the abdomen as well as improving the elasticity of the back muscles.

Marichyasana I

1 *Sit in the rod pose (see page 106) on a foam block or a folded blanket, bend your left knee, drawing your heel toward your left buttock, then grasp your shin with both hands and pull your trunk forward toward your thigh.*

2 *Press your right hand down behind you and lift from the hips. Bend your left arm, stretch it forward, and press the elbow against the inside of your bent knee. Then press your right leg and right hand down, lift your trunk, and twist to the right.*

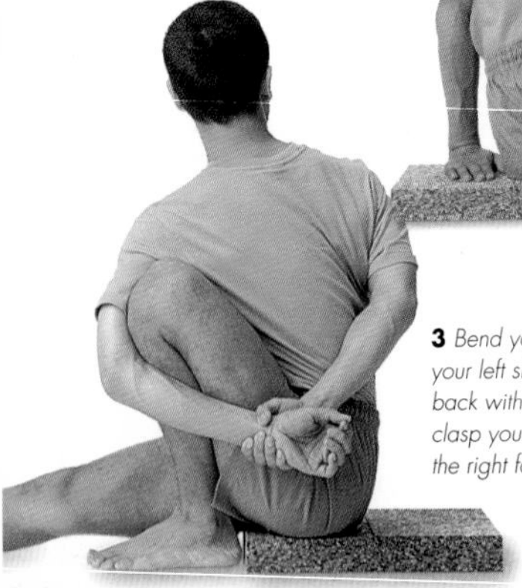

3 *Bend your left arm around your left shin, reach behind your back with your right hand to clasp your left wrist, and twist to the right for up to 15 seconds.*

Repeat and finish

Return to rod pose and repeat steps 1 and 2, bending your right leg, pressing your right elbow against your right knee, and turning left.

Marichyasana III

1 *Sit in the rod pose, bend your right knee, draw the heel toward the buttock, clasp the bent knee with your hands, and pull your trunk toward it. Pressing your left leg down, lift from the hips and keeping your spine stretching forward and up, pull on your shin.*

2 *Press your right hand on the floor behind you to assist the lift and turning from the hips, rotate your trunk to the right. Pressing your left elbow against the outside of the knee, use it to lever your trunk further to the right.*

3 *Bend your left arm around your right shin, reach behind your back with your right hand to clasp your left wrist. Hold for 15 seconds.*

Repeat and finish

Return to the rod pose, then repeat steps 1–3, bending your left leg, pressing your right elbow against the outside of your left knee, and twisting to the left.

Powered Rotation

These two poses use the elbow as a powerful lever to rotate the spine from the hips more strongly. They give the trunk an intense stretch, which increases the blood supply to the kidneys. It is essential to stretch the trunk strongly upward before turning the spine, and to propel it forward to keep it perpendicular to the floor. To do this, you clasp the shin of your bent leg with your hands, just below the knee, and pull on it, drawing your trunk toward your upstretched thigh.

Keep your spine lifting by pressing down into the floor with your outstretched leg and press one hand onto the floor or on a foam block or a thick book placed behind you.

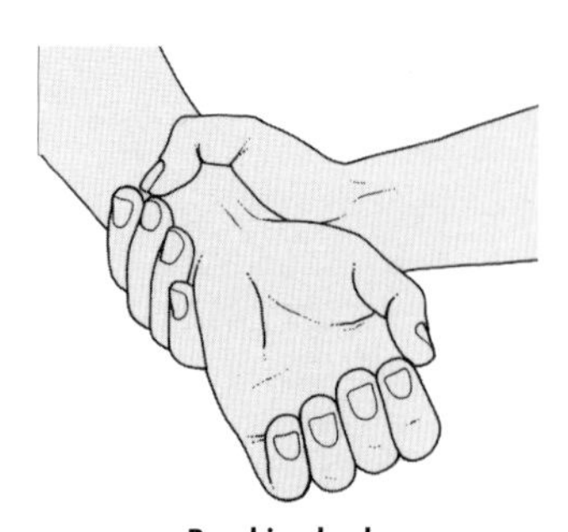

Reaching back

Reach behind your back in step 3 of both poses to grasp the wrist of the opposite arm firmly between your thumb and fingers.

Using leverage

Bringing the elbow against your bent knee in step 2 of both twists enables you to use it as a lever to turn your trunk. To do this effectively, keep the knee upright, and pull your trunk forward. There should be no space between your armpit and the top of your thigh where it rests. Breathe in before you place your elbow against your knee, and as you exhale, stretch your trunk forward and upward, and press elbow against knee and knee against elbow to rotate still more.

Involve your whole trunk in the turn, revolving your abdomen, your waist, your chest, and your head in the direction of the twist.

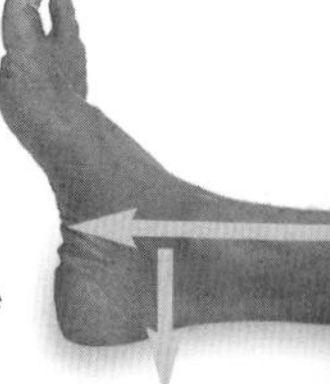

Points to Watch

- Keep your trunk lifting from the lower back—do not allow your spine to collapse downward or your buttocks to move back.
- Keep both sitting bones pressing down to the floor to keep your hips level.
- Turn your trunk as far around as you can without straining.

Marichyasana twists analyzed

This diagram shows the front view of step 3 of Marichyasana III on page 167—but the details are relevant to both twists. If you find it difficult to reach right behind your back, work on perfecting step 2 until your hip joints and spine have gained more flexibility.

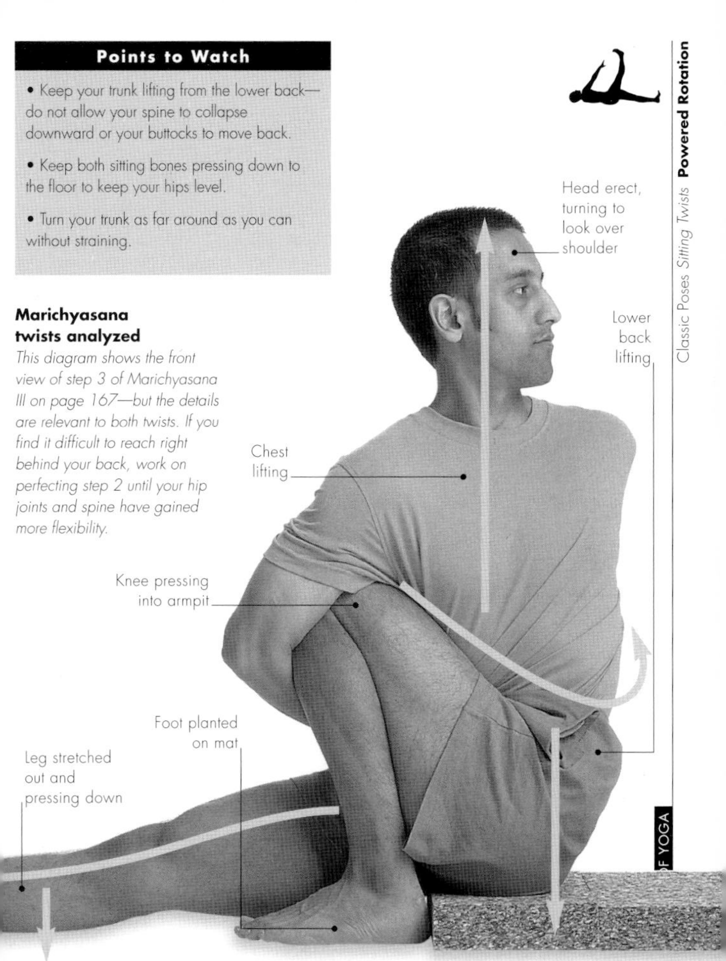

BRIDGE

The name of this pose, **sarvangasana setu bandha**, describes the bridge shape you make with your body by raising your back, using your shoulders and feet as supports. This is a good movement to follow a shoulder stand, since it gives the back a very remedial stretch.

1 *Lie on your back on the mat, your feet a hip-width apart and your arms by your sides. Bending your knees, move your heels toward your groins and stretch your sitting bones toward your heels.*

Working on the Pose

In order to give your spine even more of a stretch and to open your chest, raise the hips higher by lifting on to the balls of your feet. Then, as you retain the lift, lower your heels to the floor.

2 *Stretching your arms toward your feet and pressing arms and feet into the floor, exhale, and lift your hips, chest, and thighs. Hold the stretch for up to 20 seconds.*

Finish and rest

On an out-breath, lower your trunk and hips to the mat, stretching your sitting bones toward your feet. Rest with your legs bent.

Bending the Back

To retain its full mobility, the spine needs to be flexed backward, as well as forward and to the sides, and this section of Chapter 4 focuses on backbends performed while lying and kneeling. The bridge, which begins the sequence, involves actively lifting the back off of the floor. Begin in a good supta tadasana (see page 39), bending the legs before lifting, and stretching the sitting bones down toward the feet.

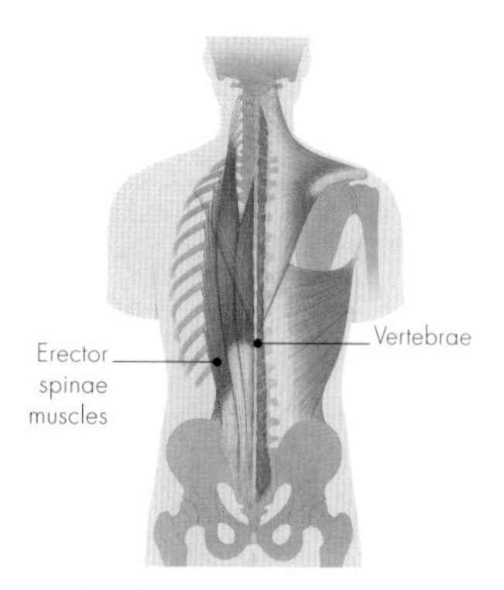

Muscles that move the spine
Many small muscles, each attached to two or three vertebrae, work together to bend the spine back, forward, to either side, and to rotate it. They are called the erector spinae because they also hold the spine upright.

Making the bridge

To lift, press your arms hard into the floor, and raise your hips, using the large muscles of your buttocks and thighs and the many muscles that control the movements of the spine. As you rise, press your feet down hard on the mat, and stretch upward from the backs of your thighs. In order to arch the back high above the mat, raise your heels, lift your hips still higher, then lower your heels, keeping your hips lifting.

At first you may be able to raise your back just a little way, and to sustain the lift for a few seconds only. However,

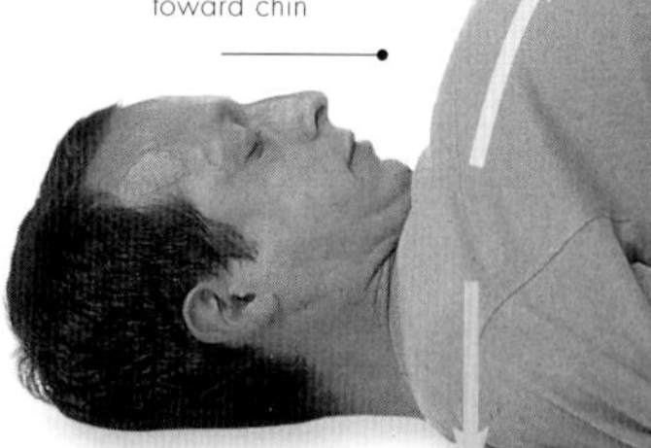

regular practice strengthens the muscles you use to lift your body, making your back more supple. Eventually, you may attempt a more advanced form of the pose—dropping the legs and feet down into the bridge from the shoulder stand, salamba sarvangasana, on pages 186–87.

Points to Watch

- To increase the lift, stretch your breastbone toward your head, and open your shoulders, pressing your shoulder blades against your ribs.
- Keep your chest, hips, tailbone, and thighs lifting throughout the pose.
- Relax your neck and your chin.

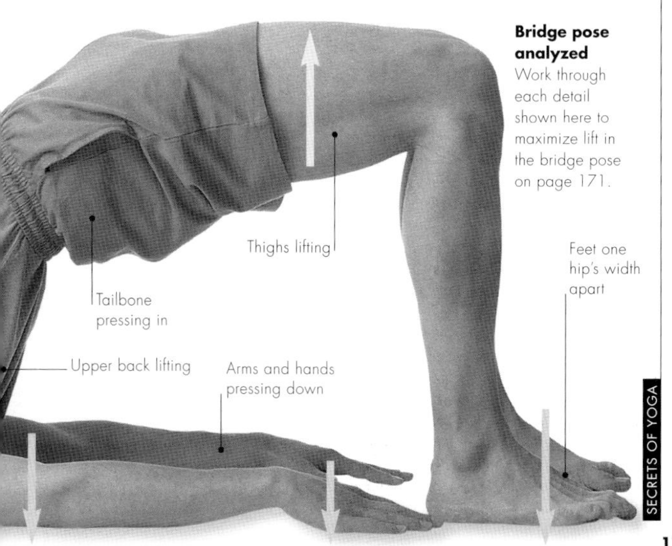

Bridge pose analyzed
Work through each detail shown here to maximize lift in the bridge pose on page 171.

LOCUST

The name of this pose is descriptive—your body imitates the shape of a locust at rest. Authorities recommend the locust pose or **salabhasana** as a gentle exercise for strengthening the muscles around any part of the spine where a disk has slipped, and it certainly relieves backaches. It is more effective than sit-ups for exercising the large muscles of the abdomen, buttocks, and thighs.

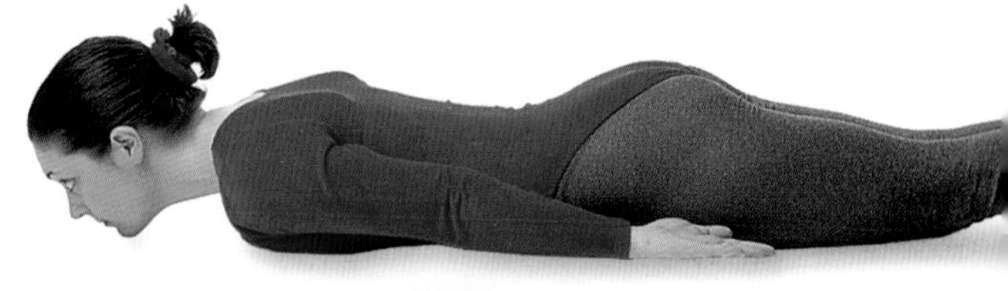

1 *Lie on your stomach with your chin resting on the mat, your eyes facing the floor, your arms by your sides and legs together, both stretching back, and your palms turned up.*

2 *Press your pelvis into the floor, inhale, and, stretching your arms and hands toward your heels, lift your head, upper body, and legs as high off the floor as you can. Stretch your arms and legs back, level with your shoulders.*

Legs and Feet

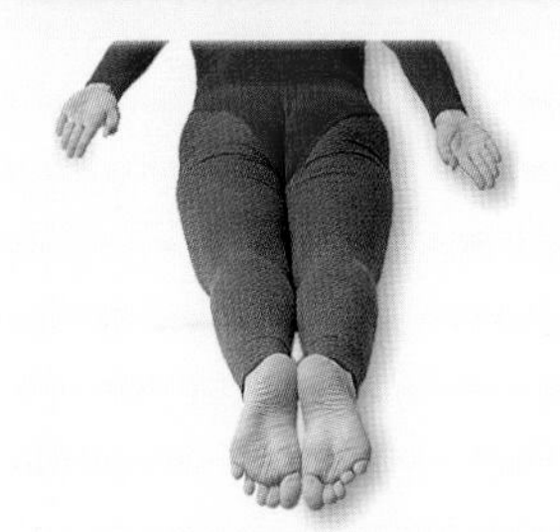

Keep your legs and feet together and your shins pointing directly downward—do not let your legs roll outward. Stretch your legs and feet away from your head. If at first you get a cramp when you stretch your feet back, stop and resume the pose when it has passed. It happens when muscles are unused to being stretched, so keep practicing and the cramps will disappear.

Finish and rest

Hold the pose for 10–20 seconds, breathing normally, gaze directed forward, then lower your head, shoulders, arms, and legs to the mat, and rest.

Arching the Back

From the neck down to the pelvis, each pair of vertebrae that form the spine is separated by a joint capable of just a small amount of movement. These partly movable joints, as they are called, all work together to give the spine its marvelous mobility. To remain fully mobile, however, the spine needs to be exercised regularly. In the course of a normal day we may occasionally bend forward to pick something up, twist around, and perhaps bend to one side or the other, but we rarely, if ever, bend the spine back.

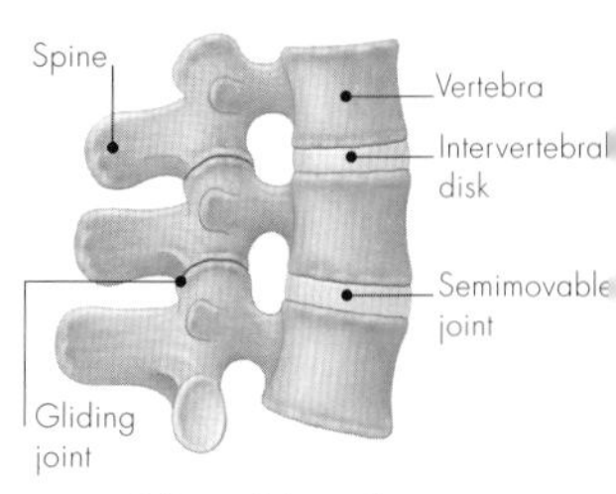

Joints of the spine

Disks of cartilage cushion the joints between vertebrae, allowing a little movement back, forward, and to the sides. When the vertebrae move, their spines glide over each other.

Creating the arch

In the locust pose on pages 174–75 you bend the back while lying on your stomach, lifting your legs and thighs and your chest and shoulders off the mat, so that you balance on your lower abdomen and hip bones.

Arching the spine helps restore suppleness to the lower back especially, reducing discomfort in that often painful area. Strengthening the muscles that control the movements of the spine

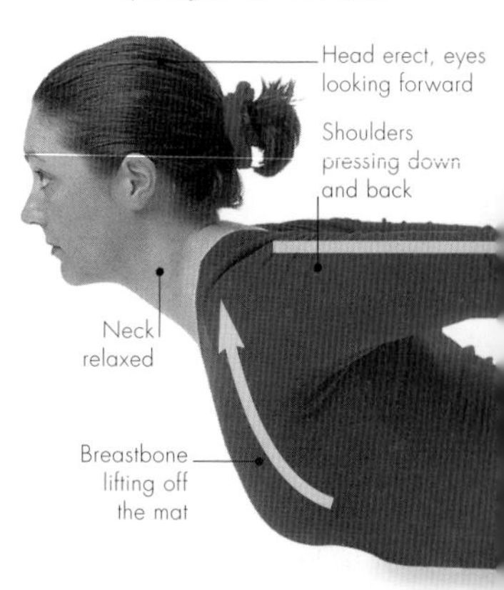

prevents disks from slipping. Arching also stimulates the digestive system, relieving indigestion and stomachache.

As you lift, you really stretch both arms and legs back, away from your head, and the trunk forward, toward it, so practicing this pose strengthens the abdominal muscles that lift the front of the body. The stronger these muscles become, the easier the pose will be.

Points to Watch

- Breathe in as you lift your chest and legs, then remember to breathe normally as you hold the pose.
- As you lift your legs and arms, really stretch them back, away from your head, and keep stretching throughout.
- Lift your breastbone as high as you can, but flatten your shoulder blades into your back.

Locust pose analyzed

The details shown here help you achieve lift in step 2 of the locust pose on page 175.

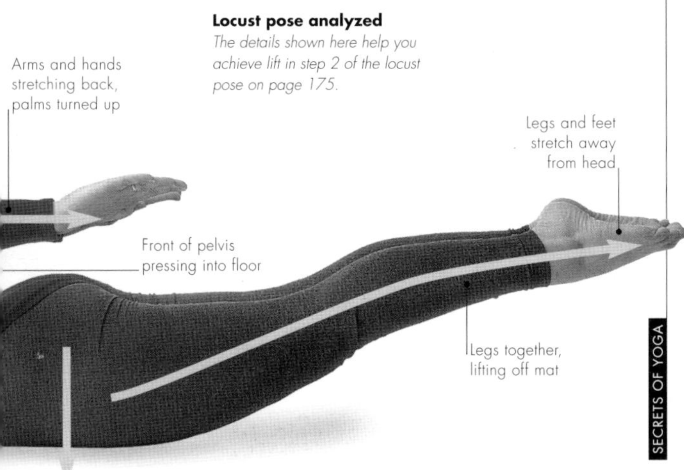

CAMEL

Ustrasana or camel pose intensifies the backward stretch of the spine, yet it is not too demanding, even if your back is stiff. It is an excellent pose for correcting poor posture—the rounded shoulders and back that result from too much sitting and slumping.

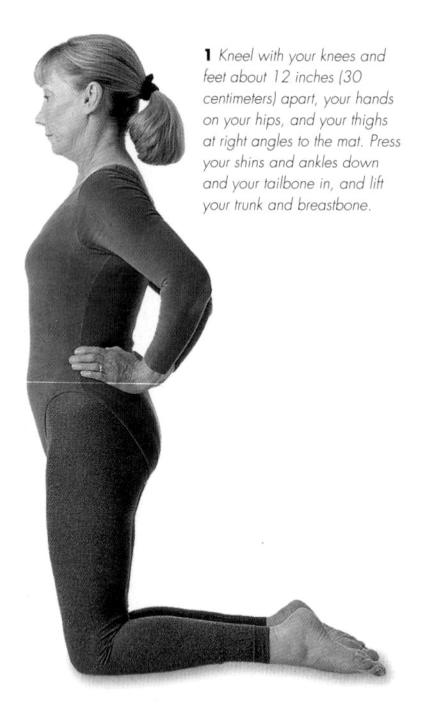

1 *Kneel with your knees and feet about 12 inches (30 centimeters) apart, your hands on your hips, and your thighs at right angles to the mat. Press your shins and ankles down and your tailbone in, and lift your trunk and breastbone.*

Working Behind the Back

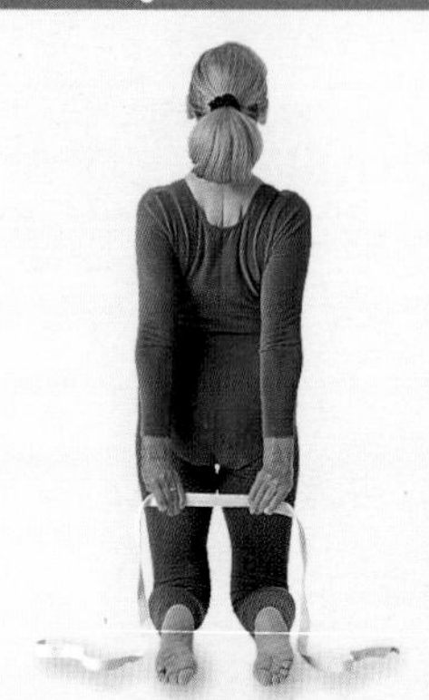

If you have trouble guiding your hands to your feet with your arms behind you, hold a belt between finger and thumb of each hand, leaving 12 inches (30 centimeters) between them. Your hands are now the same distance apart as your heels, palms turned forward, so the belt will guide your hands down to your feet.

2 *Breathe out, drop your head back, take your arms behind your back, and place the palms of your hands on your feet, fingers pointing down. Lift from your thighs, stretching your breastbone up. Hold the stretch for up to15 seconds.*

Finish and rest

Breathe in, lift your hands, and raise your head and trunk until you are kneeling upright. Relax, sitting on your heels with your hands on your thighs.

Ending the Pose

In step 2, your trunk is stretched and lifted and your head tilted back. If you drop your chest and sink onto your heels, you may strain your neck and back. Finish by repeating the step sequence in reverse, rather than just stopping midpose. Keep your spine stretching up.

Stretching the Trunk

The camel pose is more than a backbend since it stretches the whole trunk from the thighs to the neck. As you press your legs into the floor in step 1, you pull your tailbone in and stretch your sitting bones down toward the floor, and you lift your thighs and pull your trunk up from the groins and the hips to the top of the breastbone. As you move your hands back toward your heels, you stretch your shoulders back so your shoulder blades lie flat against your ribs, and the stretch runs along your arms to your hands. Keep both sides of the trunk in line so both hands reach the feet at the same time.

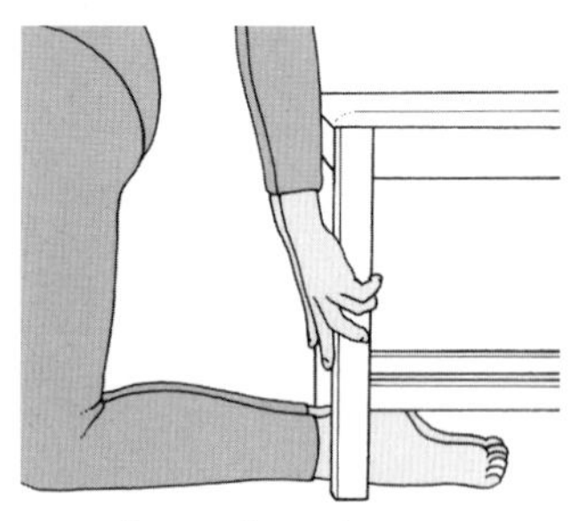

Overcoming resistance

To accustom yourself to bending your trunk back, place a chair behind you with its back against a wall, and bend backward, holding the chair legs with your hands.

Bending back

People sometimes find it difficult to bend their head and trunk back. At first, you may prefer to keep your head upright throughout until you feel comfortable enough to try bending back a little more each time you practice. Alternatively, you might place each hand on a pile of books positioned beside your ankles until you are ready to stretch right back and hold your feet. As the joints in your spine regain flexibility you will be able to bend so far back that you can see the wall behind your head.

In the backbends the whole front of the body stretches over the framework provided by the spine and the rib cage. Keeping the thighs and the trunk stretching up throughout the pose, the breastbone lifting high, and the shoulders pressing back enables you to bend the spine still further.

Points to Watch

- Keep your shins and ankles pressing down onto the mat and your body lifting up from the knees throughout the pose.
- As you bend your head back, close your mouth, and breathe normally as you hold the pose.
- Do not allow your hips to sink back onto your heels—keep your tailbone pressing in.
- Take care: if you feel any strain or pain during this Level 3 pose, unwind by reversing the step sequence, and rest.

Camel pose analyzed

The details shown here help you achieve a full stretch in step 2 of the camel pose on page 179.

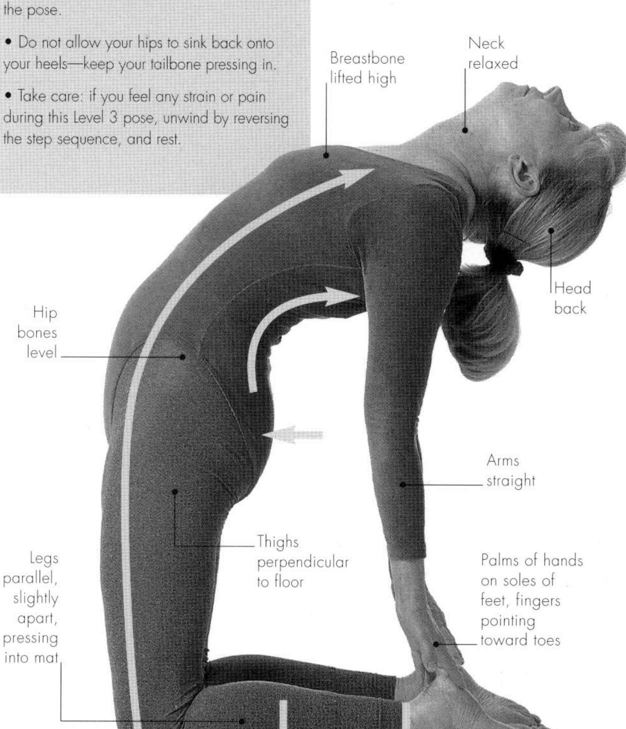

BOW

The bow pose or **dhanurasana** is a floor pose in which you stretch your whole body back and hold your ankles with your hands, so your body forms a bow shape with your arms as the bowstring. This is an extreme stretch, a demanding pose which, in time, will restore elasticity to the spine.

1 *Lie on your stomach on the mat with your legs slightly apart and your arms by your sides. Raise your legs a little and stretch them back.*

2 *Bend your knees, keeping your thighs stretched back, and press your tail down. Raise both arms and clasp your ankles. On an out-breath pull on your ankles and lift your thighs and chest off the mat.*

3 *Raise your head a little more, directing your gaze forward, and lift your shins higher breathing normally and without straining, for up to 10 seconds.*

Finish and rest

Breathe out, release your ankles, lower your legs and trunk to the mat, and rest.

An Extreme Stretch

The bow pose on pages 182–83 gives the trunk and spine an extreme stretch, extending the front of the body as well as bending the back to its fullest extent. As in the camel pose on pages 178–81, pressing the tail in and the pelvis into the floor gives you the impetus you need to raise your legs off the mat, and stretching them up helps you hold them in position. And when you are holding the pose, pressing down in this way—a technique known as challenge and resistance—will enable you to bend your back a little more, and stretch from hips to breastbone. Pull on your ankles to lift your trunk and thighs higher.

Achieving lift

If you find it difficult at first to catch your ankles, practice the pose without lifting your legs off the mat. Begin by just stretching your arms back toward your ankles, then gradually raise your head and then your chest off the mat, and then work on raising your legs at the same time. Working in this way will improve the stretch on your trunk and legs, and make your spine more flexible. Then, when you can achieve more movement you can work on holding your ankles and lifting higher.

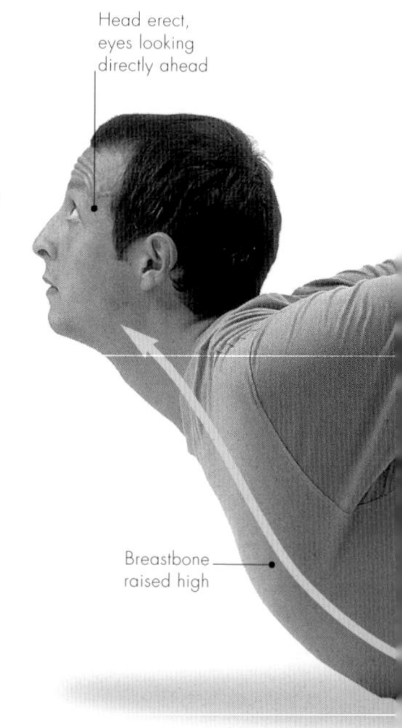

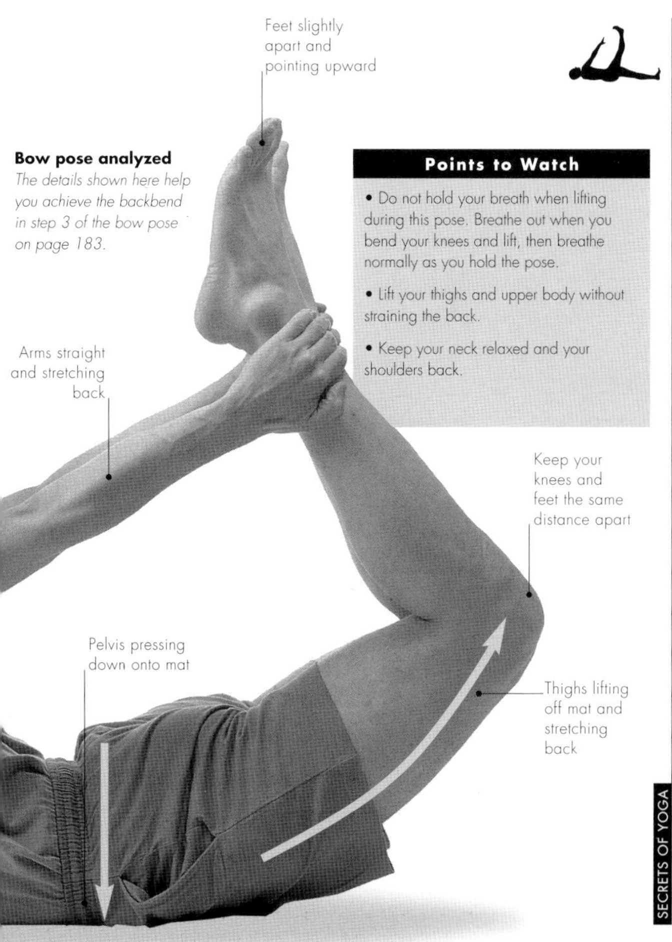

Bow pose analyzed

The details shown here help you achieve the backbend in step 3 of the bow pose on page 183.

Points to Watch

- Do not hold your breath when lifting during this pose. Breathe out when you bend your knees and lift, then breathe normally as you hold the pose.
- Lift your thighs and upper body without straining the back.
- Keep your neck relaxed and your shoulders back.

SHOULDER STAND AND PLOW

The shoulder stand, **salamba sarvangasana**, and the plow or **halasana** may be performed separately, but here they are shown together as a sequence of movements. Before you begin, position a chair so that when you lie on the mat its seat is a little more than arm's length away, behind your head.

1 *Lie in supta tadasana (see page 39), and press your shoulders and upper arms into the floor, lifting your breastbone. Bending your knees, move your heels back to your seat.*

2 *Breathe in, press your arms down, and raise your legs and hips, bringing your bent knees over your head. Bend your elbows, placing your hands on either side of your spine to support your upper back.*

3 *Place your feet on the chair behind your head in the plow pose. Straighten your legs and move your hips forward, to rest above your shoulders. Keep your elbows in. Hold for about 10 seconds.*

4 *Bend your knees, point them at the ceiling, and keeping your legs together, slowly straighten them until your feet are above your shoulders and you are doing a shoulder stand. Hold for up to 5 minutes. (With practice you will be able to do the pose from step 2 to step 5 without the use of a chair.)*

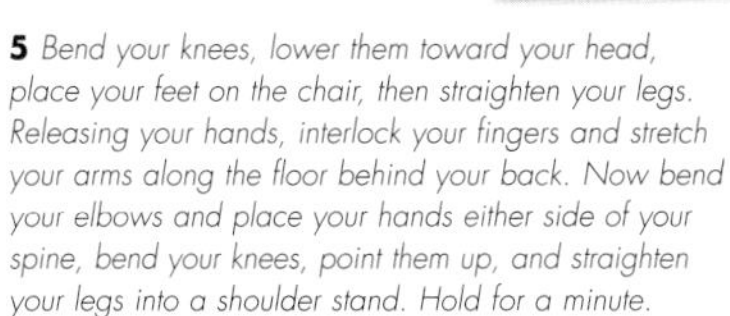

5 *Bend your knees, lower them toward your head, place your feet on the chair, then straighten your legs. Releasing your hands, interlock your fingers and stretch your arms along the floor behind your back. Now bend your elbows and place your hands either side of your spine, bend your knees, point them up, and straighten your legs into a shoulder stand. Hold for a minute.*

Finish and rest

Keeping your legs together, exhale, bend your knees and lower them toward your head, stretch your arms along the floor behind your back, pressing them down for control as you lower your hips to the floor. Rest with your legs bent.

Introducing Inverted Poses

Inverted poses have always been considered important in yoga because of their health-giving qualities. By stimulating blood and lymph circulation, they increase vitality.

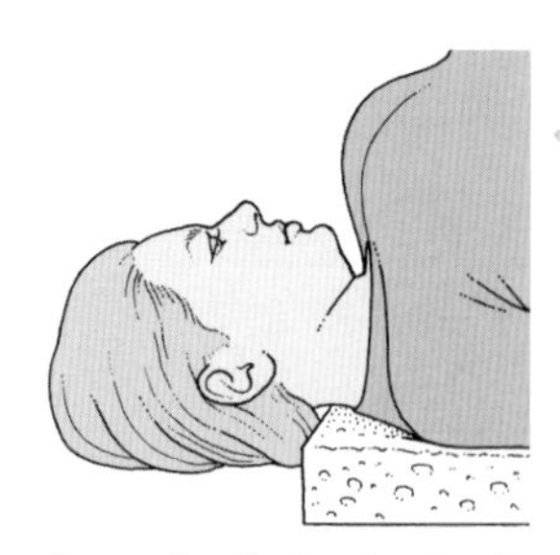

Supporting the head and neck

Begin both poses lying on your back, your upper body raised on three or four folded blankets or four foam blocks. This provides essential support for your neck.

Balance and control

Accurate alignment is important in these poses. Your head must be at right angles to your shoulders and not turned to either side. Stretching your arms toward your feet and pressing your shoulders and arms down lifts your breastbone and helps you maintain balance and control. When in the plow pose, interlocking your fingers and stretching your arms along the floor keeps your upper arms close and parallel to each other, giving you more control.

Keep your legs together throughout, and when you raise your body into a shoulder stand, stretch your thighs up so your ankles, hips, and shoulders are all in one plane. As you lower your legs into the plow pose, move your hips away from your head. When your feet touch the chair seat, straighten your bent knees, then move your hips forward toward your head so they lie above your shoulders, tuck your toes under the insteps, and stretch your thighs up to straighten your legs even more.

Lowering the feet to a chair seat is a good way of learning the plow pose. When you feel confident, attempt the full pose, lowering your feet to the mat.

Warning

Never practice this pose without raising your shoulders on foam blocks or three or four folded blankets, with your head lower. Do not do shoulder stands if you have high blood pressure or weakness or injury of the upper back, neck, or head. Women should avoid inverted poses when menstruating. Tie long hair back before practicing inverted poses.

Points to Watch

- In both poses, position your raised hips and trunk above your shoulders.
- Keep your sitting bones stretching away from your shoulders, your tail pressing in, and your thighs tucked back.
- Do not turn your head while in an inverted pose.
- Breathe normally throughout, lifting and lowering your body on an out-breath.

Shoulder stand analyzed

Check each of the points below for the shoulder stand on page 187.

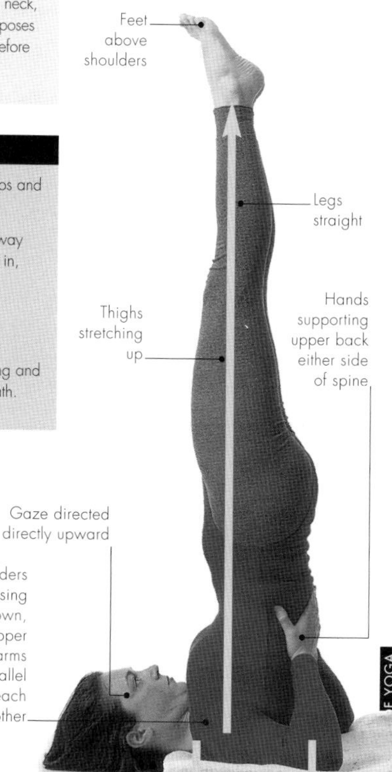

SHOULDER STAND VARIATIONS

When you have learned the shoulder stand and the plow, and you feel confident with them, vary your practice with these poses on the same theme. These pages show three poses from a sequence of more than 20 which make up the **sarvangasana** cycle—asanas based on the shoulder stand on page 186–87. These three poses follow each other with no more than a brief rest.

Eka pada sarvangasana

Keeping your left leg stretching up strongly lower your right leg to the floor or a chair seat, keeping it straight. Hold for about 10–15 seconds, then raise it beside your left leg, stretching both legs up in a shoulder stand again. Then repeat, keeping your right leg stretching up and lowering your left leg to the chair seat, then stretch up in the shoulder stand.

Parsvaika pada sarvangasana

Stretch up in a shoulder stand and turn your right leg out at the hip joint. Keeping it straight, lower it diagonally to the floor, resting your right toes in line with your right shoulder. Hold for 10–15 seconds, then raise the leg into a shoulder stand. Repeat, lowering your left leg to the floor, and stretch up into a shoulder stand.

Supta konasana

1 *Lift up in a strong shoulder stand, supporting your back with your hands. Exhale, bend your knees into plow pose (see page 186) but with your feet on the floor. Straighten your legs and spread them apart in a wide-legged plow pose.*

2 *Release your hands from your back and hold the big toes. Press your thighs up and hold the stretch for 10–15 seconds.*

Finish and rest

Release your toes, support your back with your hands, walk your feet together into plow pose. Then on an out-breath, bend your knees and return to a shoulder stand. Keeping your legs together, bend your knees, stretch your arms along the floor, and pressing your arms down, lower your hips and trunk to the floor. Rest with your knees bent.

Achieving the Pose

Breathe out before spreading your feet as wide apart as you can at the end of step 1. Grasp your big toes between the thumb and first fingers of each hand. If you cannot reach your toes, hold your ankles or your calves.

Working on Shoulder Stands

These three poses are all fairly advanced and you should try them only when you feel confident with the shoulder stand and plow pose on pages 186–87. Bear in mind that these are all balancing exercises, and since they are inverted poses it is important to be confident about lowering your body to the floor. The best way to learn the one-leg shoulder stand, eka pada sarvangasana, is to lower one leg onto a chair as you did in the plow. As you gain confidence, you can take your leg still further down—to two foam blocks, perhaps, and then to the floor. Support your upper back with your hands throughout the pose.

Focus on alignment

In eka pada sarvangasana the upward-stretching leg must face forward, toward your head, but in parsvaika pada sarvangasana, the diagonal leg-stretch to the floor, you turn your right leg out from the hip before lowering it. In both poses, keep both legs stiff as you lower one to the chair seat or the floor, and keep your hips level: as the right leg comes down, lift the right hip, and vice versa. Remember to lower and raise your legs on an out-breath.

Supta konasana on page 191 combines a wide-legged stretch with the plow. Like all inverted poses, its aims are to raise the trunk and hips above the shoulders and to stretch the whole body. Supta konasana is an extreme stretch, but like all the exercises in this section, once you have practiced it and can do it easily, it becomes a calming, relaxing pose.

Hands holding toes

Supta konasana analyzed

The image below analyzes supta konasana—the wide-legged plow pose—on page 191, but most of the details relate to all three shoulder stand variations on pages 190–91.

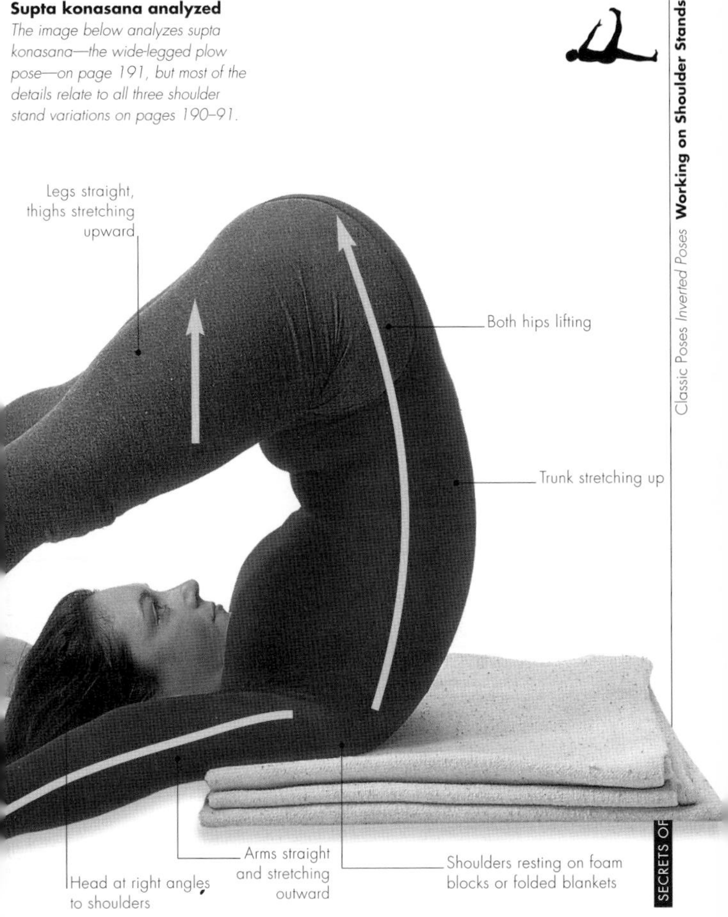

SHOULDER EXERCISES

Although some people exercise their shoulders regularly because their work demands it, most people's lives are largely sedentary nowadays, and this encourages rounded shoulders. This chapter ends with two exercises—hand clasp or **gomukhasana**, and arm twist or **garudasana**—to stretch the shoulders, arms, and hands, and open the chest.

Hand clasp

1 *Inhale, bend your left arm up behind your back, moving your forearm as close as you can to your spine, and the backs of your fingers touching your spine as high up as you can reach.*

2 *Keeping the back of your left hand against your spine, lift your right arm above your head, turn it at the shoulder until the palm faces behind you, and bend it back toward the fingers of your left hand.*

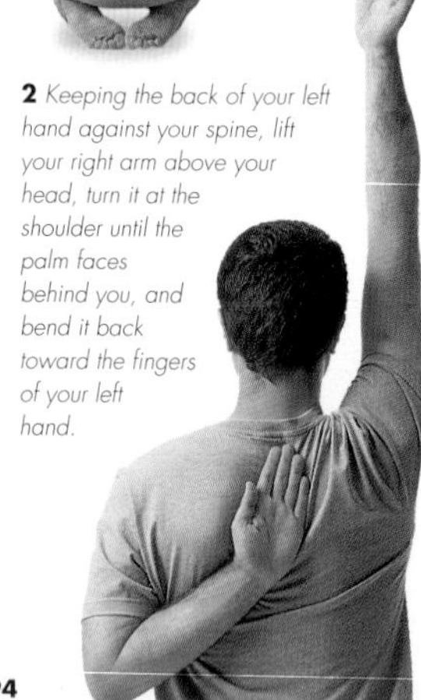

3 *Stretch your left elbow down to bring your left hand further up; and stretch your right elbow toward the ceiling to bring your right hand further down, then clasp your hands. Hold for 20 seconds.*

Repeat and finish

Release your hands, raise your right arm above your head, and lower both arms to your sides, then repeat steps 2 and 3, bending your right arm up behind your back and raising your left arm.

Twisting the Hands

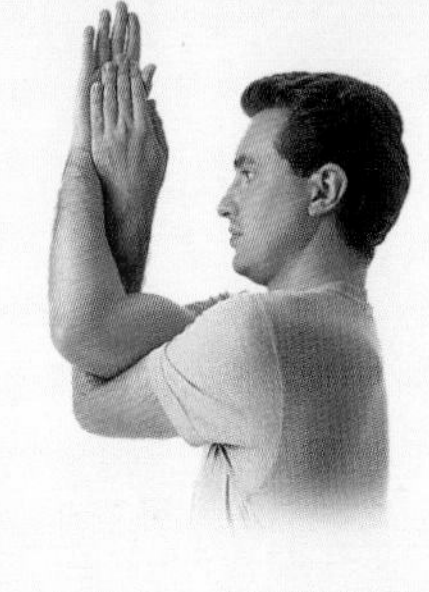

Keep your palms and thumbs touching and your fingers stretching up as you lift your elbows in step 3. If your palms do not meet, repeat steps 1 and 2, swinging your arms forward more rapidly and hugging your chest more tightly so your arms cross higher up.

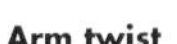

Arm twist

1 *Breathe in, stretch both arms out to the sides, and as you breathe out, swing your arms rapidly forward as if you are hugging yourself, crossing the right upper arm over the left at chest level.*

2 *Bending both arms, bring the backs of your hands together, fingers pointing up, then move your left hand toward you and your right hand slightly back, and move your hands together until the palms touch.*

3 *Keeping your shoulders down, lift your elbows level with them, and move your elbows a little away from your chest. Hold for about 20 seconds*

Repeat and finish

Release your hands and repeat steps 1–3, this time crossing the left upper arm over the right at chest level.

Mobilizing the Shoulders

Sitting at a desk, reading on a train, or reclining to watch television fill hours of many people's lives, and they do not realize how hunched their shoulders have become. In free moments, try these simple exercises to stretch your shoulders, arms, and hands. Like namaste on page 94, which is an integral part of the side-stretch, parsvottanasana, the shoulder exercises on pages 194–95 can be an integral part of a pose, or alternatively practiced alone. Begin by standing in a good tadasana (see pages 42–43), or sitting cross-legged in sukhasana (see page 38), or kneeling in the hero pose or virasana (see page 107). Before beginning, concentrate for a moment on lifting the spine and stretching across the upper chest, broadening your shoulders, and flattening your shoulder blades against your ribs.

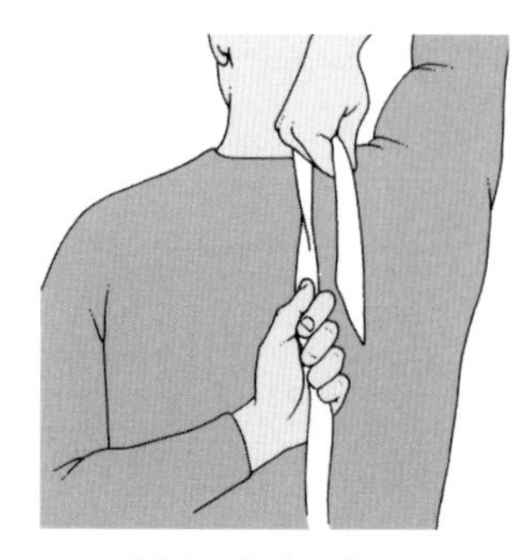

Joining the hands

If your shoulders are stiff, you may be unable to move your arm far toward the spine in the hand clasp, so that only your fingers meet. The answer is to hold a belt and walk both hands along it, toward each other.

Hand clasp

The hand clasp, gomukhasana, pulls the shoulders firmly back and stretches the upper arms. The key to this pose is to move the upward-stretching hand and arm as close to the center of the back as is possible. The aim of this pose is to clasp the hands together, and for that the upward-stretching hand needs to reach high up the back, between the shoulder blades. The downward-stretching arm also needs to be aligned accurately. As you stretch it up in step 2, keep it well back, touching the side of your head; and when you have turned it so that the hand faces behind you, keep the upper arm still as you bend the forearm down behind your back. Letting the elbow form a wing out to the side will prevent it from reaching so far.

Arm twist

Some yoga courses tell you to begin the hand twist, garudasana, by simply crossing your upper arms, but this graceful pose will be easier if you begin by throwing your arms around your chest as if giving yourself a bear-hug. That makes it easier to cross the upper arms high up.

When you bring your palms together after crossing your arms in step 2, you will be able to see your thumbs in front of your nose, the fingers stretching away behind them. Keep them at that height, but move them a little way from your body, keeping your shoulders down, and you will increase the stretch on your upper arms.

HAND EXERCISES

Most of what we do with our hands involves moving and closing them. This exercise stretches them, exercises the joints, and makes them more flexible. It improves circulation in the fingers on cold days, and is said to be a good preventive and a therapy for repetitive strain injury (RSI) and mild arthritis.

Interlocking fingers

1 *Clasp your hands in front of you by interlocking your fingers so that your right thumb lies on top.*

2 *Turn your clasped hands palms outward, and stretch your arms forward.*

3 *Keeping your fingers interlocked, stretch your arms up above your head, then back so that your upper arms lie either side of your head, brushing your ears.*

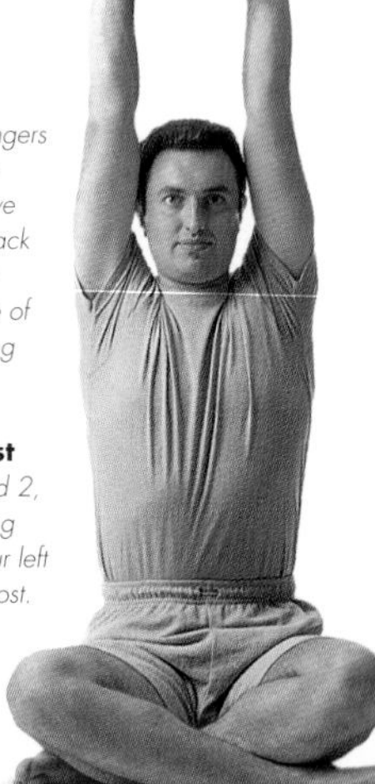

Repeat and rest

Repeat steps 1 and 2, this time interlocking your fingers so your left thumb lies uppermost.

Finger twister

1 *Hold your two hands up parallel to your chest, palms facing down, tips of your middle fingers just touching, then turn the palm of the left hand up. Stretch the index finger and the little finger of each hand out to the sides, then bend the two middle fingers of the left hand up and the two middle fingers of the right hand down. Now move your hands closer together, sliding the little finger of your right hand across the index finger of your left hand, and your right index finger across your left little finger.*

2 *Turn your left hand toward you, and straighten the two middle fingers of your left hand so they lie across the knuckle of your right index finger. Raise your right thumb and press it down on the tips of the two middle fingers. Pause to open your palms.*

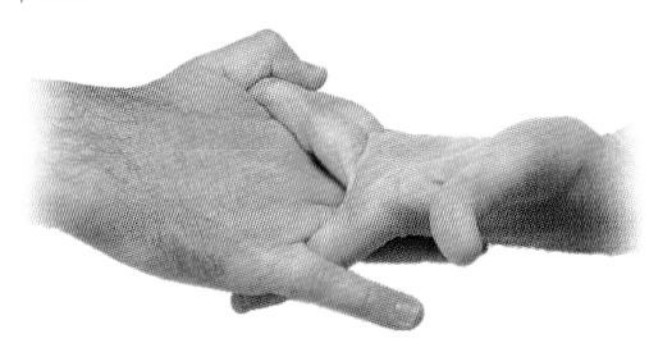

3 *Now straighten the two middle fingers of your right hand, and stretching them away from you, tuck your left thumb beneath the tips. To achieve this you may need to move your hands a little further apart, widening the gap in the center. Hold your hands up and if you have achieved the finger twist you should be able to see through the gap between the index and middle fingers.*

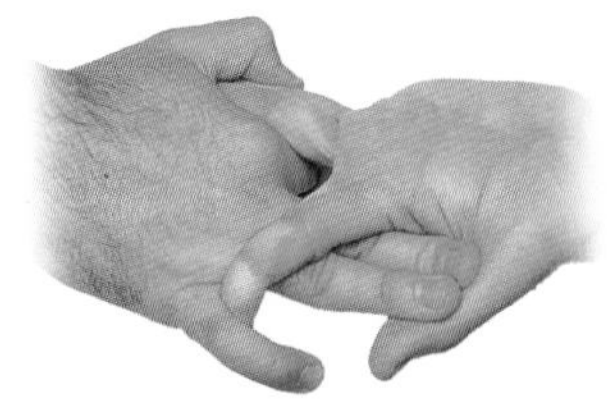

Flexing the Hands

We use our marvelously flexible hands all the time, but we rarely exercise them. We contract and relax sets of muscles to put things down and pick them up, but few of the everyday movements we make involve stretching the fingers and bending them outward, bending the wrist back, or stretching the palms. Like every part of the skeleton, the hands have joints and muscles that need to be exercised to keep them supple. If you injure your hand you need to restore flexibility to the muscles, and hand and wrist exercises may reduce the effects of diseases affecting the joints, such as arthritis, and perhaps prevent them.

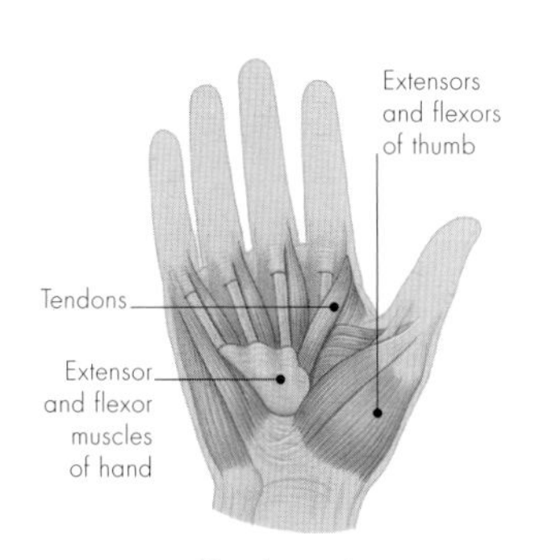

Hand muscles

More than 40 muscles, some of them tiny, move the fingers, thumb, and wrist to make the hand an extraordinarily flexible instrument.

Hand flexors

Several yoga poses incorporate hand exercises. For example, in the side-stretch (parsvottanasana on pages 94–97) the hands form the prayer pose or namaste behind your back. This movement stretches the palms and fingers laterally and longitudinally, and flexes the wrist as you turn your hands inward. The shoulder exercises on pages 194–97 also stretch the hands. You can practice hand exercises to fill free moments.

Finger twister

If you find you can do it easily, move your fingers closer together at the start to give them less space to maneuver. It is a great cold weather exercise since it improves the circulation to the fingers.

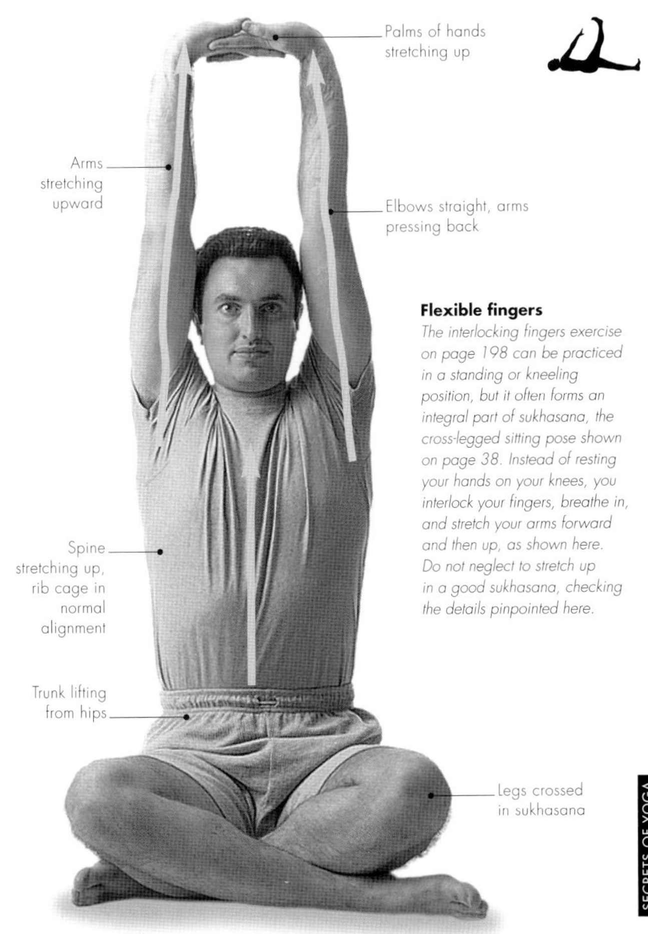

Flexible fingers

The interlocking fingers exercise on page 198 can be practiced in a standing or kneeling position, but it often forms an integral part of sukhasana, the cross-legged sitting pose shown on page 38. Instead of resting your hands on your knees, you interlock your fingers, breathe in, and stretch your arms forward and then up, as shown here. Do not neglect to stretch up in a good sukhasana, checking the details pinpointed here.

PLANNING YOUR PRACTICE

This final chapter helps you plan your own future yoga practices based on the 50 classic poses illustrated and described step by step in this book. The following two pages give guidelines for designing a program to suit your particular needs. The pages that follow show three short sample programs. Try the first program when you are ready to progress from exercises for beginners to those presenting a slightly higher level of difficulty (see page 206 for full icon key); and the second when you eventually feel ready to try more advanced poses. The chapter ends with a short practice for whenever you feel tired or stressed.

Designing your Yoga Course

The important principle in yoga is always to progress at your own pace. Start with the beginner's poses in Chapter 3, and as long as you practice regularly, concentrating on the details of each exercise, do not worry if you prefer to stay with the nine poses shown on those pages for some weeks, until you can do them well.

Standing Poses

These are the five basic standing poses in the order in which they should be practiced: hold the standing poses for 10–15 seconds each side at first, then repeat as often as you like. Breathe normally through the nose.

1 Triangle	pages 46–47
2 Extended side angle	pages 50–51
3 Warrior II	pages 78–79
4 Warrior I	pages 82–83
5 Side-stretch	pages 94–95

Expanding your repertoire

You will soon want to introduce new poses into your practice, and this book is planned to enable you to progress in whichever way suits you best. The poses in Chapter 4 are grouped into different types of exercise—standing poses, sitting poses, floor poses, and so on. Each is graded according to its level of difficulty. Beginners usually start with the standing poses, but you could try a sitting pose, a floor pose, such as the downward-facing dog pose on pages 130–31, or even the cross-legged sitting twist on pages 158–59.

There are few rules in yoga, simply because everyone's body is different, so if your body is quite flexible and you want to try one of the higher-level poses, do not feel you must wait. However, it is a good idea to begin with a simple pose.

Resting time

Between poses, the muscles and joints need a chance to recover from stretching, the breathing must be allowed to return to normal, and the mind needs to recenter itself. For example, after a standing pose, return to tadasana (pages 42–43), and to dandasana (page 106) after a sitting pose. Rest on your back at the end of a floor pose with your knees raised to your chest and your hands clasped around them. Sit on your heels after a backbend, and relax with your legs bent after a shoulder stand.

Do make your favorite poses a part of your practice—after all, you should enjoy yoga—but include a good mix of poses in your program. Start with standing poses since they tone your muscles and boost your circulation, waking you up, followed by calming sitting or floor poses, which give muscles and joints a good stretch. Then exercise the spine with an energizing sitting twist followed by a backbend. Leave new and less familiar poses until last—finish with the shoulder stand and plow (pages 186–87), for instance. And end with the corpse pose, savasana (pages 64–65), to rest your body and mind completely.

A SECOND-LEVEL PROGRAM

These four pages present a program of second-level poses. You can tackle them at any stage, but to master them you will need a degree of flexibility, especially in the hips, for they are mainly sitting poses. If you have been practicing yoga for three to four months you should have that flexibility; if not, you may need the help of foam blocks or folded blankets. This program should last about an hour, but work at your own speed. Aim to practice it at least once a week.

Levels of Difficulty

Within each category the poses appear in order of increasing complexity, and each has an icon

BEGINNERS for complete beginners

INTERMEDIATE slightly more advanced—you have worked through Chapter 3 at least once

ADVANCED more advanced poses for when your body has gained some flexibility

1 Cross-legged sitting
sukhasana with parvatasana, pages 38 and 201

2 Extended leg-stretch I
utthita hasta padangusthasana, page 70

3 Extended leg-stretch II
utthita hasta padangusthasana II, page 71

4 Cobbler
baddha konasana, page 110

5 Floor leg-stretch I
supta padangusthasana I,
page 146–4 7

6 Floor leg-stretch II
supta padangusthasana II,
page 147

7 Angled leg-stretch
upavistha konasana,
page 111

8 Head-to-knee pose
janu sirsasana,
pages 114–15

9 Three-limbed pose
triang mukhaikapada paschimottanasana,
pages 118–19

10 Sitting forward bend
paschimottanasana,
pages 122–23

11 Mermaid I
Bharadvajasana I,
pages 162–63

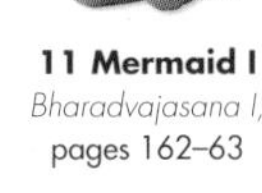

12 Sage
Marichyasana I,
page 166

13 Shoulder stand and plow
salamba sarvangasana and halasana,
pages 186–87

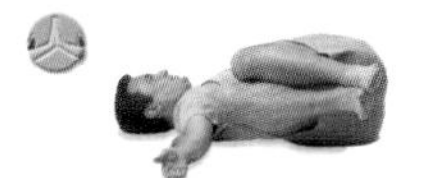

14 Revolving abdomen
jathara parivartanasana,
pages 138–39

15 Corpse
savasana I,
pages 64–65

Concentrating on Sitting Poses

Every practice needs to begin with a passive pose to quiet and focus the mind. This program starts with cross-legged sitting, a restful sitting pose in which you concentrate on stretching your arms up in parvatasana. An invigorating standing pose follows to stretch and tone your legs. As you work through the program you may find you need to rest briefly between the stretches by lying for a few seconds with your knees clasped to your chest. Between leg-stretches you concentrate on opening the hips. The second part of the practice works on the back in a succession of forward bends and twists.

Go as far as you can with each pose, supporting yourself whenever you need to on a ledge, a chair back or seat, foam blocks, or piles of books. For the safety of your neck, never attempt the shoulder stand (pose 13) without resting your shoulders and upper arms on folded blankets or foam blocks so your head lies back below their level.

1 Cross-legged sitting

Begin the the second-level program quietly in sukhasana (page 38) with your arms stretched above your head in parvatasana (page 201). Hold the pose for about 20 seconds, stretching up throughout.

2 & 3 Extended leg-stretches

Stretch your hip joints and wake up the muscles of your hips and legs with utthita hasta padangusthasana I and II (pages 70–71). Aim to hold the pose for up to a minute.

4 Cobbler

Now sit with your back against a wall and relax into baddha konasana (page 110), clasping your feet with your hands. You may want to hold this pose for more than a minute.

5 & 6 Floor leg-stretches

Return to leg-stretches—supta padangusthasana I and II (pages 146–47) performed lying on the mat. Raise each leg in turn, holding the stretch for up to a minute. End with a few seconds in a resting position.

7 Angled leg-stretch

The angled leg-stretch upavistha konasana (page 111) stretches both legs out to the sides. Remember to breathe out as you lean forward. Hold for 20 seconds, and finish in a resting pose.

8 Head-to-knee pose

Janu sirsasana (pages 114–15) marks a change of position following the two leg-stretches. Perform the pose on the right side, then on the left. Hold for about 30 seconds each side. This is a resting pose, so relax into it.

9 Three-limbed pose

Keep your hips level as you extend your trunk forward in triang mukhaikapada paschimottanasana (pages 118–19). This second sitting forward bend is a relaxing pose, so hold it for 30 seconds on each side.

10 Sitting forward bend

End this sequence of three forward bends with paschimottanasana (pages 122–23), stretching your trunk forward with both legs extended. This is a restful pose. Hold it for up to 1 minute, if you can.

11 Mermaid I

Follow a succession of forward bends with Bharadvajasana I (pages 162–63), rotating your spine first to the right, then to the left. Hold each twist for up to 30 seconds.

12 Sage

Marichyasana (page 166) gives the back a satisfying stretch. Hold it for at least 20 seconds on each side, then rest in a kneeling position for a few seconds.

13 Shoulder stand and plow

Two inverted poses, salamba sarvangasana and halasana (pages 186–87), carried out in tandem for about 3 minutes, will be invigorating.

14 Revolving abdomen

In this last active pose—jathara parivartanasana (pages 138–39)—the legs swing to one side, then the other, exercising the spine. Practice for up to 20 seconds on each side.

15 Corpse

Finish with a 10-minute rest in the corpse pose (savasana I, pages 64–65).

A THIRD-LEVEL PROGRAM

This program includes some of the basic poses from Chapter 3, such as the triangle and the kneeling forward bend. One of the reasons for this is that the body, especially the legs, needs to be strong for the more complex poses, and the standing poses at the beginning of the program are chosen to give essential preparatory stretches. The program concentrates on energizing: the standing poses at the beginning wake the body up, and the backbends stimulate the mind and body. It focuses on backbends, which mobilize the spine, giving it an extreme stretch. The sequence should take about 75 minutes, although it is important not to hurry. Repeat the program at least once a week.

1 Downward-facing dog
adho mukha svanasana,
pages 130–31

2 Triangle
utthita trikonasana,
pages 46–47

3 Warrior II
virabhadrasana II,
pages 78–79

4 Warrior I
virabhadrasana I,
pages 82–83

5 Standing forward bend
uttanasana I,
page 75

6 Gate
parighasana,
pages 134–35

7 Hero
virasana,
page 107

8 Camel
ustrasana,
pages 178–79

9 Bridge
sarvangasana setu bandha,
pages 170–71

10 Locust
salabhasana,
pages 174–74

11 Bow
dhanurasana,
pages 182–83

12 Cross-legged twist
sukhasana twist,
pages 158–59

13 Kneeling forward bend
page 54

14 Corpse
savasana I,
pages 64–65

Concentrating on Backbends

Although this is a stimulating practice, it is a good idea to begin with a few minutes sitting cross-legged or in the hero pose to quiet the mind. It incorporates some demanding poses, but the program is punctuated by restful postures, such as calming forward bends.

In the second half of the practice you work on the spine in a sequence of backbends, which elongate the whole trunk from the groin to the neck and extend the spine. The stretching opens up the chest and the front of the body. The backbends and twists give an extreme stretch, so you may need to rest briefly, sitting back on your heels, perhaps, or lying on the floor with your knees drawn up to your chest and your hands clasped over your shins after a particularly intense effort. As always, end the program with a 5–10 minute rest in the corpse pose. Afterward you will still find that the program has had an invigorating effect.

1 Downward-facing dog

Begin with the muscle-toning, body-stretching adho mukha svanasana (pages 130–31), which relaxes the heart. Hold for up to one minute.

2 Triangle

Utthita trikonasana (pages 46–47) is included here to strengthen the legs. Hold the pose for up to 20 seconds on the right and the left.

3 Warrior II

A sequence of wake-up standing poses continues with virabhadrasana II (pages 78–79). Hold the pose for up to 20 seconds each side.

4 Warrior I

Concentrate on stretching up in virabhadrasana I (pages 82–83). Hold for a maximum of 15 seconds each side.

5 Standing forward bend

The standing poses end with uttanasana I (see page 75), which slows the heartbeat and calms the nerves. Bend from the hips, keeping your legs straight. Hold for a minute or more, breathing normally through the nose.

6 Gate

Parighasana (pages 134–35) introduces a short sequence of kneeling and sitting postures at the heart of this practice. This pose stretches each side of the body in turn. Hold for up to 10 seconds on each side, feeling the stretch.

7 Hero

When performed correctly, so that your sitting bones touch the floor between your feet, virasana (page 107) stretches the feet, the ankles, and the knees. This is a relaxing pose, so hold it for more than a minute.

8 Camel

The first in the sequence of backbends, ustrasana (pages 178–79) stretches the whole spine up as well as back. Hold for up to 10 seconds, then rest, sitting back on your heels.

9 Bridge

For this second backbend, arch your back in sarvangasana setu bandha (pages 170–71). Hold the pose for up to 10 seconds, then rest with your legs bent and your feet on the mat.

10 Locust

In this backbend, salabhasana (pages 174–75) you lift your legs and upper body, giving your spine an extreme stretch. Hold for up to 10 seconds.

11 Bow

Dhanurasana (pages 182–83), the last in the backbend sequence, exercises the joints of the spine. Hold for up to 10 seconds.

12 Cross-legged twist

The sukhasana twist (pages 158–59) rotates the spine, moving it in a different direction from the backbends. Hold for up to 15 seconds.

13 Kneeling forward bend

This simple forward bend (on page 54) rests the back after the twist that precedes it. Hold the pose for two minutes or more.

14 Corpse

Five to ten minutes of full relaxation in savasana I (pages 64–65) is essential after the effort demanded by this practice.

EASING STRESS AND FATIGUE

This short practice makes an excellent pick-me-up after a hard day's work, whenever you are tired or feel stressed or anxious, or when you just need to give yourself a little tender loving care. It is a simple program of four relaxing postures, intended to be used as remedy for fatigue of any kind, because it will enable you to refresh your mind and body with minimum effort. The program works because the poses are passive—that is, although you make the effort to stretch in one pose, lift in another, or just concentrate your mind in a third, you are not actively moving or even stretching intensively. This program is estimated to take around 20–25 minutes, but relax in each pose for as long as you feel you need to.

1 Cross-legged sitting

Calm your mind by sitting cross-legged in sukhasana (page 38) for a minute or two, your eyes closed. Support your back by sitting on a foam block against a wall. Breathe normally through the nose and listen to your breathing pattern.

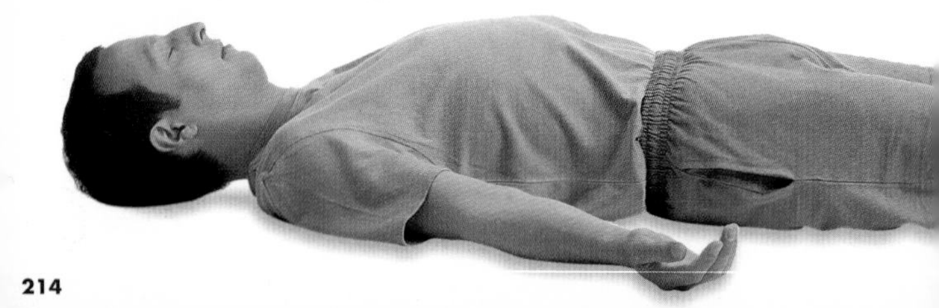

2 Cobbler floor pose
Rest your back in supta baddha konasana (pages 126–27). By now, your mind should be calm and your body relaxing. This posture is especially helpful to women during menstruation.

3 Extended leg-stretch
Relieve aching legs by lying on your back and extending them in urdhva prasarita padasana (pages 62–63) while supporting them against a wall. This pose may also alleviate an aching back.

4 Corpse pose
All practices end in the corpse pose (pages 64–65). You should now be completely relaxed. Concentrate on breathing in normally, but taking long, slow out-breaths.

GLOSSARY

Asana (pronounced "ah-sna") A yoga pose or posture.

Extend To extend a part of the body is to straighten or to stretch it.

Flex To flex a part of the body is to contract muscles in order to bend it.

Groin The groove between the bottom of the abdomen and the top of the thigh. The two groins slope out from the center of the pubic area and upward.

Hatha yoga A pathway to achieving universal wholeness or samadhi through practicing asanas, breathing, and cleansing processes; a classic school of yoga which evolved about 1,000 years ago.

Iyengar yoga A school or style of yoga founded by the Indian teacher, B.K.S. Iyengar.

Mantra Sacred words or sounds, such as "om," used to concentrate the mind.

Passive pose A yoga posture in which you stretch, but do not change position.

Pranayamas Energy-expanding techniques, including special breathing exercises.

Pratyahara Control of the senses.

Trunk The central part of the body, excluding the head, the arms, and the legs. Also called the torso.

Yoga Oneness or union.

The Asanas

SANSKRIT NAME	ENGLISH NAME
adho mukha svanasana	downward-facing dog pose
anantasana	eternal pose
ardha chandrasana	half-moon pose
ardha navasana	half-boat pose
baddha konasana	cobbler pose
Bharadvajasana	mermaid pose
chaturanga dandasana	four-limbed rod pose
dandasana	rod pose
dhanurasana	bow
eka pada sarvangasana	one-leg shoulder stand
garudasana	arm twist
gomukhasana	hand clasp
halasana	plow
janu sirsasana	head-to-knee pose
jathara parivartanasana	revolving abdomen
Marichyasana	sage pose
parighasana	gate pose
paripurna navasana	boat with oars
parivrtta trikonasana	revolved triangle
parsvaika pada sarvangasana	diagonal leg-stretch shoulder stand
parsvottanasana	side-stretch
parvatasana	interlocking fingers
paschimottanasana	sitting forward bend
prasarita padottanasana	wide leg-stretch
salabhasana	locust
salamba sarvangasana	shoulder stand
sarvangasana	shoulder stand
sarvangasana setu bandha	bridge
savasana	corpse poses
sukhasana	cross-legged sitting; cross-legged twist
supta baddha konasana	cobbler floor pose
supta konasana pose	wide-legged plow
supta padangusthasana	floor leg-stretches
supta tadasana	lying-down mountain pose
supta virasana	hero floor pose
tadasana	standing mountain pose
triang mukhaikapada paschimottanasana	three-limbed pose
upavistha konasana	angled leg-stretch
urdhva prasarita padasana	extended leg-stretch
ustrasana	camel pose
utkatasana	chair pose
uttanasana	standing forward bend
utthita hasta padangusthasana	leg-stretches
utthita parsvakonasana	extended side-angle pose
utthita trikonasana	triangle pose
virabhadrasana	warrior pose
virasana	hero pose
vrksasana	tree pose

FURTHER READING

Yoga

HITTLEMAN, RICHARD. *Yoga: A 28-Day Exercise Plan,* Bantam, UK, 1998

IYENGAR, B.K.S. *Light on Yoga,* Schocken, UK, 1996

IYENGAR, B.K.S. *Tree of Yoga,* Aquarian Press, UK, 1997

KENT, HOWARD. *Breathe Better, Feel Better,* Apple Press, UK, 1997

KENT, HOWARD. *The Complete Illustrated Guide to Yoga,* Element Books, UK, 1999

KENT, HOWARD. *Yoga for the Disabled* Sunrise Publications, Ickwell Bury, Biggleswade SG18 9EF, UK, 1985 (ISBN 0-7225-0902-2)

MEHTA, SILVA, MIRA & SHYAM. *Yoga the Iyengar Way,* Dorling Kindersley, UK, 1990

OLKIN, SILVIA KLEIN. *Positive Pregnancy Fitness, A Guide to a More Comfortable Pregnancy and Easier Birth Through Exercise and Relaxation,* Avery Publications, USA, 1996

STEWART, MARY. *Teach Yourself Yoga,* Hodder & Stoughton, UK, 998

STEWART, MARY. *Yoga Over 50,* Little, Brown, UK, 1995

STEWART, MARY, & PHILLIPS, KATHY. *Yoga for Children,* Vermilion, UK, 1992

TOBIAS, MAXINE, & SULLIVAN, JOHN, PATRICK. *The Complete Stretching Book,* Dorling Kindersley, UK, 1992

The Body

HINKLE, CARLA Z. *Fundamentals of Anatomy and Movement,* Mosby, UK, 1997

KEY, SARAH. *Back in Action,* Vermilion, UK, 1993

KEY, SARAH. *The Back Sufferer's Bible,* Telegraph Books, UK, 2000

KEY, SARAH. *Body in Action,* BBC Books, UK, 1992

Classic Yoga Texts

IYENGAR, B.K.S. *Light on the Yoga Sutras of Patañjali,* Aquarian Press, UK, 1992

MASCARO, JUAN, (trans.). *The Bhagavad Gita,* Penguin Books, UK, 1998

MASCARO, JUAN, (trans.). *The Upanishads,* Penguin Books, UK, 1998

NIKHILANANDA, S. (trans.). *The Upanishads,* Ramakrishna-Vivekananda Center, New York, USA, 1993

YOGANANDA, PRAMAHANSA. *Autobiography of a Yogi,* Rider, UK, 1991

The Yoga Sutras of Patañjali, Asian Humanities Press, USA, 1993

USEFUL ADDRESSES

The consultant for this book, Jennie Bittleston, a qualified yoga teacher, began practising yoga 25 years ago.
She can be contacted at:

The Brighton Natural Health Centre
27 Regent Street
Brighton BN1 1UL
Tel: (011 44 273) 600 010
An educational center for alternative health and complementary learning, which offers a range of healing therapies plus classes in yoga and other exercise techniques.

Divine Life Society
Shivananddear
PT Tehri-Garhwal
Uttar Pradesh
India
An organization aimed at promoting yoga worldwide.

Sivananda Yoga
Vedanta Center
243 West Street,
24th Street,
New York 10011
Tel: 212 255-4560
email:
newyork@sivananda.org
Information on Sivananda yoga, a style based on breathing and meditation.

United States Yoga Association
The San Francisco Yoga Studio
2159 Filbert Street
San Francisco, CA
94123
Tel: 1-415-931-YOGA
www.usyoga.org

Yogaville
Yogaville
Rt 1, Box 1720
Buckingham, Virginia
23921
www.yogaville.org

B.K.S. Iyengar National Association of the United States
Toll free number: 1-800-889-YOGA (1-800-889-9642)
www.comnet.org/iynaus
The website contains a list of regional associations throughout North America

Yoga Journal
www.yogajournal.com
A magazine with useful information on all branches of yoga.

Yoga Site
www.yogasite.com
A general information website.

INDEX

ACKNOWLEDGMENTS

The publisher would like to thank Deborah Fielding
for reading and commenting on the text.

Special thanks go to Louise Beglin, Carla Carrington, Linda de Comarmond,
Fiona Grantham, Kay Macmullan, Ben Morgan, Maria Rivans, David Ronchetti,
and Arup Sen for help with photography.
With thanks to Dancia International, London for the kind loan of props.

PICTURE ACKNOWLEDGMENTS

Every effort has been made to trace copyright holders and obtain permission.
The publishers apologize for any omissions and would be pleased
to make any necessary changes at subsequent printings

The Bridgeman Art Library/ British Library, London, UK 16t/
British Museum, London, UK 14b; **Corbis**/ Morton Beebe 18t/ Alison Wright
15t; **The Image Bank** 20; **Rex Features**/ The Times 8, 18b, 19t;
Tony Stone Images/ Laurie Campbell 30b/ Davies and Starr 14t/
Darrell Gulin 58t/ Donald Johnston 42t.